W.i.t.c.h.

Will   Irma   Taranee   Cornelia   Hay Lin

Part IX.
100% W.I.T.C.H.
Volume 3

CONTENTS

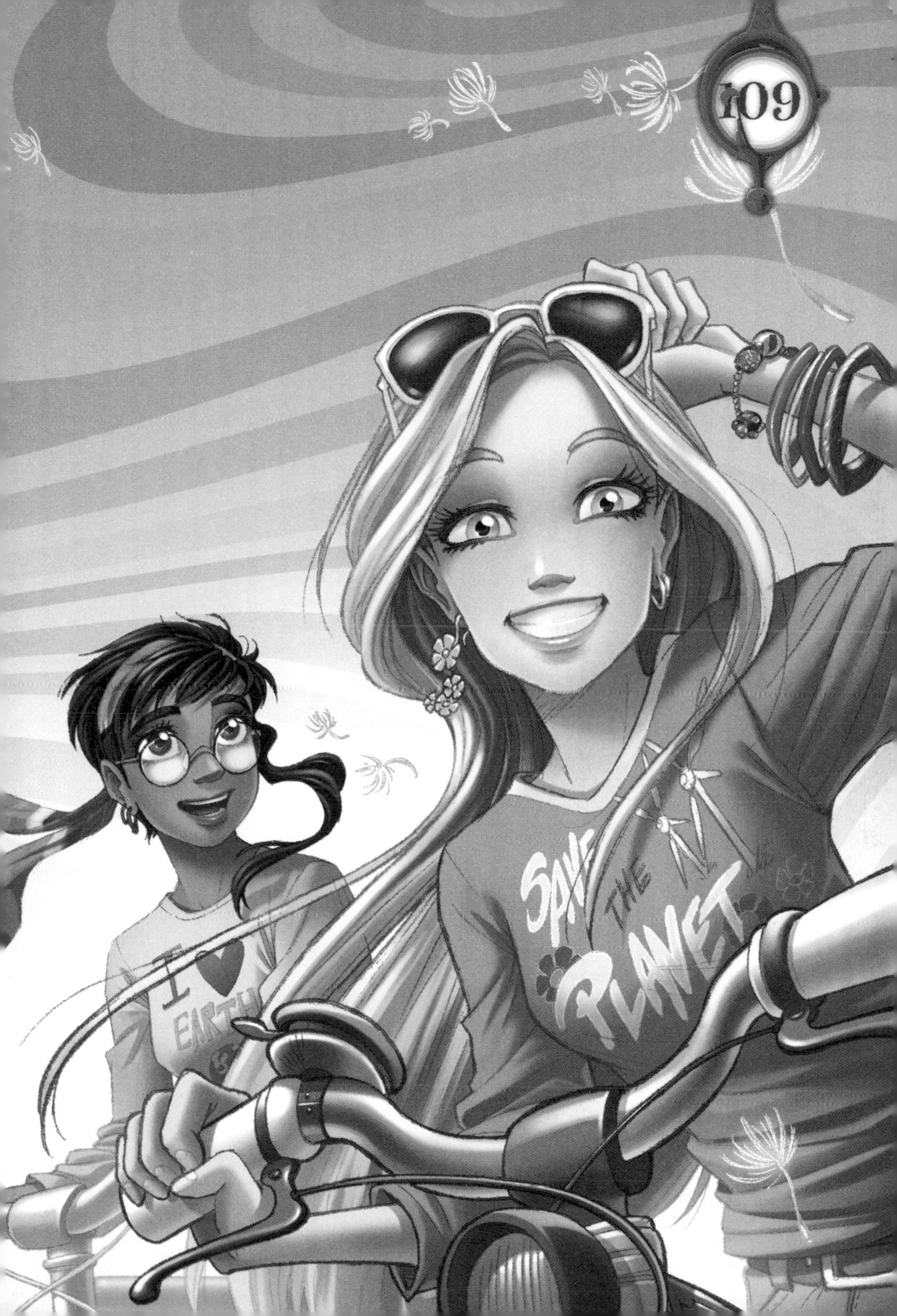
109
SAVE THE PLANET
I ♥ EARTH

W.i.t.c.h.

Will Irma Taranee Cornelia Hay Lin

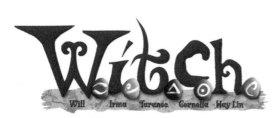

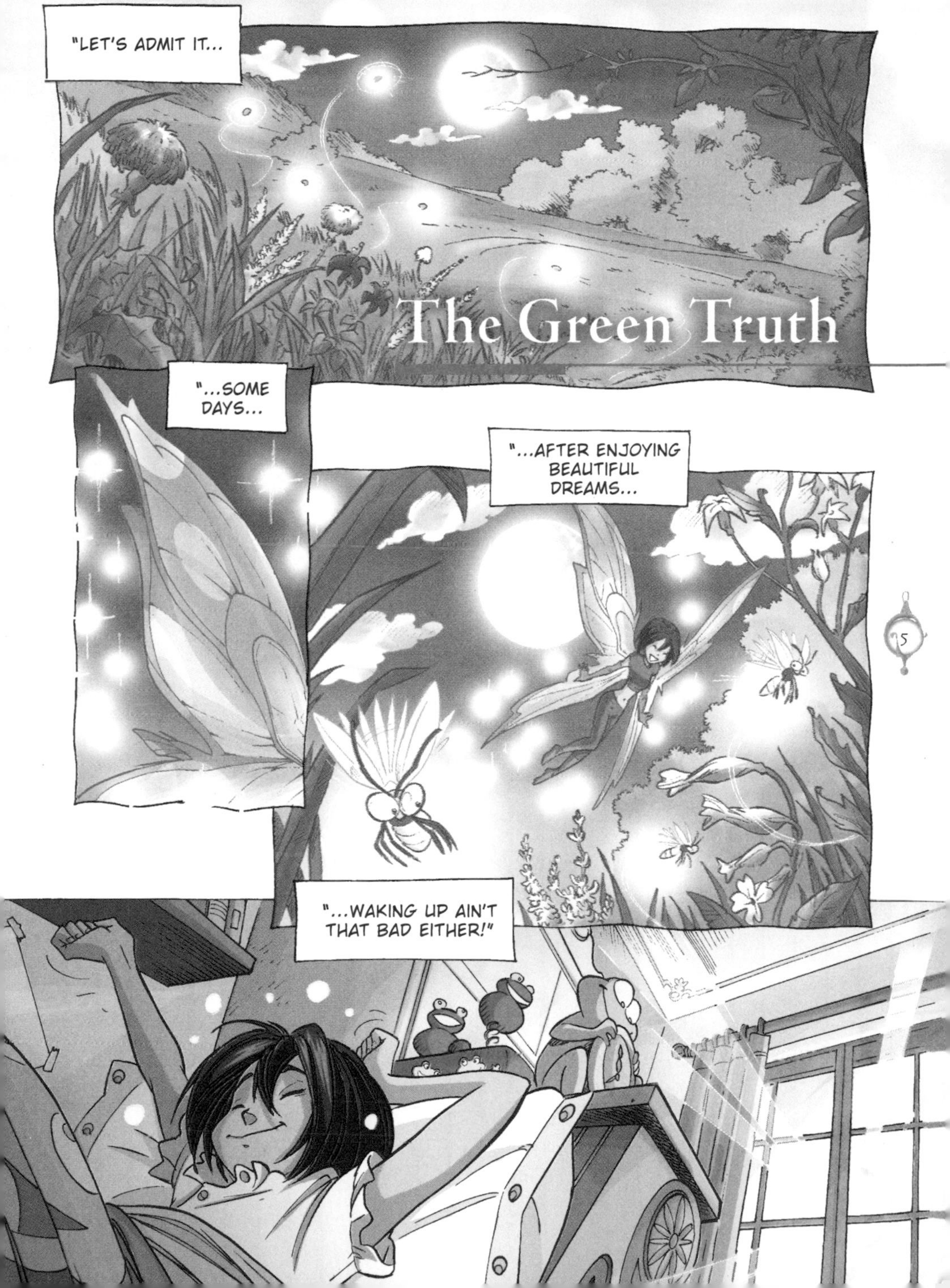
"LET'S ADMIT IT...
The Green Truth
"...SOME DAYS...
"...AFTER ENJOYING BEAUTIFUL DREAMS...
"...WAKING UP AIN'T THAT BAD EITHER!"

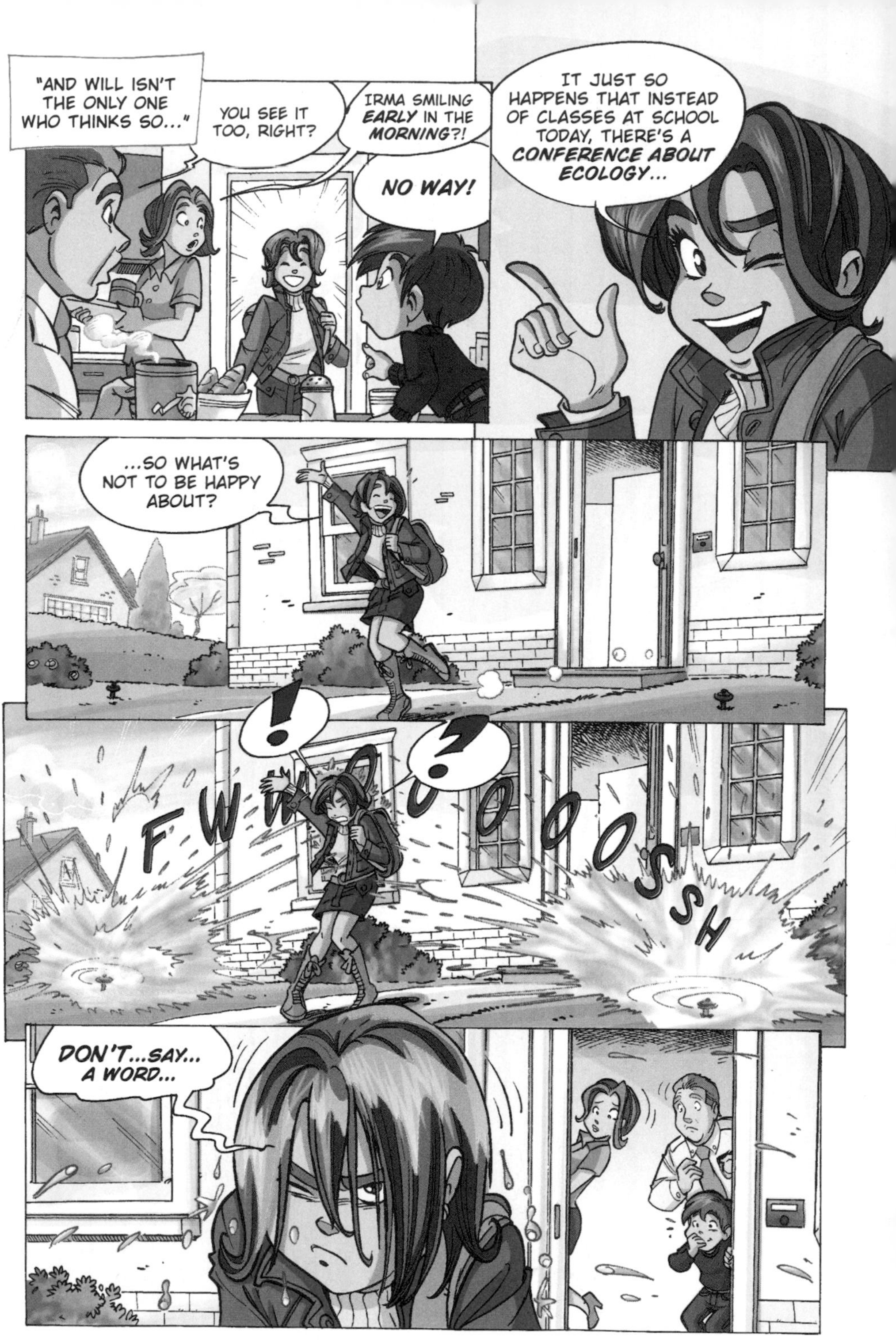
"AND WILL ISN'T THE ONLY ONE WHO THINKS SO..."
YOU SEE IT TOO, RIGHT?
IRMA SMILING *EARLY* IN THE *MORNING*?!
NO WAY!
IT JUST SO HAPPENS THAT INSTEAD OF CLASSES AT SCHOOL TODAY, THERE'S A *CONFERENCE ABOUT ECOLOGY*...
...SO WHAT'S NOT TO BE HAPPY ABOUT?
!
?
FWWOOOOOOSSH
DON'T...SAY... A WORD...

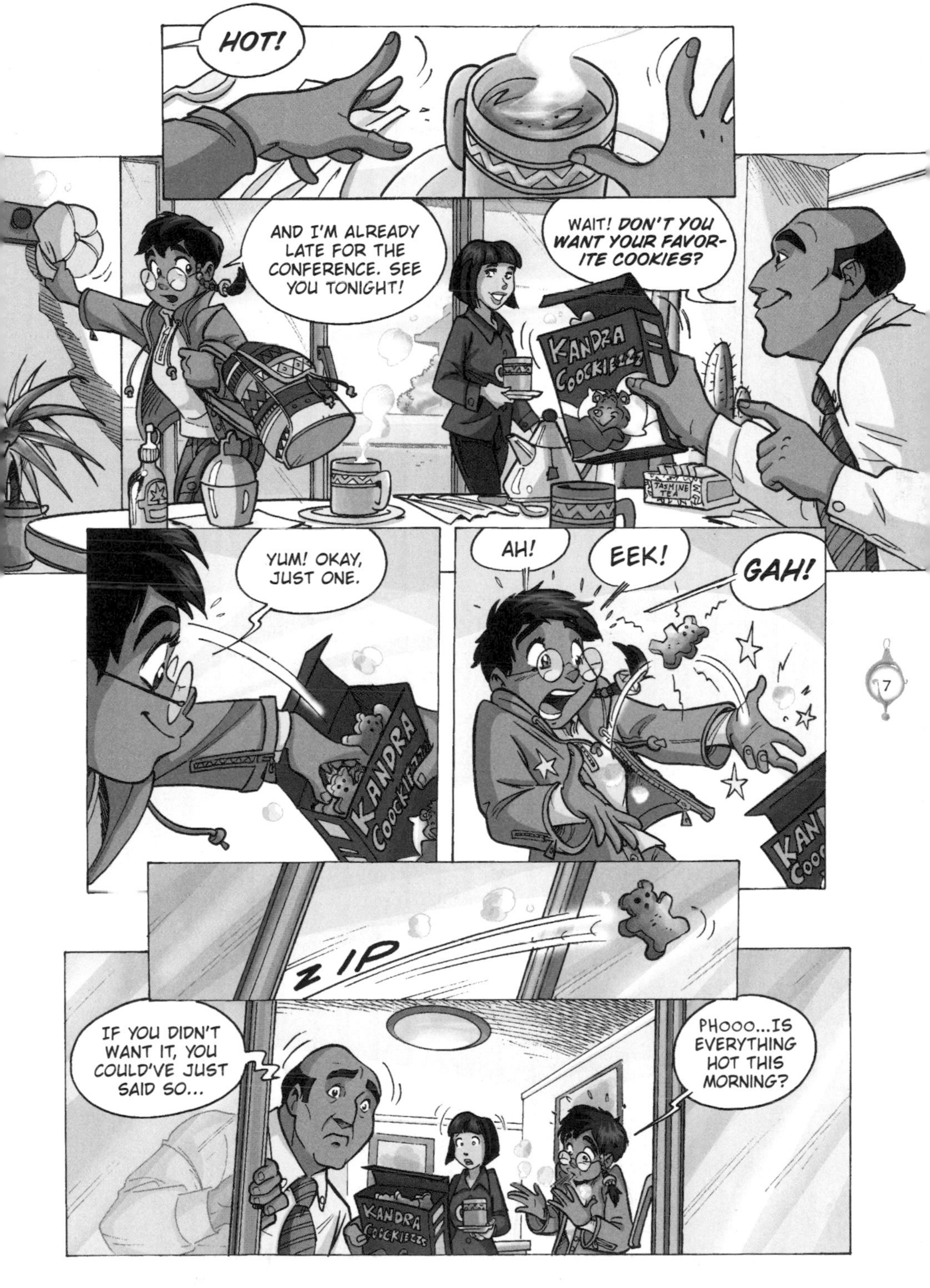
HOT!
AND I'M ALREADY LATE FOR THE CONFERENCE. SEE YOU TONIGHT!
WAIT! DON'T YOU WANT YOUR FAVOR-ITE COOKIES?
KANDRA COOCKIEZZZ
JASMINE TEA
YUM! OKAY, JUST ONE.
AH!
EEK!
GAH!
ZIP
IF YOU DIDN'T WANT IT, YOU COULD'VE JUST SAID SO...
PHOOO...IS EVERYTHING HOT THIS MORNING?
KANDRA COOCKIEZZZ

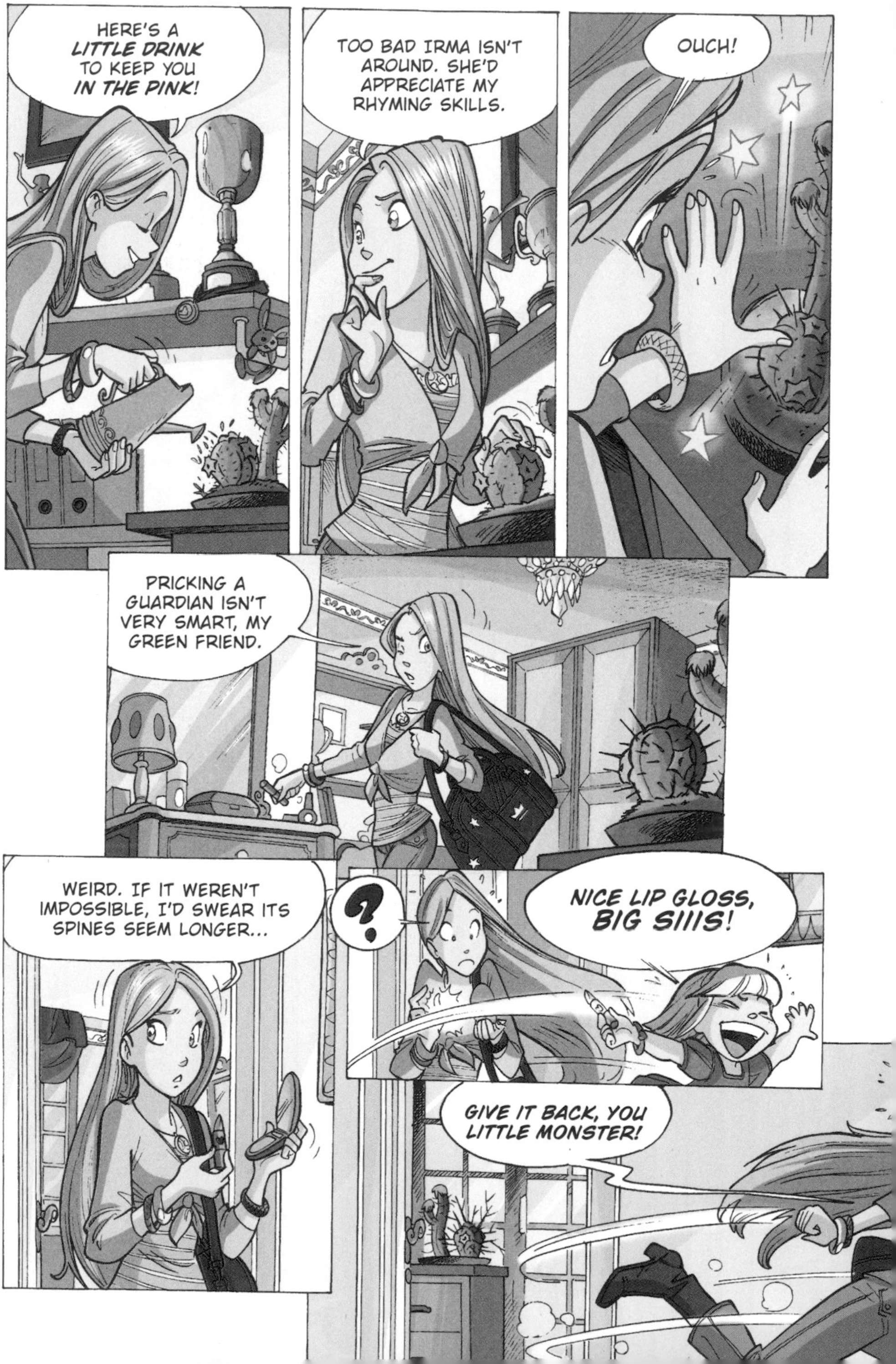
HERE'S A *LITTLE DRINK* TO KEEP YOU *IN THE PINK*!
TOO BAD IRMA ISN'T AROUND. SHE'D APPRECIATE MY RHYMING SKILLS.
OUCH!
PRICKING A GUARDIAN ISN'T VERY SMART, MY GREEN FRIEND.
WEIRD. IF IT WEREN'T IMPOSSIBLE, I'D SWEAR ITS SPINES SEEM LONGER...
?
NICE LIP GLOSS, BIG SIIIS!
GIVE IT BACK, YOU LITTLE MONSTER!

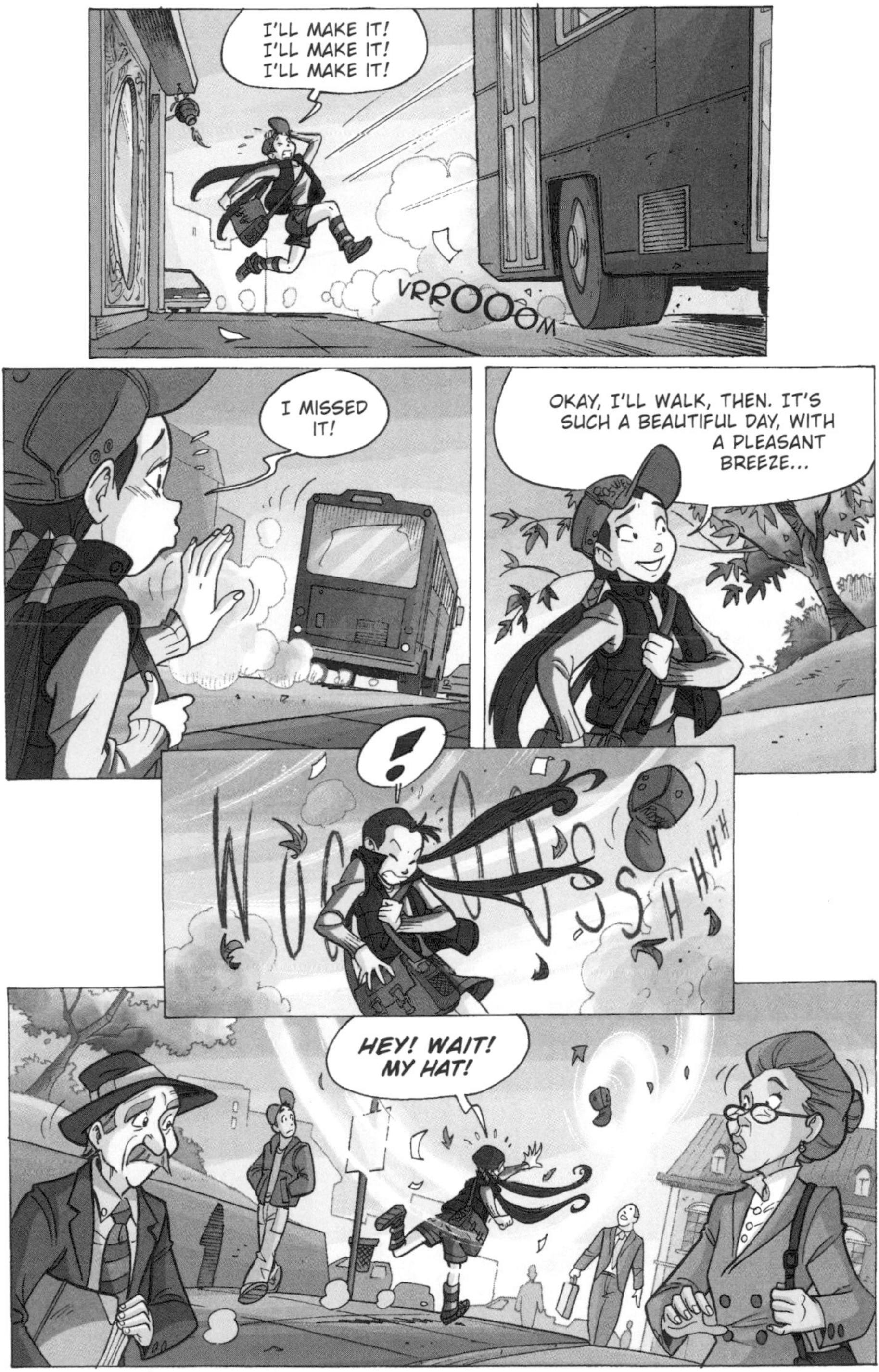
I'LL MAKE IT! I'LL MAKE IT! I'LL MAKE IT!
VRROOOM
I MISSED IT!
OKAY, I'LL WALK, THEN. IT'S SUCH A BEAUTIFUL DAY, WITH A PLEASANT BREEZE...
!
HEY! WAIT! MY HAT!

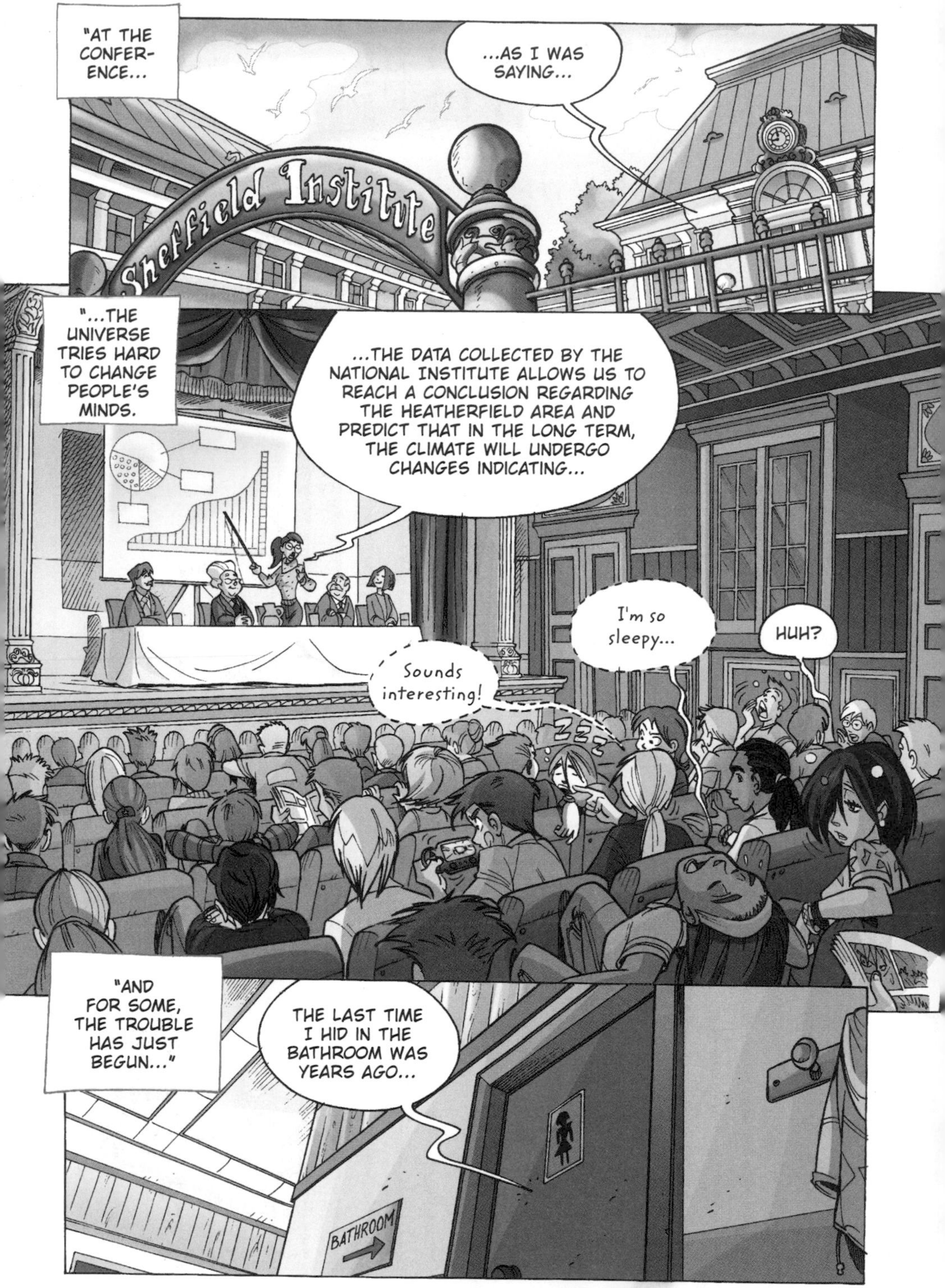
"AT THE CONFERENCE...
...AS I WAS SAYING...
Sheffield Institute
"...THE UNIVERSE TRIES HARD TO CHANGE PEOPLE'S MINDS.
...THE DATA COLLECTED BY THE NATIONAL INSTITUTE ALLOWS US TO REACH A CONCLUSION REGARDING THE HEATHERFIELD AREA AND PREDICT THAT IN THE LONG TERM, THE CLIMATE WILL UNDERGO CHANGES INDICATING...
Sounds interesting!
ZZZ
I'm so sleepy...
HUH?
"AND FOR SOME, THE TROUBLE HAS JUST BEGUN..."
THE LAST TIME I HID IN THE BATHROOM WAS YEARS AGO...
BATHROOM

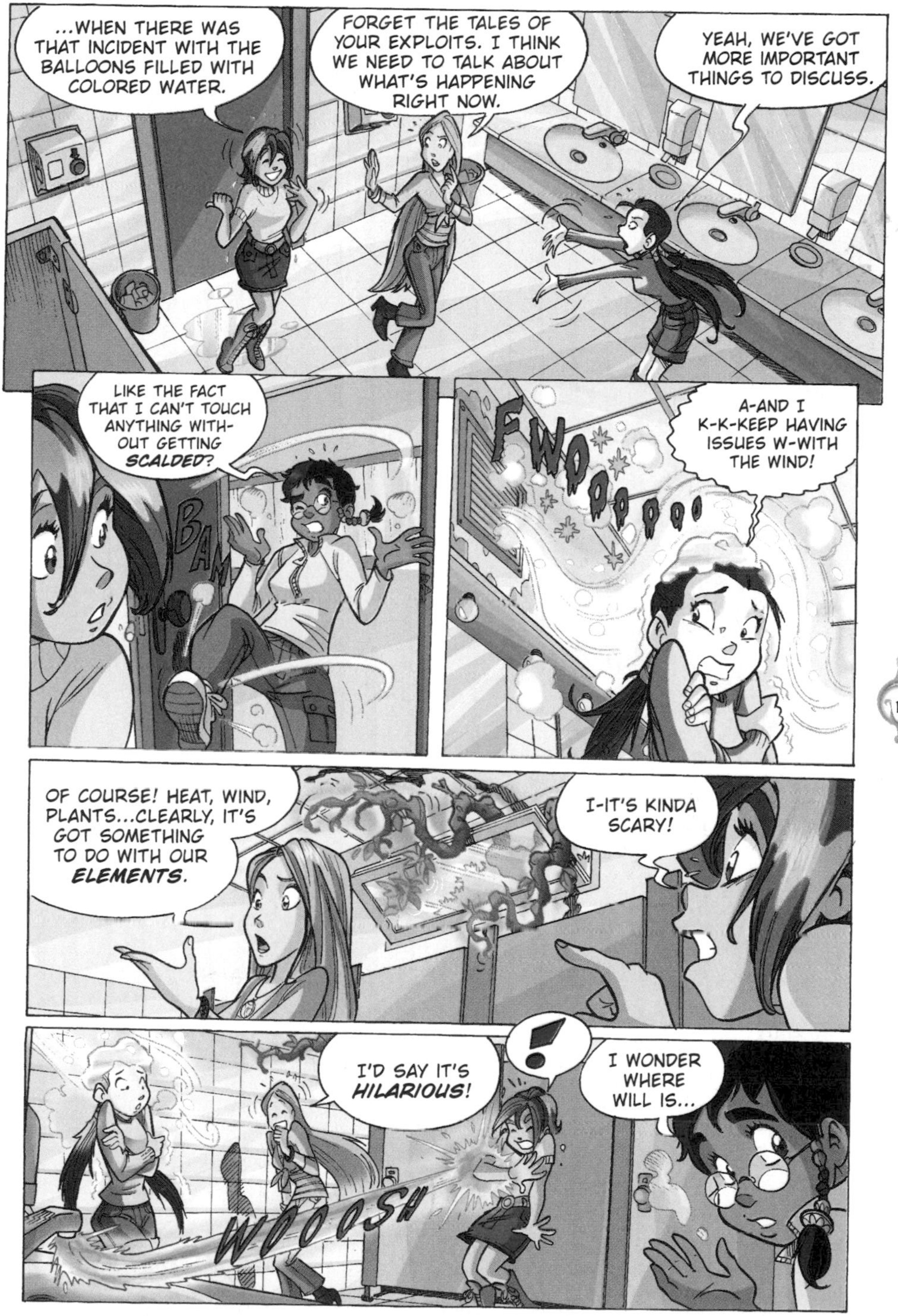
...WHEN THERE WAS THAT INCIDENT WITH THE BALLOONS FILLED WITH COLORED WATER.
FORGET THE TALES OF YOUR EXPLOITS. I THINK WE NEED TO TALK ABOUT WHAT'S HAPPENING RIGHT NOW.
YEAH, WE'VE GOT MORE IMPORTANT THINGS TO DISCUSS.
LIKE THE FACT THAT I CAN'T TOUCH ANYTHING WITHOUT GETTING SCALDED?
BAM
FWOOOOOO
A-AND I K-K-KEEP HAVING ISSUES W-WITH THE WIND!
OF COURSE! HEAT, WIND, PLANTS...CLEARLY, IT'S GOT SOMETHING TO DO WITH OUR ELEMENTS.
I-IT'S KINDA SCARY!
I'D SAY IT'S HILARIOUS!
!
I WONDER WHERE WILL IS...
WOOOSH

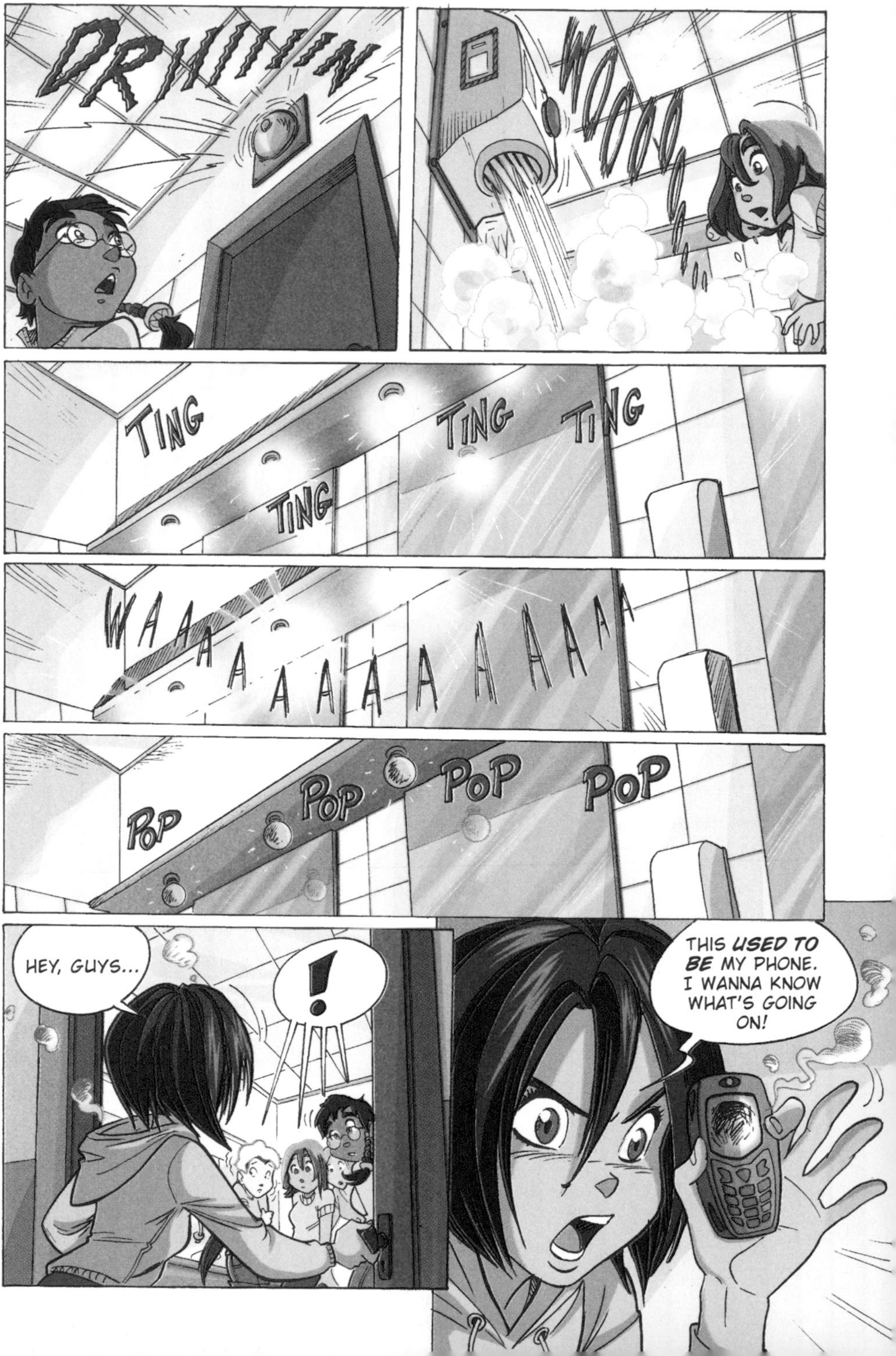

DRHIIIN
WOOOOOOOO
TING
TING
TING
TING
WAAAAAAAAAAAA
POP
POP
POP
POP
HEY, GUYS...
!
THIS USED TO BE MY PHONE. I WANNA KNOW WHAT'S GOING ON!

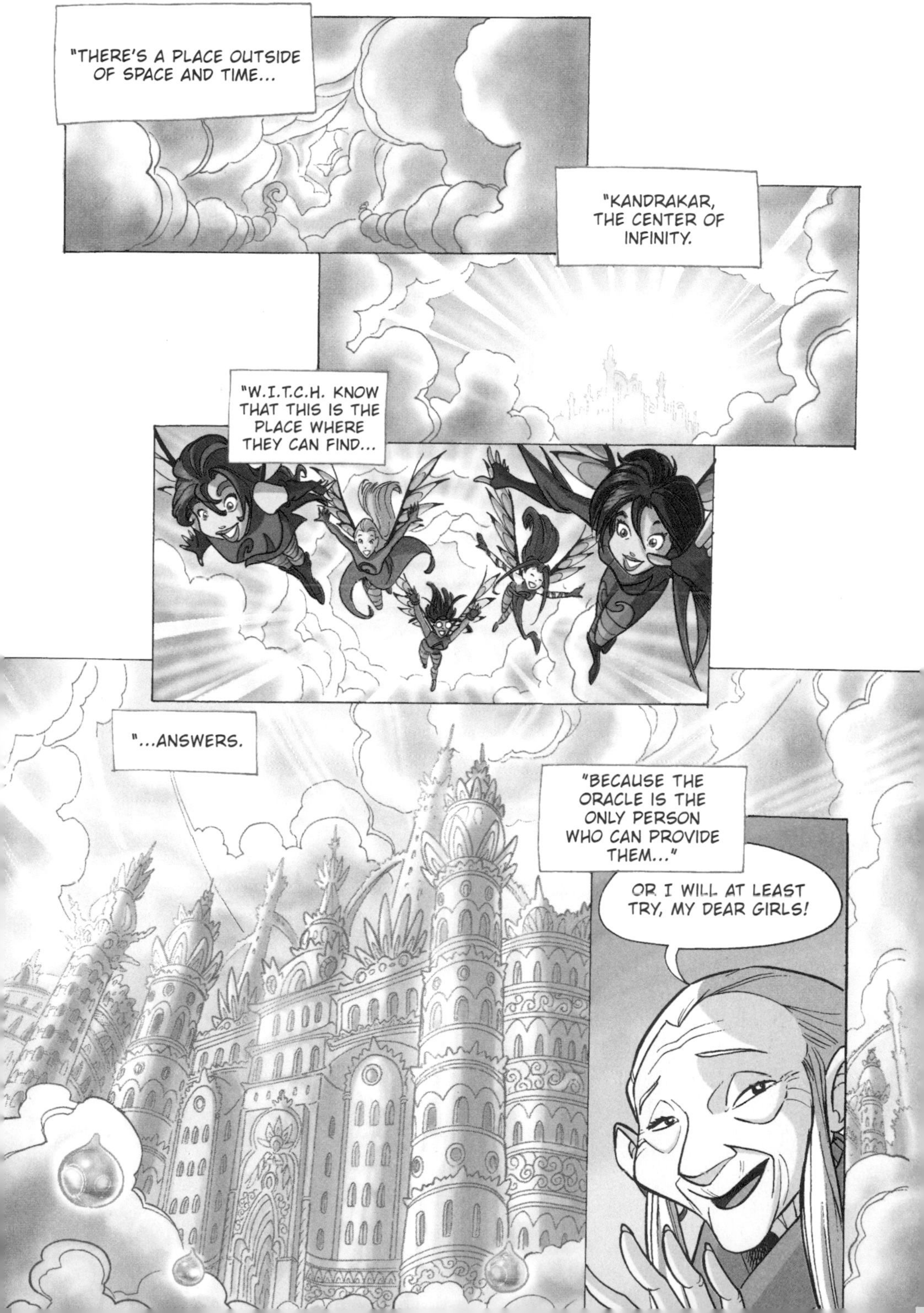
"THERE'S A PLACE OUTSIDE OF SPACE AND TIME...
"KANDRAKAR, THE CENTER OF INFINITY.
"W.I.T.C.H. KNOW THAT THIS IS THE PLACE WHERE THEY CAN FIND...
"...ANSWERS.
"BECAUSE THE ORACLE IS THE ONLY PERSON WHO CAN PROVIDE THEM..."
OR I WILL AT LEAST TRY, MY DEAR GIRLS!

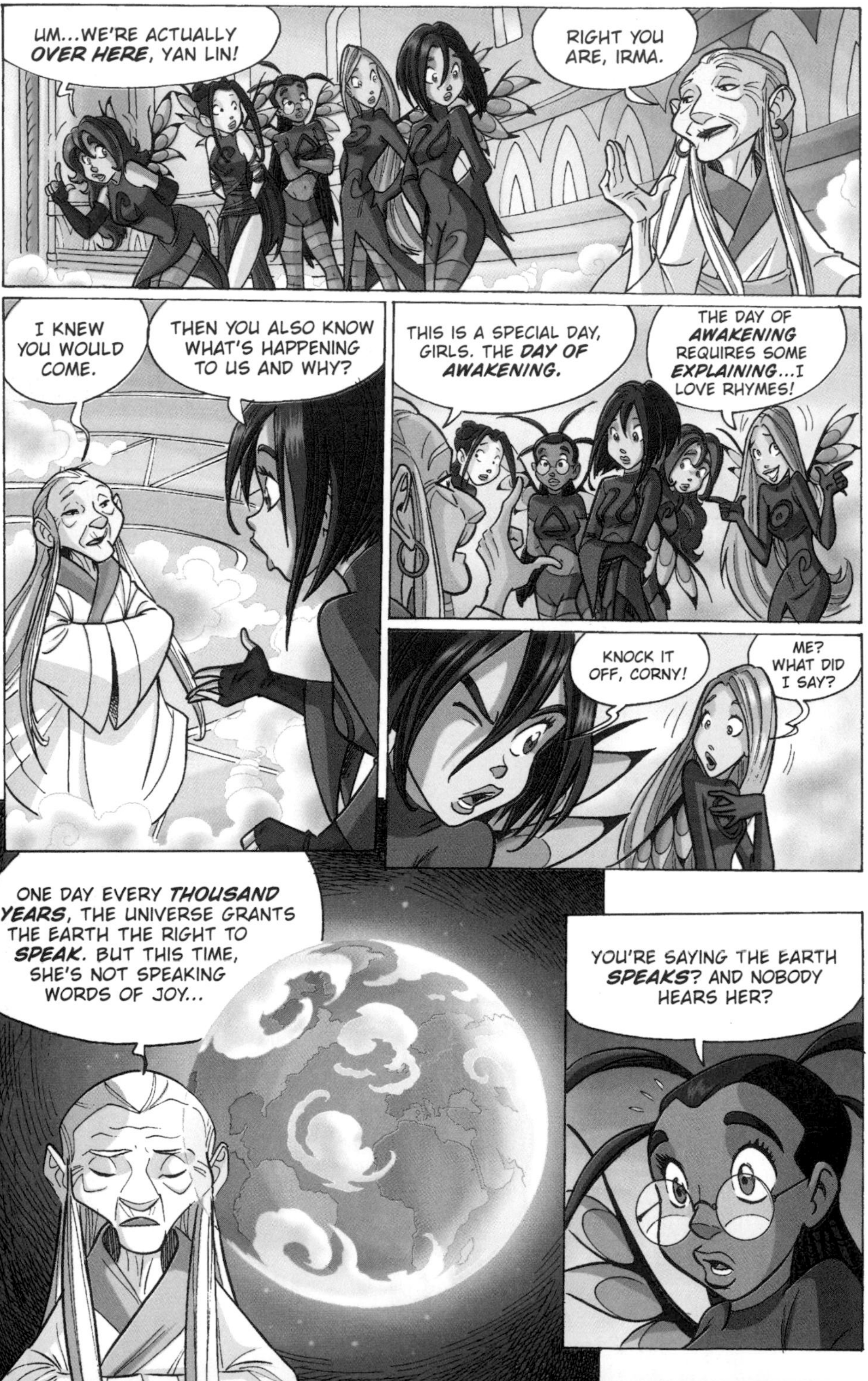
UM...WE'RE ACTUALLY OVER HERE, YAN LIN!
RIGHT YOU ARE, IRMA.
I KNEW YOU WOULD COME.
THEN YOU ALSO KNOW WHAT'S HAPPENING TO US AND WHY?
THIS IS A SPECIAL DAY, GIRLS. THE DAY OF AWAKENING.
THE DAY OF AWAKENING REQUIRES SOME EXPLAINING...I LOVE RHYMES!
KNOCK IT OFF, CORNY!
ME? WHAT DID I SAY?
ONE DAY EVERY THOUSAND YEARS, THE UNIVERSE GRANTS THE EARTH THE RIGHT TO SPEAK. BUT THIS TIME, SHE'S NOT SPEAKING WORDS OF JOY...
YOU'RE SAYING THE EARTH SPEAKS? AND NOBODY HEARS HER?

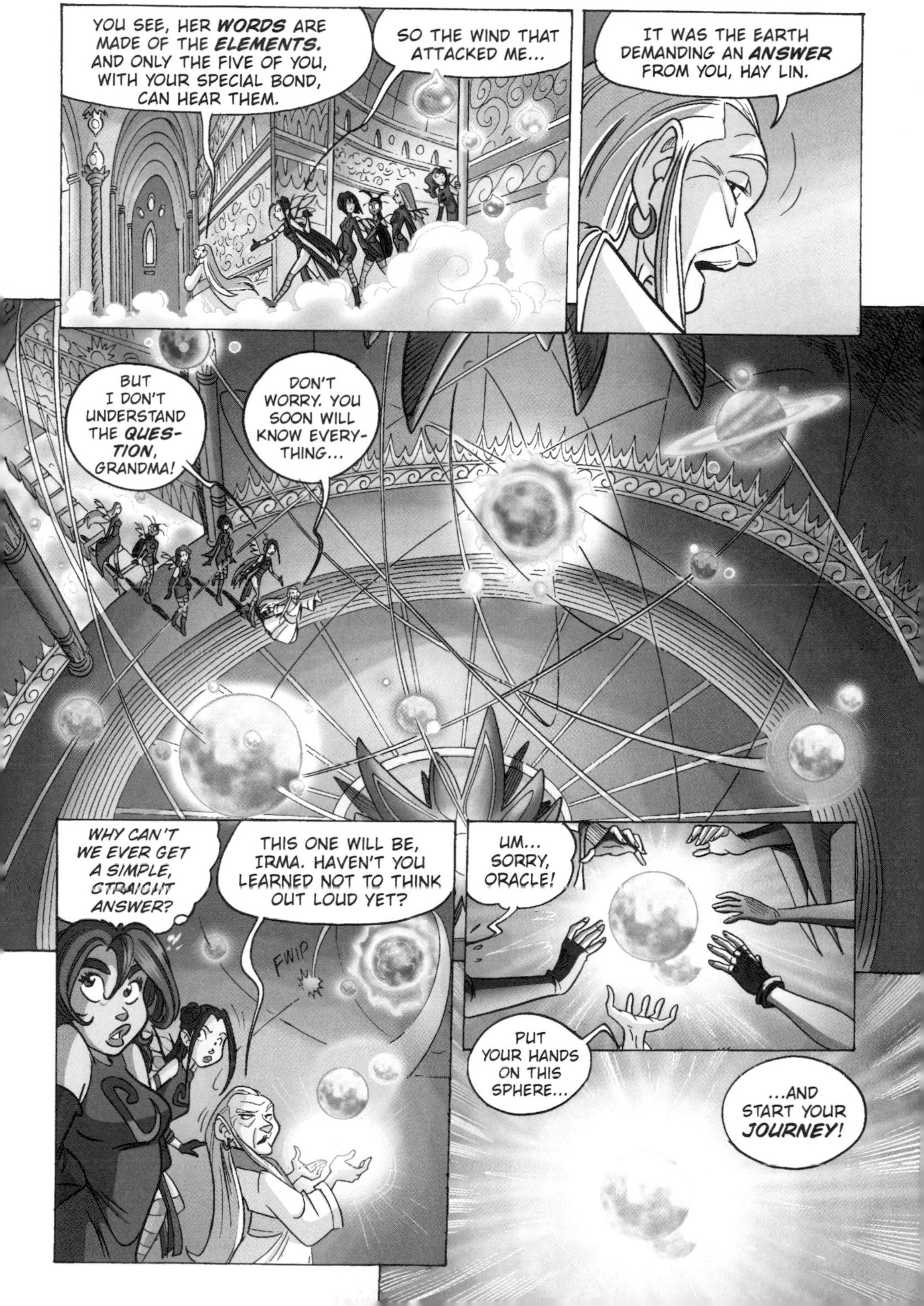
YOU SEE, HER WORDS ARE MADE OF THE ELEMENTS. AND ONLY THE FIVE OF YOU, WITH YOUR SPECIAL BOND, CAN HEAR THEM.
SO THE WIND THAT ATTACKED ME...
IT WAS THE EARTH DEMANDING AN ANSWER FROM YOU, HAY LIN.
BUT I DON'T UNDERSTAND THE QUESTION, GRANDMA!
DON'T WORRY. YOU SOON WILL KNOW EVERYTHING...
WHY CAN'T WE EVER GET A SIMPLE, STRAIGHT ANSWER?
THIS ONE WILL BE, IRMA. HAVEN'T YOU LEARNED NOT TO THINK OUT LOUD YET?
FWIP
UM... SORRY, ORACLE!
PUT YOUR HANDS ON THIS SPHERE...
...AND START YOUR JOURNEY!

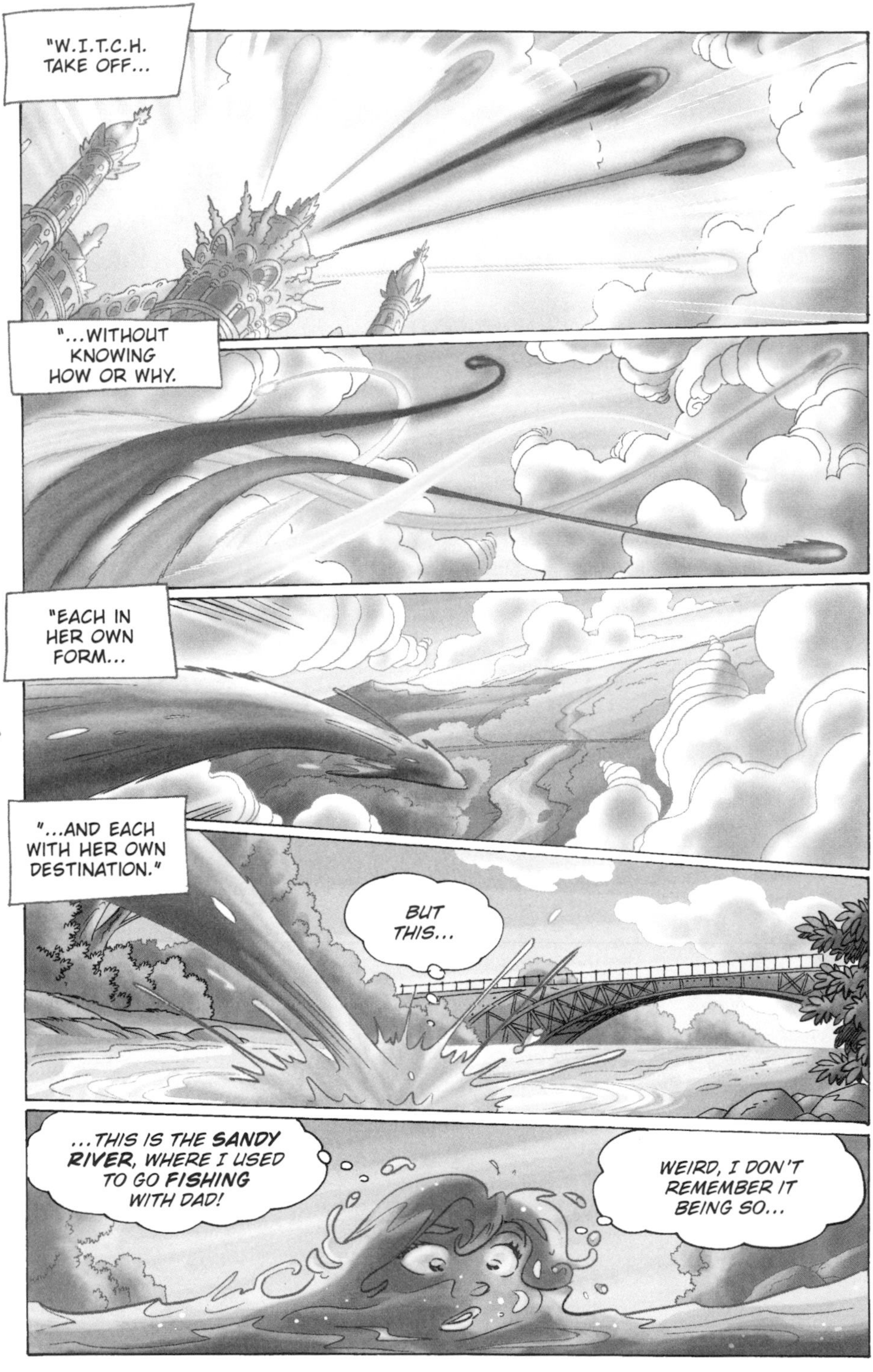
"W.I.T.C.H. TAKE OFF...
"...WITHOUT KNOWING HOW OR WHY.
"EACH IN HER OWN FORM...
"...AND EACH WITH HER OWN DESTINATION."
BUT THIS...
...THIS IS THE **SANDY RIVER**, WHERE I USED TO GO **FISHING** WITH DAD!
WEIRD, I DON'T REMEMBER IT BEING SO...

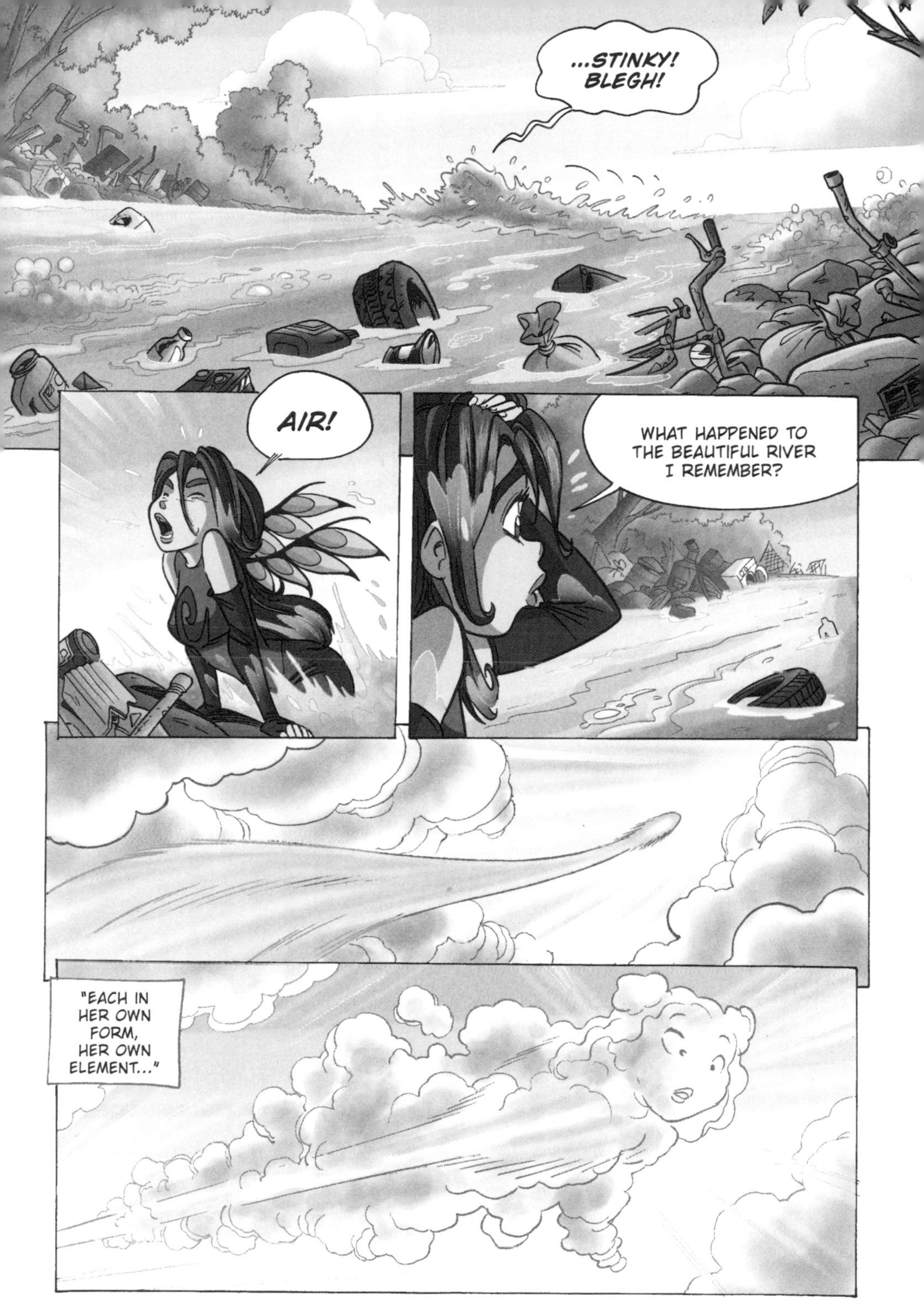
...STINKY! BLEGH!
AIR!
WHAT HAPPENED TO THE BEAUTIFUL RIVER I REMEMBER?
"EACH IN HER OWN FORM, HER OWN ELEMENT..."

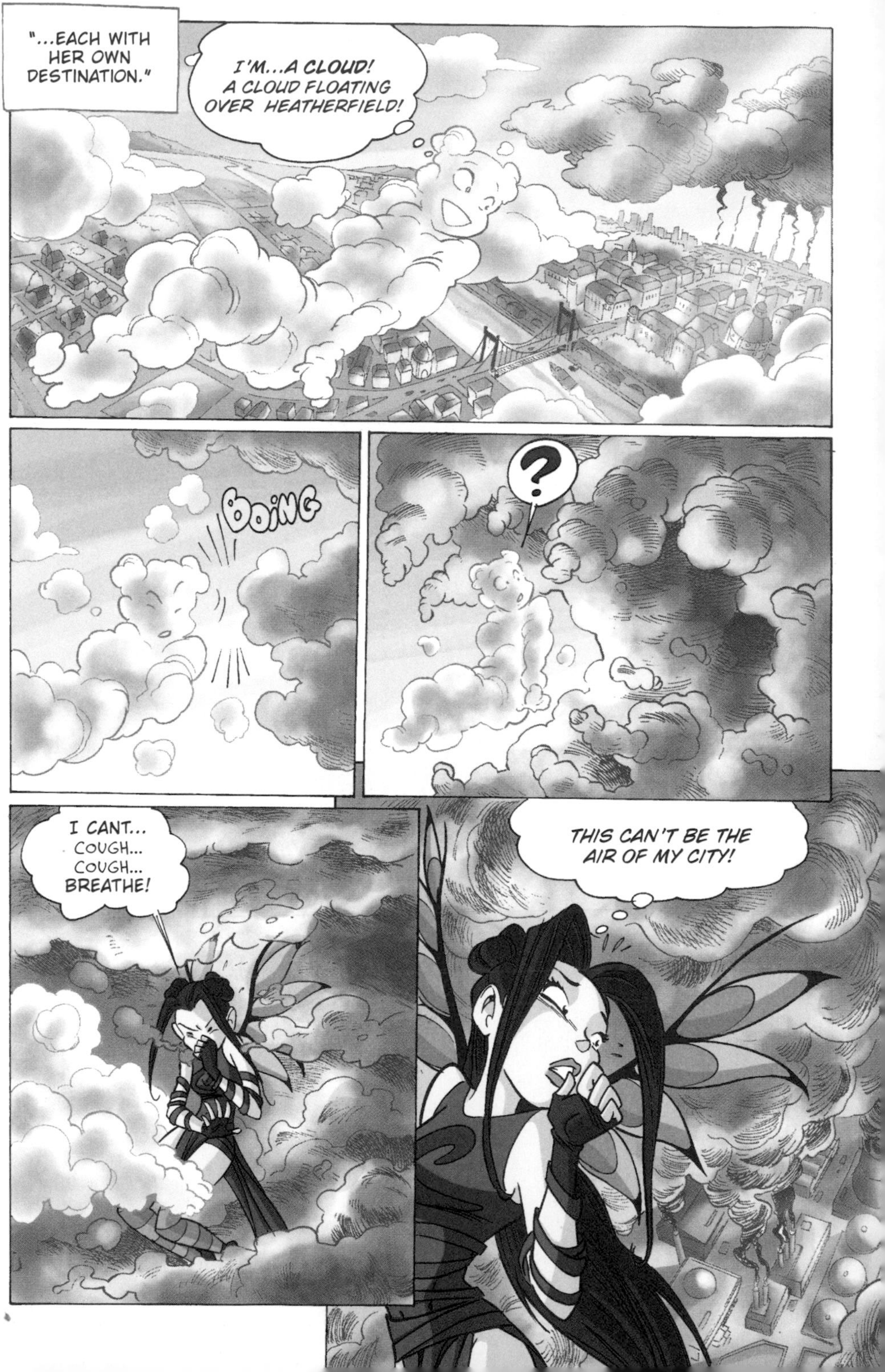
"...EACH WITH HER OWN DESTINATION."
I'M...A CLOUD! A CLOUD FLOATING OVER HEATHERFIELD!
BOING
?
I CANT... COUGH... COUGH... BREATHE!
THIS CAN'T BE THE AIR OF MY CITY!

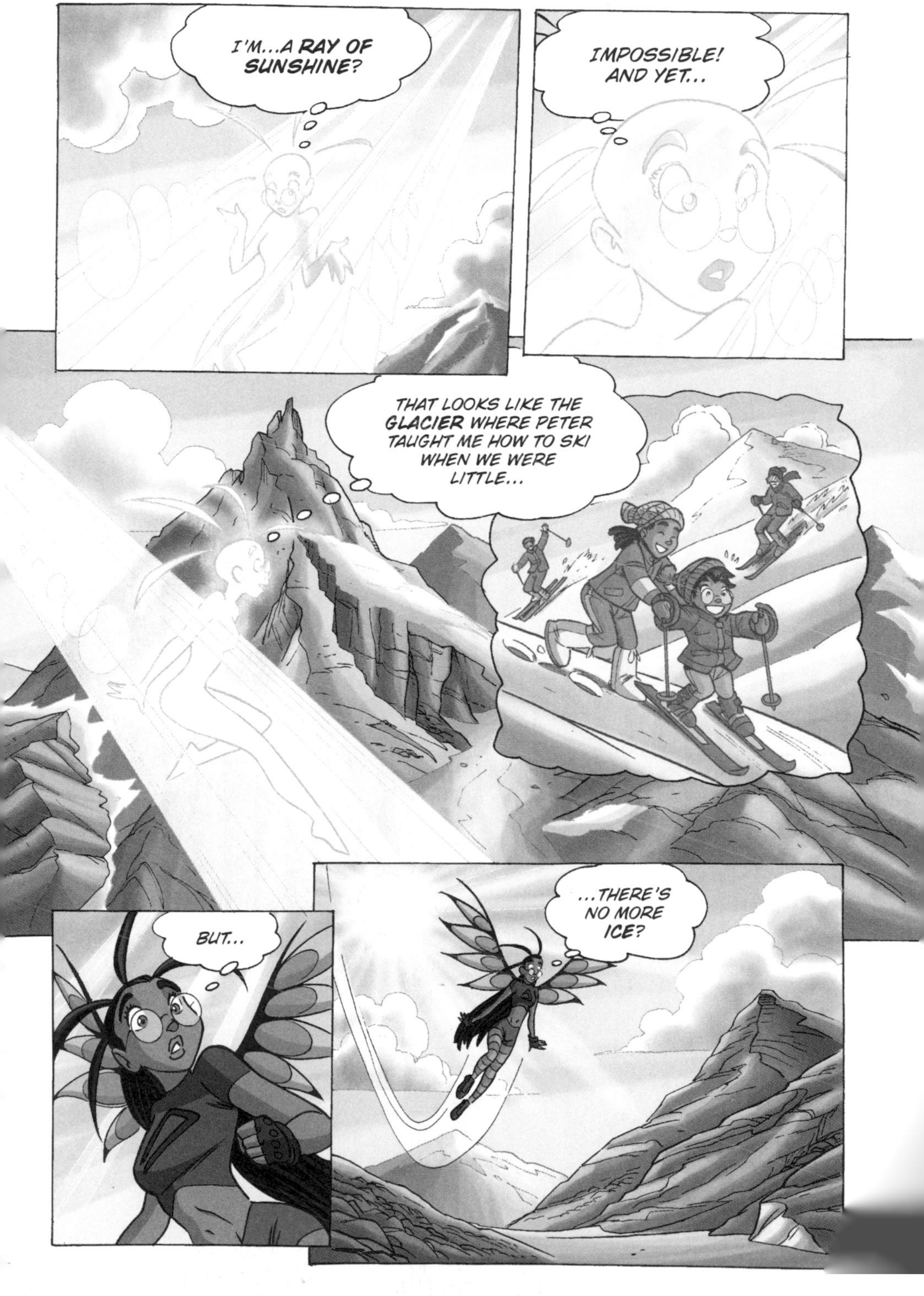
I'M...A RAY OF SUNSHINE?
IMPOSSIBLE! AND YET...
THAT LOOKS LIKE THE GLACIER WHERE PETER TAUGHT ME HOW TO SKI WHEN WE WERE LITTLE...
BUT...
...THERE'S NO MORE ICE?

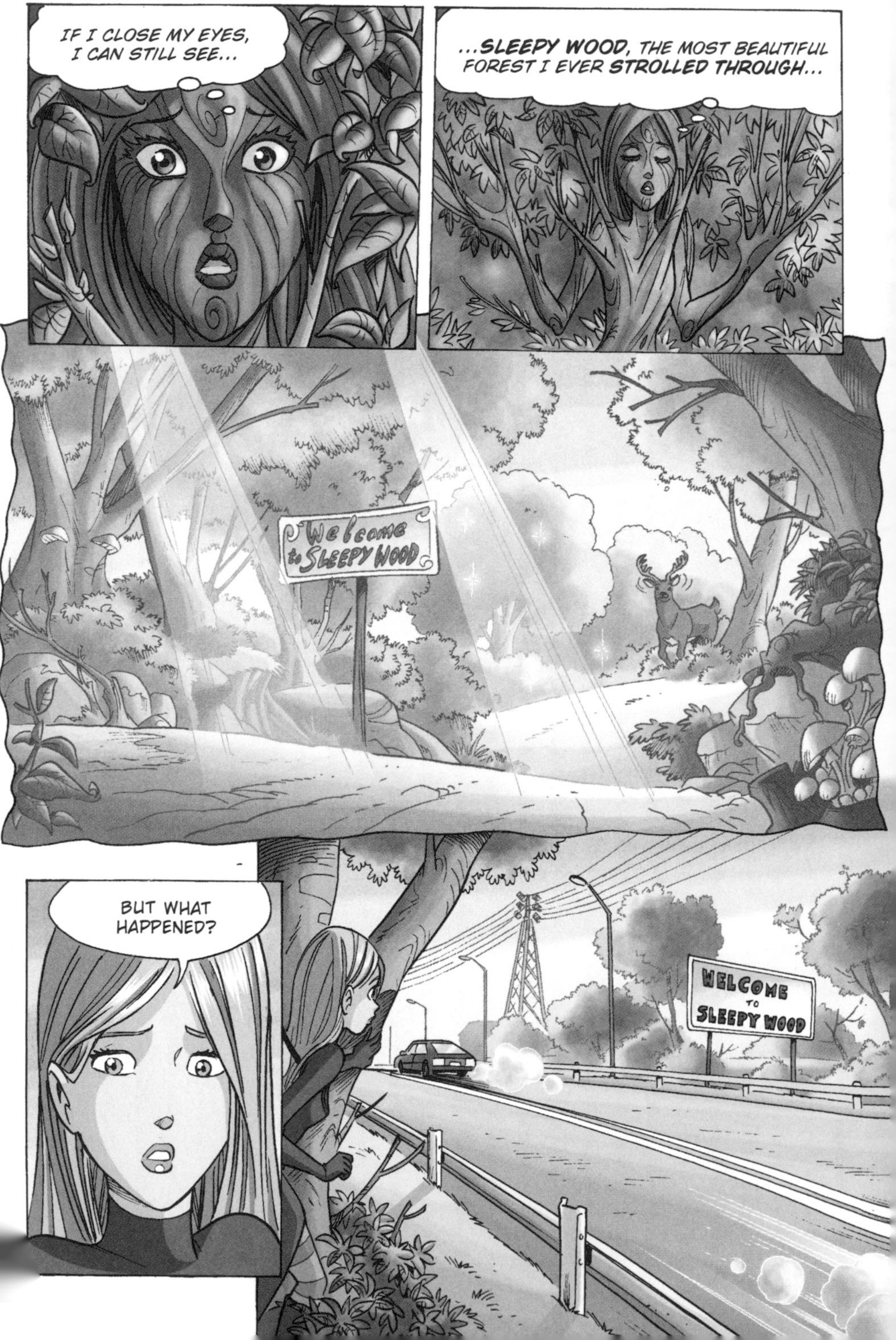
IF I CLOSE MY EYES, I CAN STILL SEE...
...SLEEPY WOOD, THE MOST BEAUTIFUL FOREST I EVER STROLLED THROUGH...
Welcome to SLEEPY WOOD
BUT WHAT HAPPENED?
WELCOME TO SLEEPY WOOD

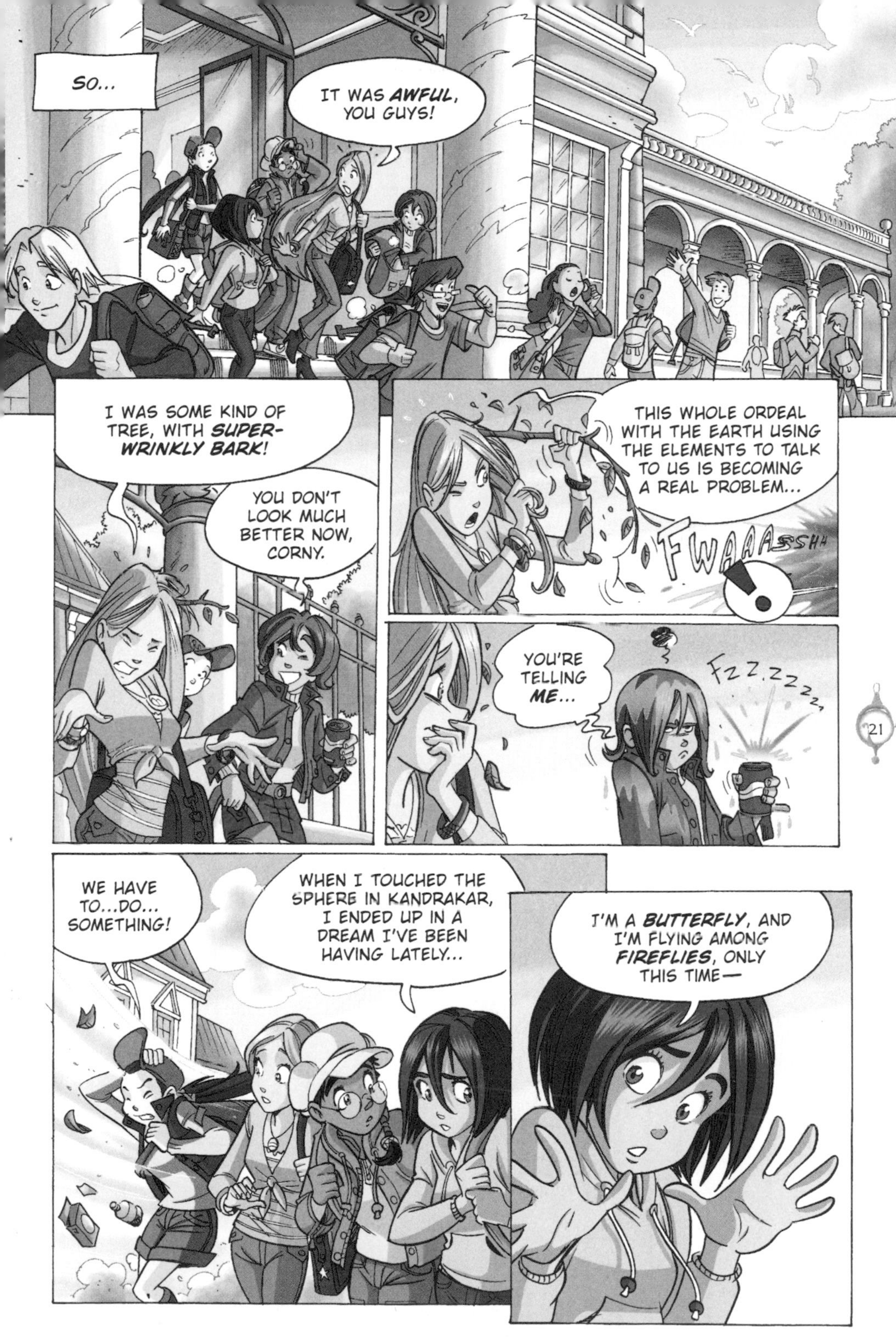
SO...
IT WAS AWFUL, YOU GUYS!
I WAS SOME KIND OF TREE, WITH SUPER-WRINKLY BARK!
YOU DON'T LOOK MUCH BETTER NOW, CORNY.
THIS WHOLE ORDEAL WITH THE EARTH USING THE ELEMENTS TO TALK TO US IS BECOMING A REAL PROBLEM...
FWAAASSHH
!
YOU'RE TELLING ME...
FZZZZZZZ
WE HAVE TO...DO... SOMETHING!
WHEN I TOUCHED THE SPHERE IN KANDRAKAR, I ENDED UP IN A DREAM I'VE BEEN HAVING LATELY...
I'M A BUTTERFLY, AND I'M FLYING AMONG FIREFLIES, ONLY THIS TIME—

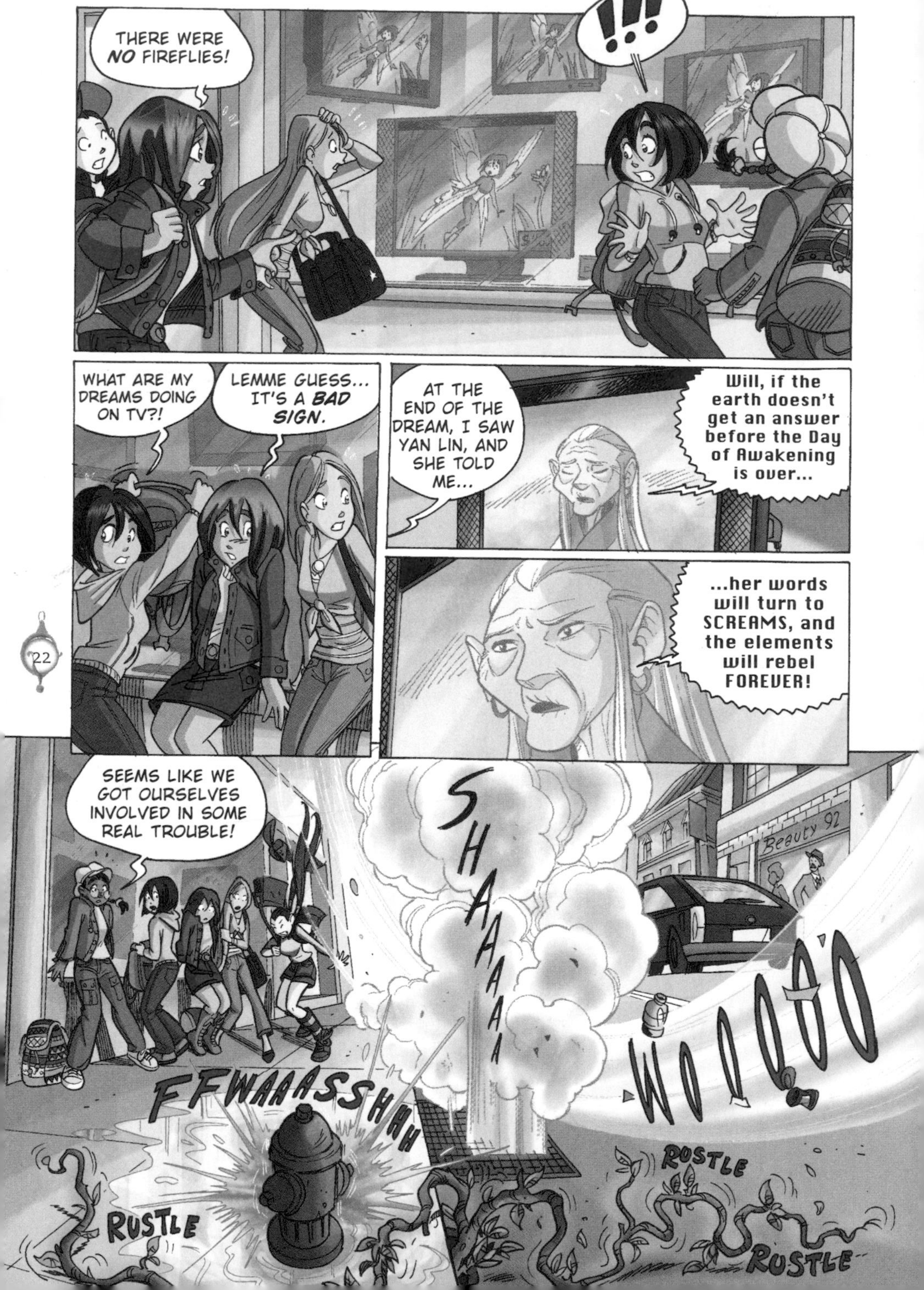

THERE WERE NO FIREFLIES!
!!!
WHAT ARE MY DREAMS DOING ON TV?!
LEMME GUESS... IT'S A BAD SIGN.
AT THE END OF THE DREAM, I SAW YAN LIN, AND SHE TOLD ME...
Will, if the earth doesn't get an answer before the Day of Awakening is over...
...her words will turn to SCREAMS, and the elements will rebel FOREVER!
SEEMS LIKE WE GOT OURSELVES INVOLVED IN SOME REAL TROUBLE!
SHAAAAA
FFWAAASSHHH
WOOOOO
Beauty 92
RUSTLE
RUSTLE
RUSTLE

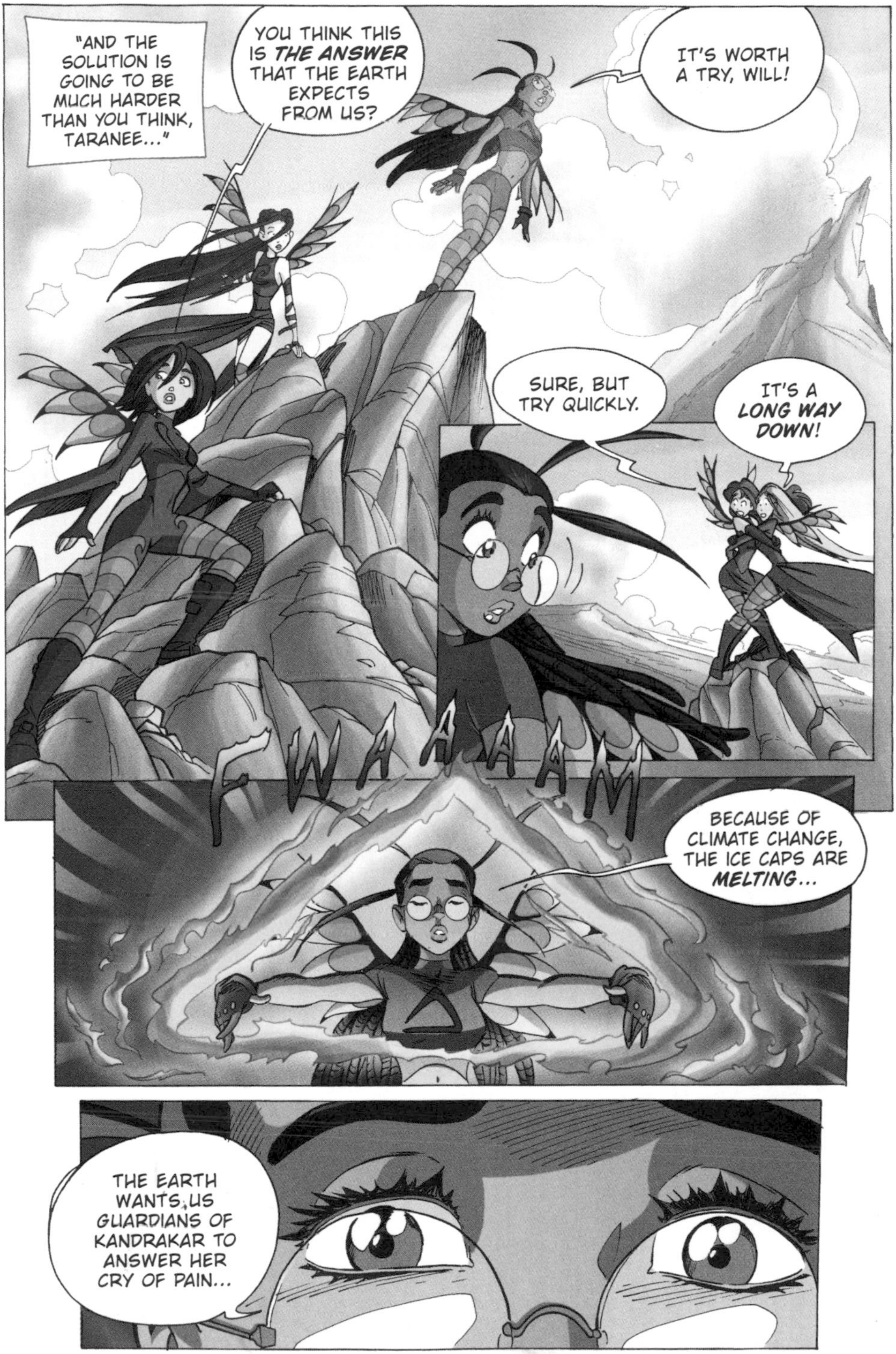
"AND THE SOLUTION IS GOING TO BE MUCH HARDER THAN YOU THINK, TARANEE..."
YOU THINK THIS IS THE ANSWER THAT THE EARTH EXPECTS FROM US?
IT'S WORTH A TRY, WILL!
SURE, BUT TRY QUICKLY.
IT'S A LONG WAY DOWN!
FWAAAAM
BECAUSE OF CLIMATE CHANGE, THE ICE CAPS ARE MELTING...
THE EARTH WANTS US GUARDIANS OF KANDRAKAR TO ANSWER HER CRY OF PAIN...

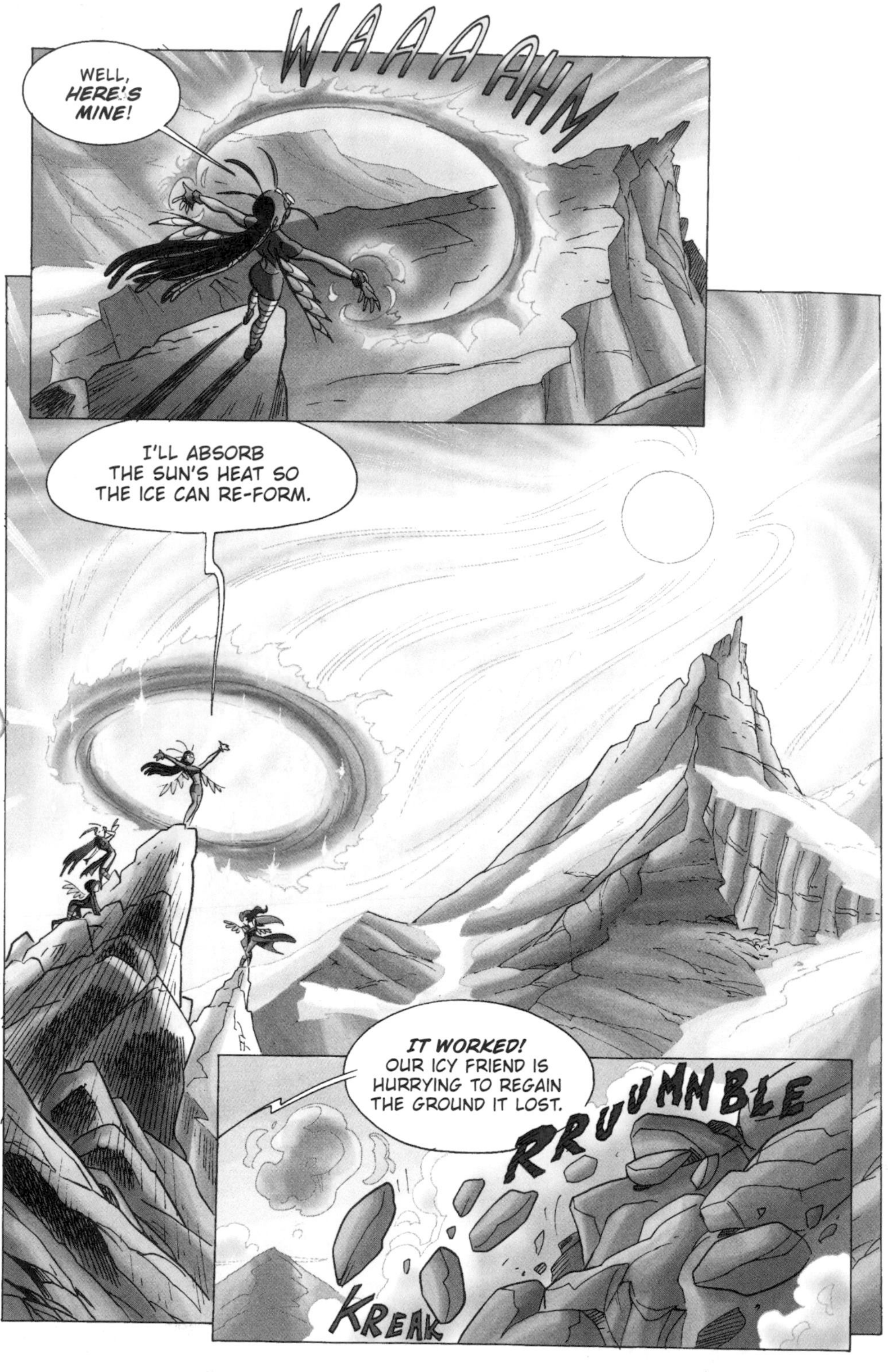
WAAAAHM
WELL, HERE'S MINE!
I'LL ABSORB THE SUN'S HEAT SO THE ICE CAN RE-FORM.
IT WORKED! OUR ICY FRIEND IS HURRYING TO REGAIN THE GROUND IT LOST.
RRUUMNBLE
KREAK

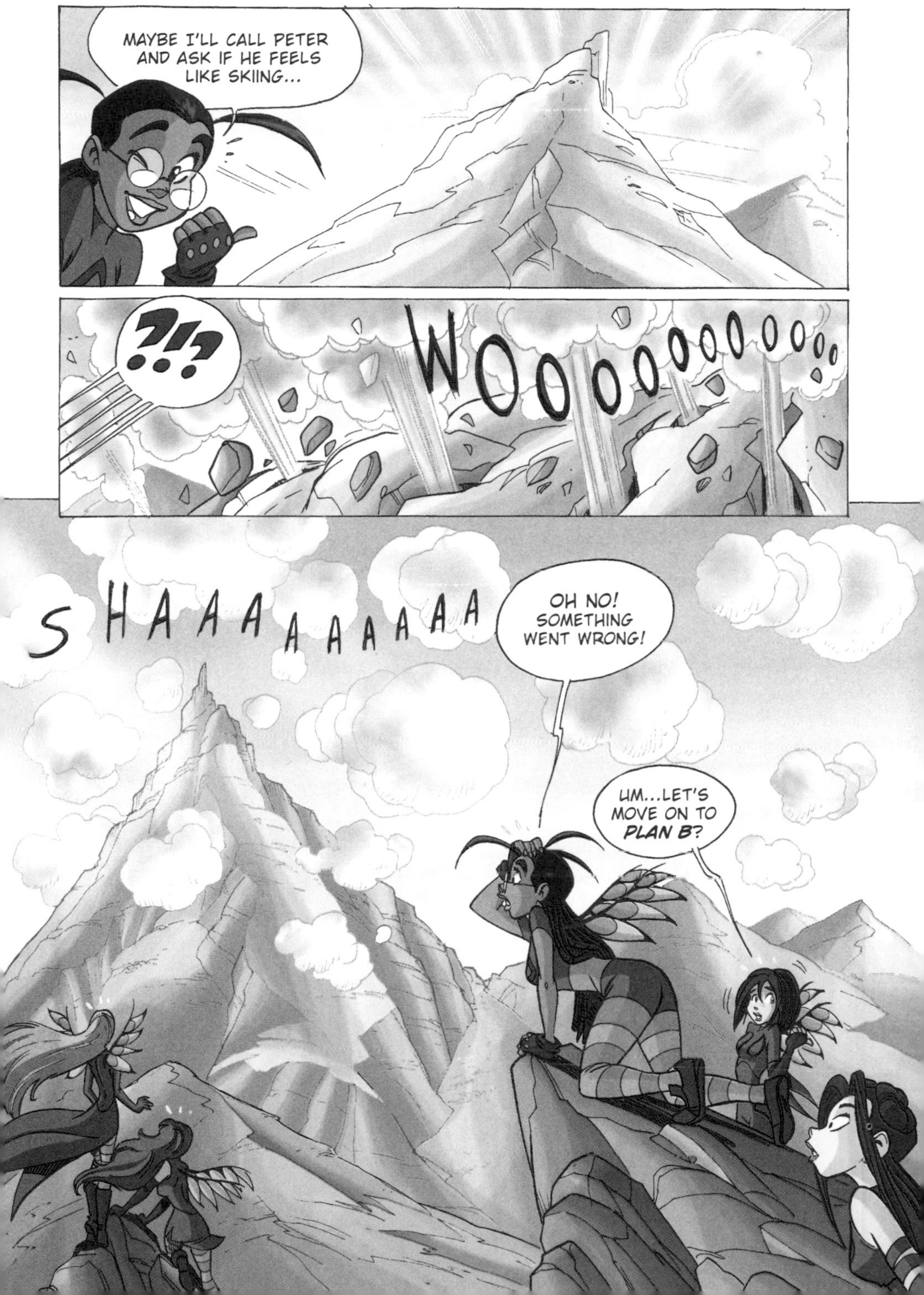
MAYBE I'LL CALL PETER AND ASK IF HE FEELS LIKE SKIING...
?!?
WOOOOOOOOOOOOO
SHAAAAAAAAAA
OH NO! SOMETHING WENT WRONG!
UM...LET'S MOVE ON TO **PLAN B**?

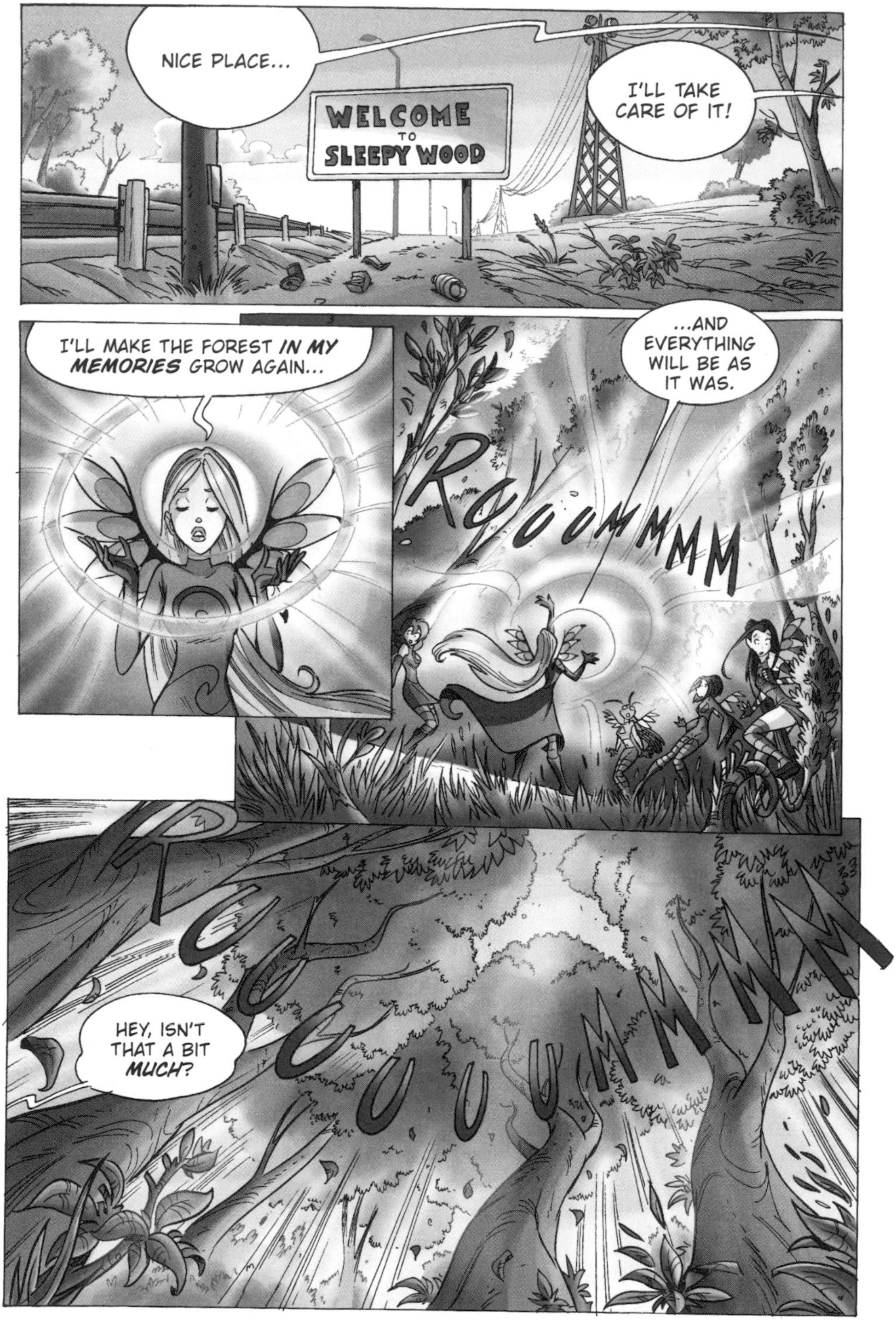
NICE PLACE...
WELCOME TO SLEEPY WOOD
I'LL TAKE CARE OF IT!
I'LL MAKE THE FOREST *IN MY MEMORIES* GROW AGAIN...
...AND EVERYTHING WILL BE AS IT WAS.
HEY, ISN'T THAT A BIT *MUCH*?

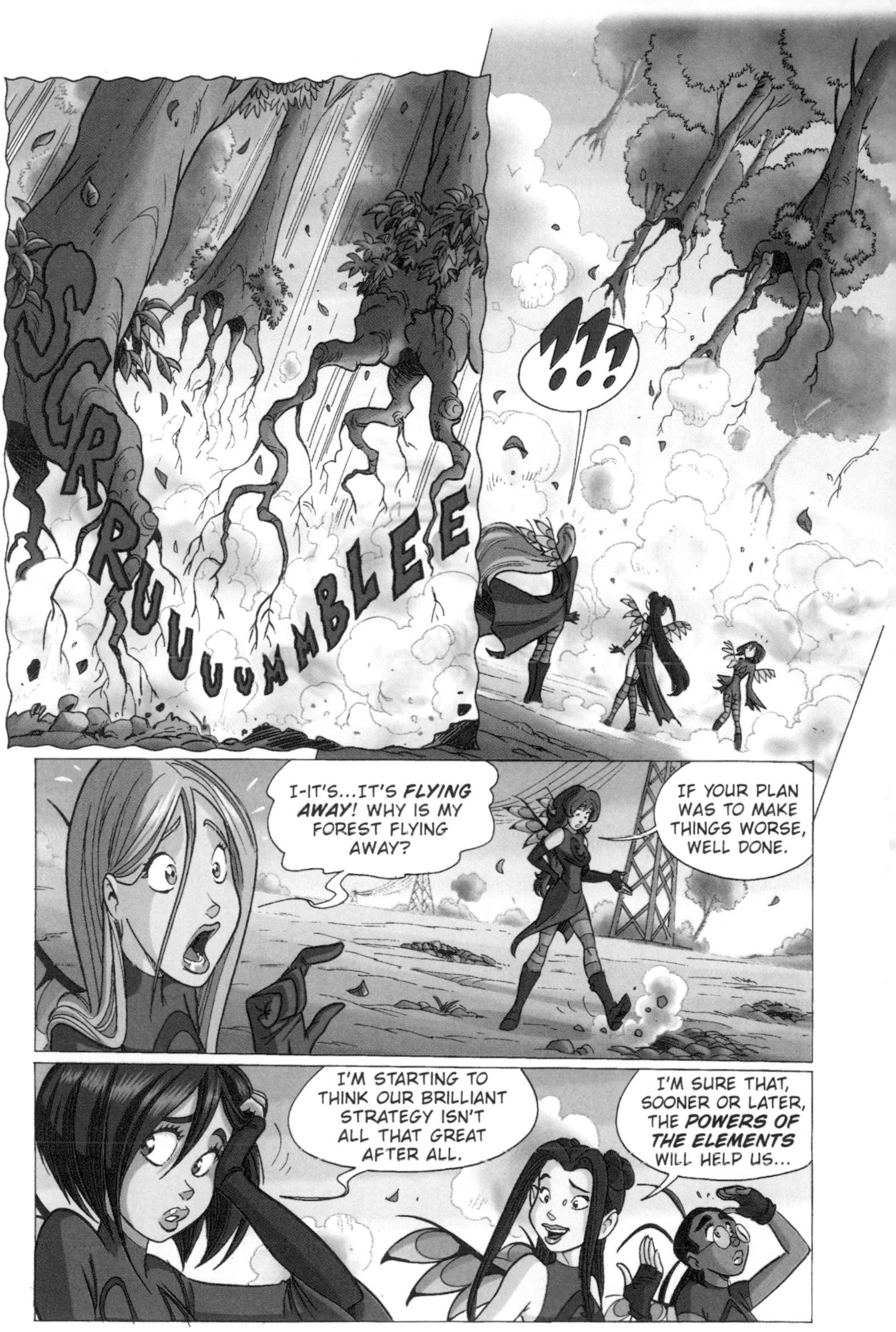
SCRRUUUUMMBLEE
???
I-IT'S...IT'S *FLYING AWAY!* WHY IS MY FOREST FLYING AWAY?
IF YOUR PLAN WAS TO MAKE THINGS WORSE, WELL DONE.
I'M STARTING TO THINK OUR BRILLIANT STRATEGY ISN'T ALL THAT GREAT AFTER ALL.
I'M SURE THAT, SOONER OR LATER, THE *POWERS OF THE ELEMENTS* WILL HELP US...

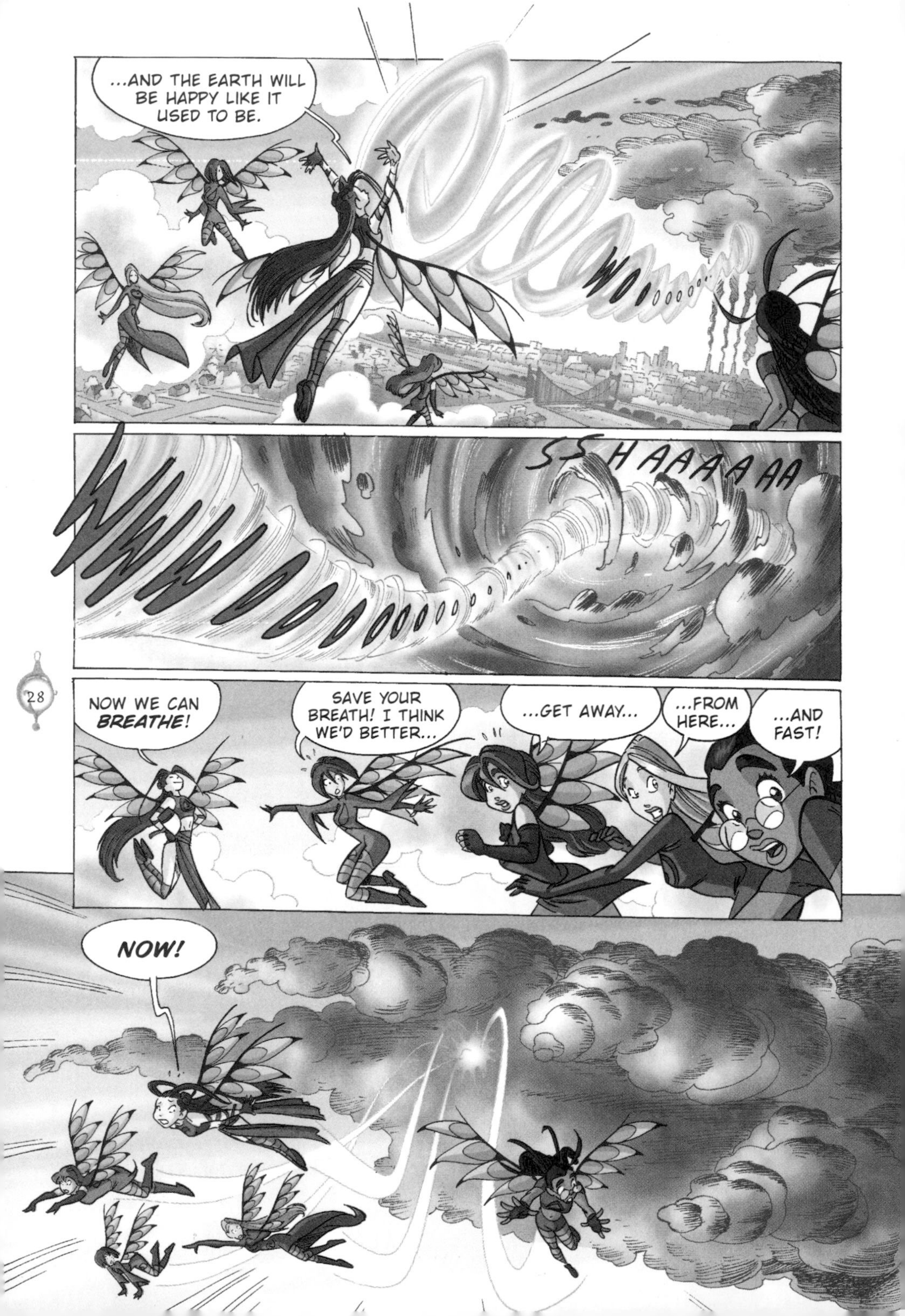

...AND THE EARTH WILL BE HAPPY LIKE IT USED TO BE.
WOOOOOO...
SSHAAAAAAA
WWWWOOOOOOOOOOO...
NOW WE CAN *BREATHE*!
SAVE YOUR BREATH! I THINK WE'D BETTER...
...GET AWAY...
...FROM HERE...
...AND FAST!
NOW!

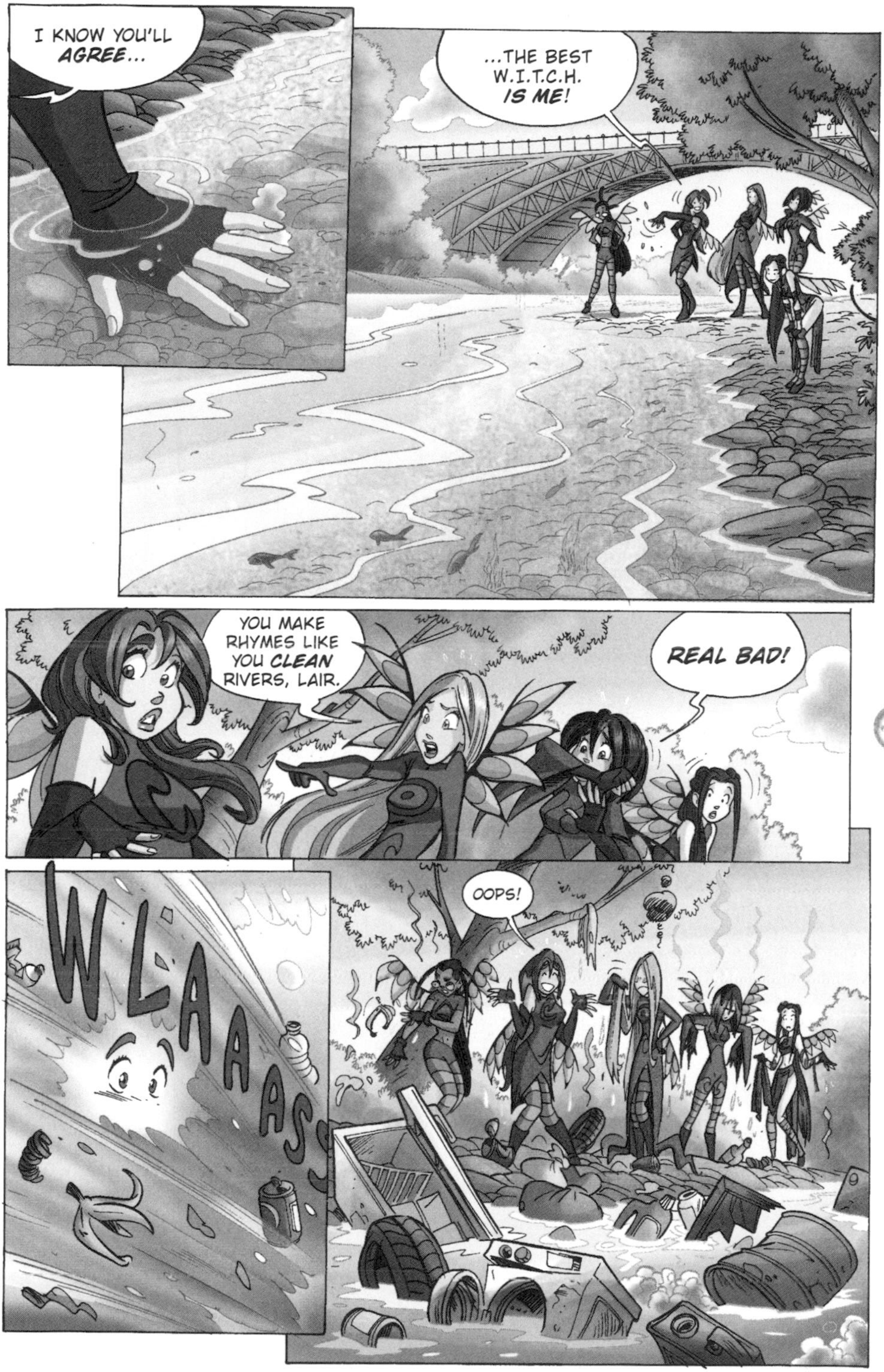

I KNOW YOU'LL **AGREE**...
...THE BEST W.I.T.C.H. **IS ME**!
YOU MAKE RHYMES LIKE YOU **CLEAN** RIVERS, LAIR.
REAL BAD!
WLAAAAS
OOPS!

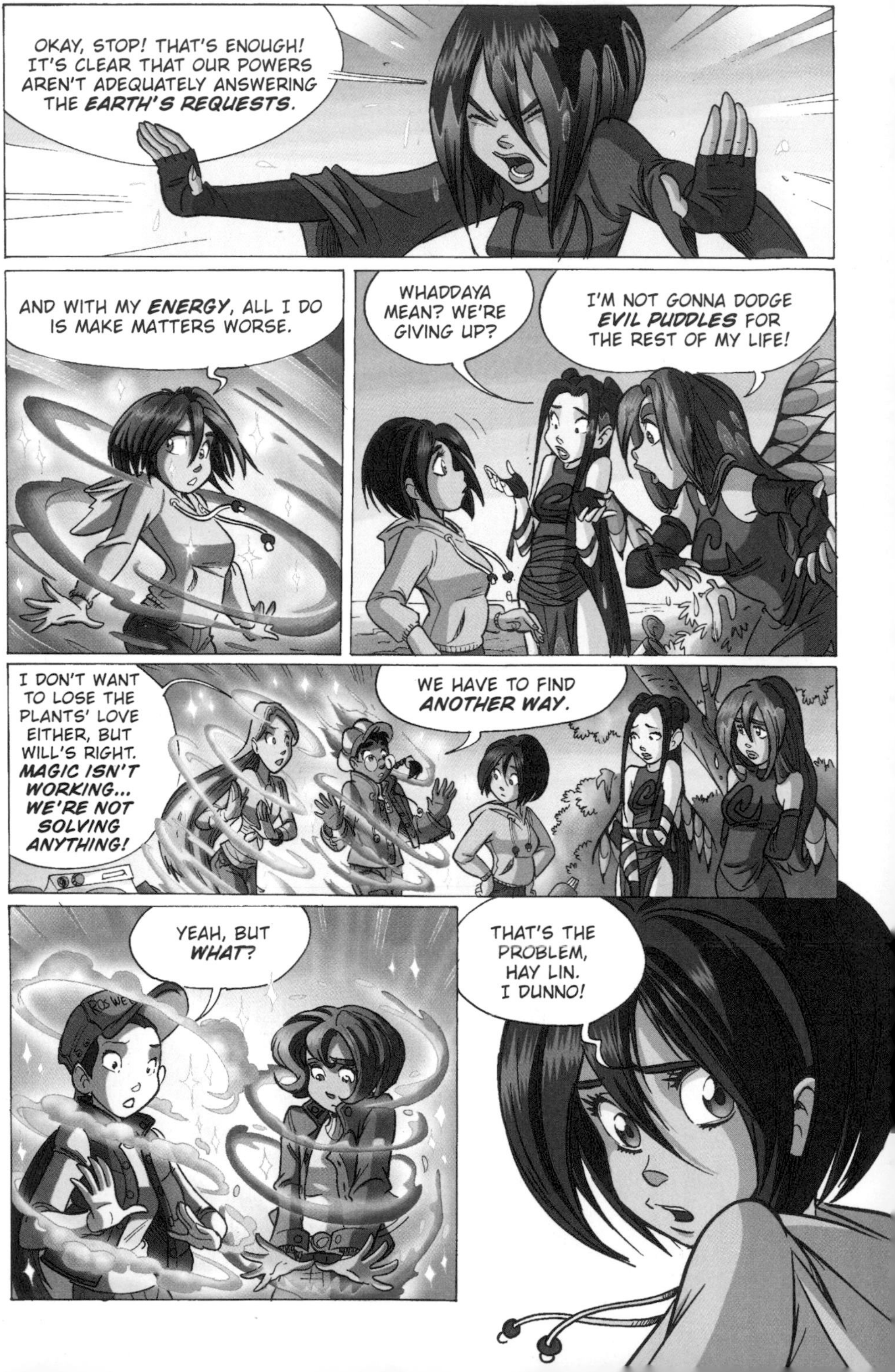
OKAY, STOP! THAT'S ENOUGH! IT'S CLEAR THAT OUR POWERS AREN'T ADEQUATELY ANSWERING THE EARTH'S REQUESTS.
AND WITH MY ENERGY, ALL I DO IS MAKE MATTERS WORSE.
WHADDAYA MEAN? WE'RE GIVING UP?
I'M NOT GONNA DODGE EVIL PUDDLES FOR THE REST OF MY LIFE!
I DON'T WANT TO LOSE THE PLANTS' LOVE EITHER, BUT WILL'S RIGHT. MAGIC ISN'T WORKING... WE'RE NOT SOLVING ANYTHING!
WE HAVE TO FIND ANOTHER WAY.
YEAH, BUT WHAT?
THAT'S THE PROBLEM, HAY LIN. I DUNNO!

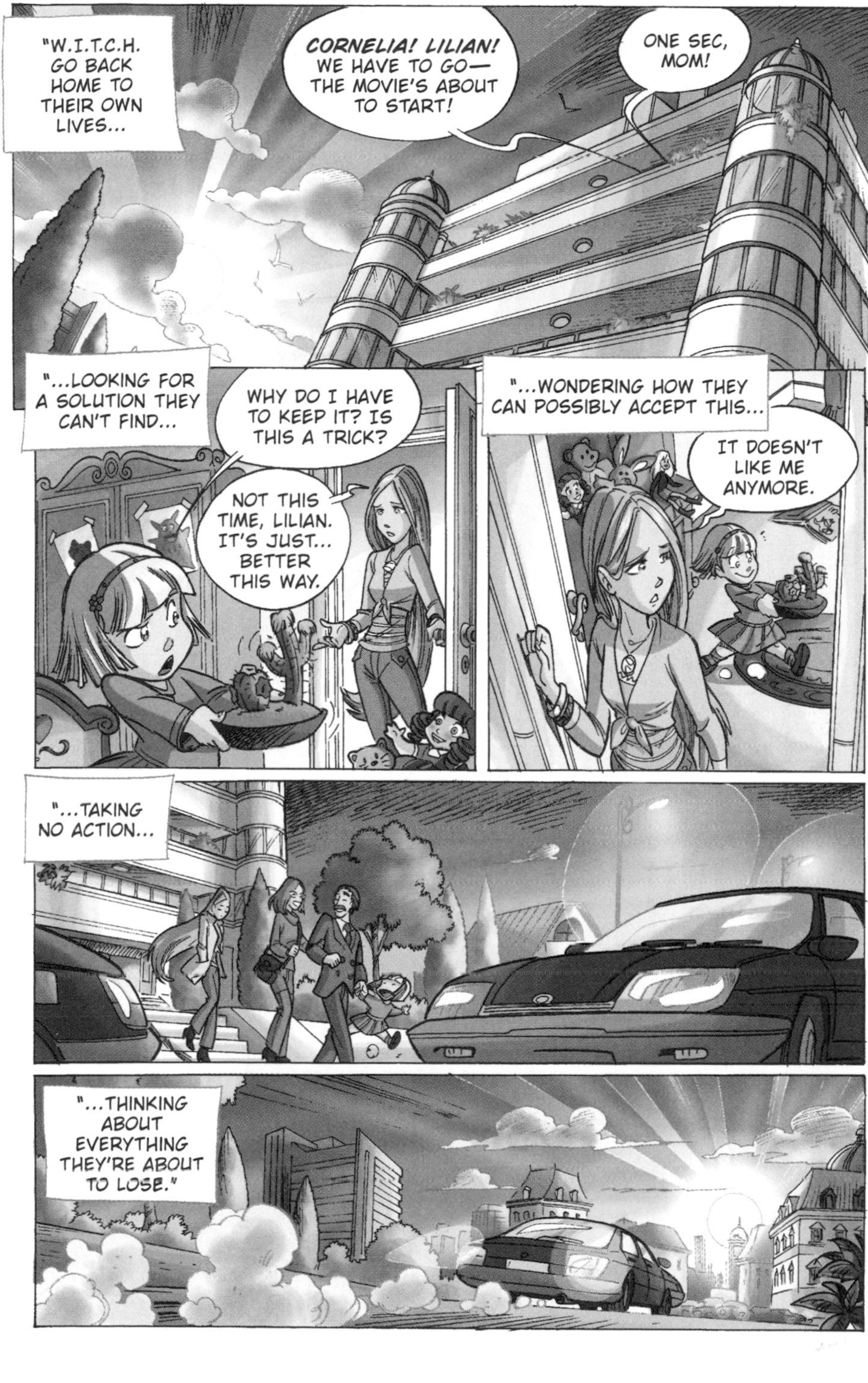
"W.I.T.C.H. GO BACK HOME TO THEIR OWN LIVES...
CORNELIA! LILIAN! WE HAVE TO GO— THE MOVIE'S ABOUT TO START!
ONE SEC, MOM!
"...LOOKING FOR A SOLUTION THEY CAN'T FIND...
WHY DO I HAVE TO KEEP IT? IS THIS A TRICK?
NOT THIS TIME, LILIAN. IT'S JUST... BETTER THIS WAY.
"...WONDERING HOW THEY CAN POSSIBLY ACCEPT THIS...
IT DOESN'T LIKE ME ANYMORE.
"...TAKING NO ACTION...
"...THINKING ABOUT EVERYTHING THEY'RE ABOUT TO LOSE."

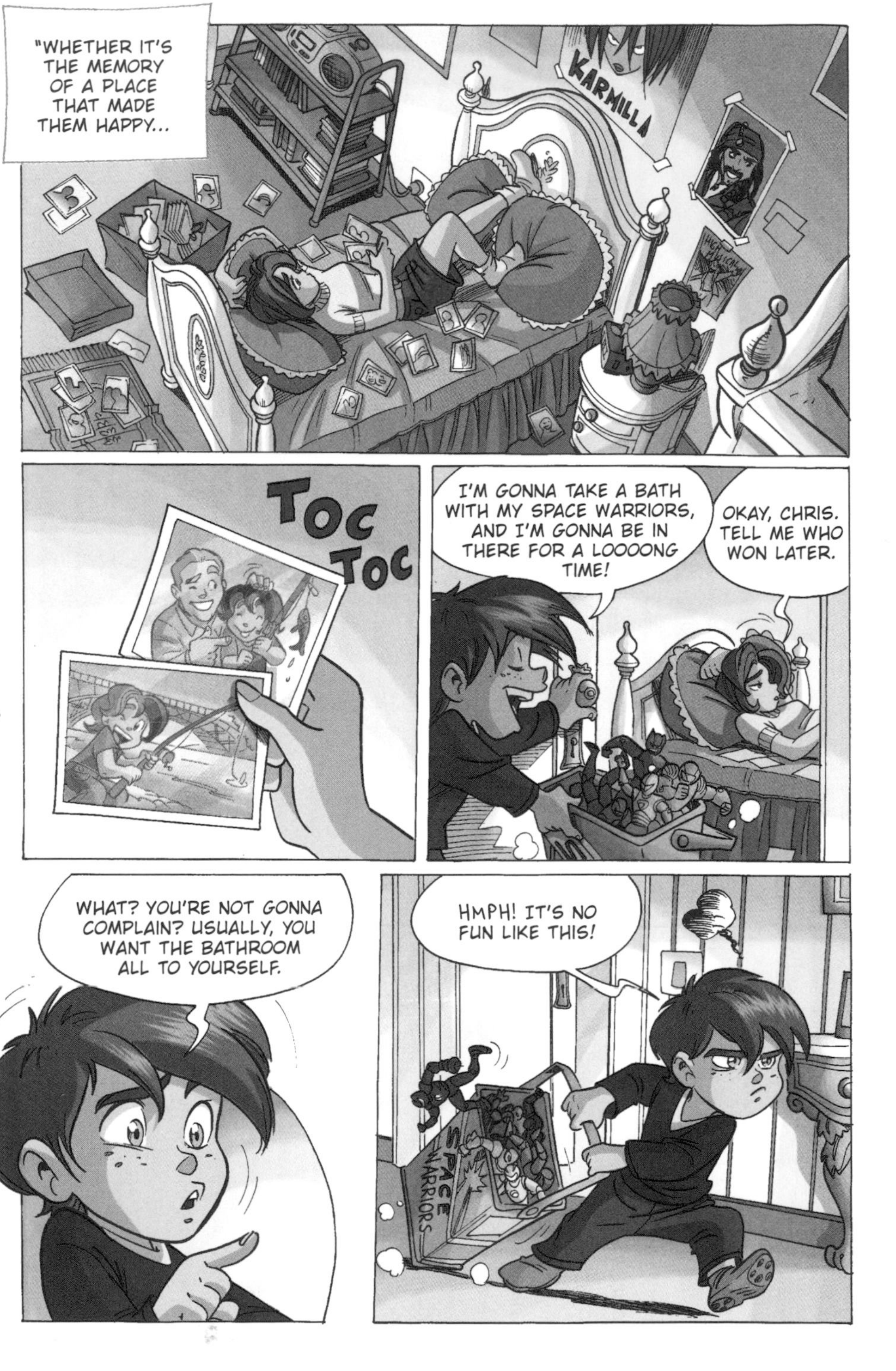
"WHETHER IT'S THE MEMORY OF A PLACE THAT MADE THEM HAPPY...
KARMILLA
TOC TOC
I'M GONNA TAKE A BATH WITH MY SPACE WARRIORS, AND I'M GONNA BE IN THERE FOR A LOOOONG TIME!
OKAY, CHRIS. TELL ME WHO WON LATER.
WHAT? YOU'RE NOT GONNA COMPLAIN? USUALLY, YOU WANT THE BATHROOM ALL TO YOURSELF.
HMPH! IT'S NO FUN LIKE THIS!
SPACE WARRIORS

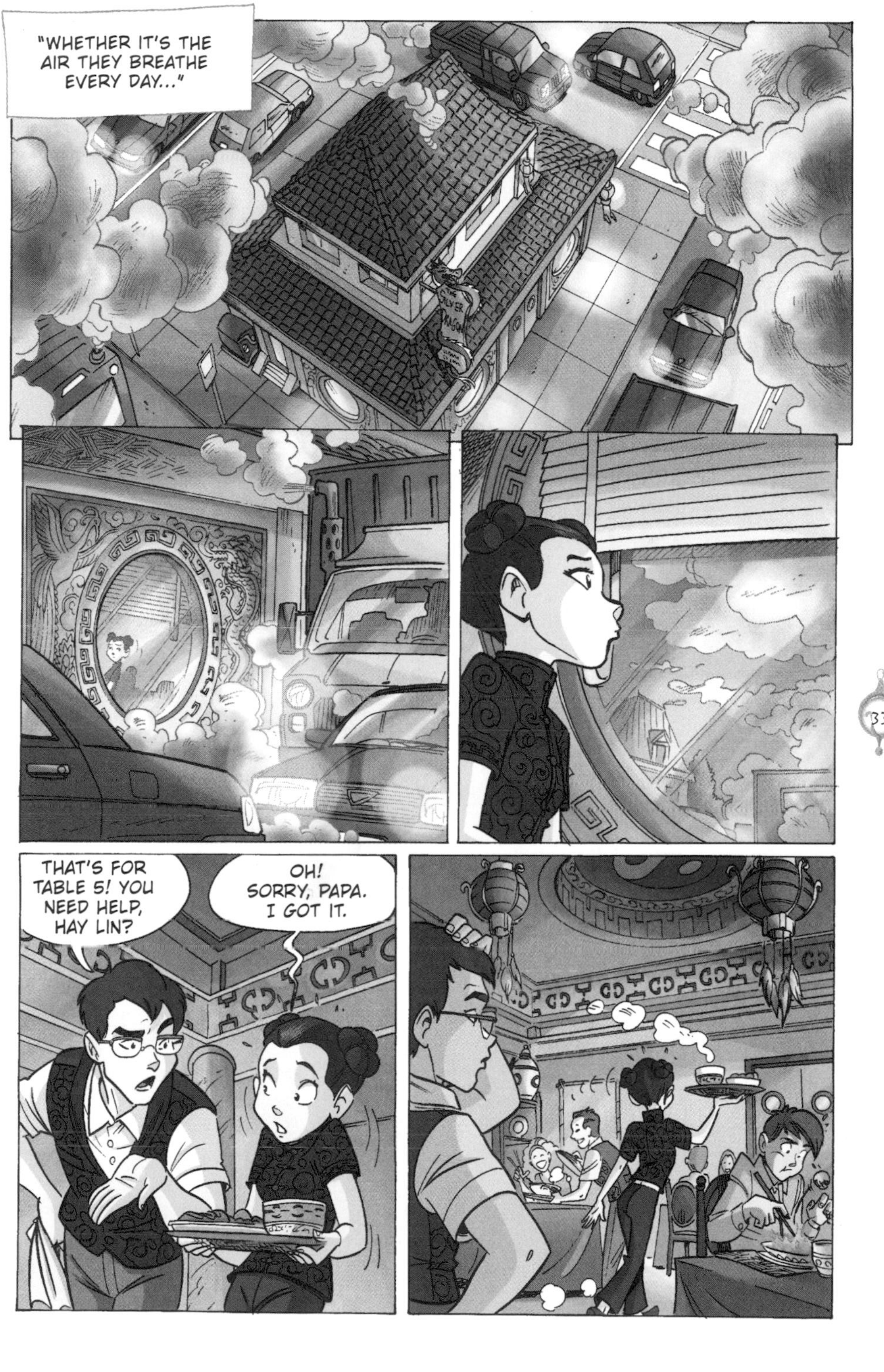
"WHETHER IT'S THE AIR THEY BREATHE EVERY DAY..."
THAT'S FOR TABLE 5! YOU NEED HELP, HAY LIN?
OH! SORRY, PAPA. I GOT IT.

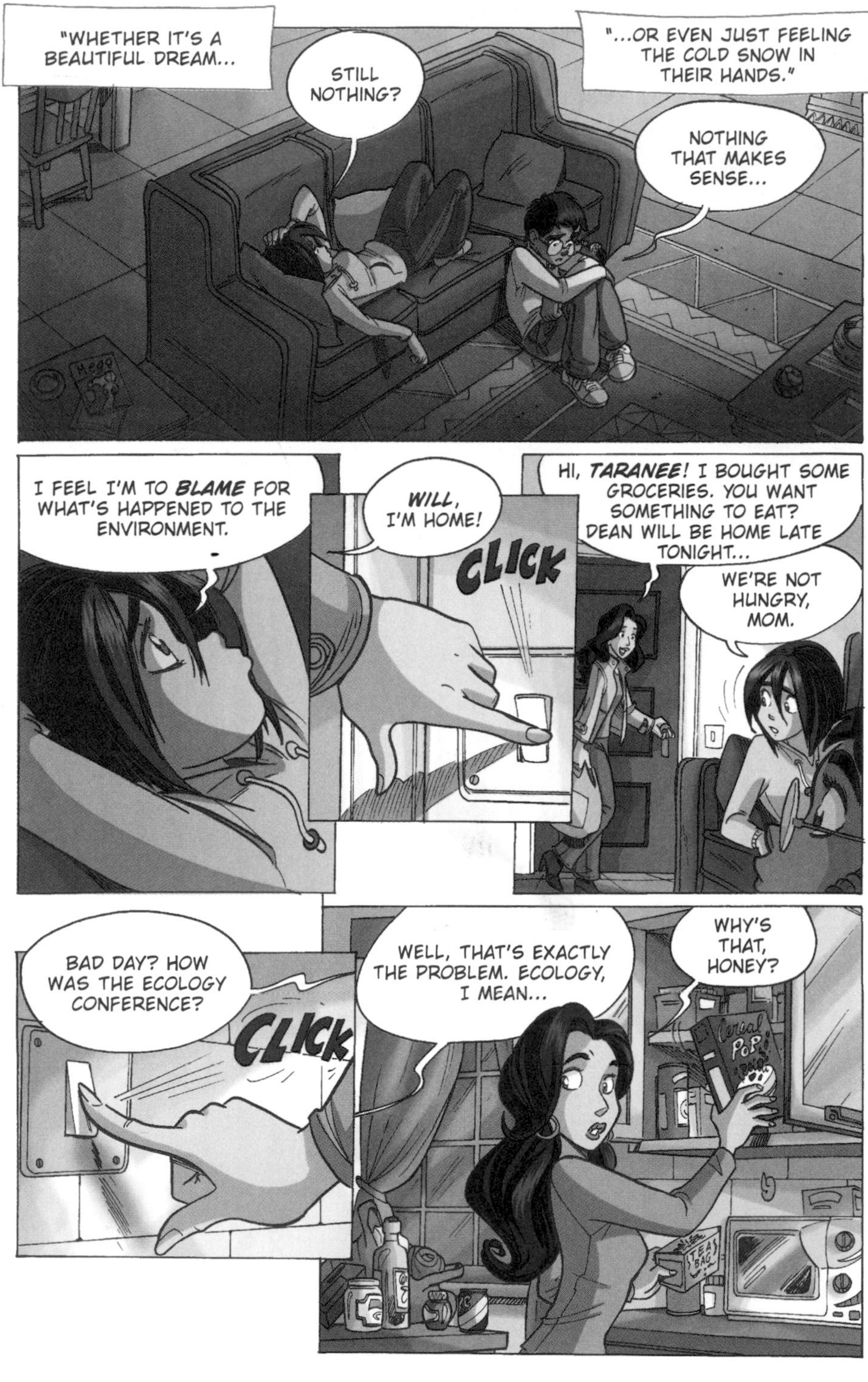

"WHETHER IT'S A BEAUTIFUL DREAM...
STILL NOTHING?
"...OR EVEN JUST FEELING THE COLD SNOW IN THEIR HANDS."
NOTHING THAT MAKES SENSE...
I FEEL I'M TO BLAME FOR WHAT'S HAPPENED TO THE ENVIRONMENT.
WILL, I'M HOME!
CLICK
HI, TARANEE! I BOUGHT SOME GROCERIES. YOU WANT SOMETHING TO EAT? DEAN WILL BE HOME LATE TONIGHT...
WE'RE NOT HUNGRY, MOM.
BAD DAY? HOW WAS THE ECOLOGY CONFERENCE?
CLICK
WELL, THAT'S EXACTLY THE PROBLEM. ECOLOGY, I MEAN...
WHY'S THAT, HONEY?
Cereal PoP
TEA BAG

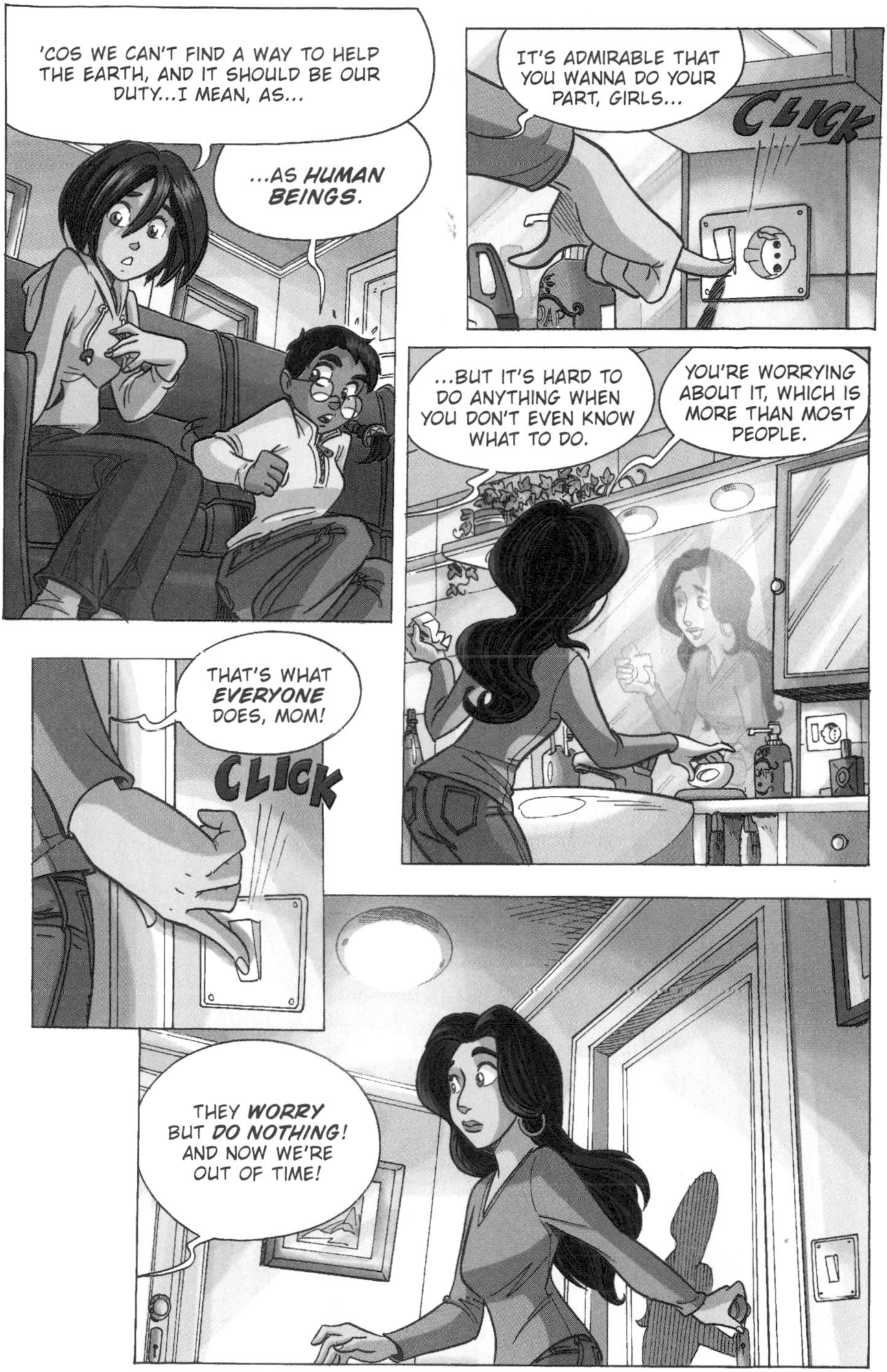
'COS WE CAN'T FIND A WAY TO HELP THE EARTH, AND IT SHOULD BE OUR DUTY...I MEAN, AS...
...AS **HUMAN BEINGS**.
IT'S ADMIRABLE THAT YOU WANNA DO YOUR PART, GIRLS...
CLICK
...BUT IT'S HARD TO DO ANYTHING WHEN YOU DON'T EVEN KNOW WHAT TO DO.
YOU'RE WORRYING ABOUT IT, WHICH IS MORE THAN MOST PEOPLE.
THAT'S WHAT **EVERYONE** DOES, MOM!
CLICK
THEY **WORRY** BUT **DO NOTHING**! AND NOW WE'RE OUT OF TIME!

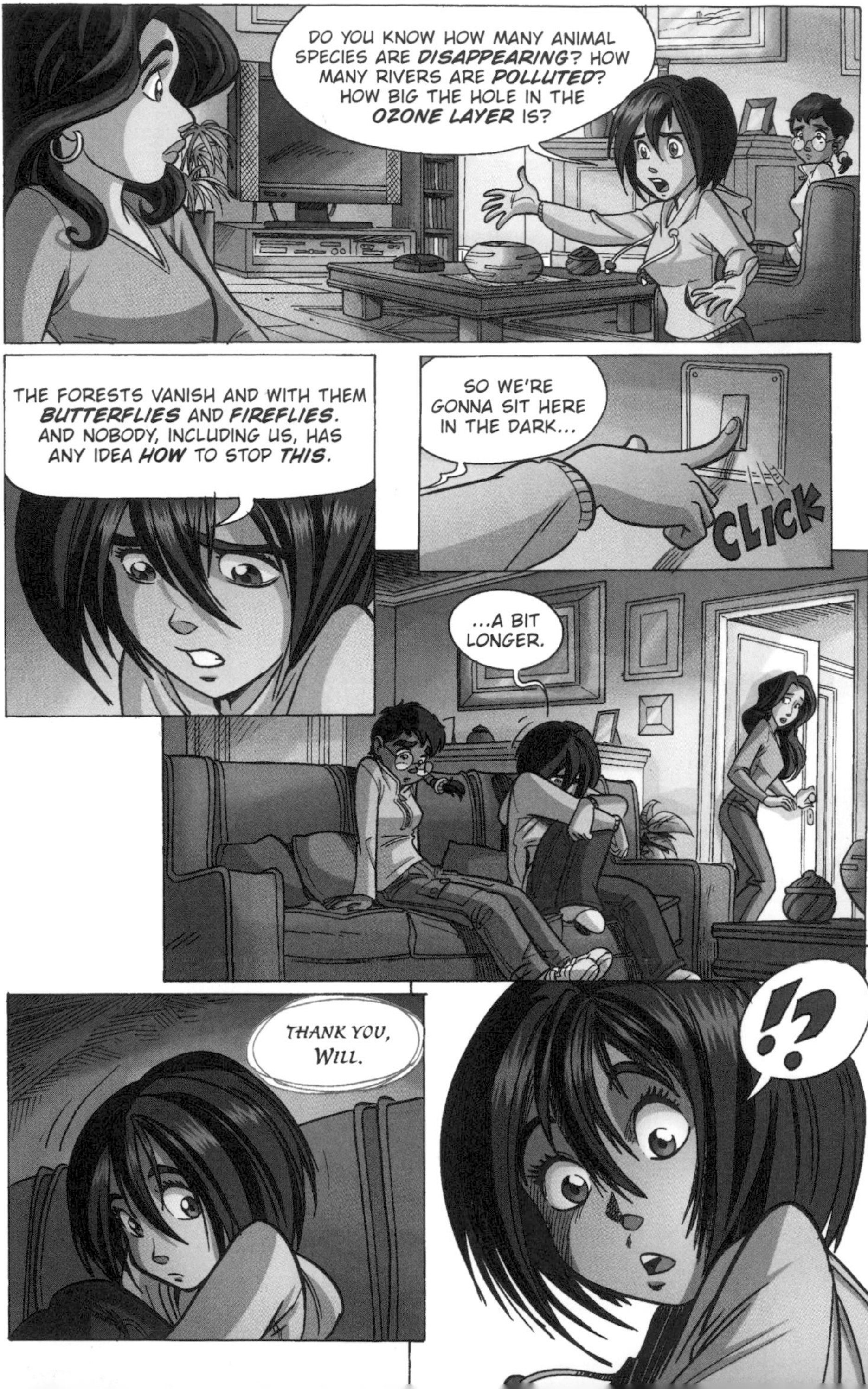
DO YOU KNOW HOW MANY ANIMAL SPECIES ARE DISAPPEARING? HOW MANY RIVERS ARE POLLUTED? HOW BIG THE HOLE IN THE OZONE LAYER IS?
THE FORESTS VANISH AND WITH THEM BUTTERFLIES AND FIREFLIES. AND NOBODY, INCLUDING US, HAS ANY IDEA HOW TO STOP THIS.
SO WE'RE GONNA SIT HERE IN THE DARK...
CLICK
...A BIT LONGER.
THANK YOU, WILL.
!?

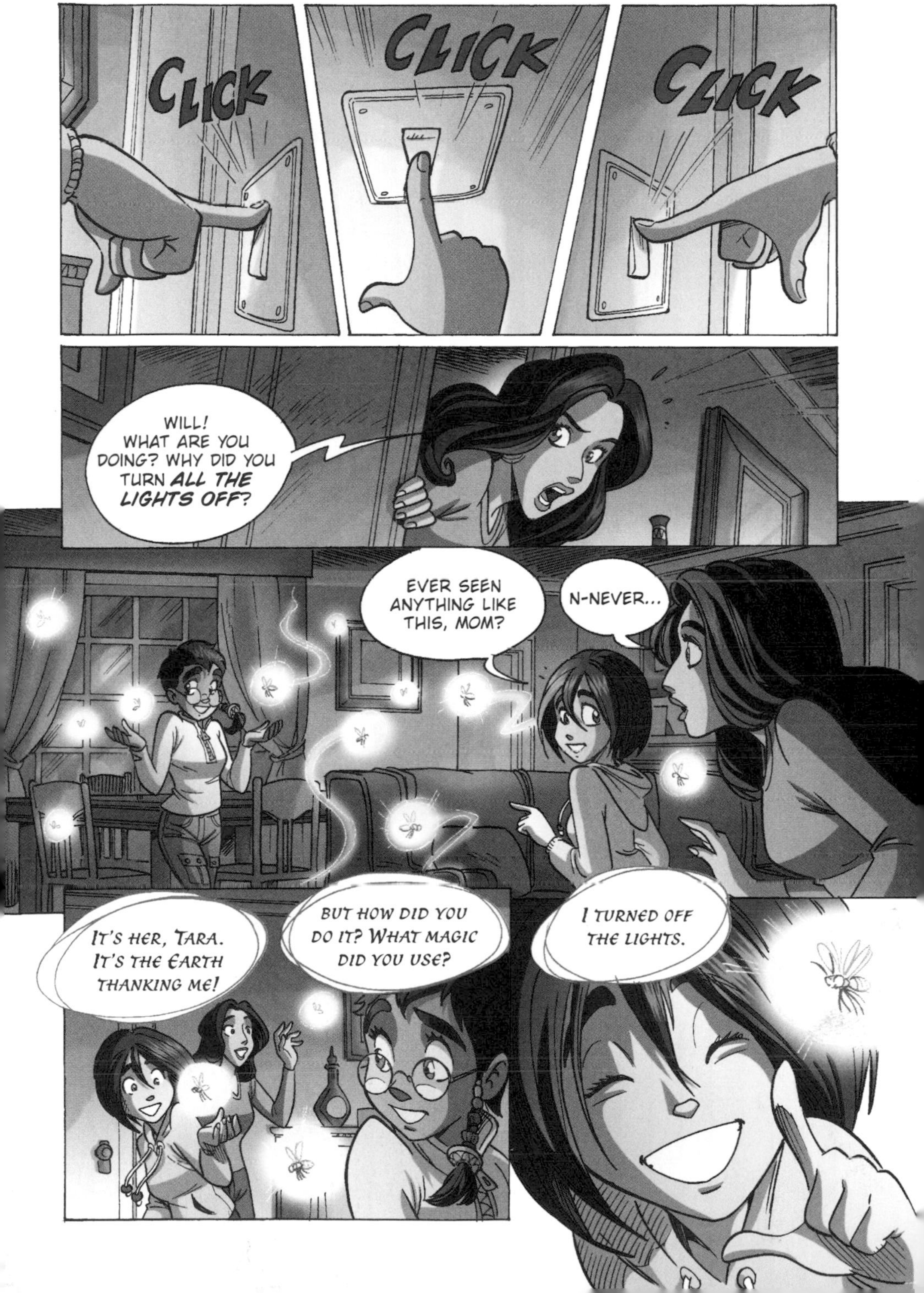
CLICK
CLICK
CLICK
WILL! WHAT ARE YOU DOING? WHY DID YOU TURN **ALL THE LIGHTS OFF**?
EVER SEEN ANYTHING LIKE THIS, MOM?
N-NEVER...
IT'S HER, TARA. IT'S THE EARTH THANKING ME!
BUT HOW DID YOU DO IT? WHAT MAGIC DID YOU USE?
I TURNED OFF THE LIGHTS.

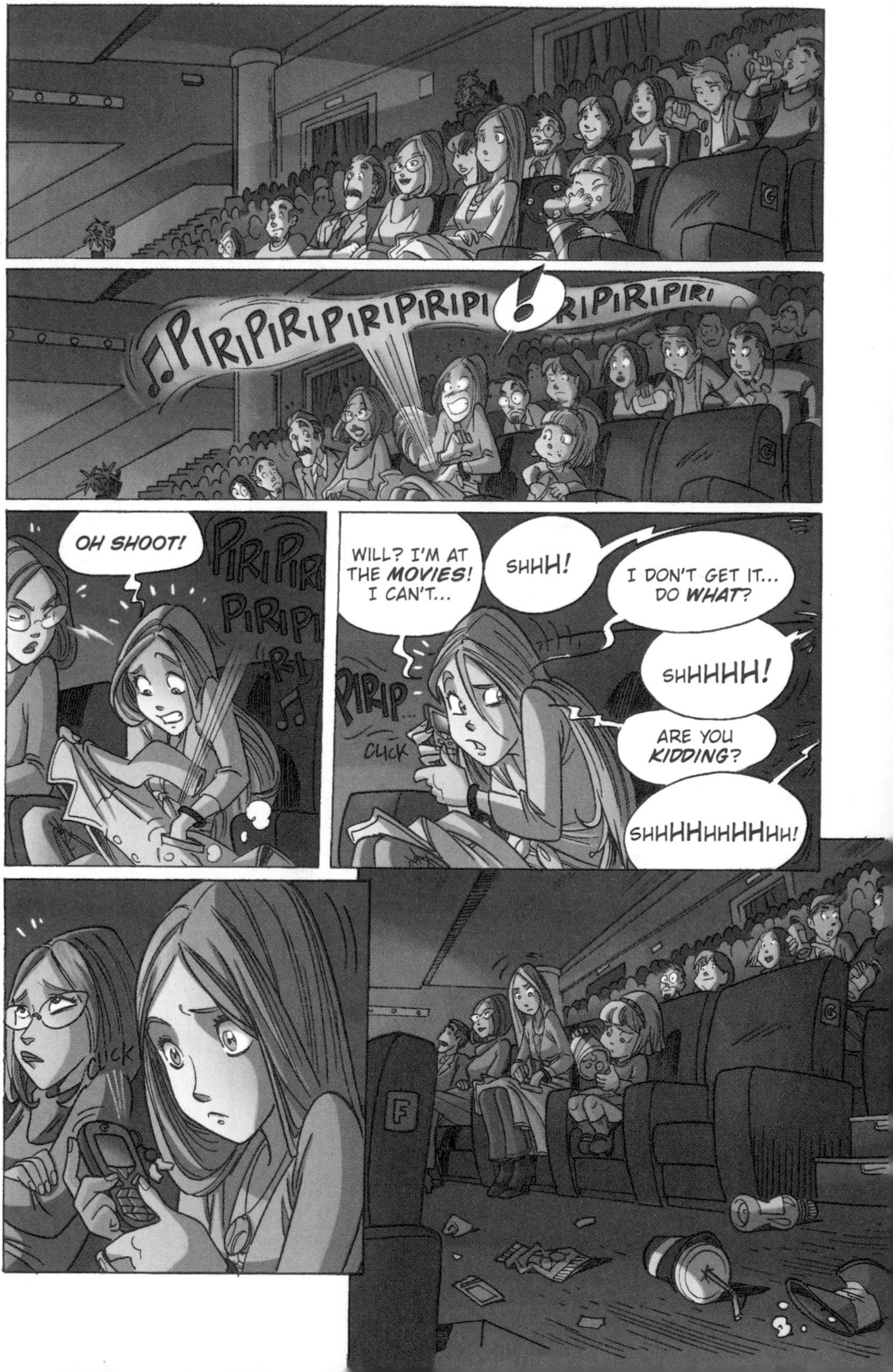
PIRIPIRIPIRIPIRIPI ! RIPIRIPIRI
OH SHOOT!
PIRIPIRI PIRIPI RI
WILL? I'M AT THE MOVIES! I CAN'T...
SHHH!
I DON'T GET IT... DO WHAT?
PIRIP...
CLICK
SHHHHH!
ARE YOU KIDDING?
SHHHHHHHHHH!
CLICK

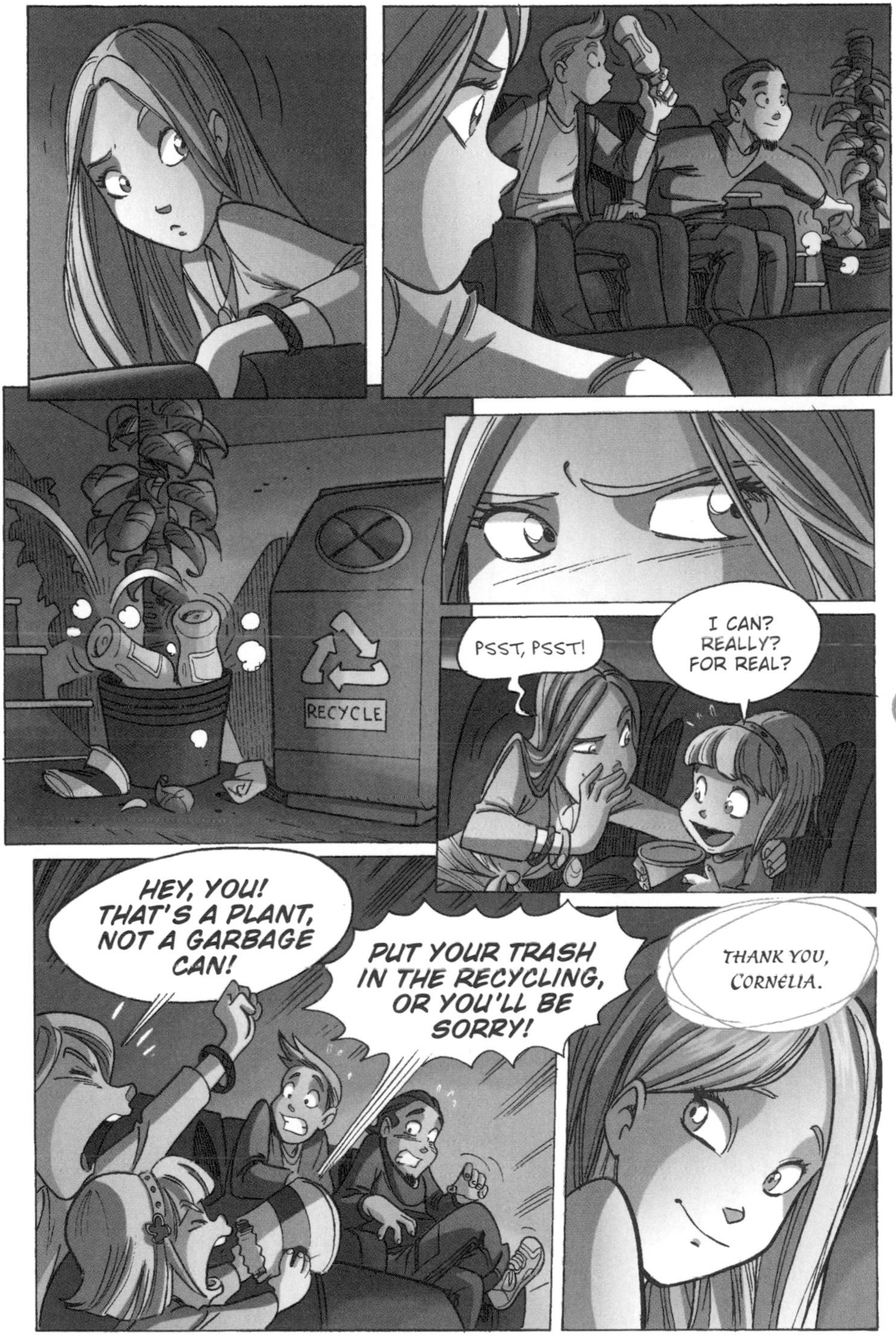

PSST, PSST!
I CAN? REALLY? FOR REAL?
RECYCLE
HEY, YOU! THAT'S A PLANT, NOT A GARBAGE CAN!
PUT YOUR TRASH IN THE RECYCLING, OR YOU'LL BE SORRY!
THANK YOU, CORNELIA.

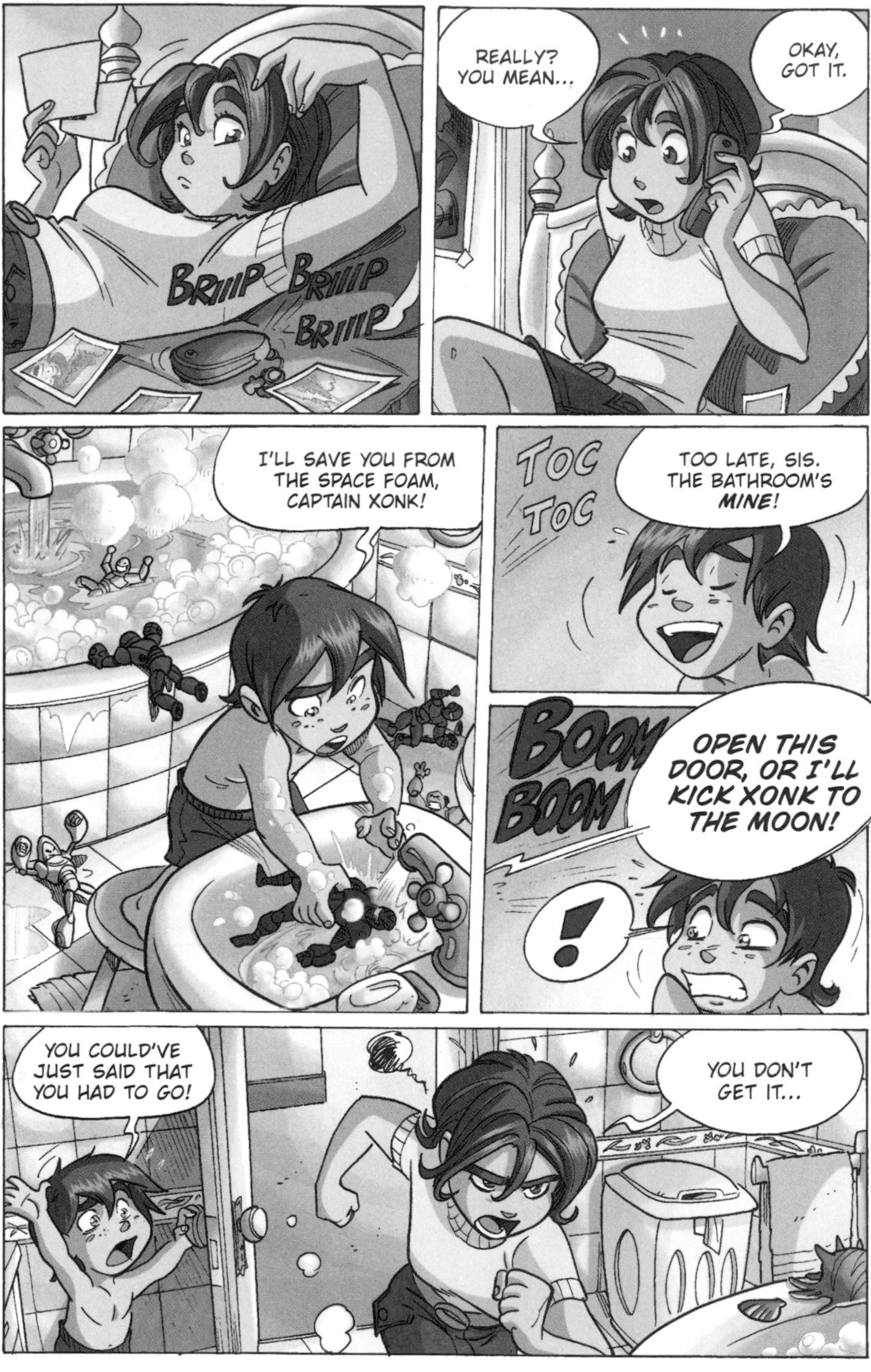
BRIIIP BRIIIP
BRIIIP
REALLY? YOU MEAN...
OKAY, GOT IT.
I'LL SAVE YOU FROM THE SPACE FOAM, CAPTAIN XONK!
TOC TOC
TOO LATE, SIS. THE BATHROOM'S *MINE*!
BOOM BOOM
OPEN THIS DOOR, OR I'LL KICK XONK TO THE MOON!
!
YOU COULD'VE JUST SAID THAT YOU HAD TO GO!
YOU DON'T GET IT...

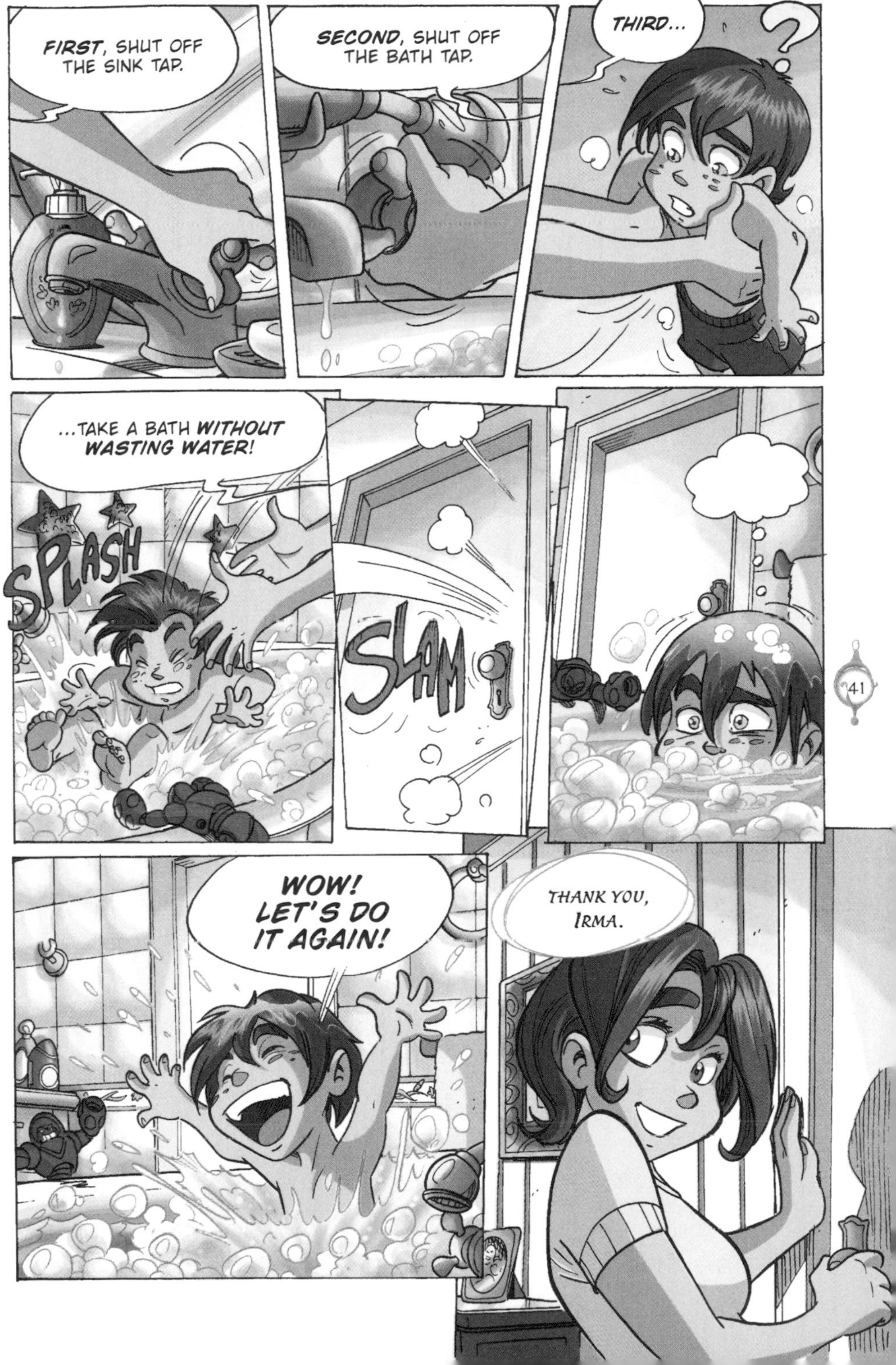
FIRST, SHUT OFF THE SINK TAP.
SECOND, SHUT OFF THE BATH TAP.
THIRD...
...TAKE A BATH WITHOUT WASTING WATER!
SPLASH
SLAM
WOW! LET'S DO IT AGAIN!
THANK YOU, IRMA.

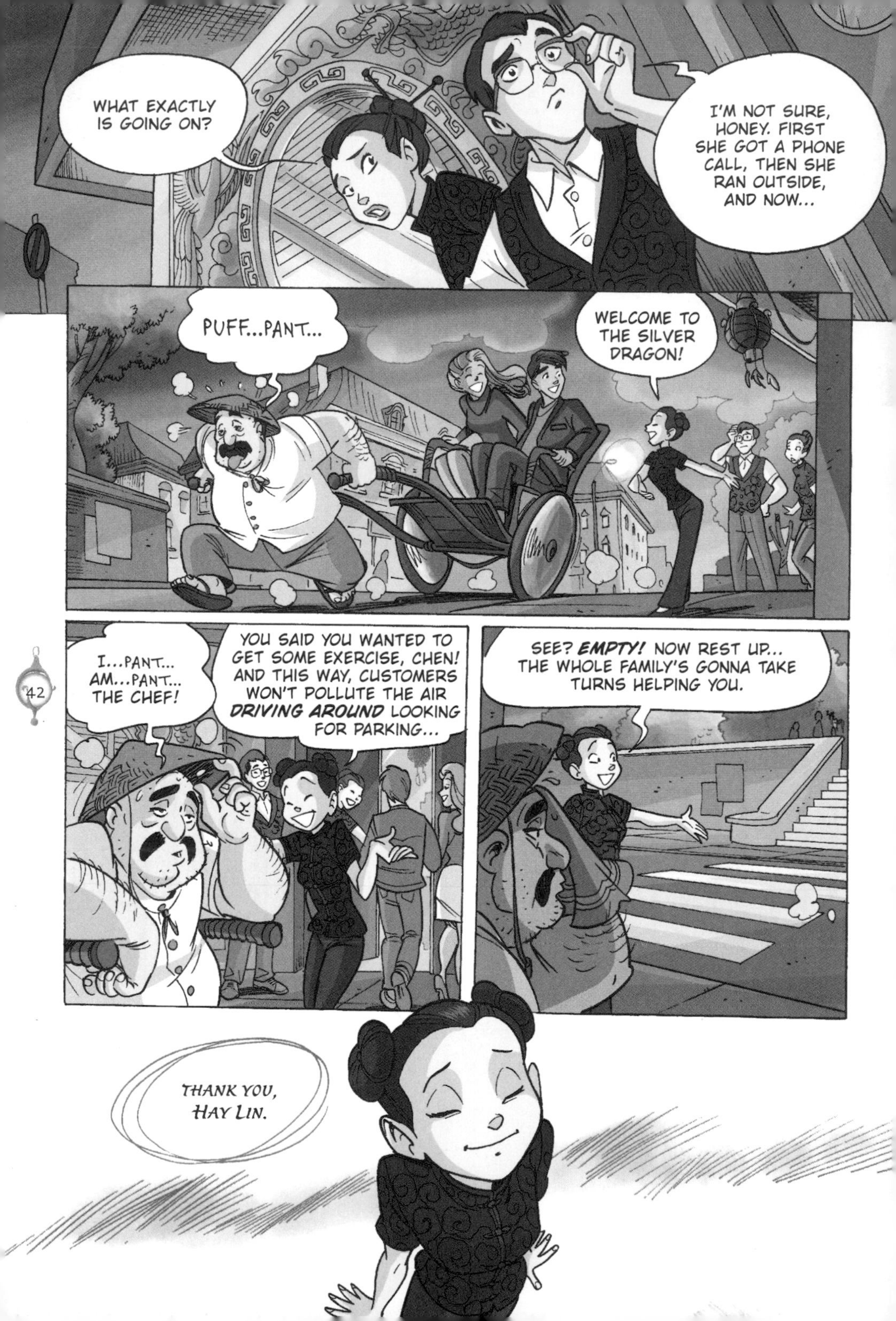

WHAT EXACTLY IS GOING ON?
I'M NOT SURE, HONEY. FIRST SHE GOT A PHONE CALL, THEN SHE RAN OUTSIDE, AND NOW...
PUFF...PANT...
WELCOME TO THE SILVER DRAGON!
I...PANT... AM...PANT... THE CHEF!
YOU SAID YOU WANTED TO GET SOME EXERCISE, CHEN! AND THIS WAY, CUSTOMERS WON'T POLLUTE THE AIR *DRIVING AROUND* LOOKING FOR PARKING...
SEE? *EMPTY!* NOW REST UP... THE WHOLE FAMILY'S GONNA TAKE TURNS HELPING YOU.
THANK YOU, HAY LIN.

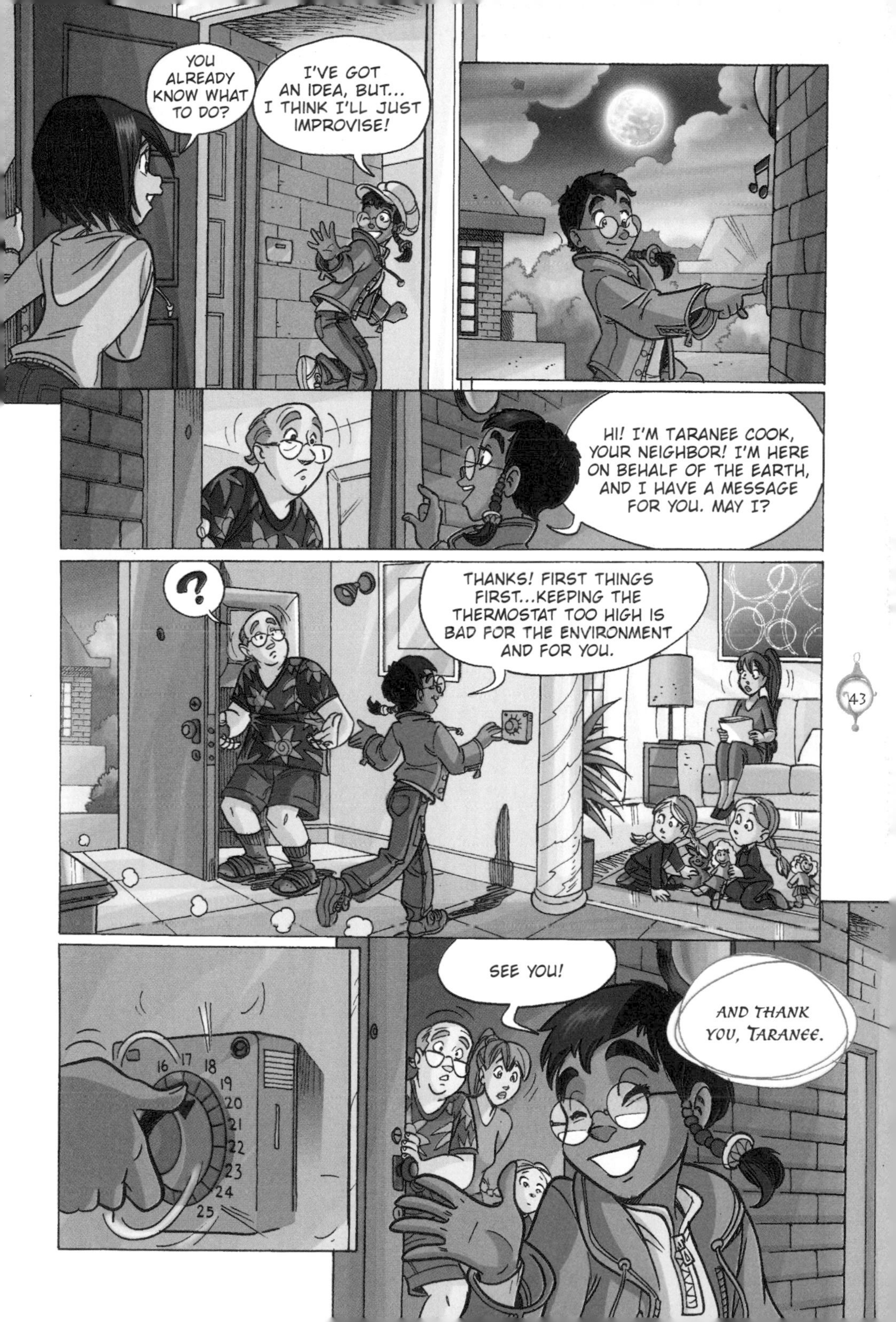

YOU ALREADY KNOW WHAT TO DO?
I'VE GOT AN IDEA, BUT... I THINK I'LL JUST IMPROVISE!
HI! I'M TARANEE COOK, YOUR NEIGHBOR! I'M HERE ON BEHALF OF THE EARTH, AND I HAVE A MESSAGE FOR YOU. MAY I?
?
THANKS! FIRST THINGS FIRST...KEEPING THE THERMOSTAT TOO HIGH IS BAD FOR THE ENVIRONMENT AND FOR YOU.
16 17 18 19 20 21 22 23 24 25
SEE YOU!
AND THANK YOU, TARANEE.

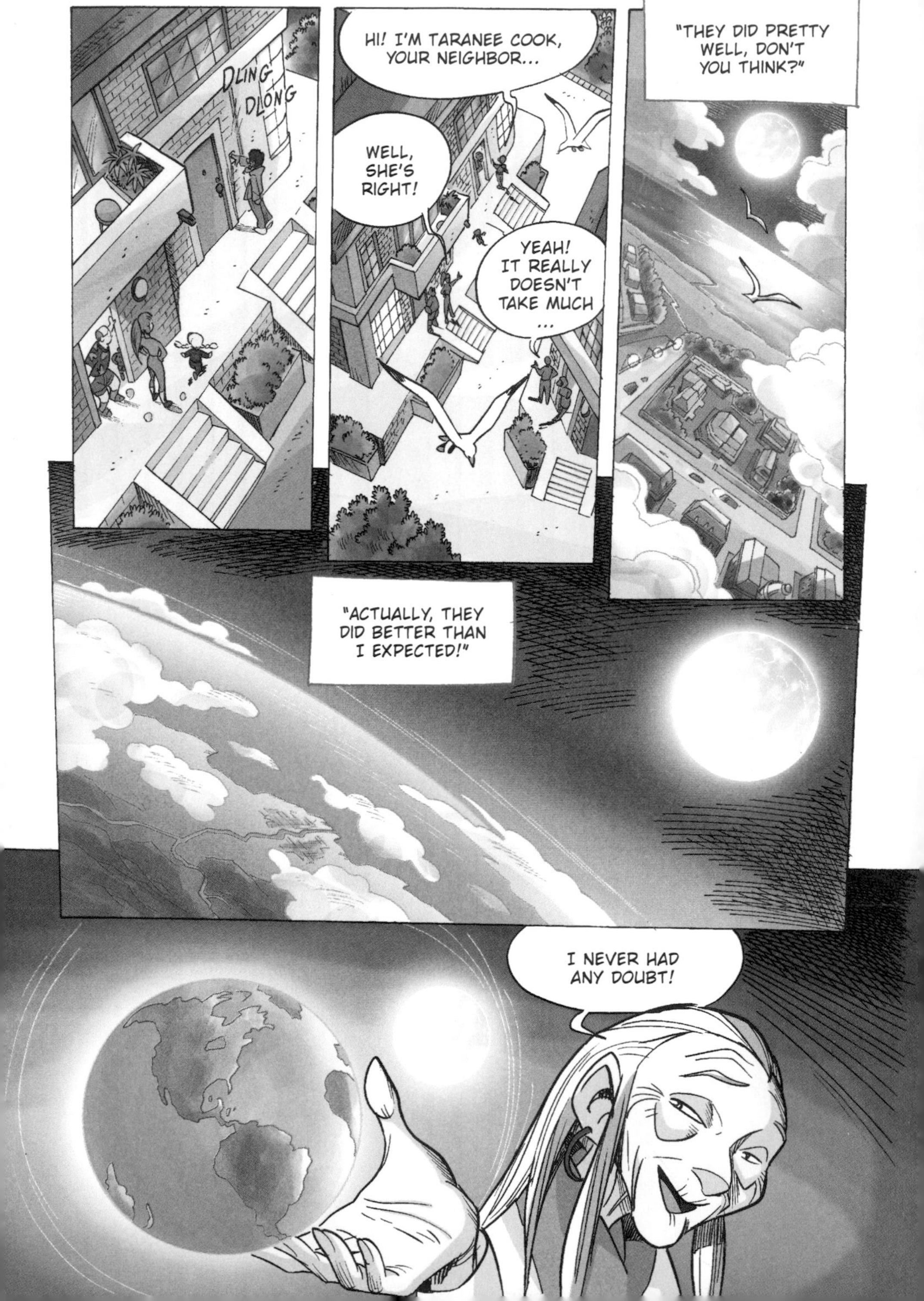
DLING DLONG
HI! I'M TARANEE COOK, YOUR NEIGHBOR...
WELL, SHE'S RIGHT!
YEAH! IT REALLY DOESN'T TAKE MUCH ...
"THEY DID PRETTY WELL, DON'T YOU THINK?"
"ACTUALLY, THEY DID BETTER THAN I EXPECTED!"
I NEVER HAD ANY DOUBT!

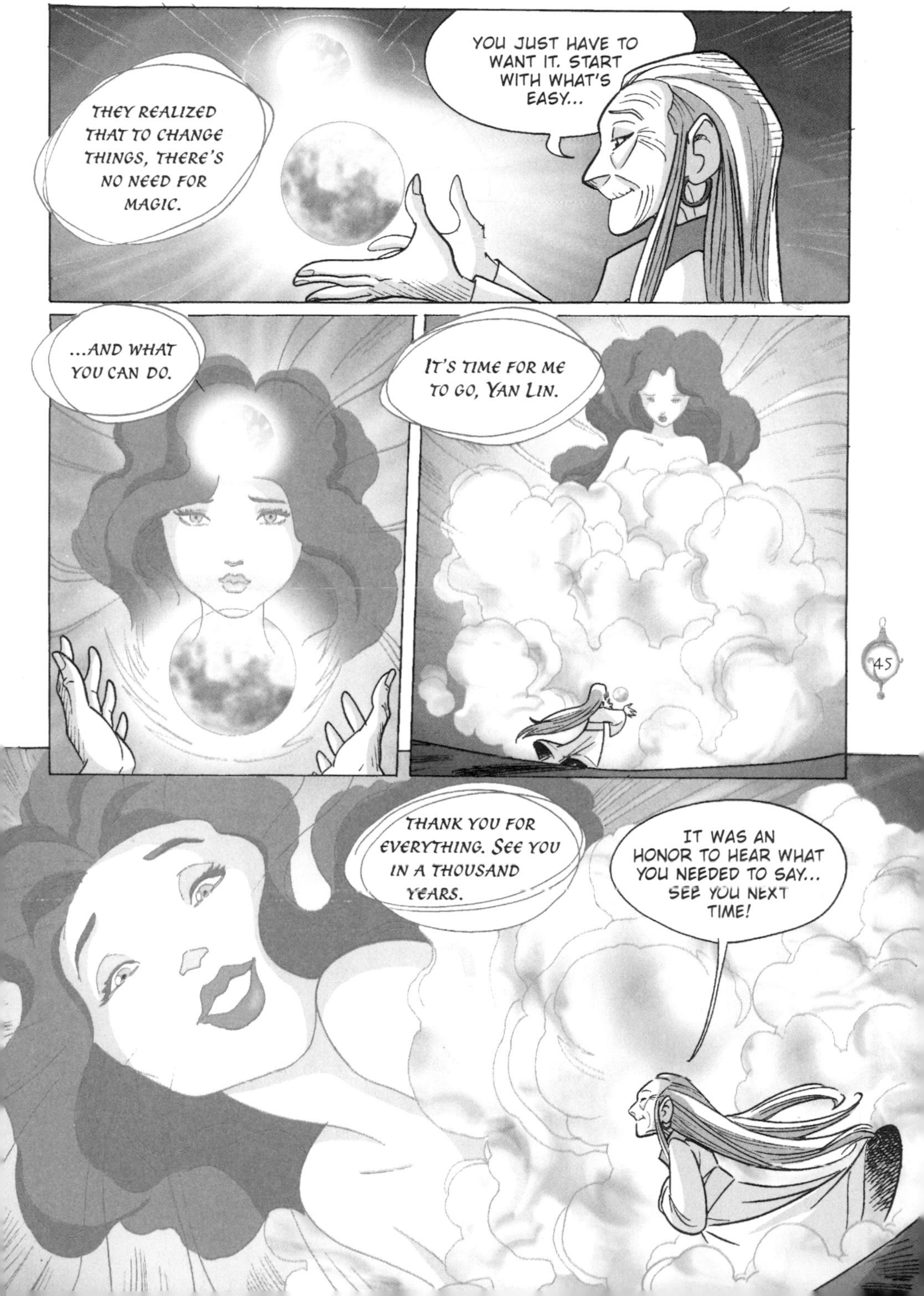
YOU JUST HAVE TO WANT IT. START WITH WHAT'S EASY...
THEY REALIZED THAT TO CHANGE THINGS, THERE'S NO NEED FOR MAGIC.
...AND WHAT YOU CAN DO.
IT'S TIME FOR ME TO GO, YAN LIN.
THANK YOU FOR EVERYTHING. SEE YOU IN A THOUSAND YEARS.
IT WAS AN HONOR TO HEAR WHAT YOU NEEDED TO SAY... SEE YOU NEXT TIME!

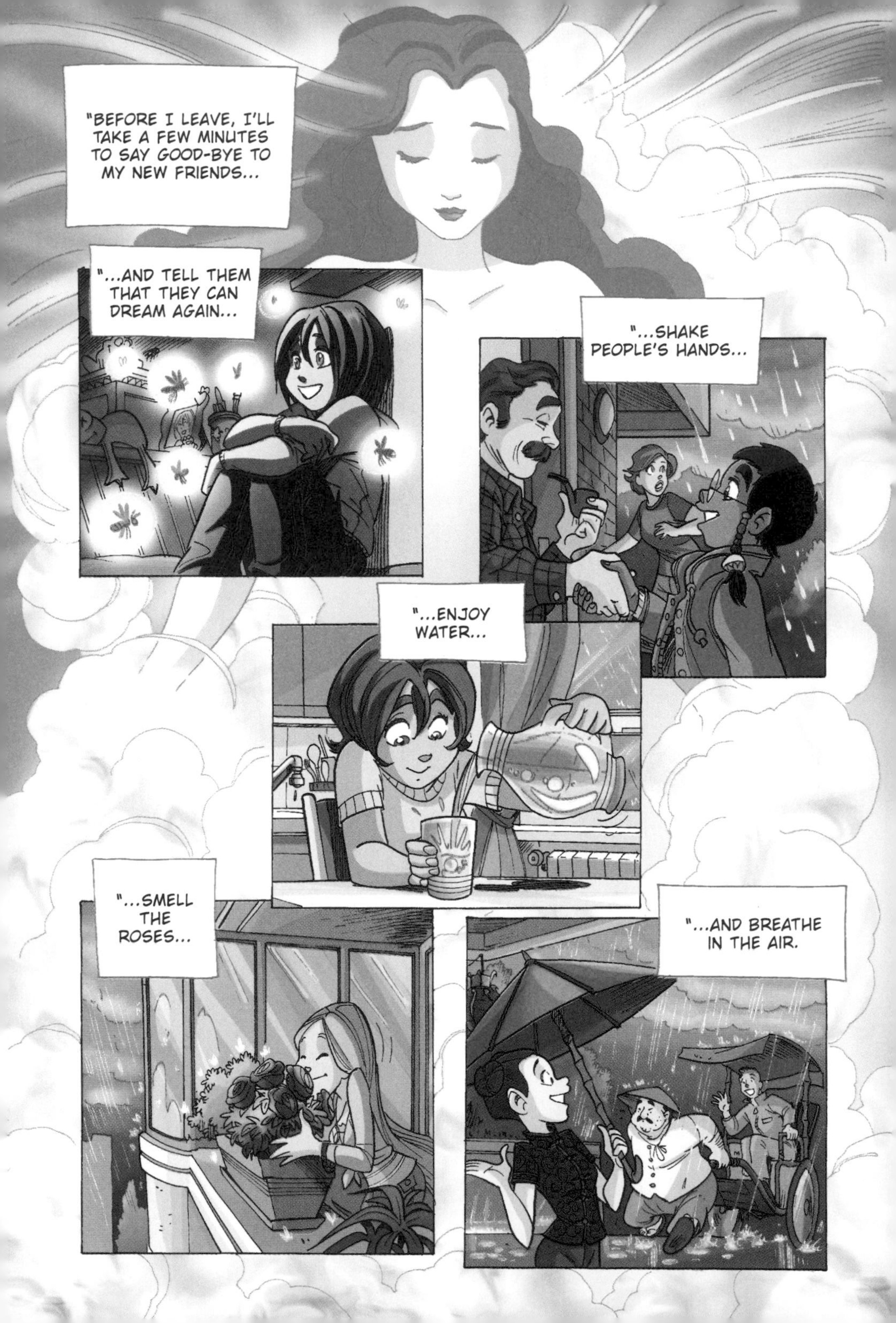

"BEFORE I LEAVE, I'LL TAKE A FEW MINUTES TO SAY GOOD-BYE TO MY NEW FRIENDS...
"...AND TELL THEM THAT THEY CAN DREAM AGAIN...
"...SHAKE PEOPLE'S HANDS...
"...ENJOY WATER...
"...SMELL THE ROSES...
"...AND BREATHE IN THE AIR.

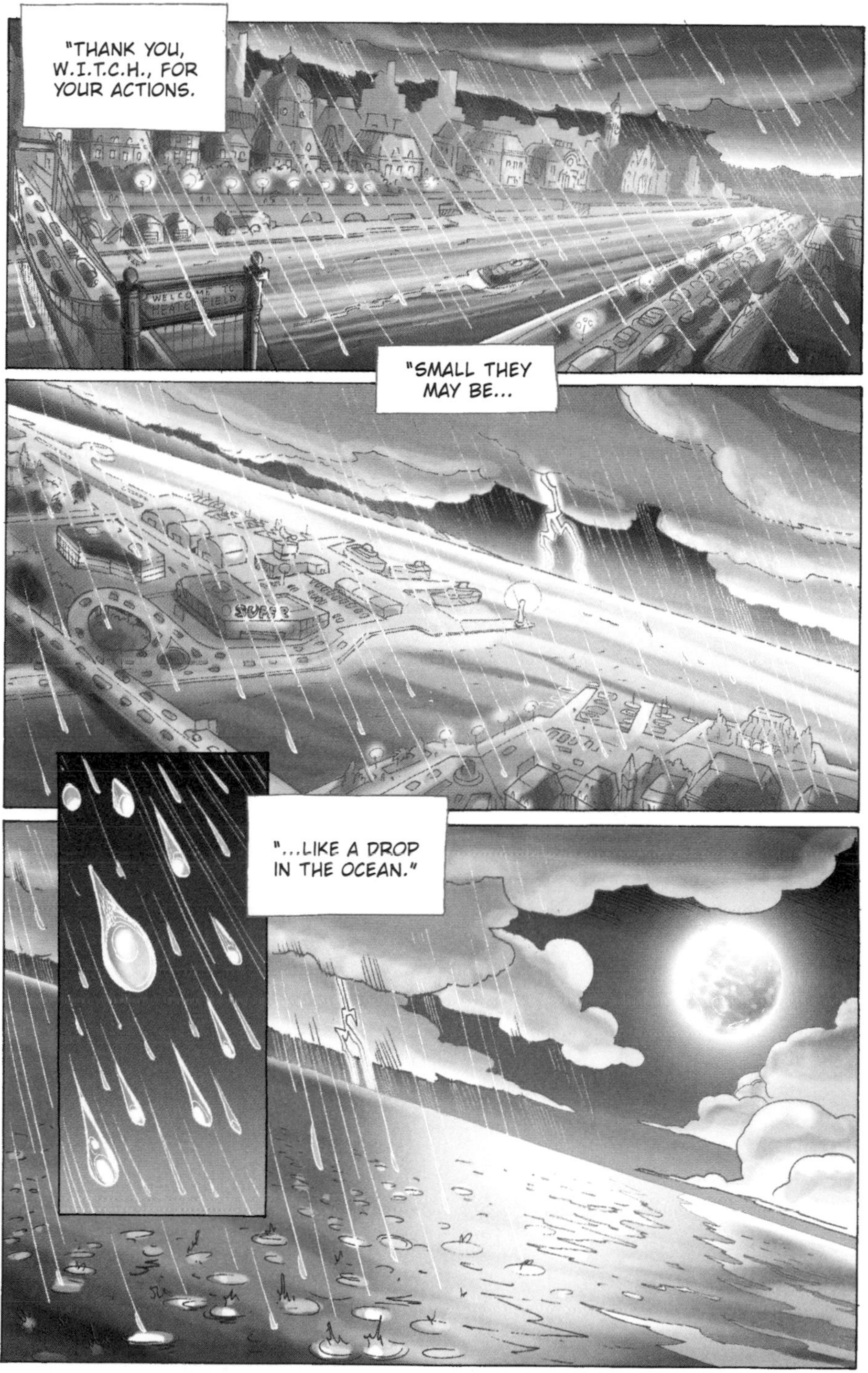
"THANK YOU, W.I.T.C.H., FOR YOUR ACTIONS.
"SMALL THEY MAY BE...
"...LIKE A DROP IN THE OCEAN."

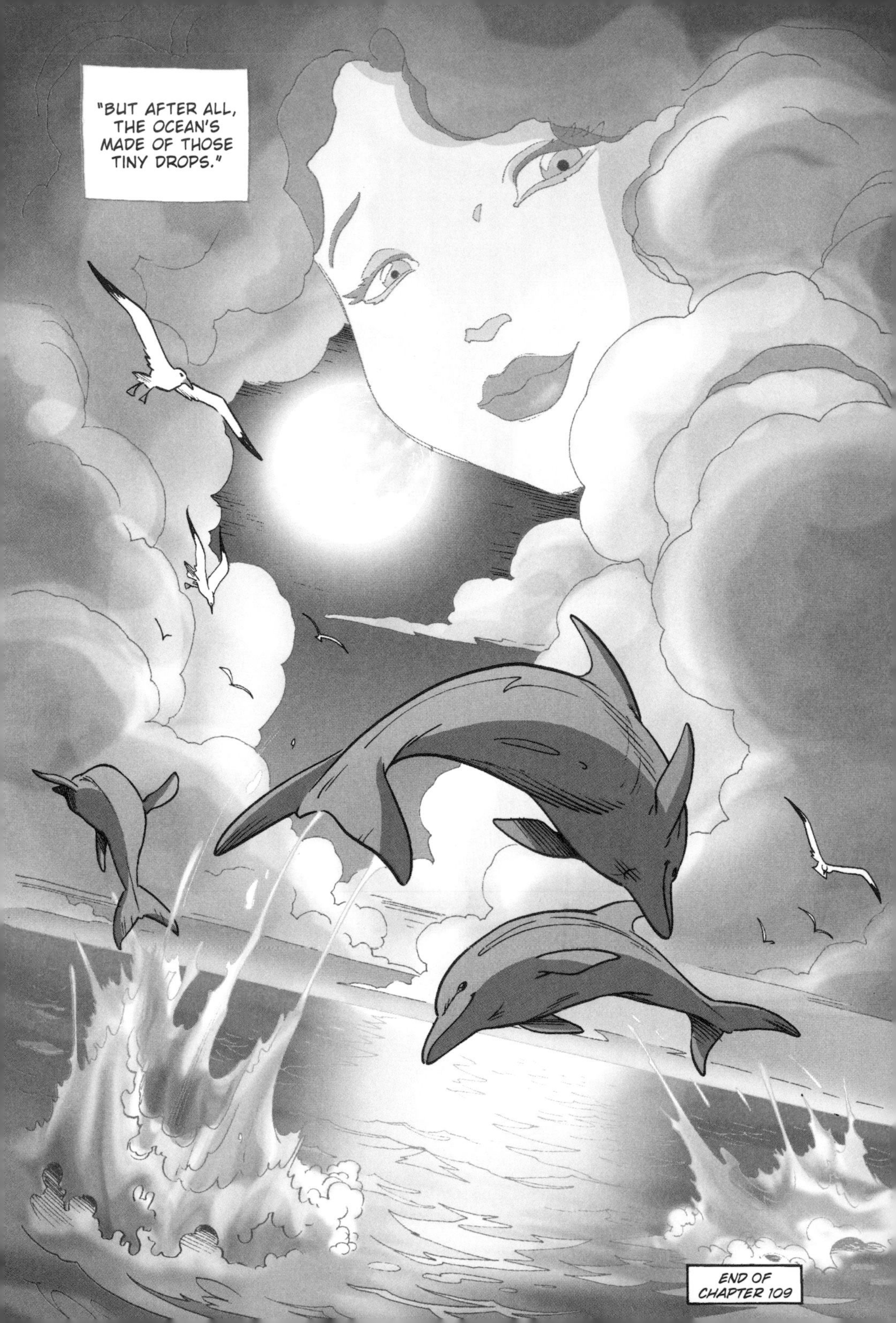
"BUT AFTER ALL, THE OCEAN'S MADE OF THOSE TINY DROPS."
END OF CHAPTER 109

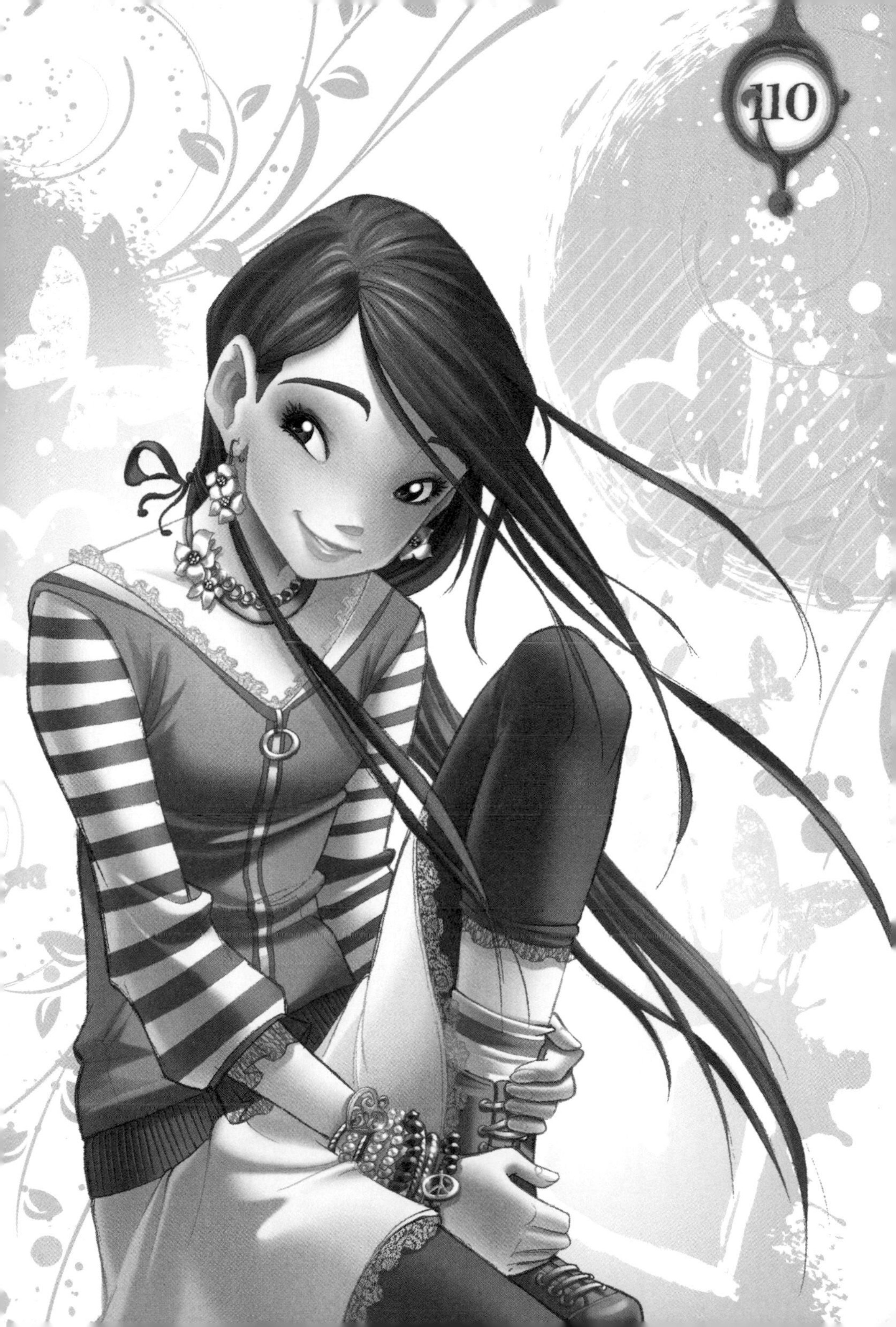

W.i.t.c.h.

Will Irma Taranee Cornelia Hay Lin

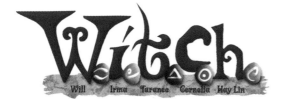

Magical Moms

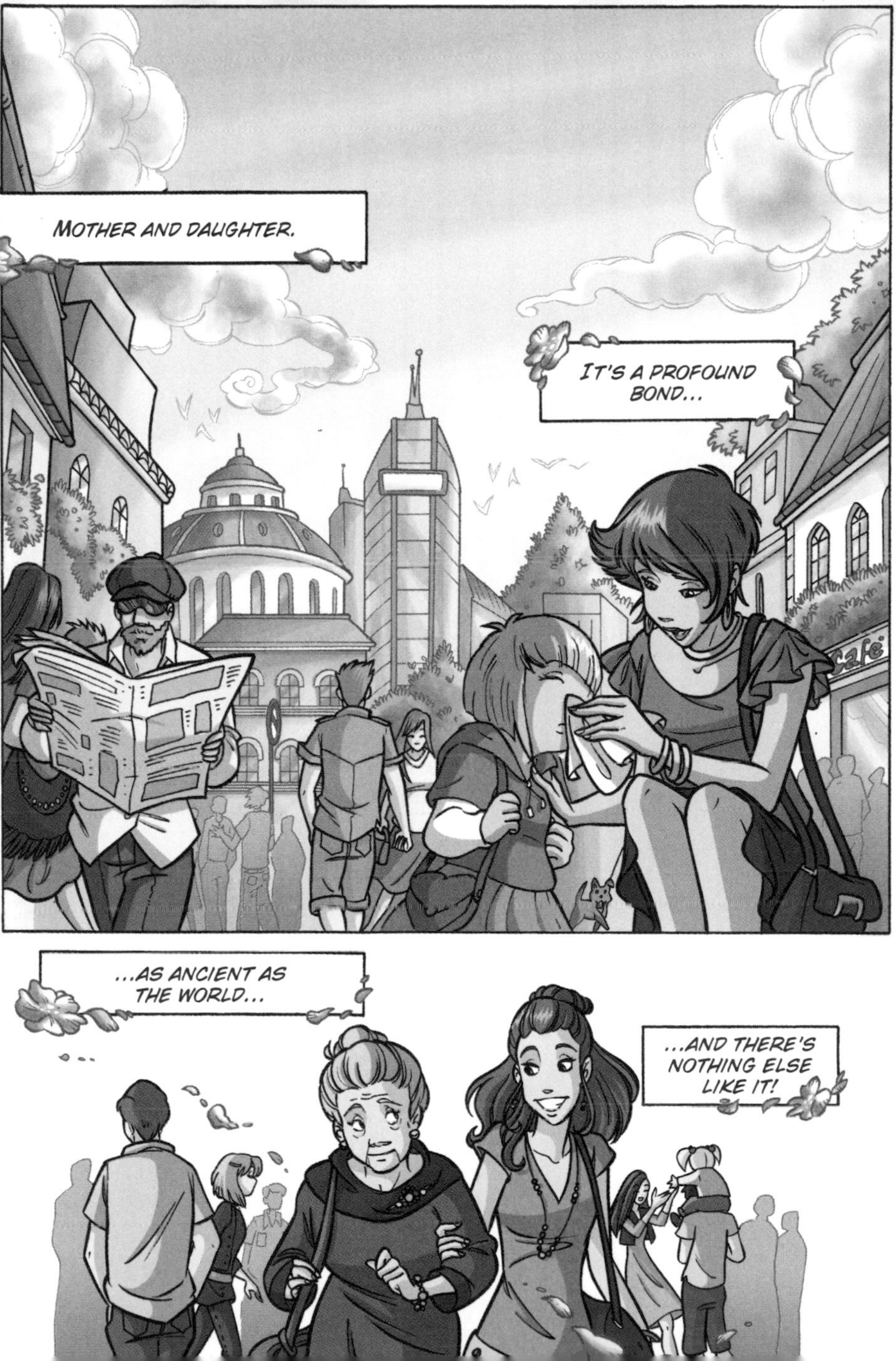

MOTHER AND DAUGHTER.
IT'S A PROFOUND BOND...
Cafe
...AS ANCIENT AS THE WORLD...
...AND THERE'S NOTHING ELSE LIKE IT!

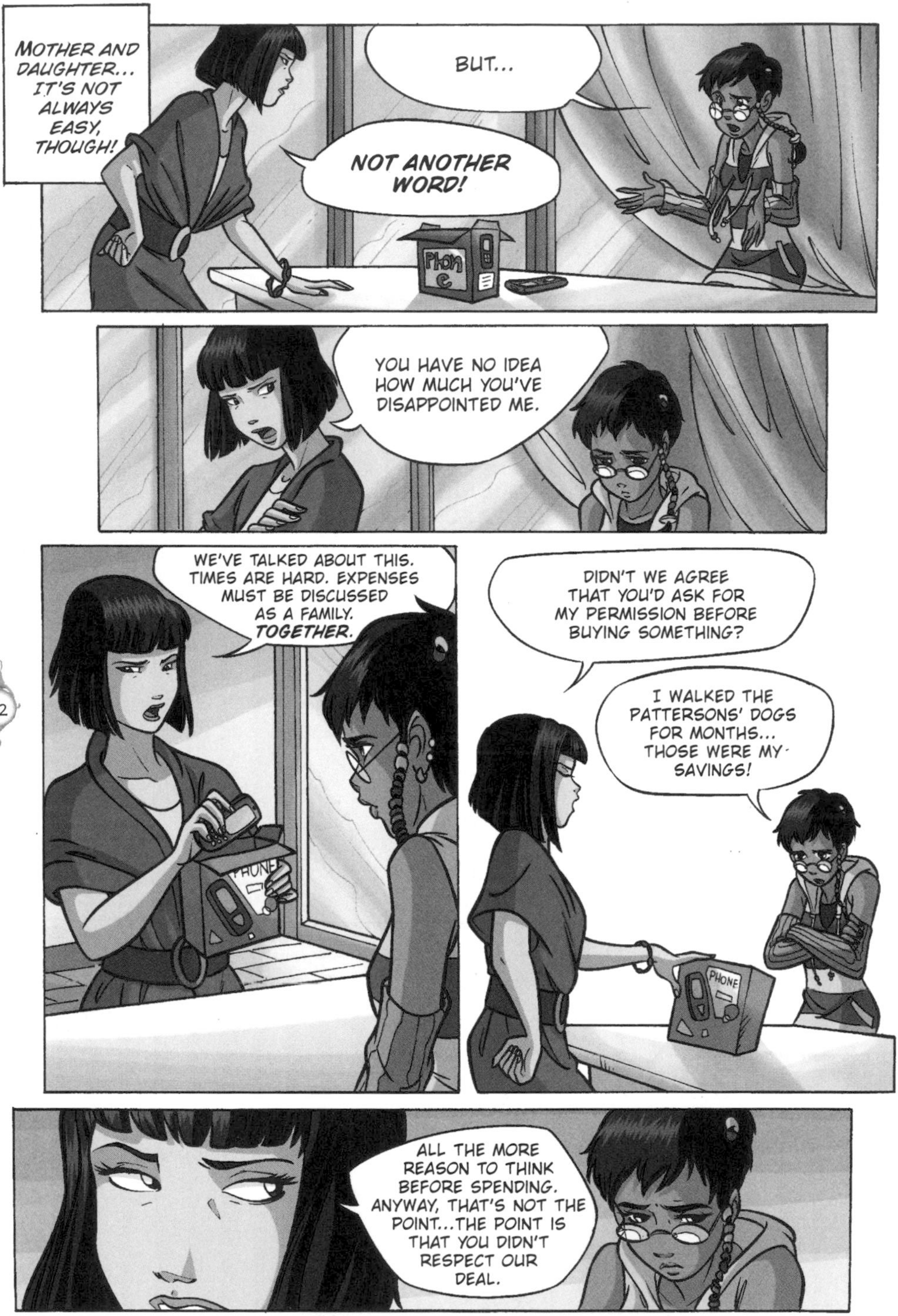

MOTHER AND DAUGHTER... IT'S NOT ALWAYS EASY, THOUGH!
BUT...
NOT ANOTHER WORD!
PHONE
YOU HAVE NO IDEA HOW MUCH YOU'VE DISAPPOINTED ME.
WE'VE TALKED ABOUT THIS. TIMES ARE HARD. EXPENSES MUST BE DISCUSSED AS A FAMILY. *TOGETHER*.
PHONE
DIDN'T WE AGREE THAT YOU'D ASK FOR MY PERMISSION BEFORE BUYING SOMETHING?
I WALKED THE PATTERSONS' DOGS FOR MONTHS... THOSE WERE MY SAVINGS!
PHONE
ALL THE MORE REASON TO THINK BEFORE SPENDING. ANYWAY, THAT'S NOT THE POINT...THE POINT IS THAT YOU DIDN'T RESPECT OUR DEAL.

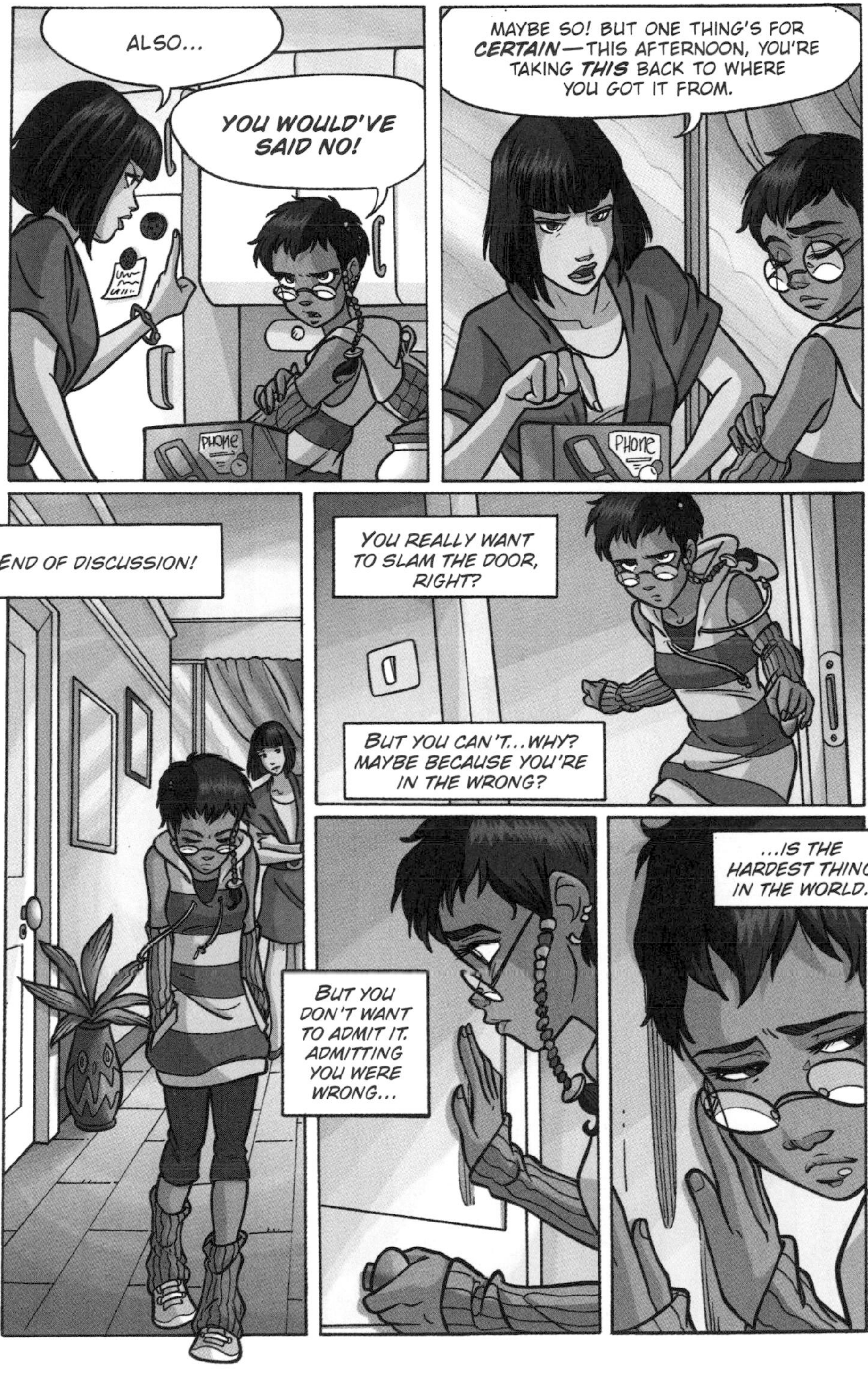
ALSO...
YOU WOULD'VE SAID NO!
PHONE
MAYBE SO! BUT ONE THING'S FOR CERTAIN—THIS AFTERNOON, YOU'RE TAKING THIS BACK TO WHERE YOU GOT IT FROM.
PHONE
END OF DISCUSSION!
YOU REALLY WANT TO SLAM THE DOOR, RIGHT?
BUT YOU CAN'T...WHY? MAYBE BECAUSE YOU'RE IN THE WRONG?
BUT YOU DON'T WANT TO ADMIT IT. ADMITTING YOU WERE WRONG...
...IS THE HARDEST THING IN THE WORLD.

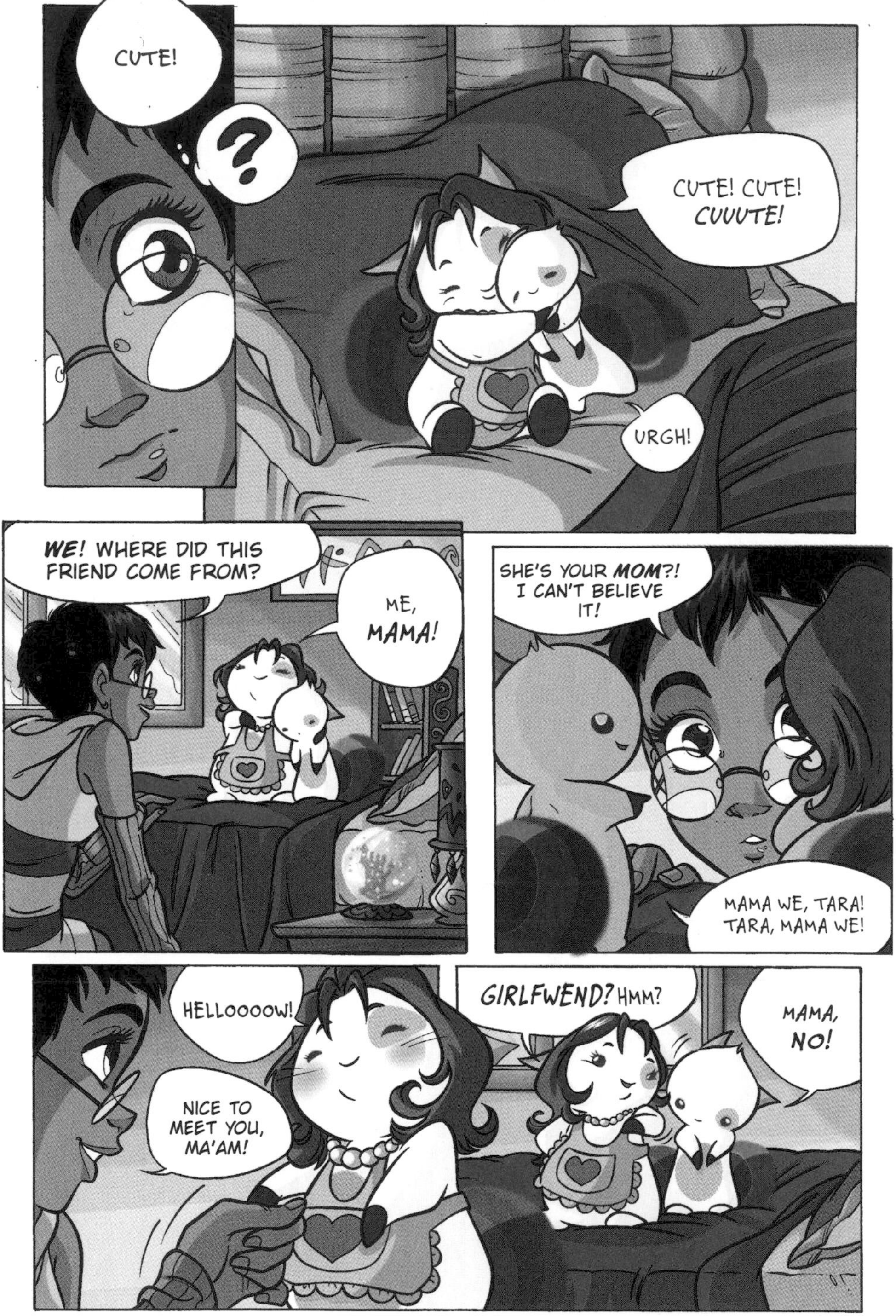
CUTE!
?
CUTE! CUTE! CUUUTE!
URGH!
WE! WHERE DID THIS FRIEND COME FROM?
ME, MAMA!
SHE'S YOUR MOM?! I CAN'T BELIEVE IT!
MAMA WE, TARA! TARA, MAMA WE!
HELLOOOOW!
NICE TO MEET YOU, MA'AM!
GIRLFWEND? HMM?
MAMA, NO!

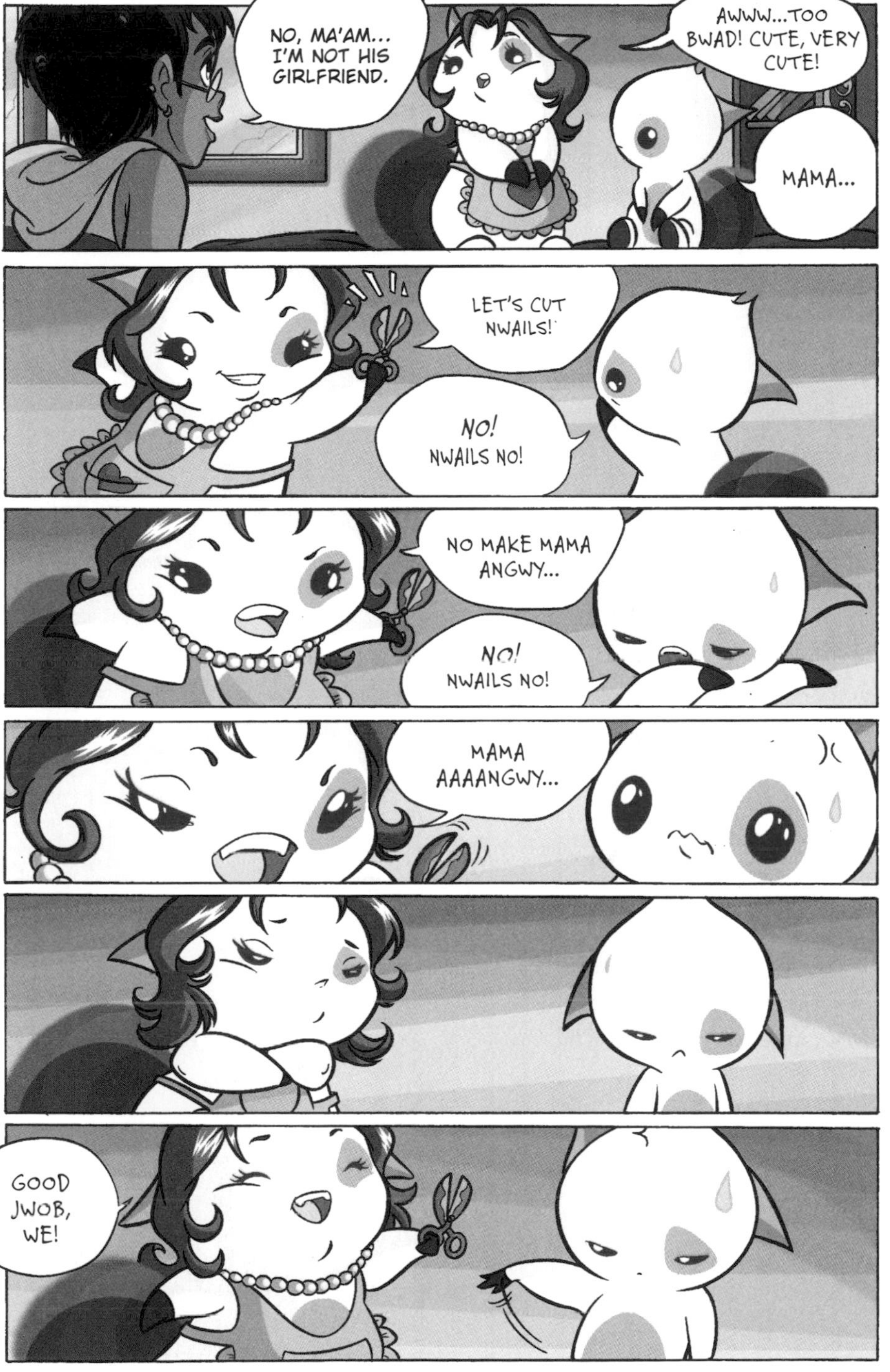
NO, MA'AM... I'M NOT HIS GIRLFRIEND.
AWWW...TOO BWAD! CUTE, VERY CUTE!
MAMA...
LET'S CUT NWAILS!
NO! NWAILS NO!
NO MAKE MAMA ANGWY...
NO! NWAILS NO!
MAMA AAAANGWY...
GOOD JWOB, WE!

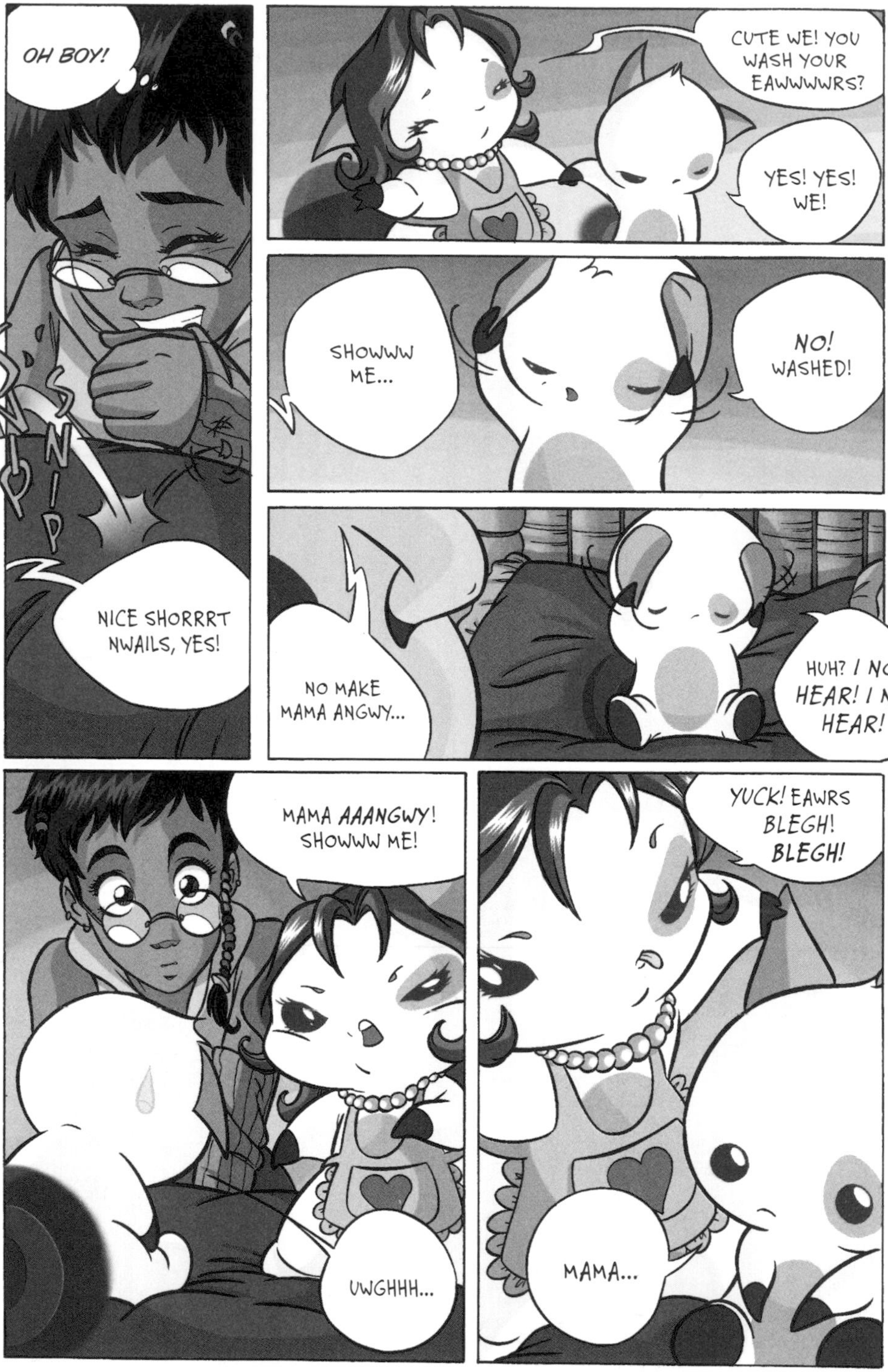

OH BOY!
CUTE WE! YOU WASH YOUR EAWWWWRS?
YES! YES! WE!
SHOWWW ME...
NO! WASHED!
SNIP
SNIP
NICE SHORRRT NWAILS, YES!
NO MAKE MAMA ANGWY...
HUH? I NO HEAR! I NO HEAR!
MAMA AAANGWY! SHOWWW ME!
UWGHHH...
YUCK! EAWRS BLEGH! BLEGH!
MAMA...

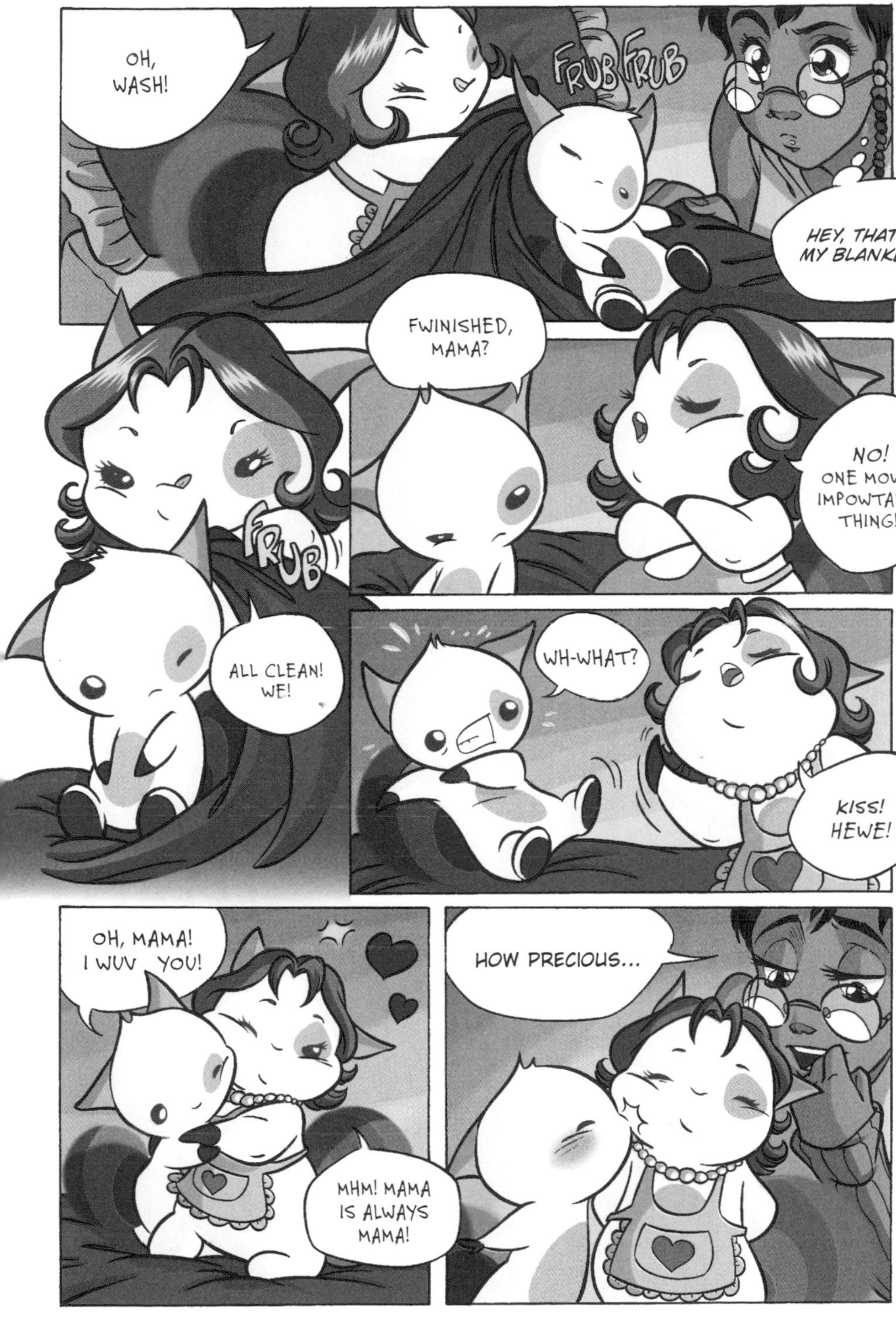
OH, WASH!
FRUB FRUB
HEY, THAT'S MY BLANKET!
FWINISHED, MAMA?
FRUB
NO! ONE MOWE IMPOWTANT THING!
ALL CLEAN! WE!
WH-WHAT?
KISS! HEWE!
OH, MAMA! I WUV YOU!
MHM! MAMA IS ALWAYS MAMA!
HOW PRECIOUS...

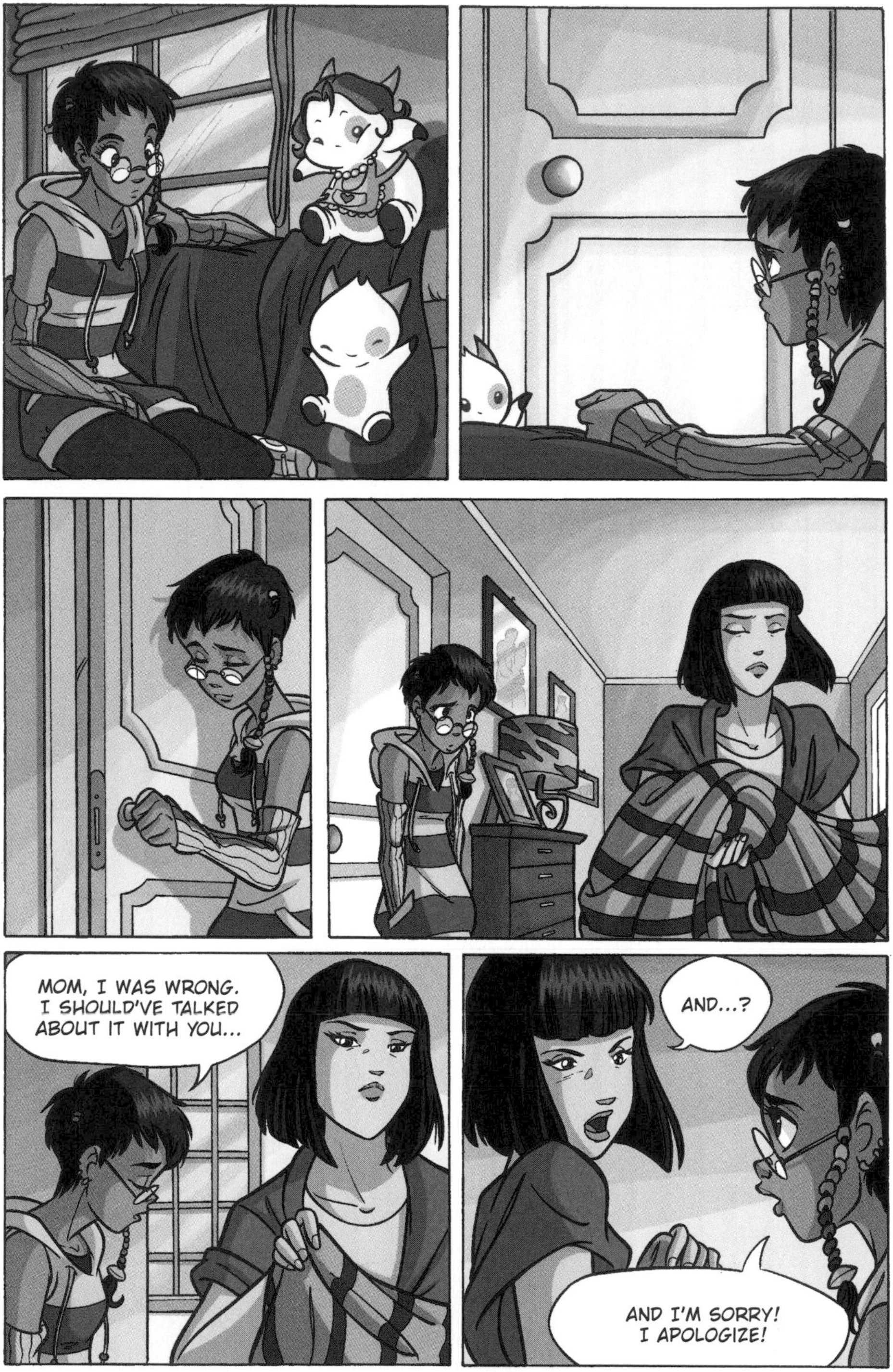
MOM, I WAS WRONG. I SHOULD'VE TALKED ABOUT IT WITH YOU...
AND...?
AND I'M SORRY! I APOLOGIZE!

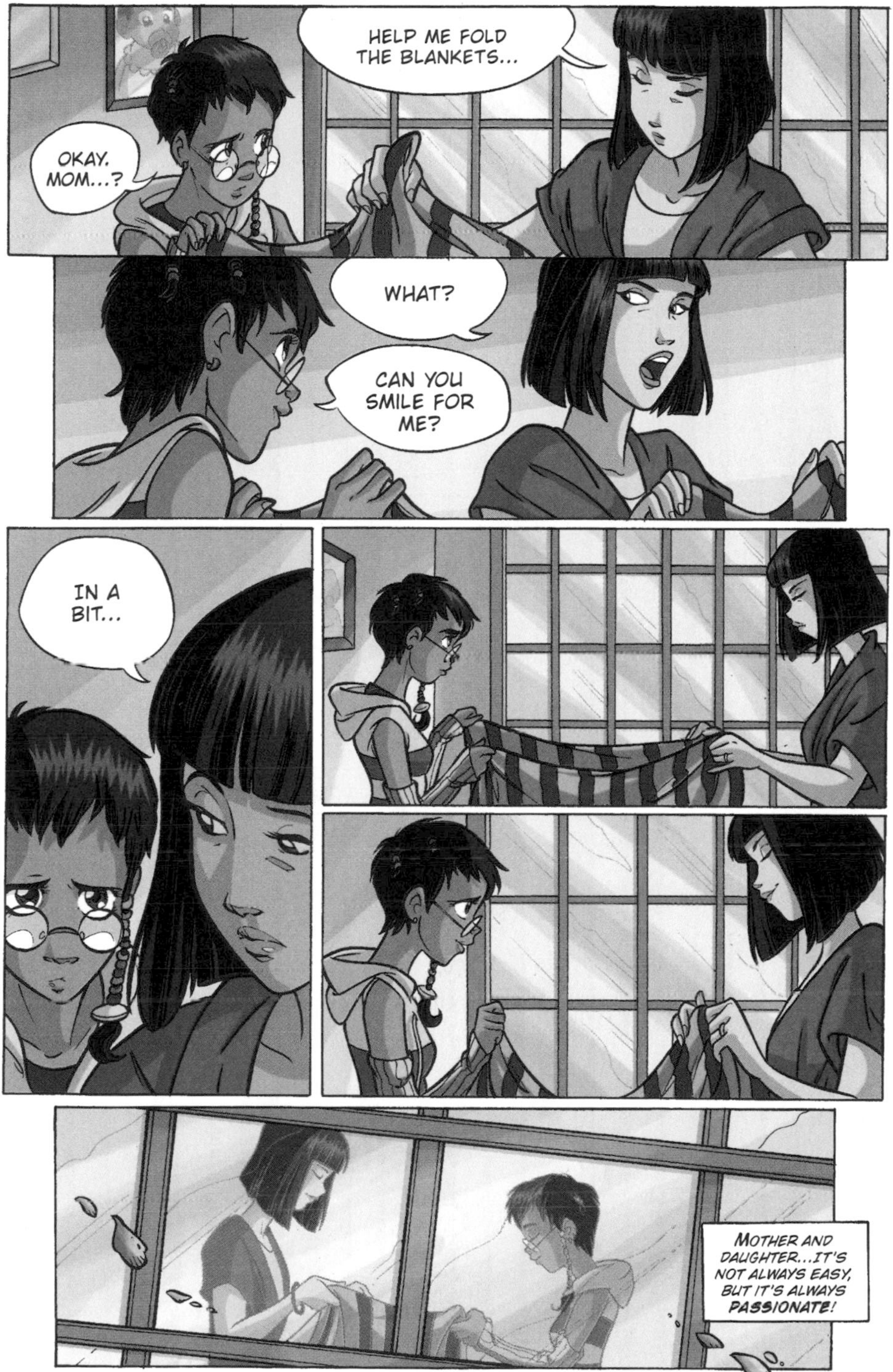

HELP ME FOLD THE BLANKETS...
OKAY. MOM...?
WHAT?
CAN YOU SMILE FOR ME?
IN A BIT...
MOTHER AND DAUGHTER...IT'S NOT ALWAYS EASY, BUT IT'S ALWAYS **PASSIONATE**!

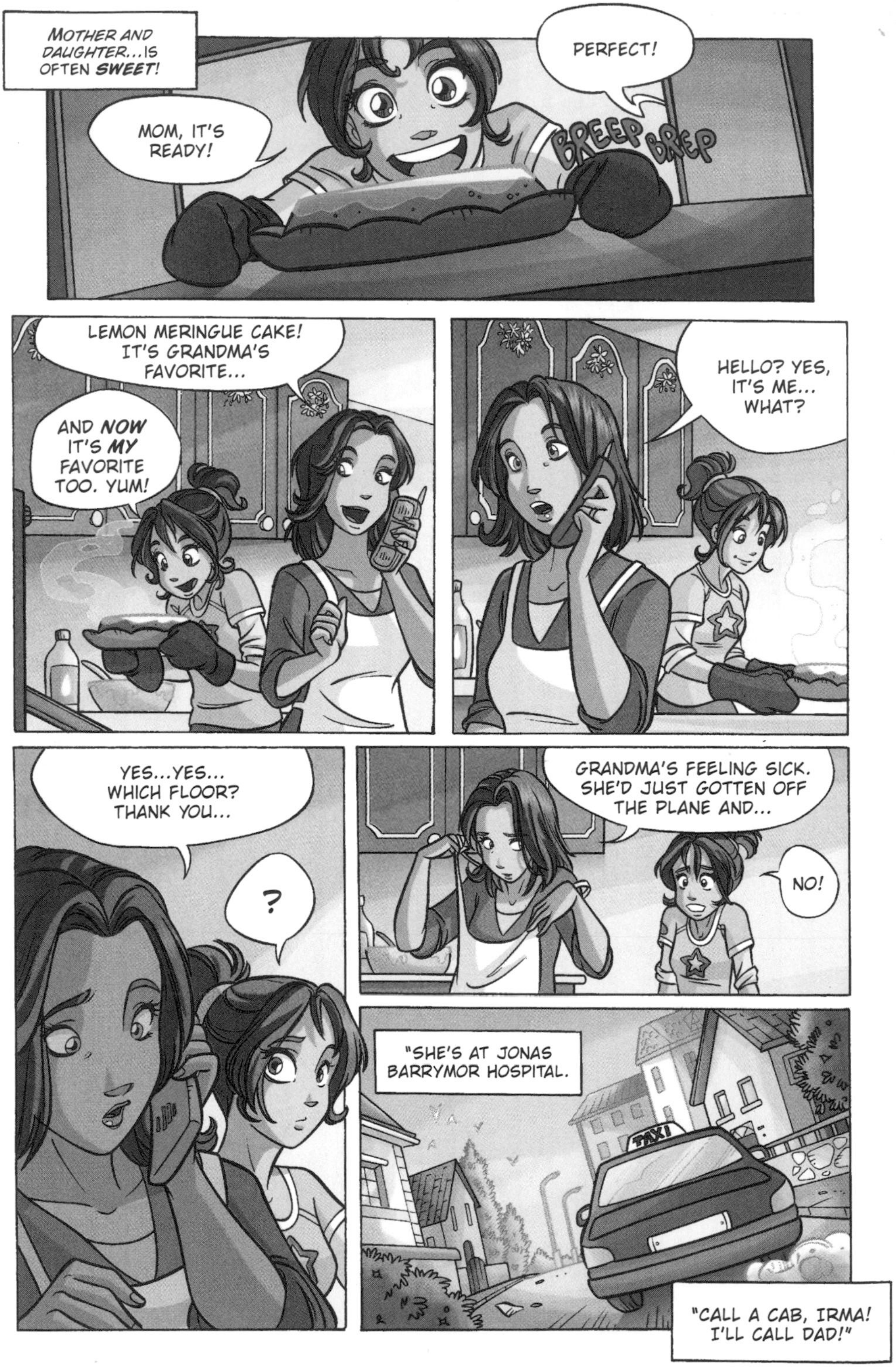

MOTHER AND DAUGHTER...IS OFTEN SWEET!
MOM, IT'S READY!
PERFECT!
BREEP BREP
LEMON MERINGUE CAKE! IT'S GRANDMA'S FAVORITE...
AND NOW IT'S MY FAVORITE TOO. YUM!
HELLO? YES, IT'S ME... WHAT?
YES...YES... WHICH FLOOR? THANK YOU...
?
GRANDMA'S FEELING SICK. SHE'D JUST GOTTEN OFF THE PLANE AND...
NO!
"SHE'S AT JONAS BARRYMOR HOSPITAL.
TAXI
"CALL A CAB, IRMA! I'LL CALL DAD!"

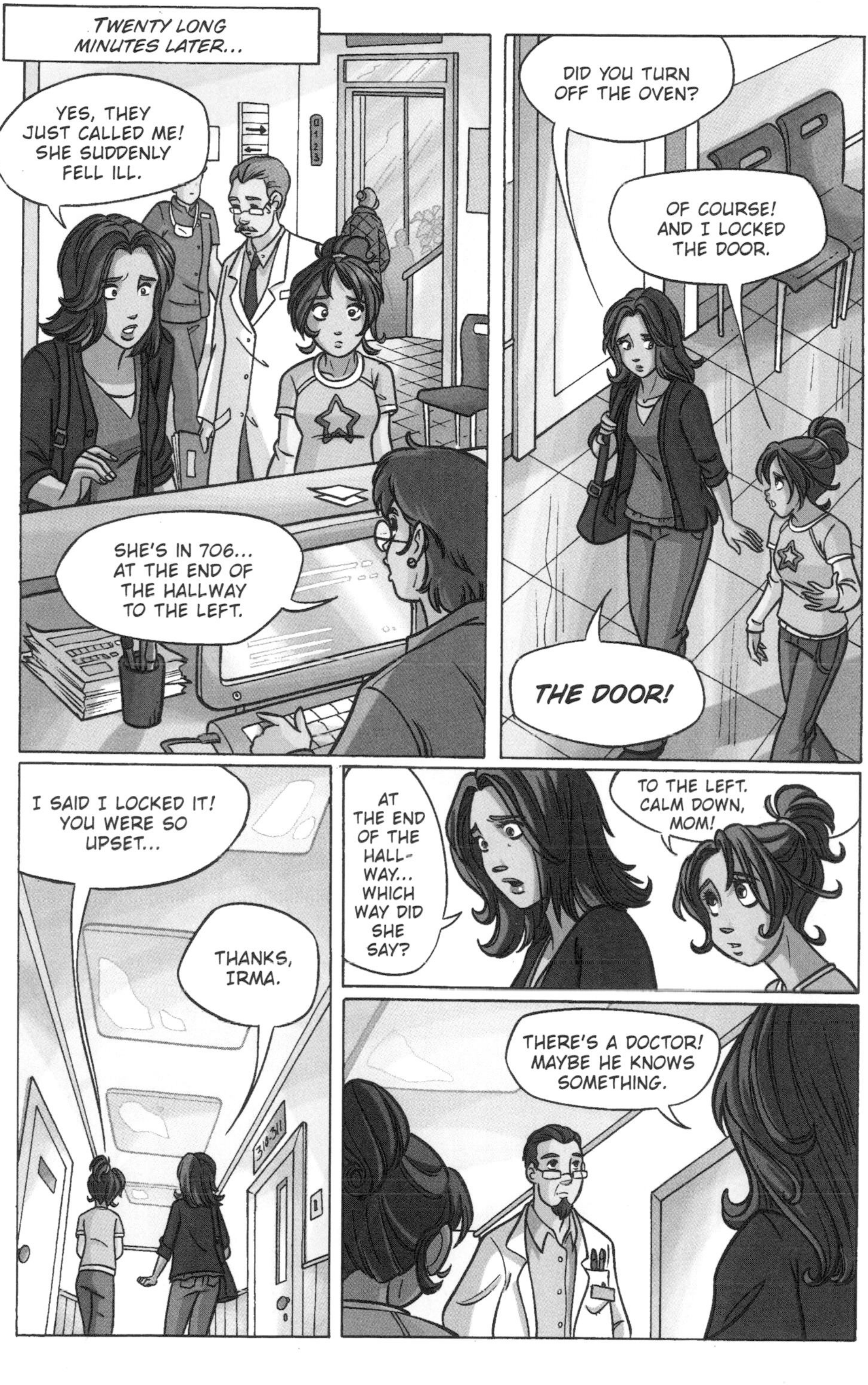
TWENTY LONG MINUTES LATER...
YES, THEY JUST CALLED ME! SHE SUDDENLY FELL ILL.
SHE'S IN 706... AT THE END OF THE HALLWAY TO THE LEFT.
DID YOU TURN OFF THE OVEN?
OF COURSE! AND I LOCKED THE DOOR.
THE DOOR!
I SAID I LOCKED IT! YOU WERE SO UPSET...
THANKS, IRMA.
AT THE END OF THE HALL-WAY... WHICH WAY DID SHE SAY?
TO THE LEFT. CALM DOWN, MOM!
THERE'S A DOCTOR! MAYBE HE KNOWS SOMETHING.

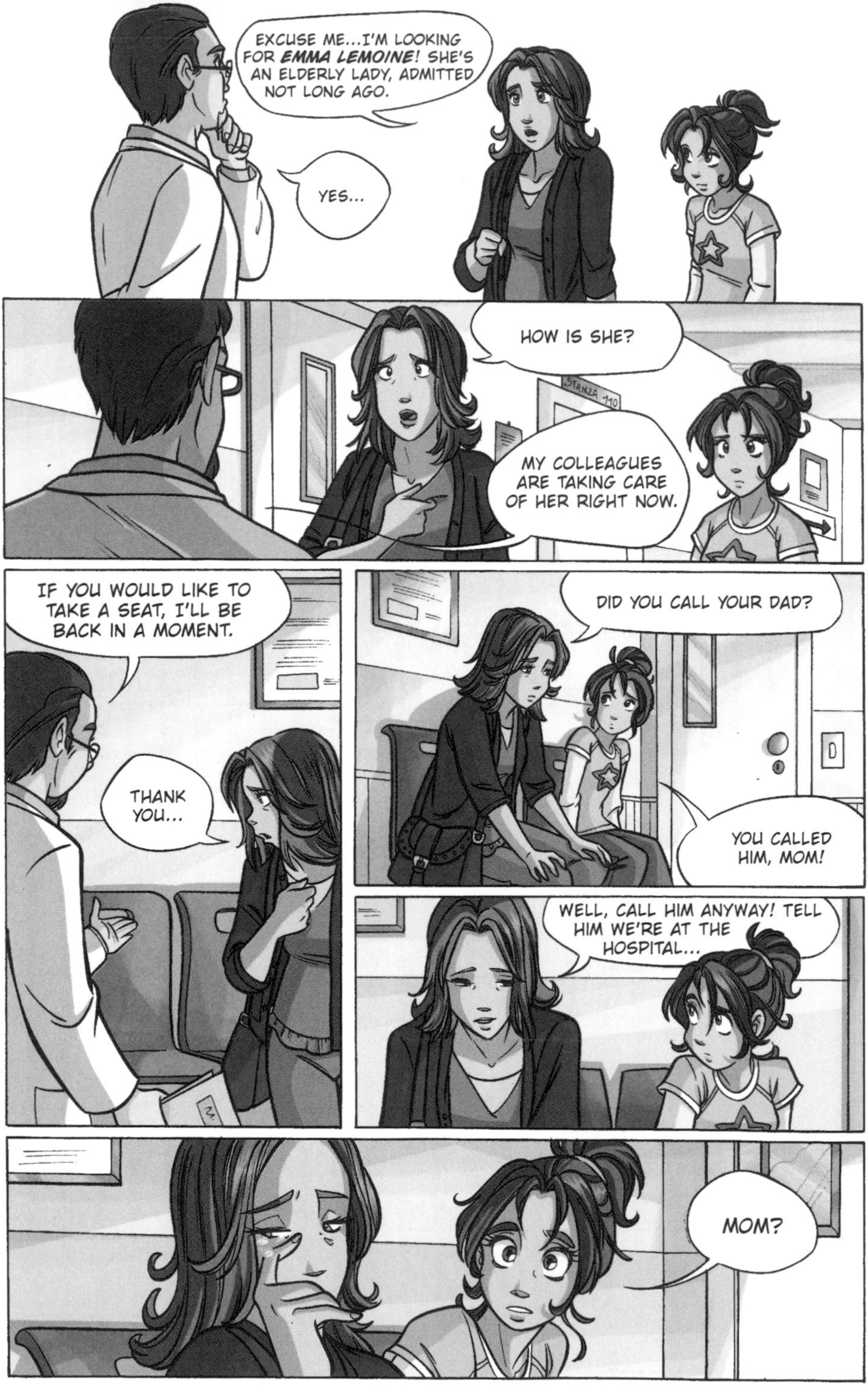

EXCUSE ME...I'M LOOKING FOR **EMMA LEMOINE**! SHE'S AN ELDERLY LADY, ADMITTED NOT LONG AGO.
YES...
HOW IS SHE?
STANZA 110
MY COLLEAGUES ARE TAKING CARE OF HER RIGHT NOW.
IF YOU WOULD LIKE TO TAKE A SEAT, I'LL BE BACK IN A MOMENT.
THANK YOU...
DID YOU CALL YOUR DAD?
YOU CALLED HIM, MOM!
WELL, CALL HIM ANYWAY! TELL HIM WE'RE AT THE HOSPITAL...
MOM?

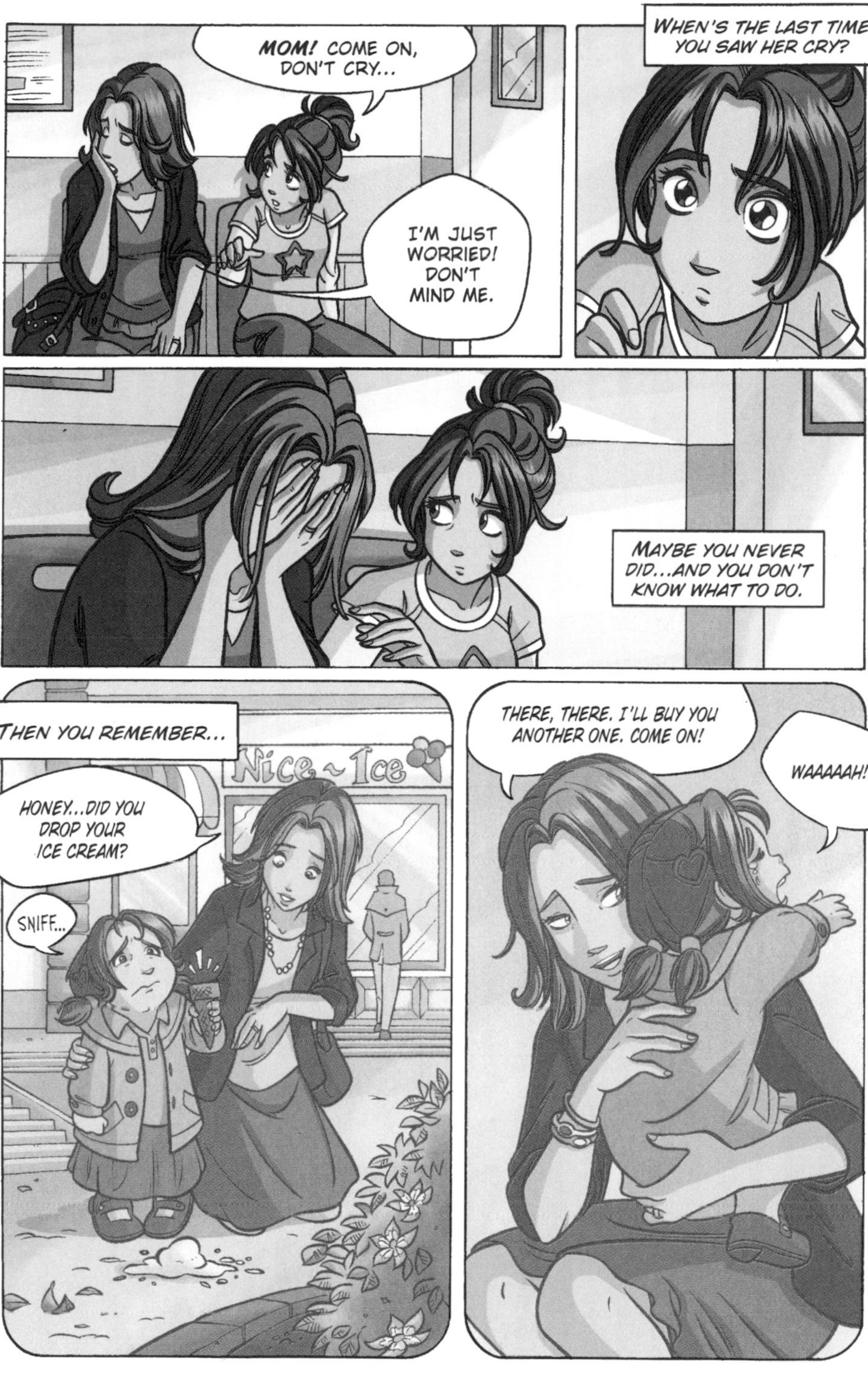

MOM! COME ON, DON'T CRY...
I'M JUST WORRIED! DON'T MIND ME.
WHEN'S THE LAST TIME YOU SAW HER CRY?
MAYBE YOU NEVER DID...AND YOU DON'T KNOW WHAT TO DO.
THEN YOU REMEMBER...
Nice ~ Ice
HONEY...DID YOU DROP YOUR ICE CREAM?
SNIFF...
THERE, THERE. I'LL BUY YOU ANOTHER ONE. COME ON!
WAAAAAH!

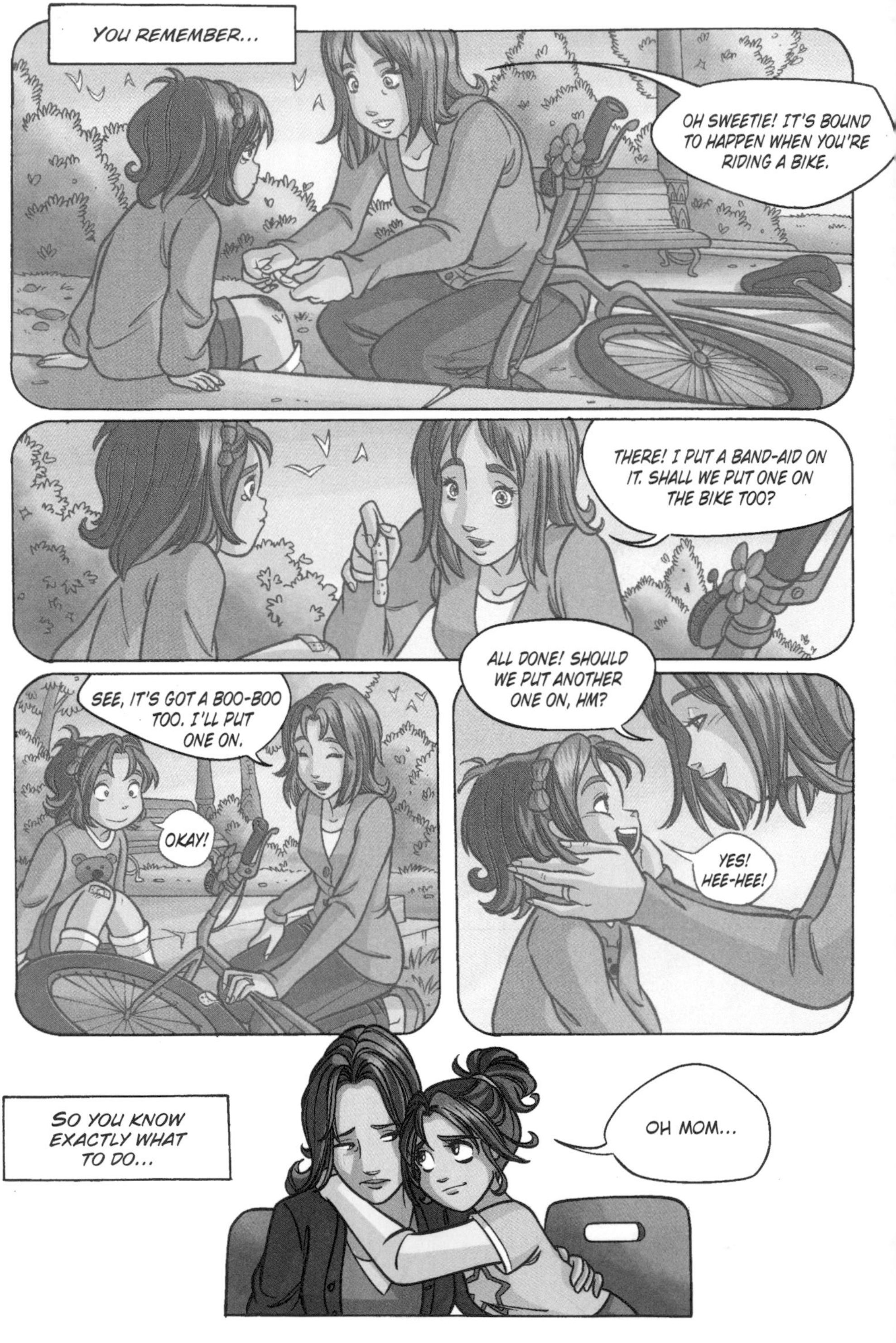
YOU REMEMBER...
OH SWEETIE! IT'S BOUND TO HAPPEN WHEN YOU'RE RIDING A BIKE.
THERE! I PUT A BAND-AID ON IT. SHALL WE PUT ONE ON THE BIKE TOO?
SEE, IT'S GOT A BOO-BOO TOO. I'LL PUT ONE ON.
OKAY!
ALL DONE! SHOULD WE PUT ANOTHER ONE ON, HM?
YES! HEE-HEE!
SO YOU KNOW EXACTLY WHAT TO DO...
OH MOM...

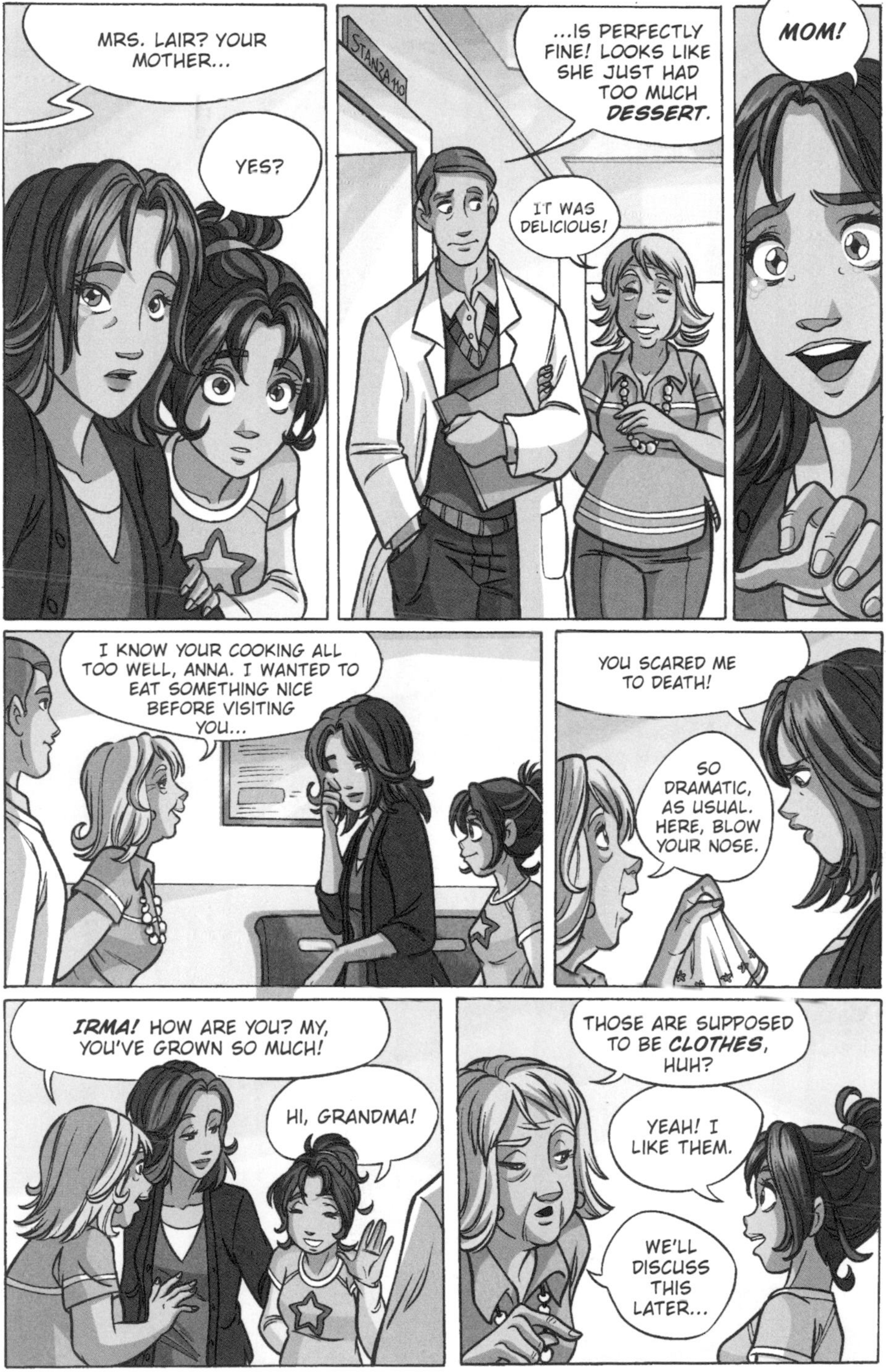
MRS. LAIR? YOUR MOTHER...
YES?
STANZA 110
...IS PERFECTLY FINE! LOOKS LIKE SHE JUST HAD TOO MUCH **DESSERT**.
IT WAS DELICIOUS!
MOM!
I KNOW YOUR COOKING ALL TOO WELL, ANNA. I WANTED TO EAT SOMETHING NICE BEFORE VISITING YOU...
YOU SCARED ME TO DEATH!
SO DRAMATIC, AS USUAL. HERE, BLOW YOUR NOSE.
IRMA! HOW ARE YOU? MY, YOU'VE GROWN SO MUCH!
HI, GRANDMA!
THOSE ARE SUPPOSED TO BE ***CLOTHES***, HUH?
YEAH! I LIKE THEM.
WE'LL DISCUSS THIS LATER...

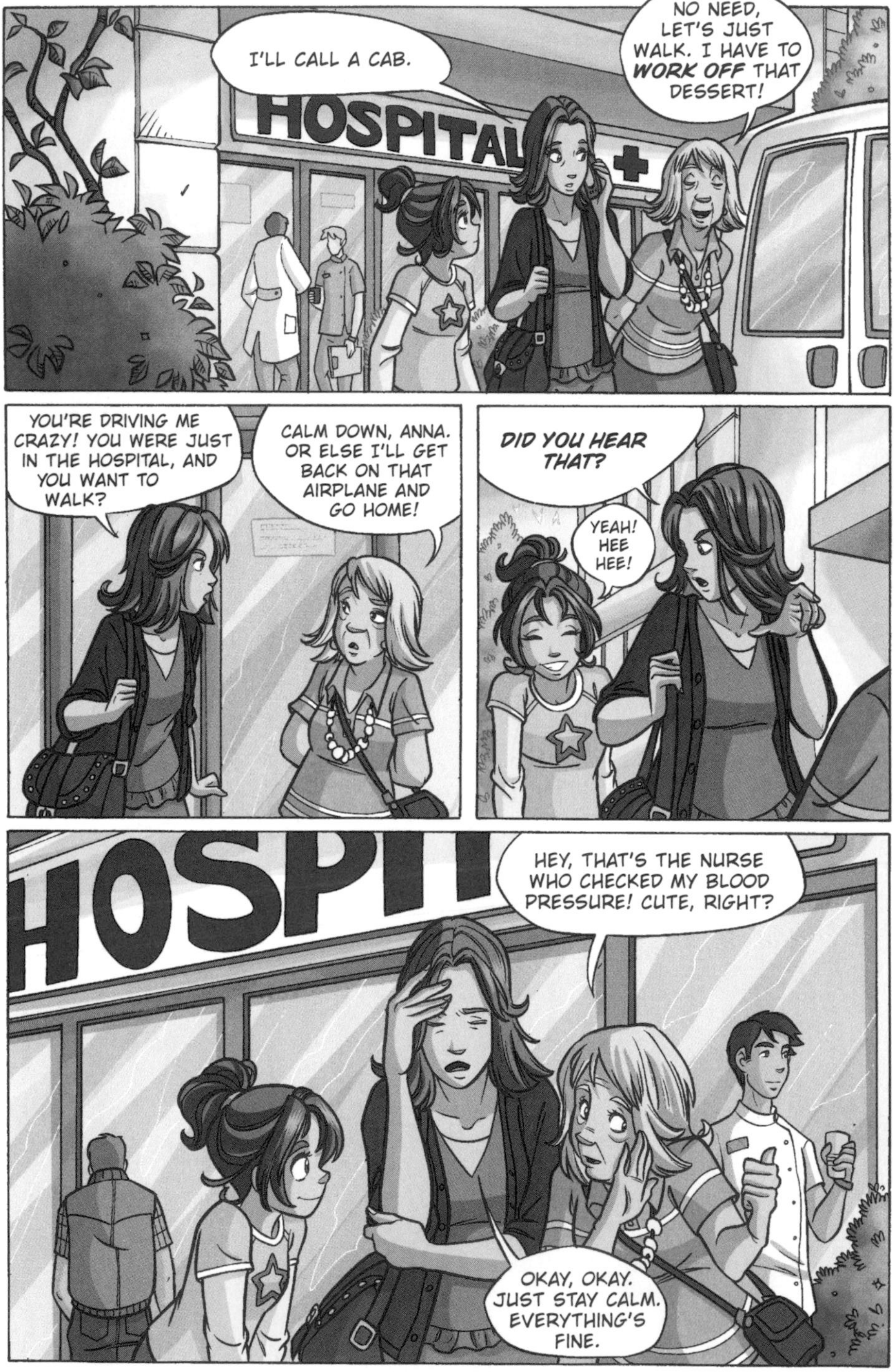

HOSPITAL
I'LL CALL A CAB.
NO NEED, LET'S JUST WALK. I HAVE TO **WORK OFF** THAT DESSERT!
YOU'RE DRIVING ME CRAZY! YOU WERE JUST IN THE HOSPITAL, AND YOU WANT TO WALK?
CALM DOWN, ANNA. OR ELSE I'LL GET BACK ON THAT AIRPLANE AND GO HOME!
DID YOU HEAR THAT?
YEAH! HEE HEE!
HOSPI
HEY, THAT'S THE NURSE WHO CHECKED MY BLOOD PRESSURE! CUTE, RIGHT?
OKAY, OKAY. JUST STAY CALM. EVERYTHING'S FINE.

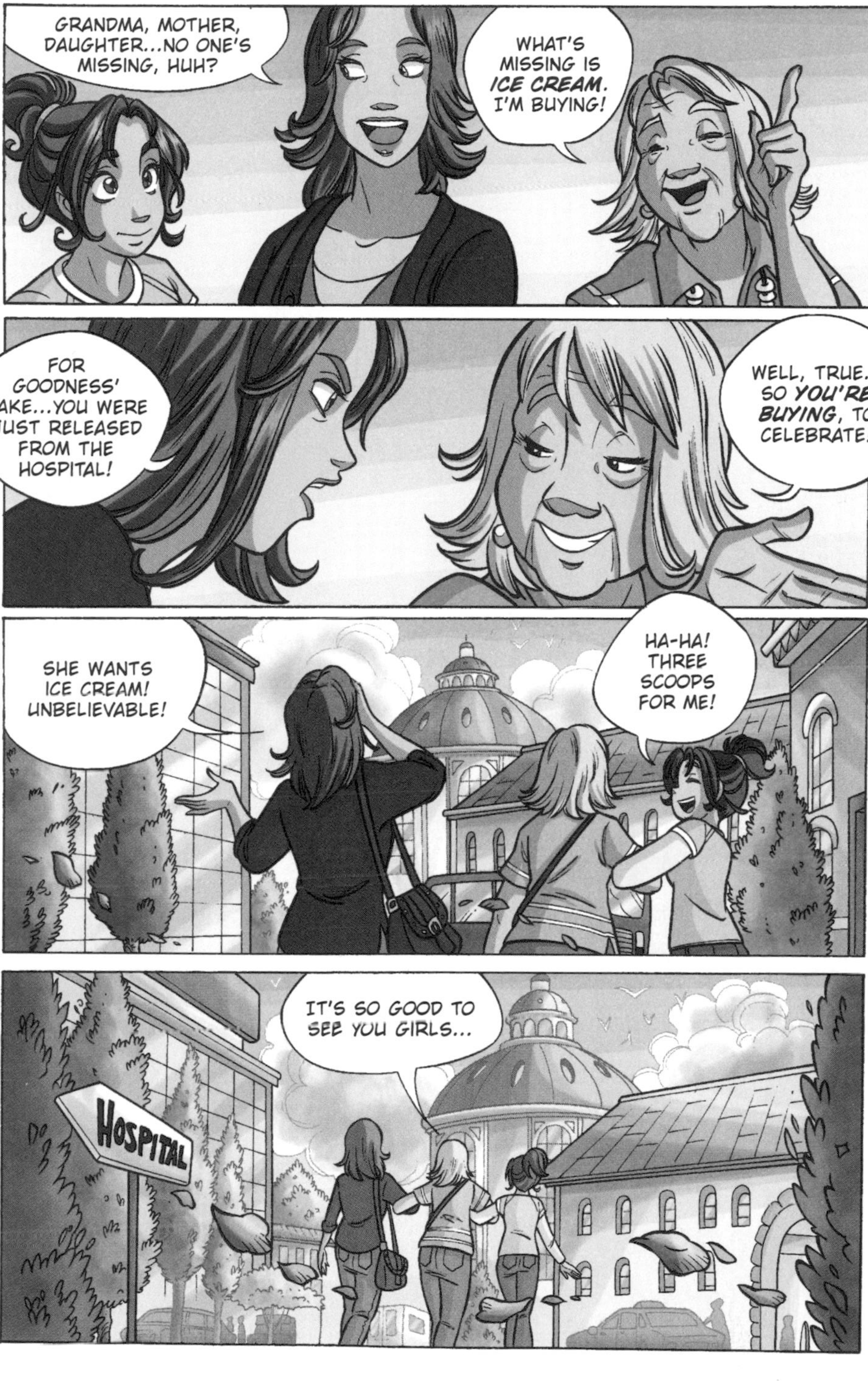
GRANDMA, MOTHER, DAUGHTER...NO ONE'S MISSING, HUH?
WHAT'S MISSING IS *ICE CREAM*. I'M BUYING!
FOR GOODNESS' SAKE...YOU WERE JUST RELEASED FROM THE HOSPITAL!
WELL, TRUE... SO *YOU'RE BUYING*, TO CELEBRATE!
SHE WANTS ICE CREAM! UNBELIEVABLE!
HA-HA! THREE SCOOPS FOR ME!
IT'S SO GOOD TO SEE YOU GIRLS...
HOSPITAL

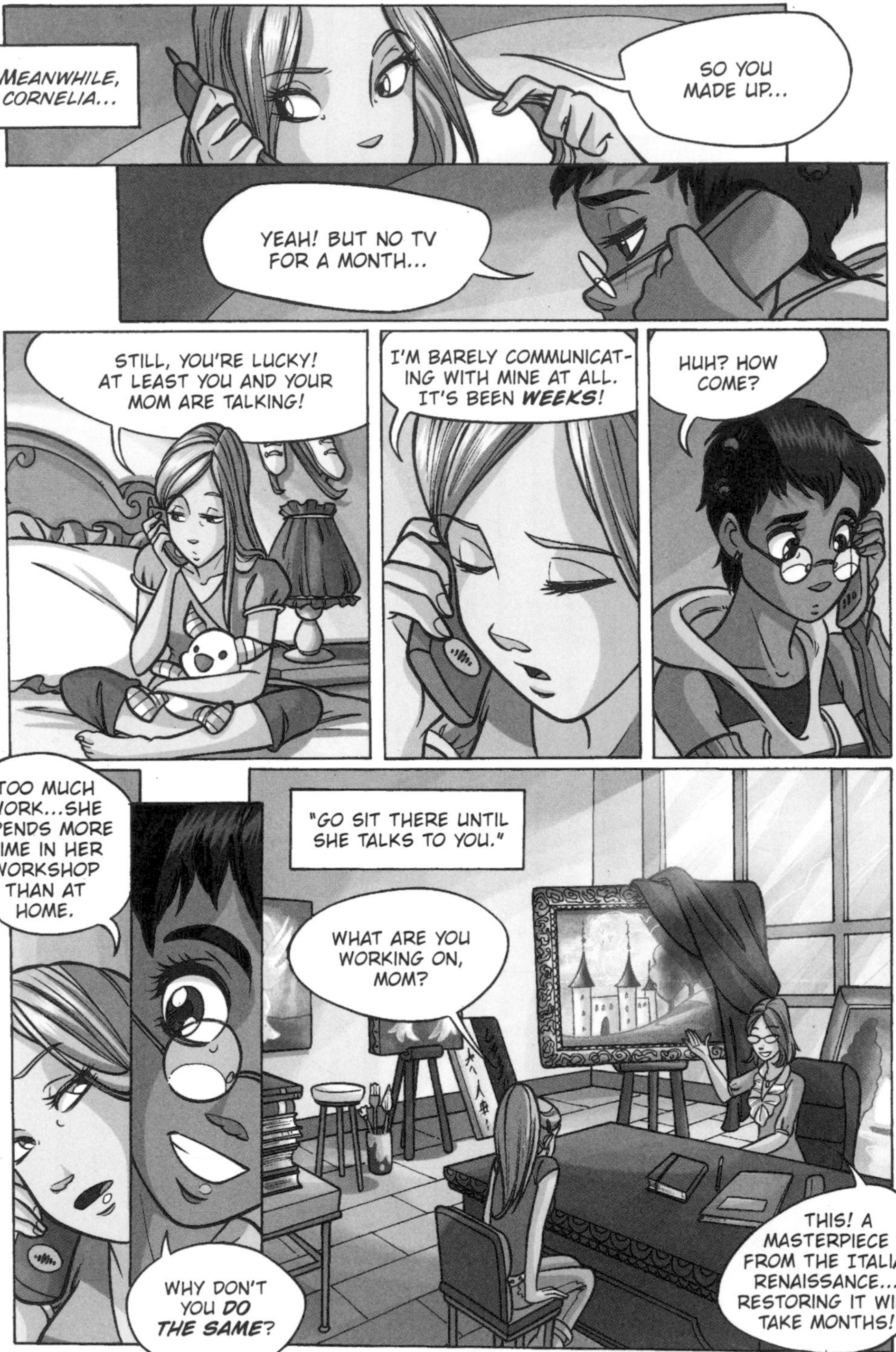

MEANWHILE, CORNELIA...
SO YOU MADE UP...
YEAH! BUT NO TV FOR A MONTH...
STILL, YOU'RE LUCKY! AT LEAST YOU AND YOUR MOM ARE TALKING!
I'M BARELY COMMUNICATING WITH MINE AT ALL. IT'S BEEN *WEEKS*!
HUH? HOW COME?
TOO MUCH WORK...SHE SPENDS MORE TIME IN HER WORKSHOP THAN AT HOME.
WHY DON'T YOU *DO THE SAME*?
"GO SIT THERE UNTIL SHE TALKS TO YOU."
WHAT ARE YOU WORKING ON, MOM?
THIS! A MASTERPIECE FROM THE ITALIAN RENAISSANCE... RESTORING IT WILL TAKE MONTHS!

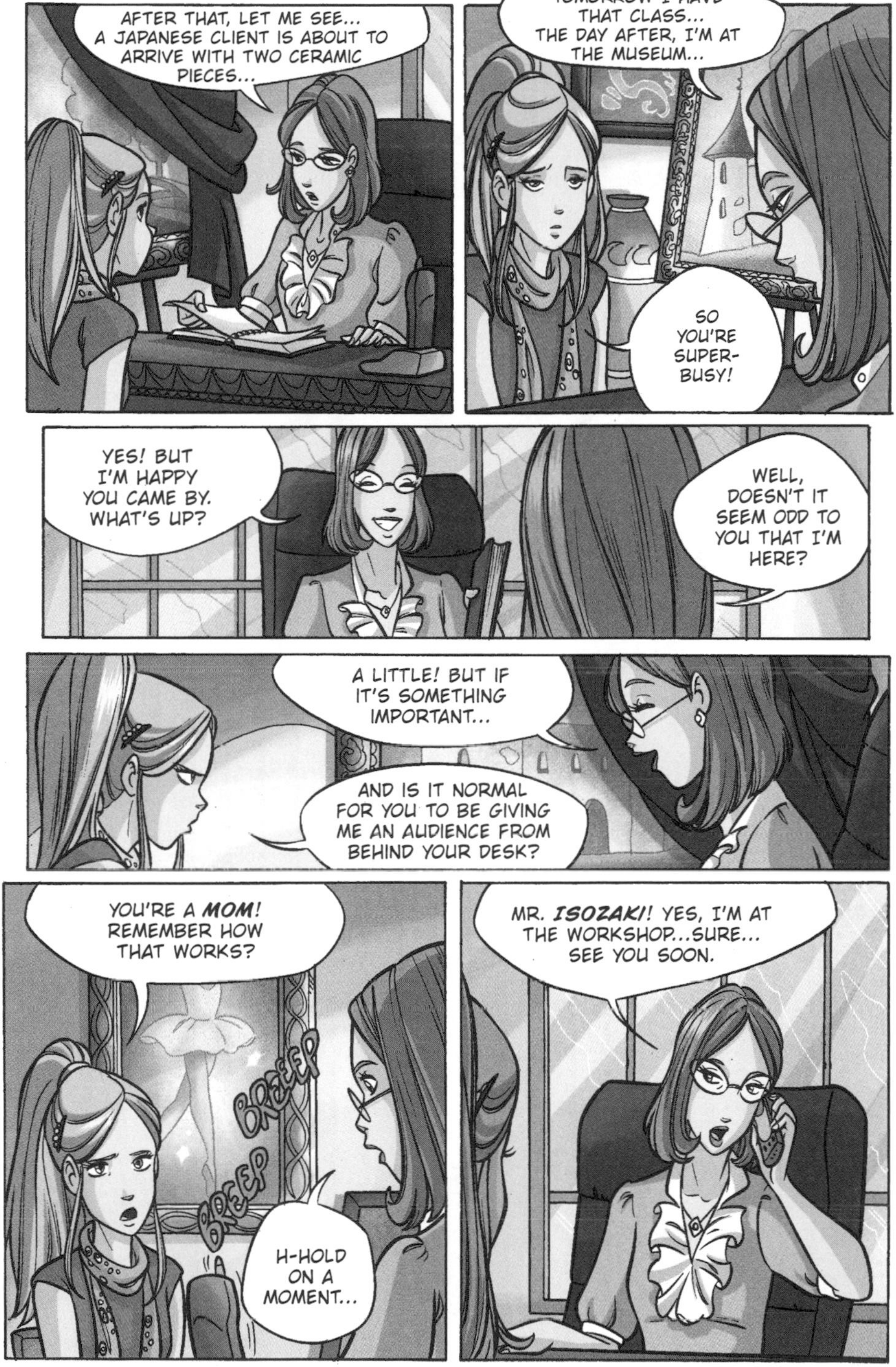
AFTER THAT, LET ME SEE... A JAPANESE CLIENT IS ABOUT TO ARRIVE WITH TWO CERAMIC PIECES...
TOMORROW I HAVE THAT CLASS... THE DAY AFTER, I'M AT THE MUSEUM...
SO YOU'RE SUPER-BUSY!
YES! BUT I'M HAPPY YOU CAME BY. WHAT'S UP?
WELL, DOESN'T IT SEEM ODD TO YOU THAT I'M HERE?
A LITTLE! BUT IF IT'S SOMETHING IMPORTANT...
AND IS IT NORMAL FOR YOU TO BE GIVING ME AN AUDIENCE FROM BEHIND YOUR DESK?
YOU'RE A **MOM**! REMEMBER HOW THAT WORKS?
BREEP BREEP
H-HOLD ON A MOMENT...
MR. ***ISOZAKI***! YES, I'M AT THE WORKSHOP...SURE... SEE YOU SOON.

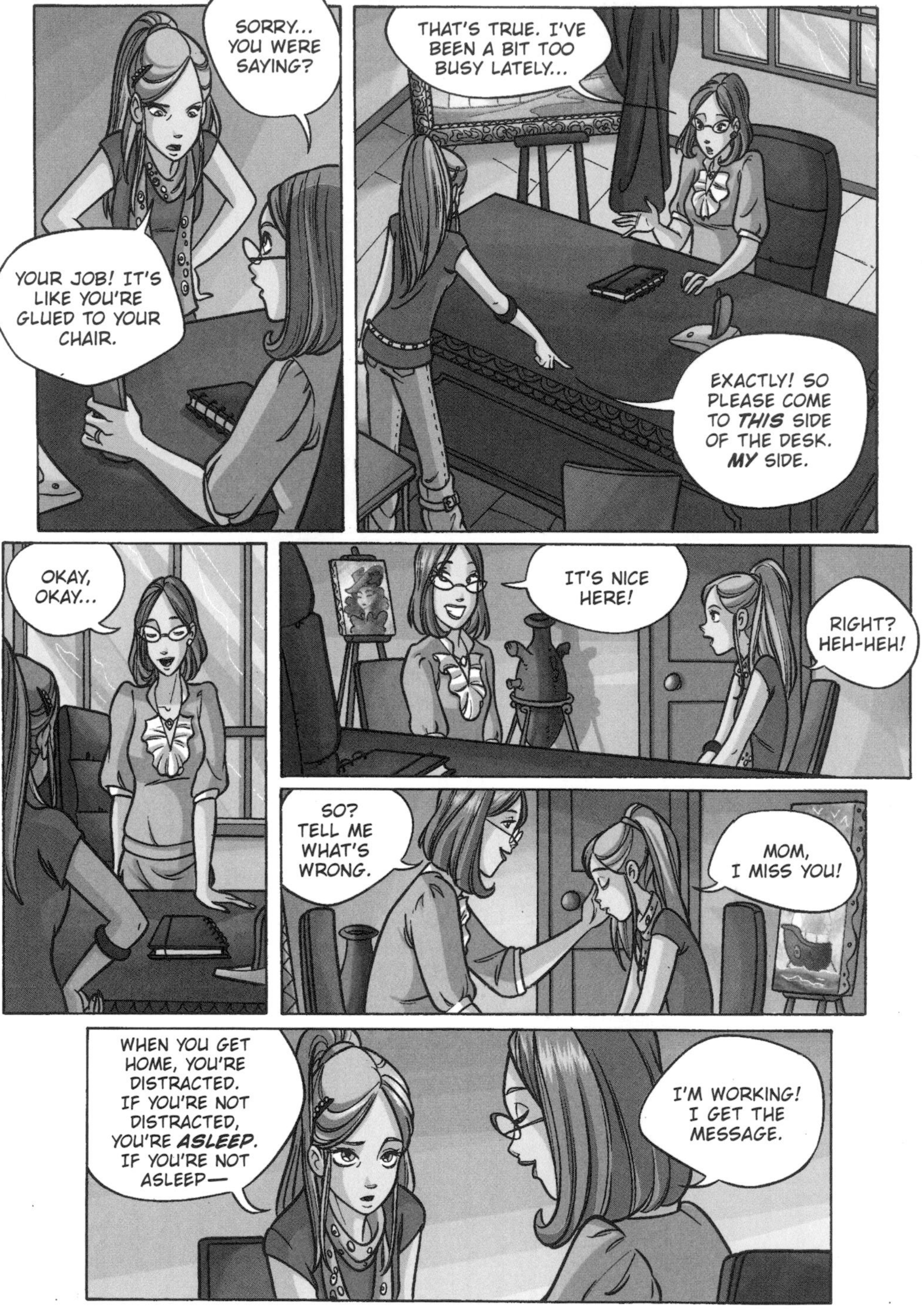
SORRY... YOU WERE SAYING?
YOUR JOB! IT'S LIKE YOU'RE GLUED TO YOUR CHAIR.
THAT'S TRUE. I'VE BEEN A BIT TOO BUSY LATELY...
EXACTLY! SO PLEASE COME TO THIS SIDE OF THE DESK. MY SIDE.
OKAY, OKAY...
IT'S NICE HERE!
RIGHT? HEH-HEH!
SO? TELL ME WHAT'S WRONG.
MOM, I MISS YOU!
WHEN YOU GET HOME, YOU'RE DISTRACTED. IF YOU'RE NOT DISTRACTED, YOU'RE ASLEEP. IF YOU'RE NOT ASLEEP—
I'M WORKING! I GET THE MESSAGE.

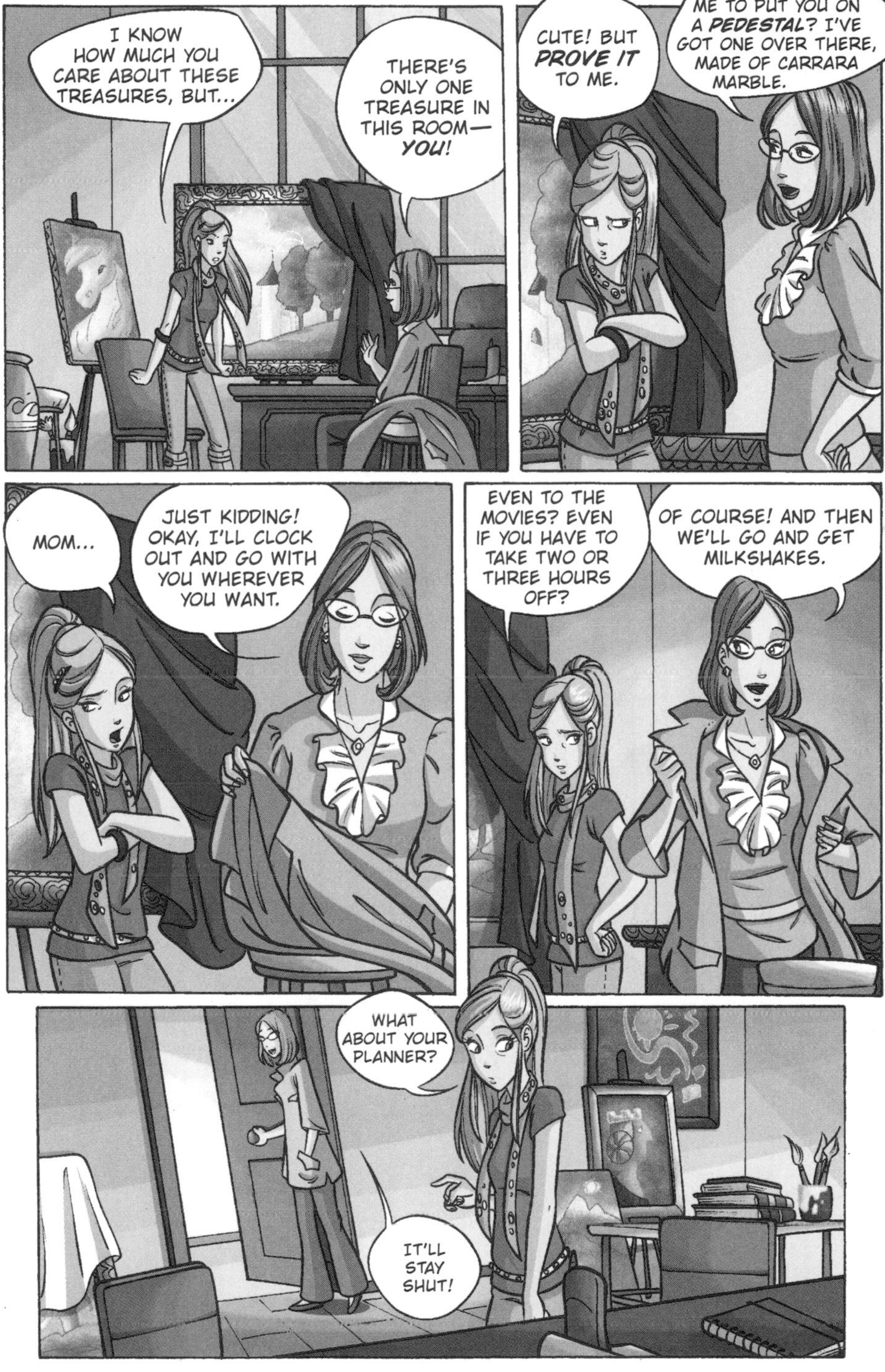
I KNOW HOW MUCH YOU CARE ABOUT THESE TREASURES, BUT...
THERE'S ONLY ONE TREASURE IN THIS ROOM— ***YOU!***
CUTE! BUT ***PROVE IT*** TO ME.
YOU WANT ME TO PUT YOU ON A ***PEDESTAL***? I'VE GOT ONE OVER THERE, MADE OF CARRARA MARBLE.
MOM...
JUST KIDDING! OKAY, I'LL CLOCK OUT AND GO WITH YOU WHEREVER YOU WANT.
EVEN TO THE MOVIES? EVEN IF YOU HAVE TO TAKE TWO OR THREE HOURS OFF?
OF COURSE! AND THEN WE'LL GO AND GET MILKSHAKES.
WHAT ABOUT YOUR PLANNER?
IT'LL STAY SHUT!

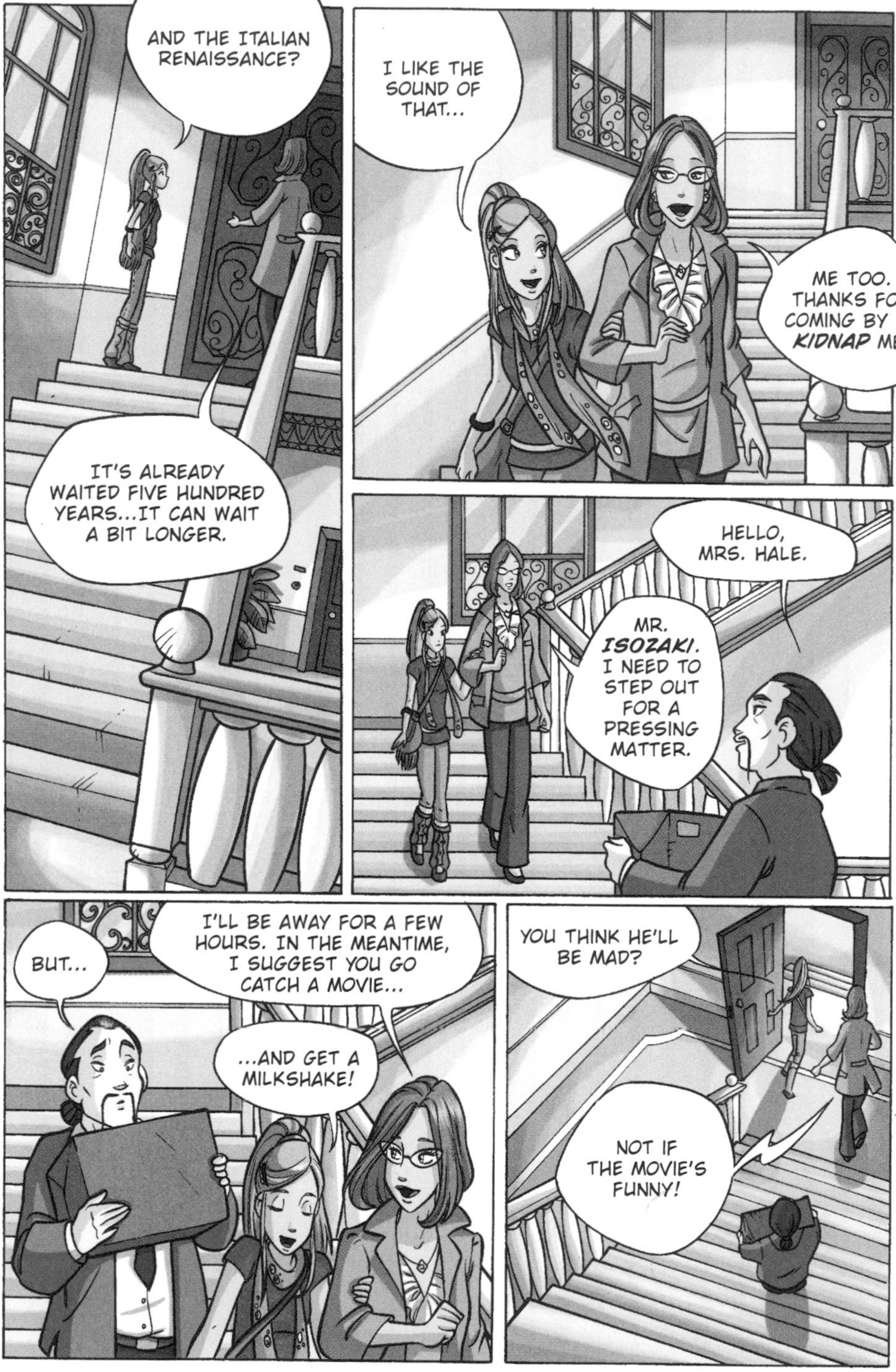
AND THE ITALIAN RENAISSANCE?
IT'S ALREADY WAITED FIVE HUNDRED YEARS...IT CAN WAIT A BIT LONGER.
I LIKE THE SOUND OF THAT...
ME TOO. THANKS FOR COMING BY TO *KIDNAP* ME.
HELLO, MRS. HALE.
MR. *ISOZAKI*. I NEED TO STEP OUT FOR A PRESSING MATTER.
BUT...
I'LL BE AWAY FOR A FEW HOURS. IN THE MEANTIME, I SUGGEST YOU GO CATCH A MOVIE...
...AND GET A MILKSHAKE!
YOU THINK HE'LL BE MAD?
NOT IF THE MOVIE'S FUNNY!

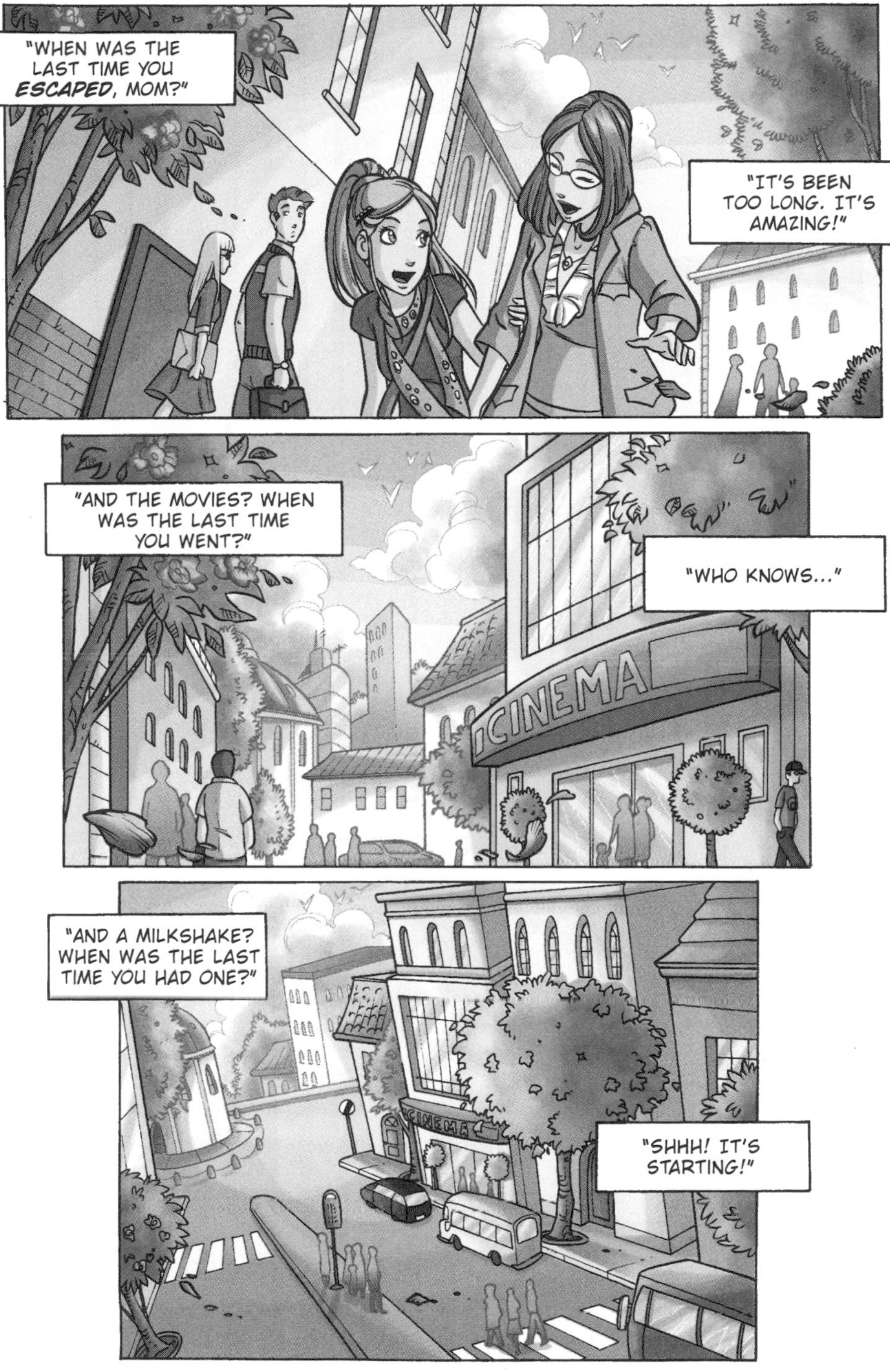
"WHEN WAS THE LAST TIME YOU **ESCAPED**, MOM?"
"IT'S BEEN TOO LONG. IT'S AMAZING!"
"AND THE MOVIES? WHEN WAS THE LAST TIME YOU WENT?"
"WHO KNOWS..."
CINEMA
"AND A MILKSHAKE? WHEN WAS THE LAST TIME YOU HAD ONE?"
CINEMA
"SHHH! IT'S STARTING!"

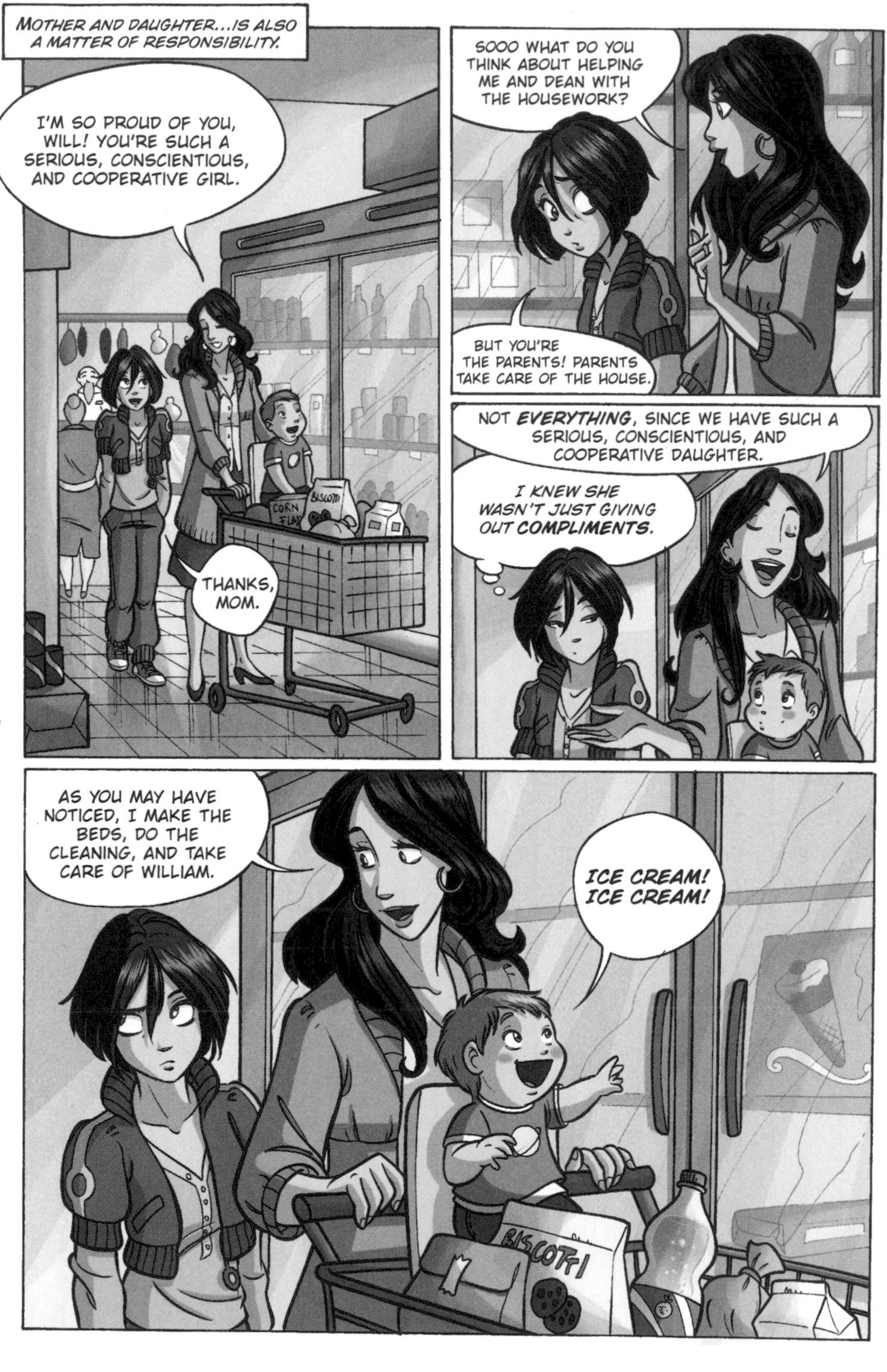
MOTHER AND DAUGHTER...IS ALSO A MATTER OF RESPONSIBILITY.
I'M SO PROUD OF YOU, WILL! YOU'RE SUCH A SERIOUS, CONSCIENTIOUS, AND COOPERATIVE GIRL.
THANKS, MOM.
SOOO WHAT DO YOU THINK ABOUT HELPING ME AND DEAN WITH THE HOUSEWORK?
BUT YOU'RE THE PARENTS! PARENTS TAKE CARE OF THE HOUSE.
NOT EVERYTHING, SINCE WE HAVE SUCH A SERIOUS, CONSCIENTIOUS, AND COOPERATIVE DAUGHTER.
I KNEW SHE WASN'T JUST GIVING OUT COMPLIMENTS.
AS YOU MAY HAVE NOTICED, I MAKE THE BEDS, DO THE CLEANING, AND TAKE CARE OF WILLIAM.
ICE CREAM! ICE CREAM!

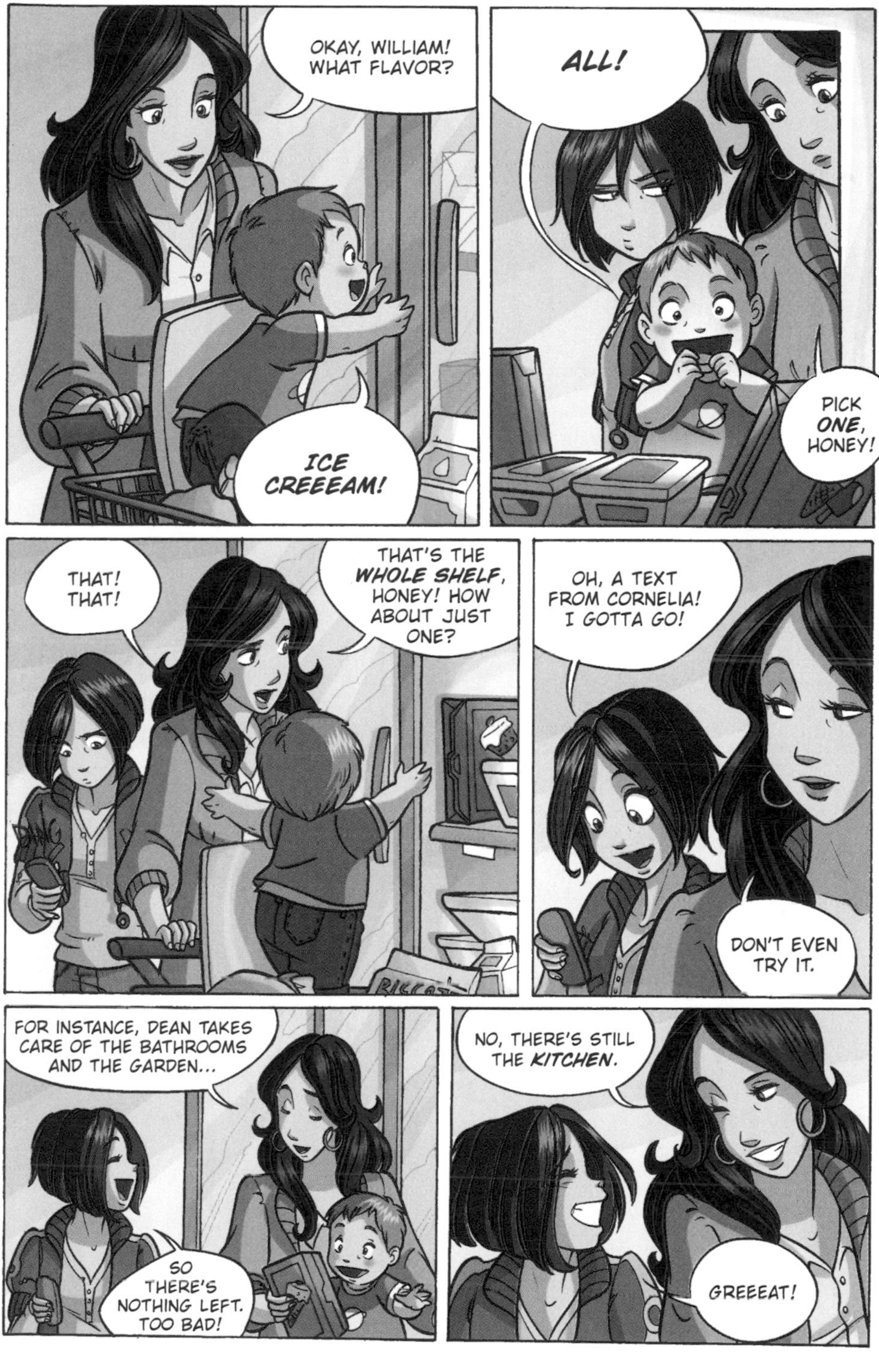
OKAY, WILLIAM! WHAT FLAVOR?
ICE CREEEAM!
ALL!
PICK ONE, HONEY!
THAT! THAT!
THAT'S THE WHOLE SHELF, HONEY! HOW ABOUT JUST ONE?
OH, A TEXT FROM CORNELIA! I GOTTA GO!
DON'T EVEN TRY IT.
FOR INSTANCE, DEAN TAKES CARE OF THE BATHROOMS AND THE GARDEN...
SO THERE'S NOTHING LEFT. TOO BAD!
NO, THERE'S STILL THE KITCHEN.
GREEEAT!

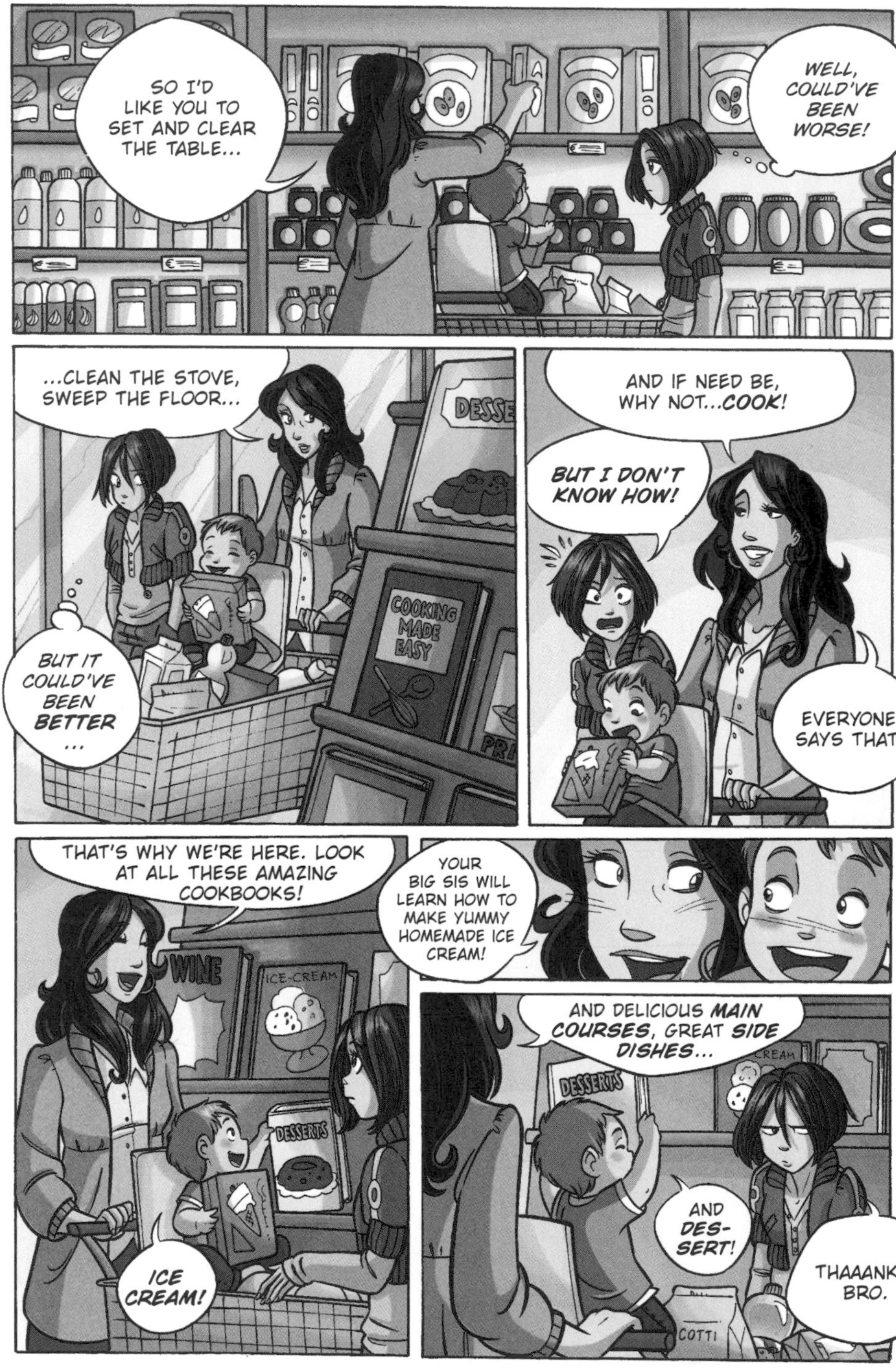
SO I'D LIKE YOU TO SET AND CLEAR THE TABLE...
WELL, COULD'VE BEEN WORSE!
...CLEAN THE STOVE, SWEEP THE FLOOR...
DESSE
BUT IT COULD'VE BEEN BETTER ...
COOKING MADE EASY
AND IF NEED BE, WHY NOT...COOK!
BUT I DON'T KNOW HOW!
EVERYONE SAYS THAT.
THAT'S WHY WE'RE HERE. LOOK AT ALL THESE AMAZING COOKBOOKS!
WINE
ICE-CREAM
DESSERTS
ICE CREAM!
YOUR BIG SIS WILL LEARN HOW TO MAKE YUMMY HOMEMADE ICE CREAM!
AND DELICIOUS MAIN COURSES, GREAT SIDE DISHES...
DESSERTS
CREAM
AND DES-SERT!
THAAANKS, BRO.
COTTI

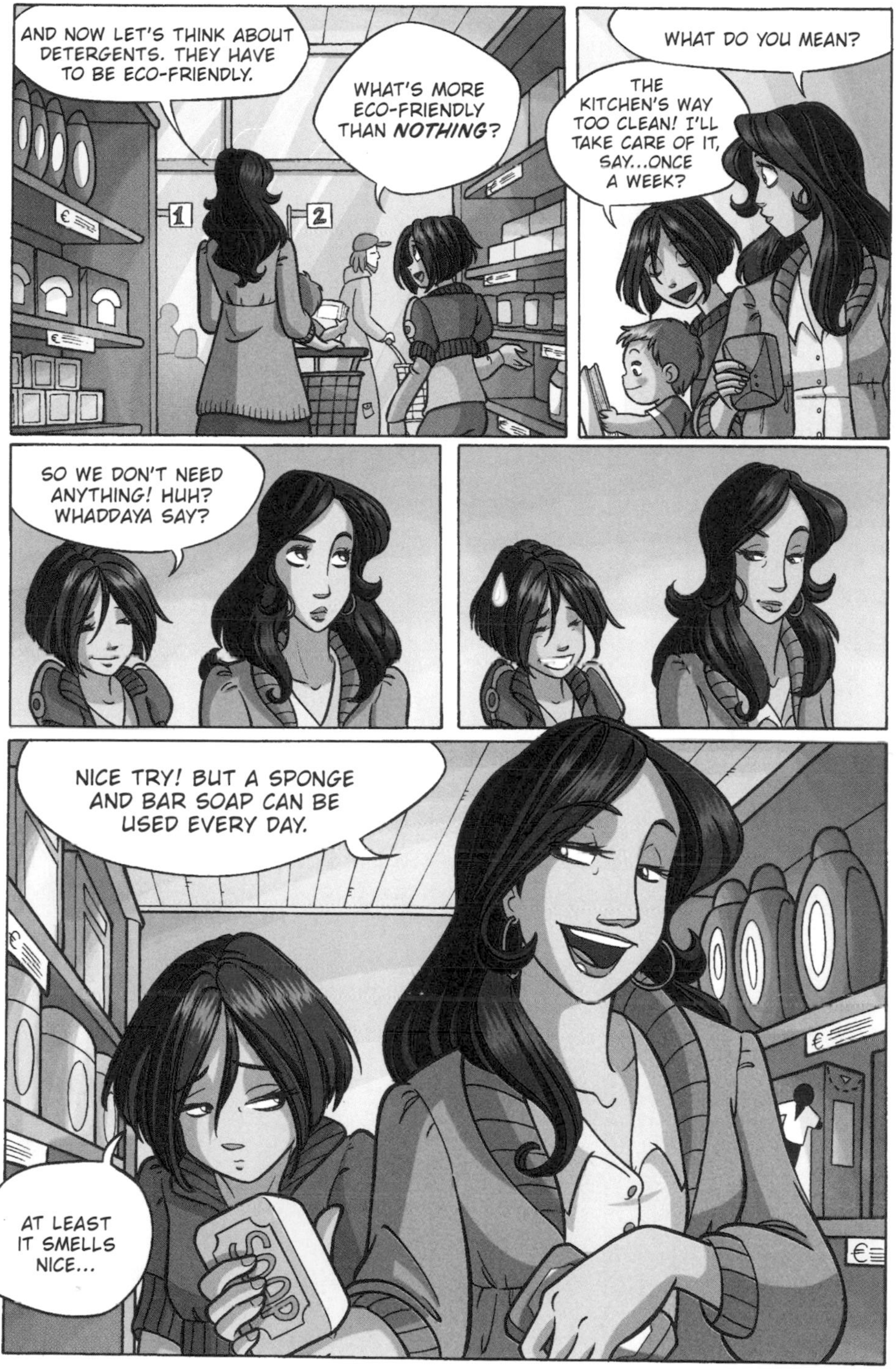
AND NOW LET'S THINK ABOUT DETERGENTS. THEY HAVE TO BE ECO-FRIENDLY.
WHAT'S MORE ECO-FRIENDLY THAN *NOTHING*?
WHAT DO YOU MEAN?
THE KITCHEN'S WAY TOO CLEAN! I'LL TAKE CARE OF IT, SAY...ONCE A WEEK?
SO WE DON'T NEED ANYTHING! HUH? WHADDAYA SAY?
NICE TRY! BUT A SPONGE AND BAR SOAP CAN BE USED EVERY DAY.
AT LEAST IT SMELLS NICE...

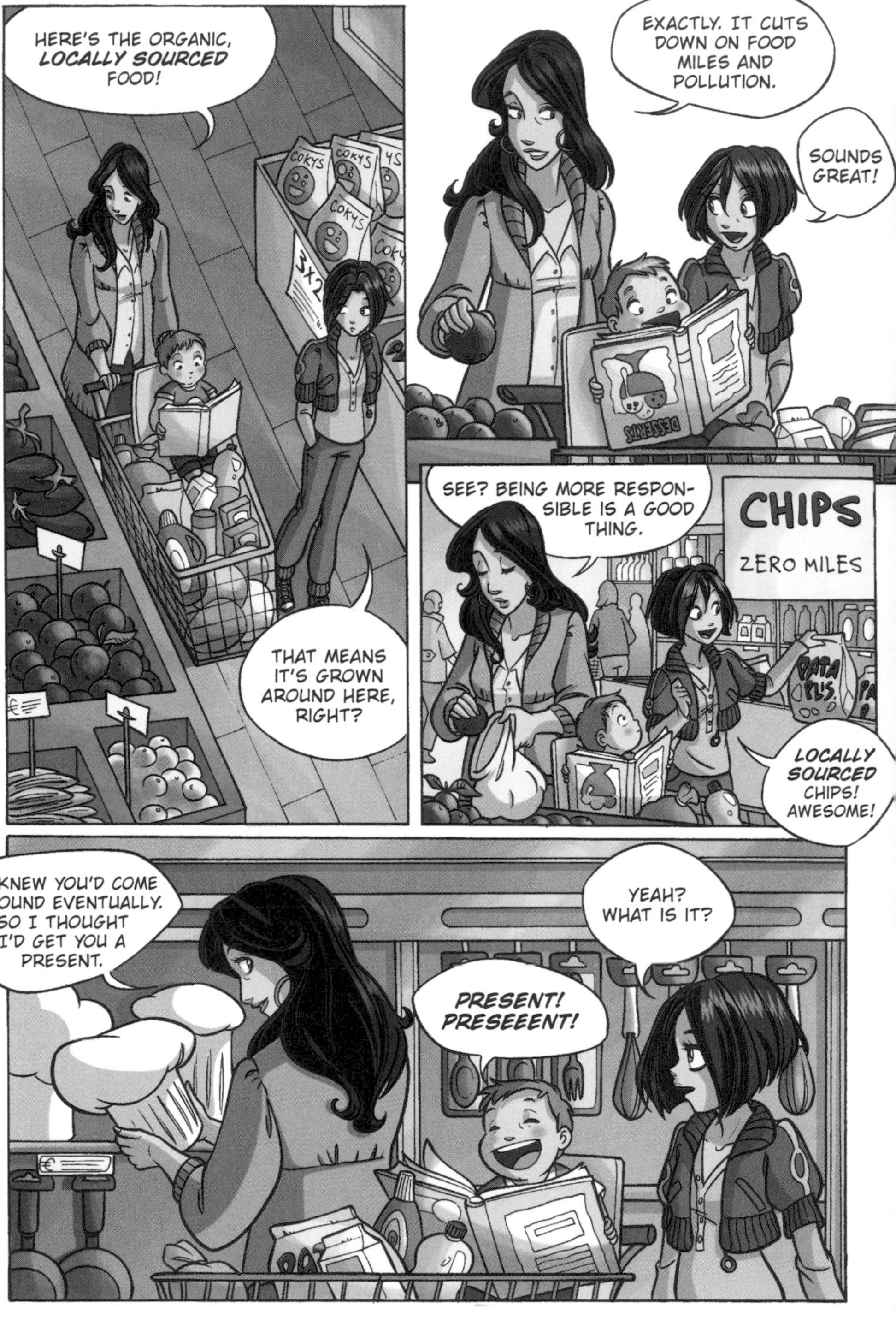
HERE'S THE ORGANIC, *LOCALLY SOURCED* FOOD!
COKYS
3x2
THAT MEANS IT'S GROWN AROUND HERE, RIGHT?
EXACTLY. IT CUTS DOWN ON FOOD MILES AND POLLUTION.
SOUNDS GREAT!
DESSERTS
SEE? BEING MORE RESPONSIBLE IS A GOOD THING.
CHIPS
ZERO MILES
LOCALLY SOURCED CHIPS! AWESOME!
I KNEW YOU'D COME AROUND EVENTUALLY. SO I THOUGHT I'D GET YOU A PRESENT.
YEAH? WHAT IS IT?
PRESENT! PRESEEENT!

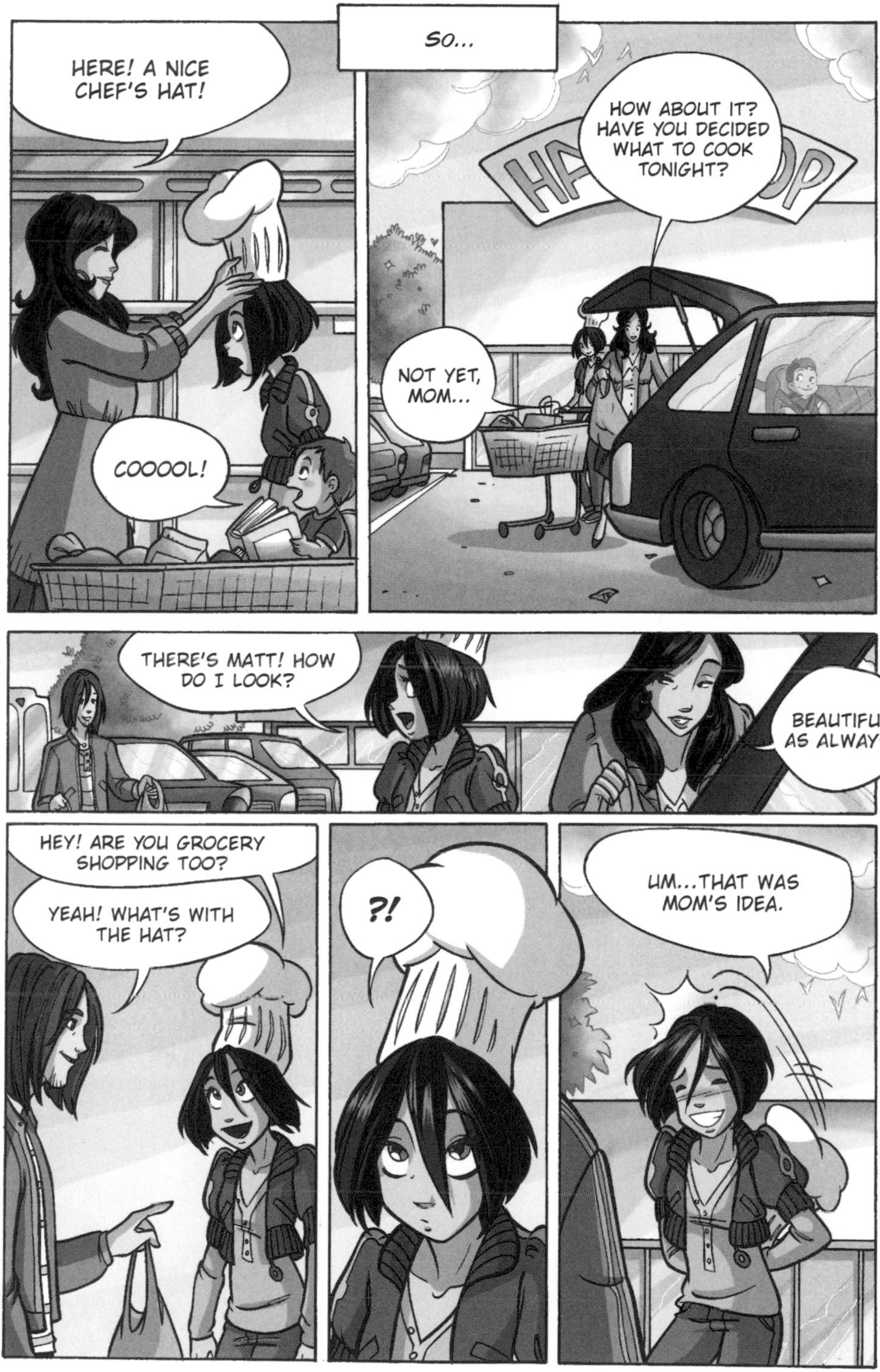
HERE! A NICE CHEF'S HAT!
COOOOL!
SO...
HOW ABOUT IT? HAVE YOU DECIDED WHAT TO COOK TONIGHT?
NOT YET, MOM...
THERE'S MATT! HOW DO I LOOK?
BEAUTIFUL AS ALWAYS.
HEY! ARE YOU GROCERY SHOPPING TOO?
YEAH! WHAT'S WITH THE HAT?
?!
UM...THAT WAS MOM'S IDEA.

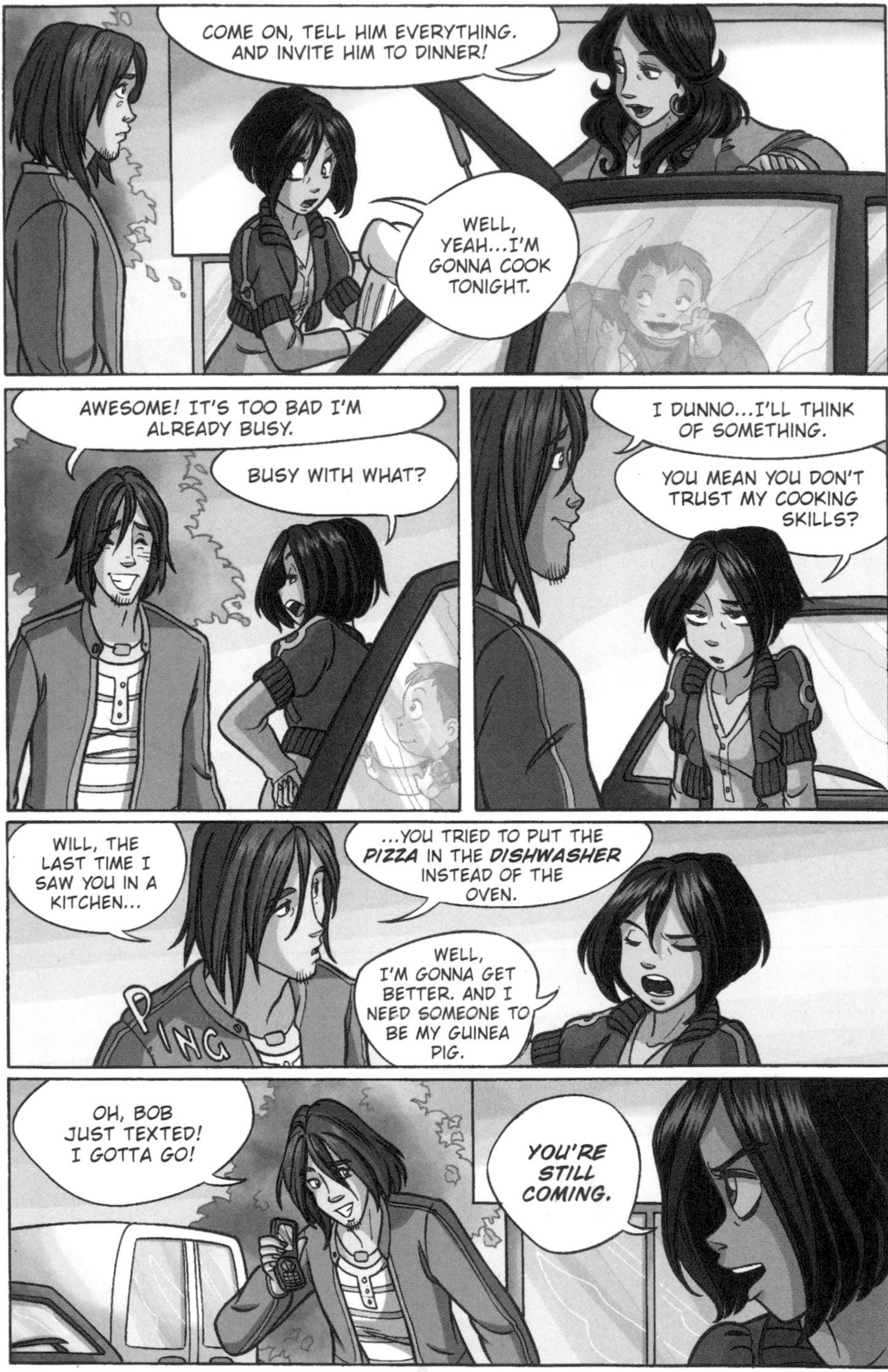
COME ON, TELL HIM EVERYTHING. AND INVITE HIM TO DINNER!
WELL, YEAH...I'M GONNA COOK TONIGHT.
AWESOME! IT'S TOO BAD I'M ALREADY BUSY.
BUSY WITH WHAT?
I DUNNO...I'LL THINK OF SOMETHING.
YOU MEAN YOU DON'T TRUST MY COOKING SKILLS?
WILL, THE LAST TIME I SAW YOU IN A KITCHEN...
...YOU TRIED TO PUT THE ***PIZZA*** IN THE ***DISHWASHER*** INSTEAD OF THE OVEN.
WELL, I'M GONNA GET BETTER. AND I NEED SOMEONE TO BE MY GUINEA PIG.
PING
OH, BOB JUST TEXTED! I GOTTA GO!
YOU'RE STILL COMING.

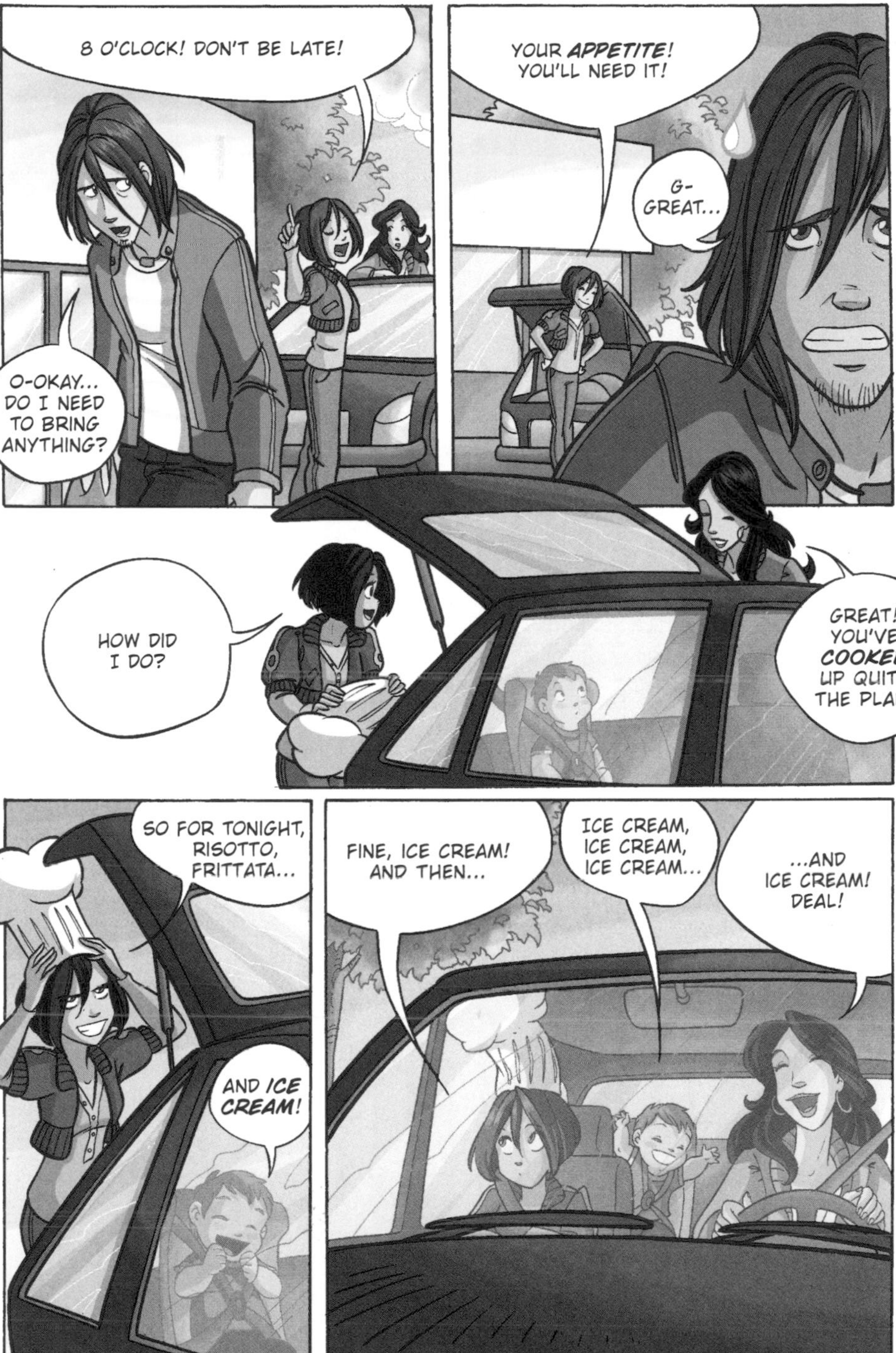
8 O'CLOCK! DON'T BE LATE!
O-OKAY... DO I NEED TO BRING ANYTHING?
YOUR APPETITE! YOU'LL NEED IT!
G- GREAT...
HOW DID I DO?
GREAT! YOU'VE COOKED UP QUITE THE PLAN.
SO FOR TONIGHT, RISOTTO, FRITTATA...
AND ICE CREAM!
FINE, ICE CREAM! AND THEN...
ICE CREAM, ICE CREAM, ICE CREAM...
...AND ICE CREAM! DEAL!

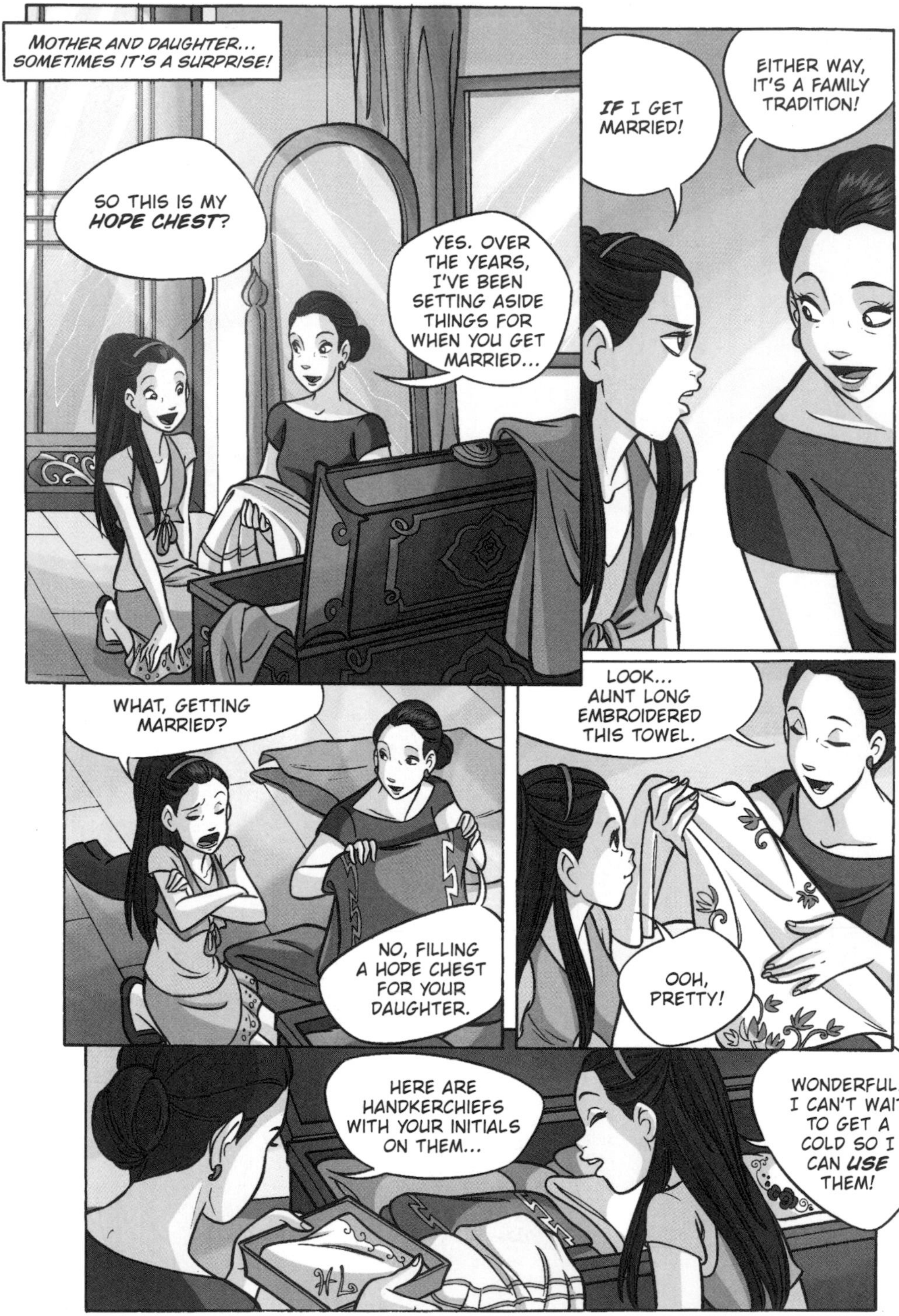
MOTHER AND DAUGHTER... SOMETIMES IT'S A SURPRISE!
SO THIS IS MY ***HOPE CHEST***?
YES. OVER THE YEARS, I'VE BEEN SETTING ASIDE THINGS FOR WHEN YOU GET MARRIED...
IF I GET MARRIED!
EITHER WAY, IT'S A FAMILY TRADITION!
WHAT, GETTING MARRIED?
NO, FILLING A HOPE CHEST FOR YOUR DAUGHTER.
LOOK... AUNT LONG EMBROIDERED THIS TOWEL.
OOH, PRETTY!
HERE ARE HANDKERCHIEFS WITH YOUR INITIALS ON THEM...
WONDERFUL! I CAN'T WAIT TO GET A COLD SO I CAN ***USE*** THEM!

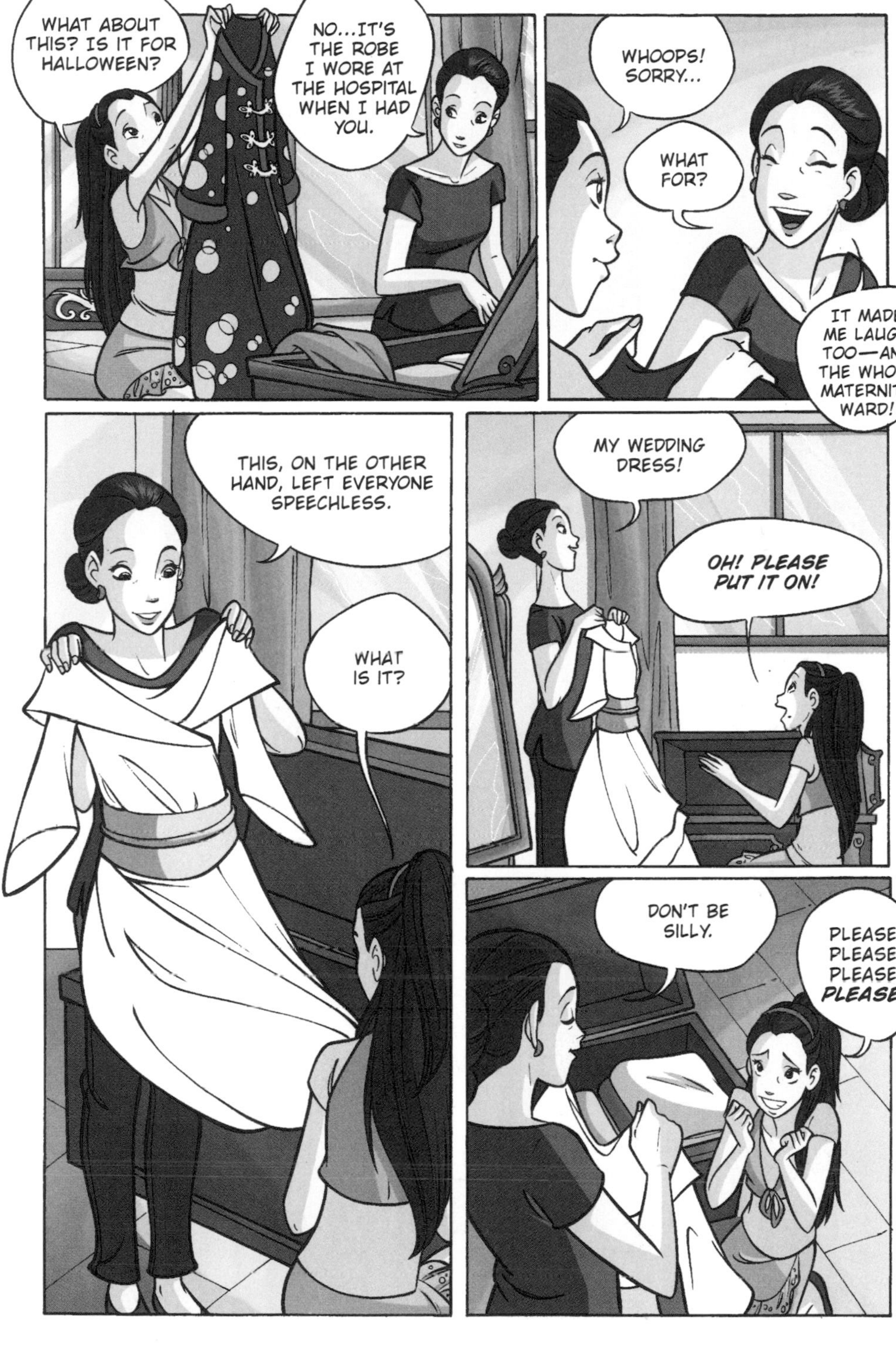
WHAT ABOUT THIS? IS IT FOR HALLOWEEN?
NO...IT'S THE ROBE I WORE AT THE HOSPITAL WHEN I HAD YOU.
WHOOPS! SORRY...
WHAT FOR?
IT MADE ME LAUGH TOO—AND THE WHOLE MATERNITY WARD!
THIS, ON THE OTHER HAND, LEFT EVERYONE SPEECHLESS.
WHAT IS IT?
MY WEDDING DRESS!
OH! PLEASE PUT IT ON!
DON'T BE SILLY.
PLEASE, PLEASE, PLEASE, PLEASE!

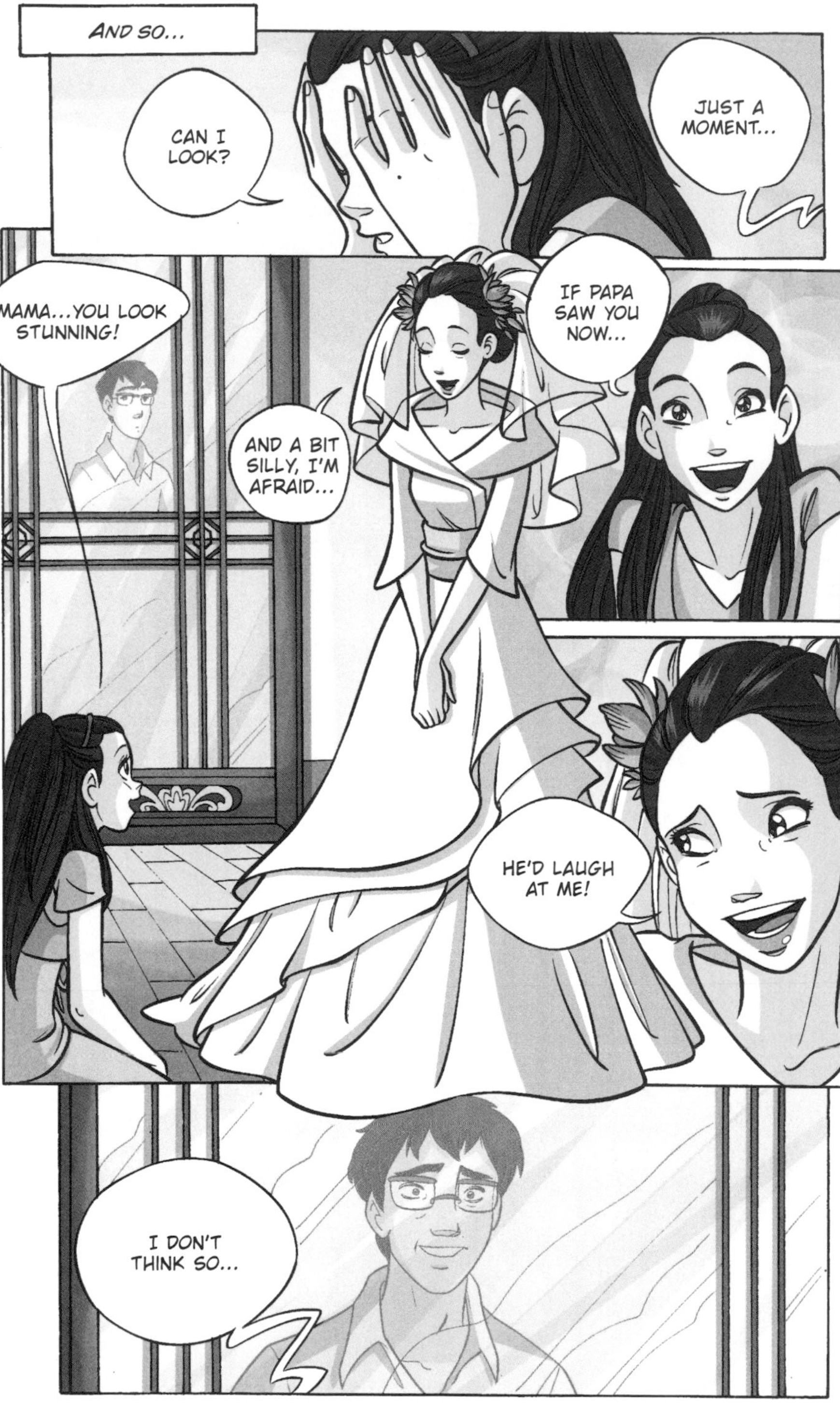
AND SO...
CAN I LOOK?
JUST A MOMENT...
MAMA...YOU LOOK STUNNING!
IF PAPA SAW YOU NOW...
AND A BIT SILLY, I'M AFRAID...
HE'D LAUGH AT ME!
I DON'T THINK SO...

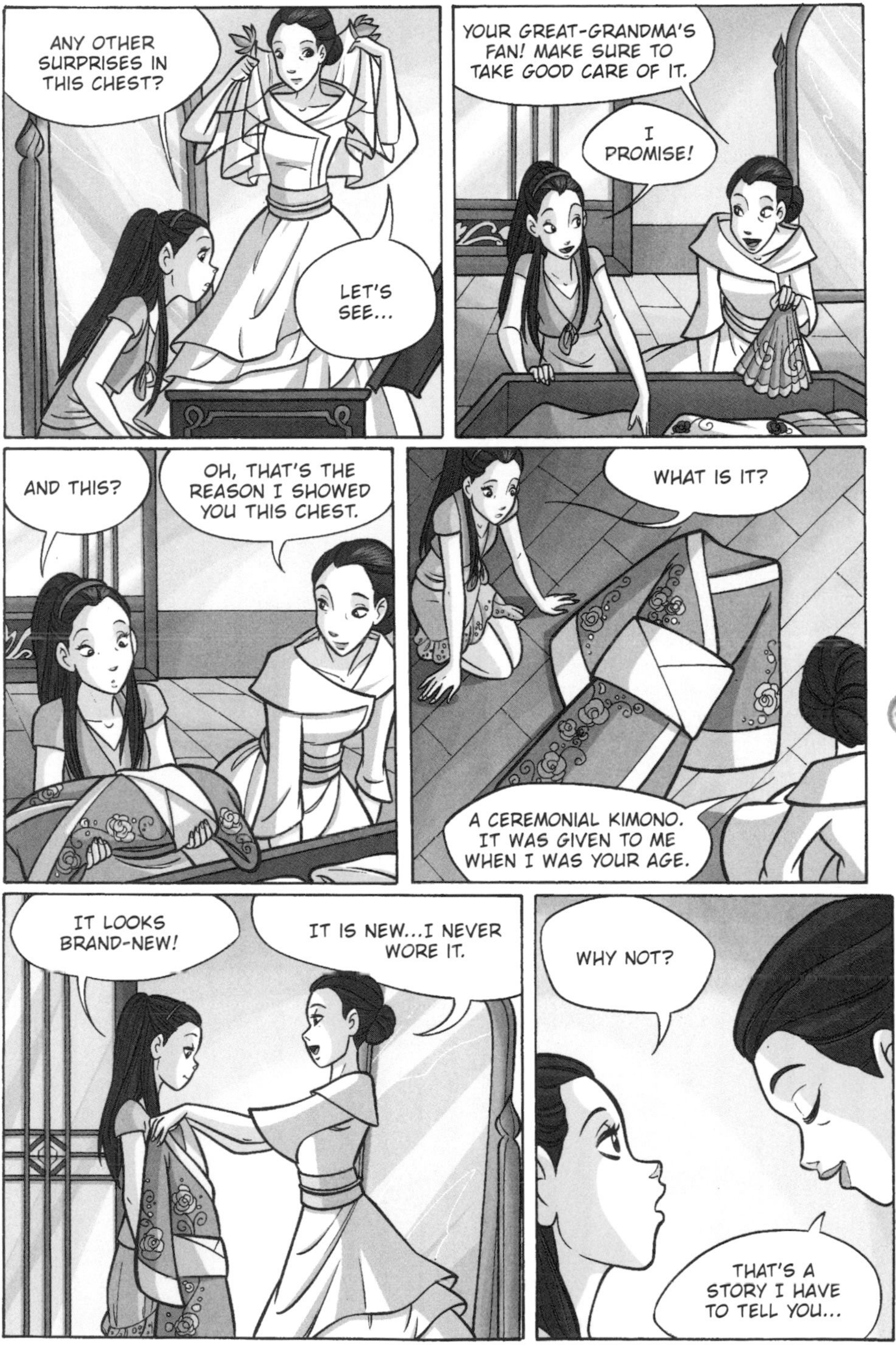
ANY OTHER SURPRISES IN THIS CHEST?
LET'S SEE...
YOUR GREAT-GRANDMA'S FAN! MAKE SURE TO TAKE GOOD CARE OF IT.
I PROMISE!
AND THIS?
OH, THAT'S THE REASON I SHOWED YOU THIS CHEST.
WHAT IS IT?
A CEREMONIAL KIMONO. IT WAS GIVEN TO ME WHEN I WAS YOUR AGE.
IT LOOKS BRAND-NEW!
IT IS NEW...I NEVER WORE IT.
WHY NOT?
THAT'S A STORY I HAVE TO TELL YOU...

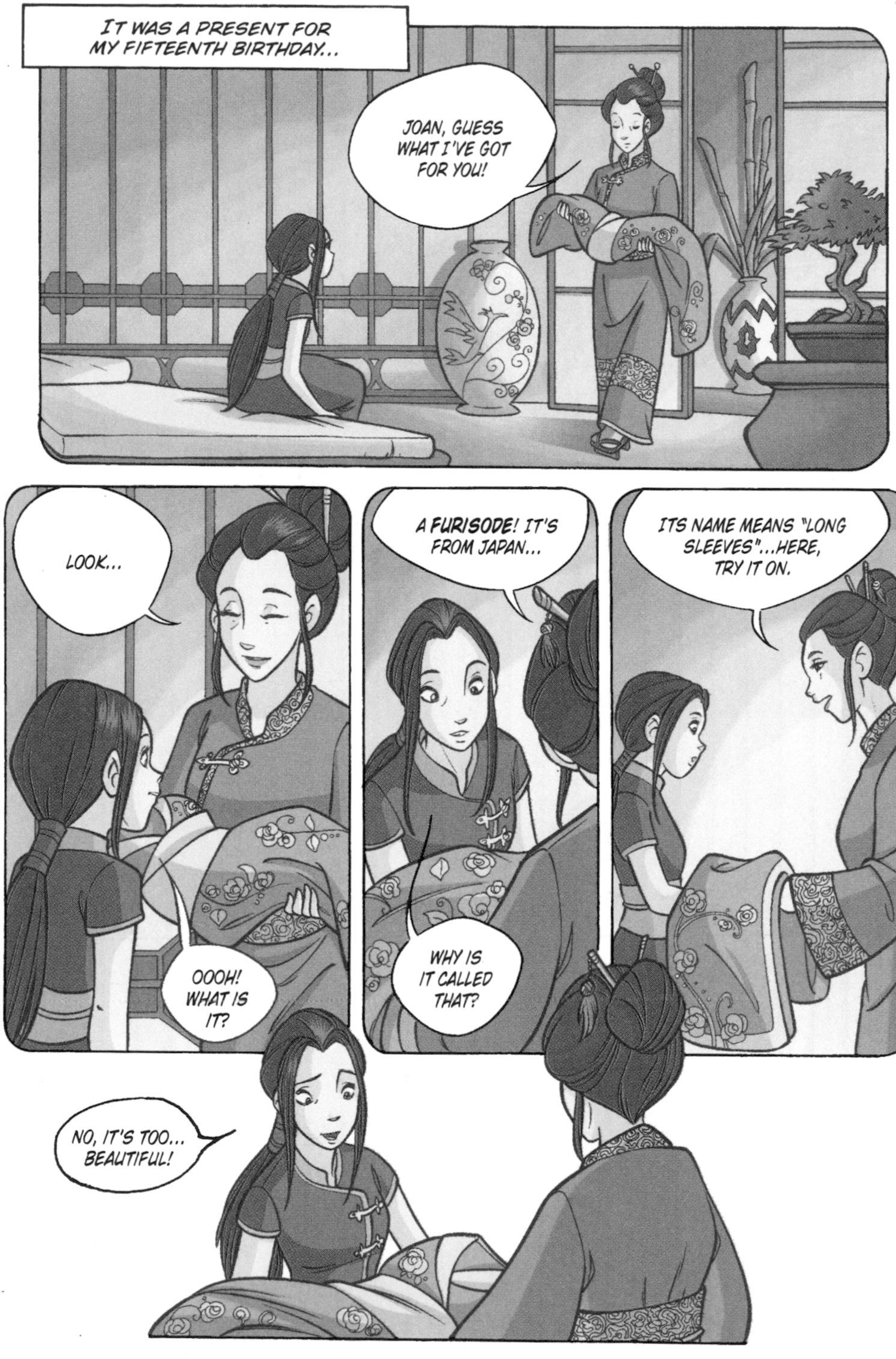
IT WAS A PRESENT FOR MY FIFTEENTH BIRTHDAY...
JOAN, GUESS WHAT I'VE GOT FOR YOU!
LOOK...
OOOH! WHAT IS IT?
A FURISODE! IT'S FROM JAPAN...
WHY IS IT CALLED THAT?
ITS NAME MEANS "LONG SLEEVES"...HERE, TRY IT ON.
NO, IT'S TOO... BEAUTIFUL!

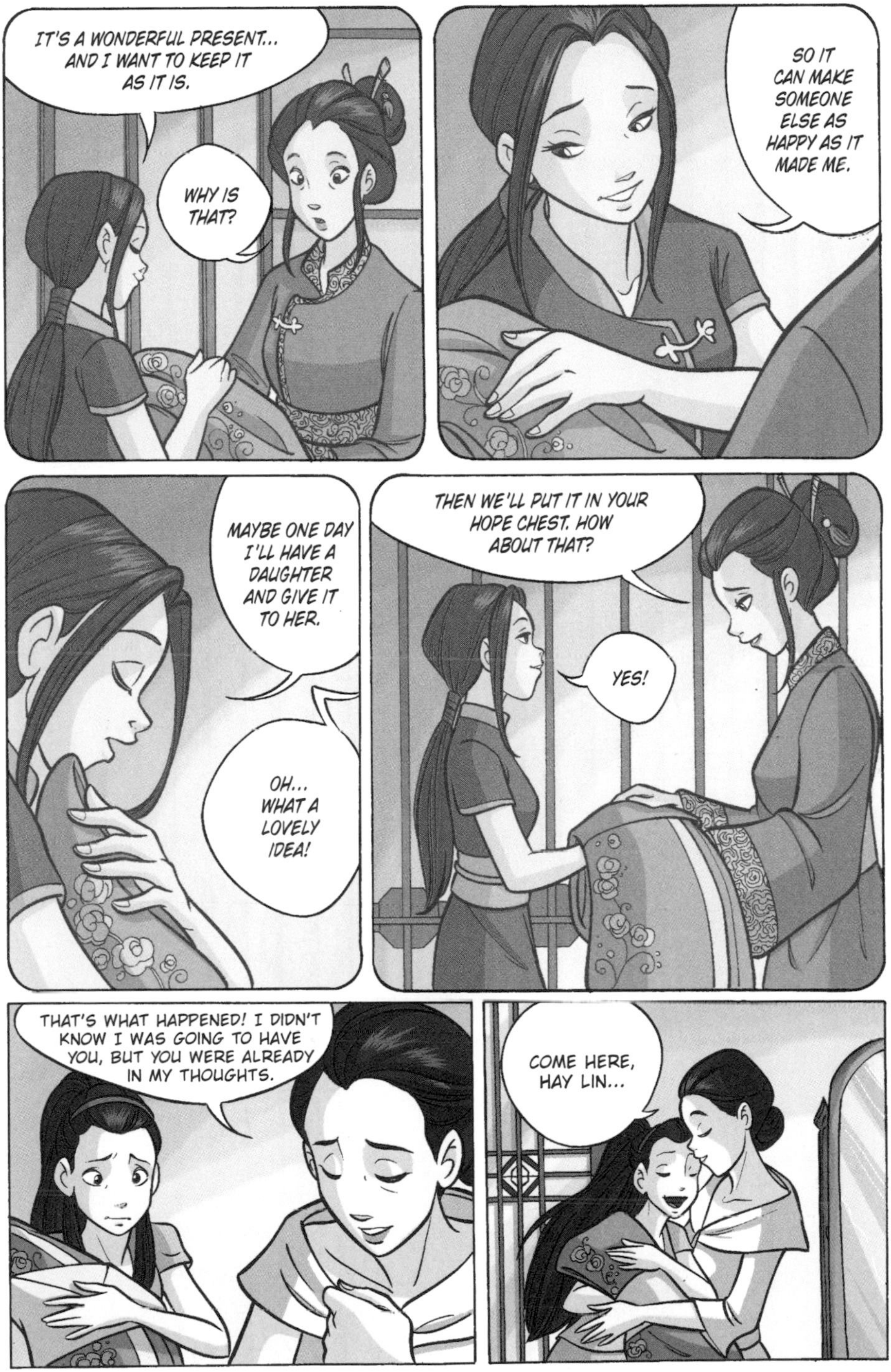
IT'S A WONDERFUL PRESENT... AND I WANT TO KEEP IT AS IT IS.
WHY IS THAT?
SO IT CAN MAKE SOMEONE ELSE AS HAPPY AS IT MADE ME.
MAYBE ONE DAY I'LL HAVE A DAUGHTER AND GIVE IT TO HER.
OH... WHAT A LOVELY IDEA!
THEN WE'LL PUT IT IN YOUR HOPE CHEST. HOW ABOUT THAT?
YES!
THAT'S WHAT HAPPENED! I DIDN'T KNOW I WAS GOING TO HAVE YOU, BUT YOU WERE ALREADY IN MY THOUGHTS.
COME HERE, HAY LIN...

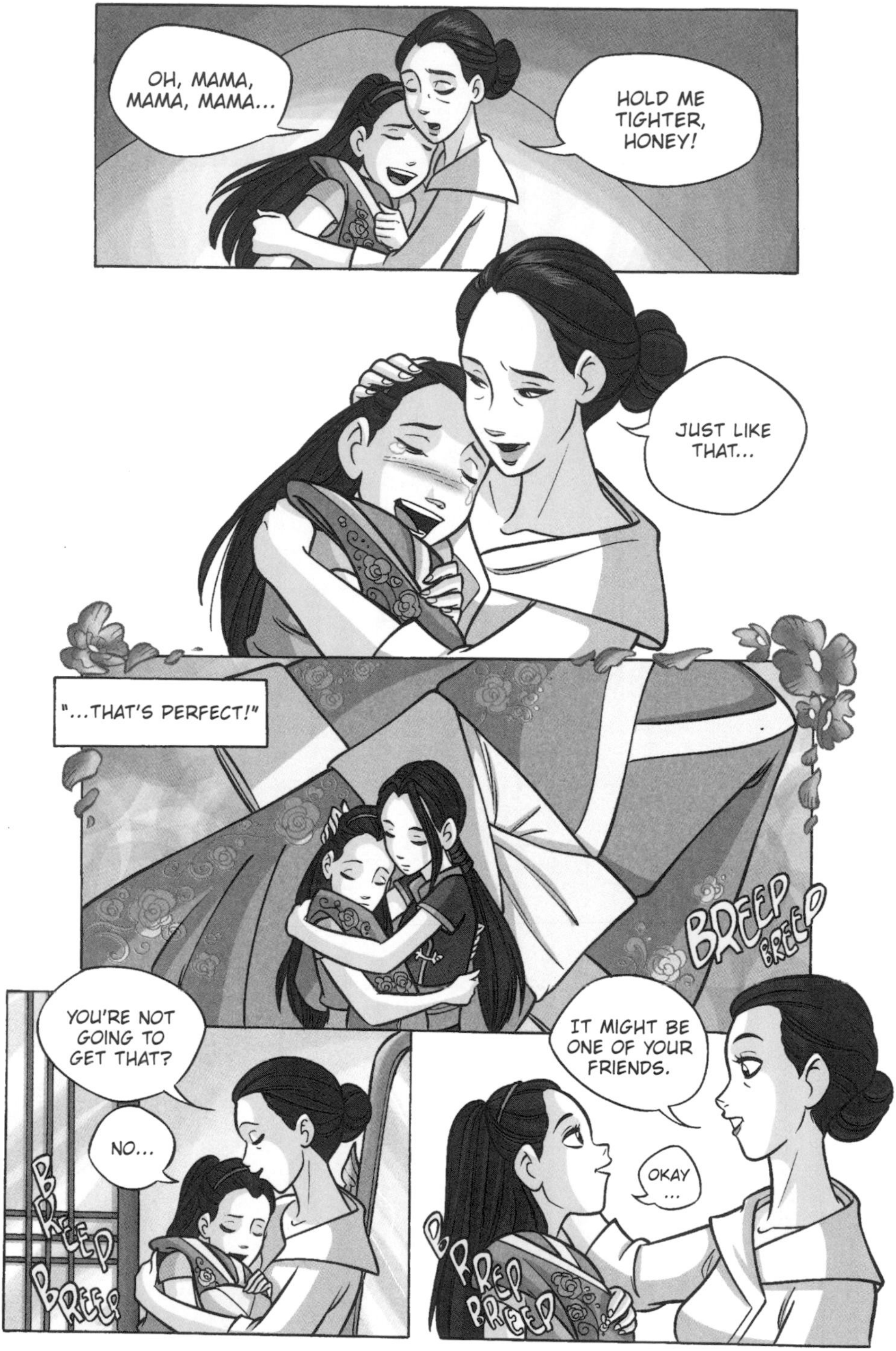

OH, MAMA, MAMA, MAMA...
HOLD ME TIGHTER, HONEY!
JUST LIKE THAT...
"...THAT'S PERFECT!"
BREEP BREEP
YOU'RE NOT GOING TO GET THAT?
NO...
BREEP BREEP
IT MIGHT BE ONE OF YOUR FRIENDS.
OKAY ...
BRREP BREEP

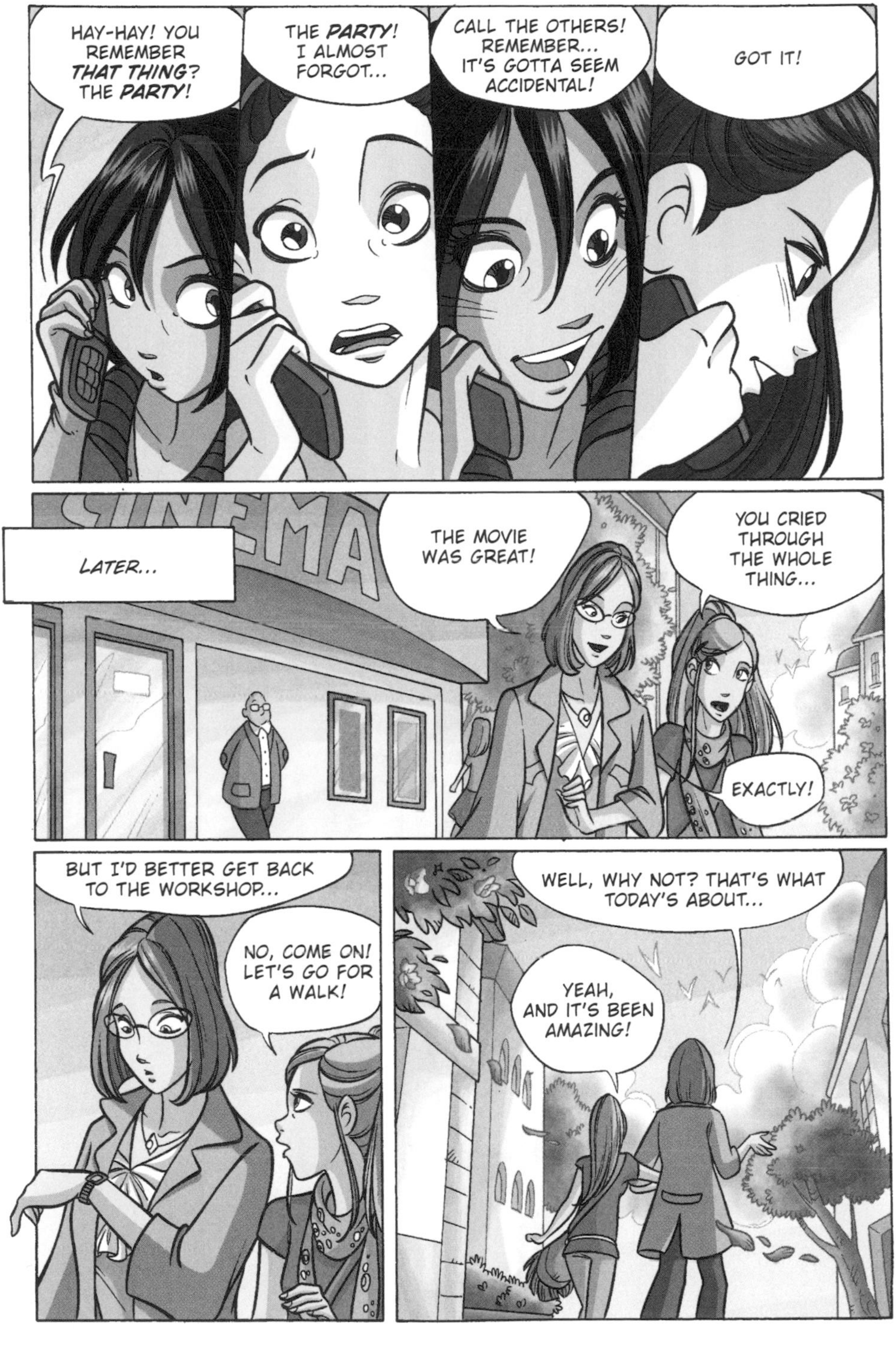

HAY-HAY! YOU REMEMBER *THAT THING*? THE *PARTY*!
THE *PARTY*! I ALMOST FORGOT...
CALL THE OTHERS! REMEMBER... IT'S GOTTA SEEM ACCIDENTAL!
GOT IT!
SINEMA
LATER...
THE MOVIE WAS GREAT!
YOU CRIED THROUGH THE WHOLE THING...
EXACTLY!
BUT I'D BETTER GET BACK TO THE WORKSHOP...
NO, COME ON! LET'S GO FOR A WALK!
WELL, WHY NOT? THAT'S WHAT TODAY'S ABOUT...
YEAH, AND IT'S BEEN AMAZING!

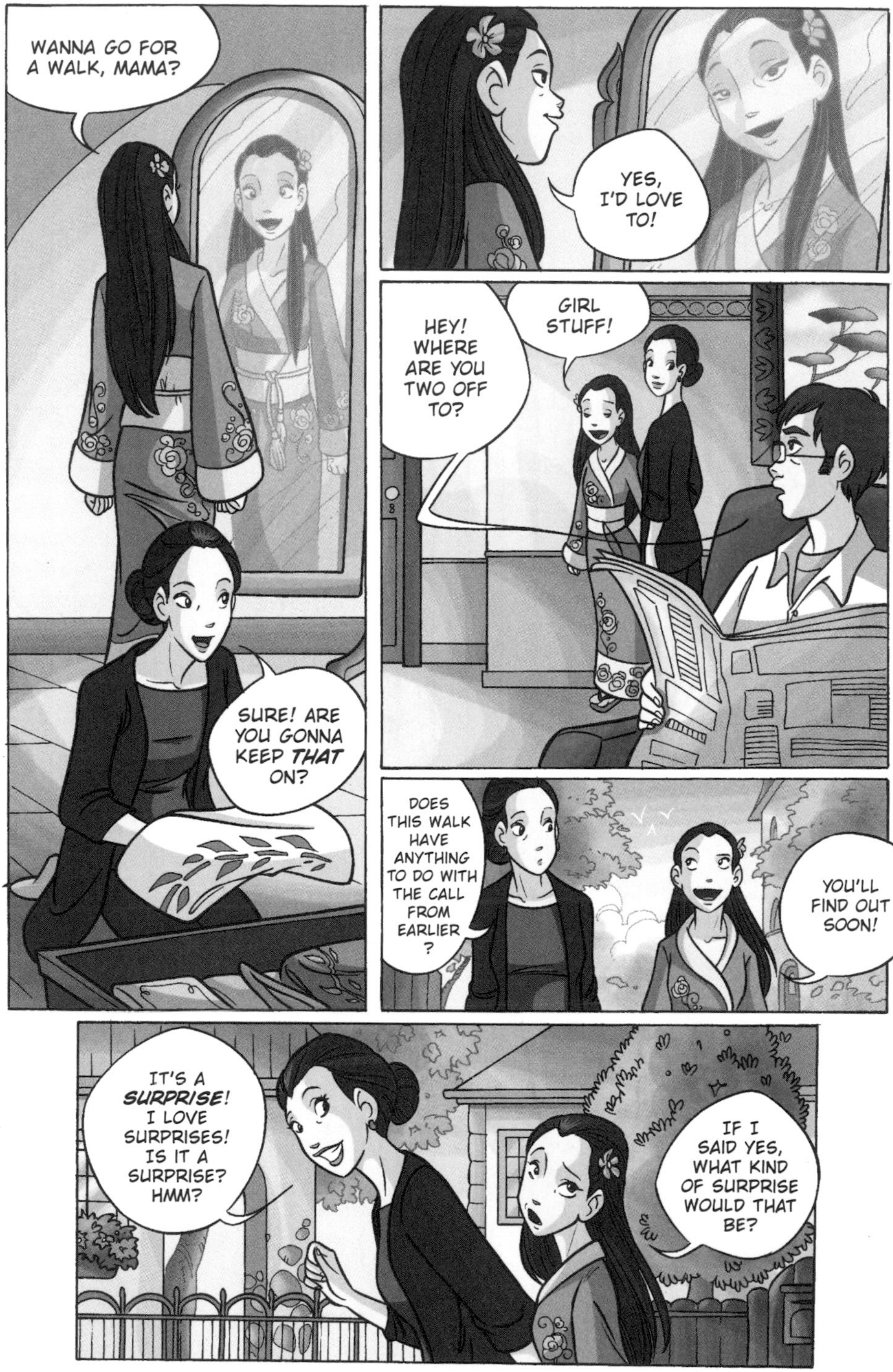
WANNA GO FOR A WALK, MAMA?
YES, I'D LOVE TO!
SURE! ARE YOU GONNA KEEP THAT ON?
HEY! WHERE ARE YOU TWO OFF TO?
GIRL STUFF!
DOES THIS WALK HAVE ANYTHING TO DO WITH THE CALL FROM EARLIER?
YOU'LL FIND OUT SOON!
IT'S A SURPRISE! I LOVE SURPRISES! IS IT A SURPRISE? HMM?
IF I SAID YES, WHAT KIND OF SURPRISE WOULD THAT BE?

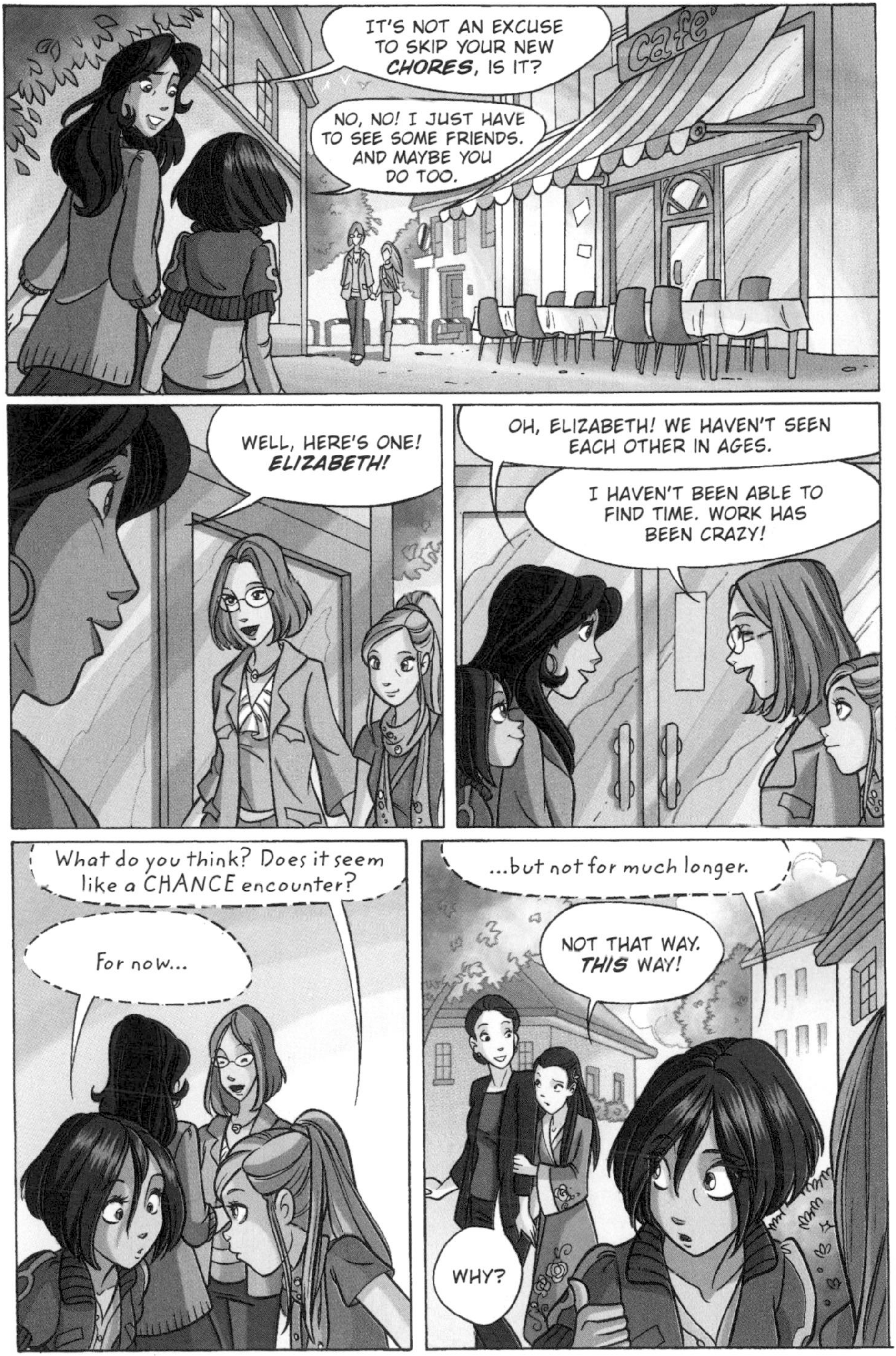
IT'S NOT AN EXCUSE TO SKIP YOUR NEW CHORES, IS IT?
NO, NO! I JUST HAVE TO SEE SOME FRIENDS. AND MAYBE YOU DO TOO.
WELL, HERE'S ONE! ELIZABETH!
OH, ELIZABETH! WE HAVEN'T SEEN EACH OTHER IN AGES.
I HAVEN'T BEEN ABLE TO FIND TIME. WORK HAS BEEN CRAZY!
What do you think? Does it seem like a CHANCE encounter?
For now...
...but not for much longer.
NOT THAT WAY. THIS WAY!
WHY?

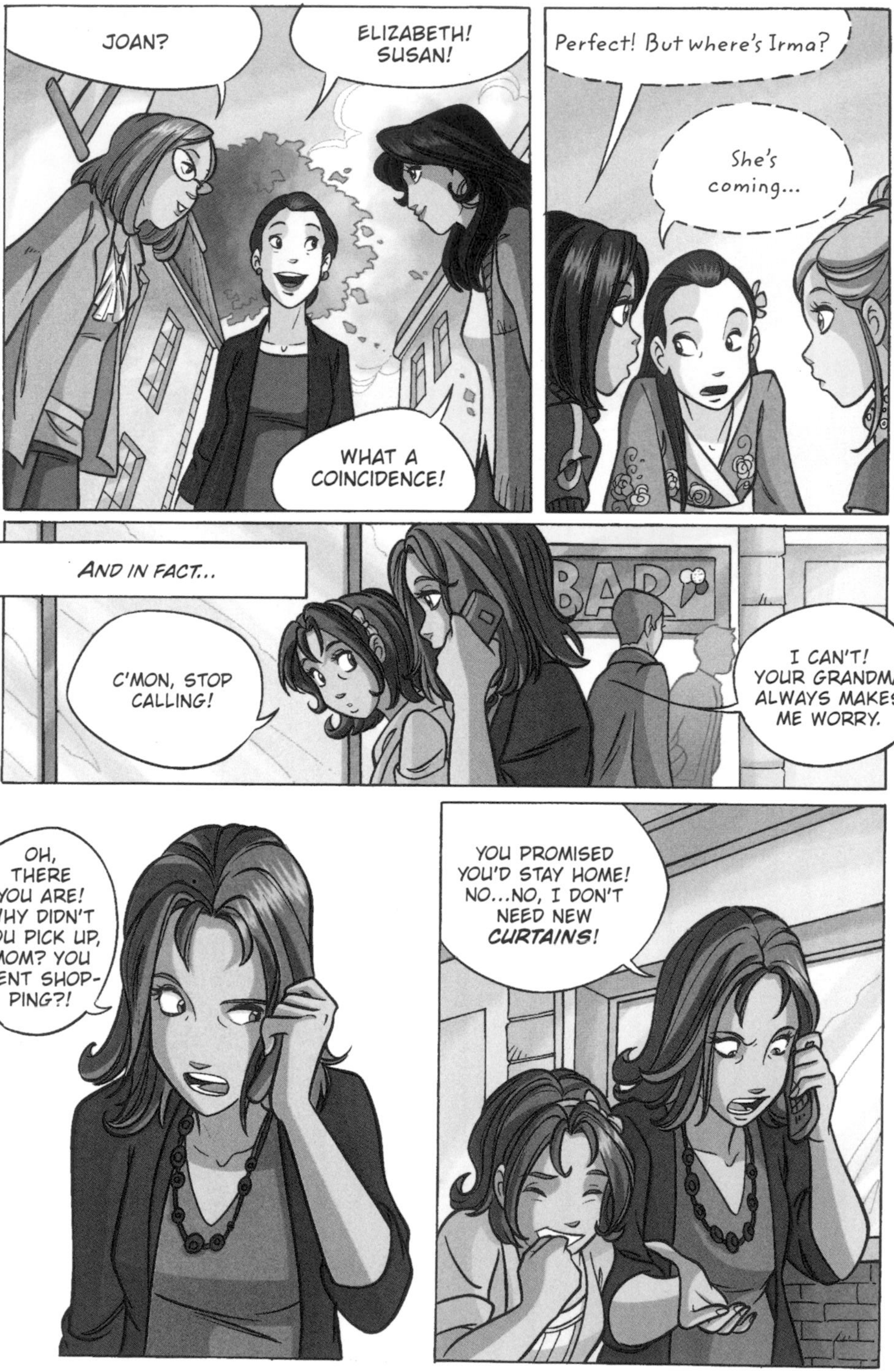
JOAN?
ELIZABETH! SUSAN!
WHAT A COINCIDENCE!
Perfect! But where's Irma?
She's coming...
AND IN FACT...
C'MON, STOP CALLING!
I CAN'T! YOUR GRANDMA ALWAYS MAKES ME WORRY.
OH, THERE YOU ARE! WHY DIDN'T YOU PICK UP, MOM? YOU WENT SHOP-PING?!
YOU PROMISED YOU'D STAY HOME! NO...NO, I DON'T NEED NEW *CURTAINS*!

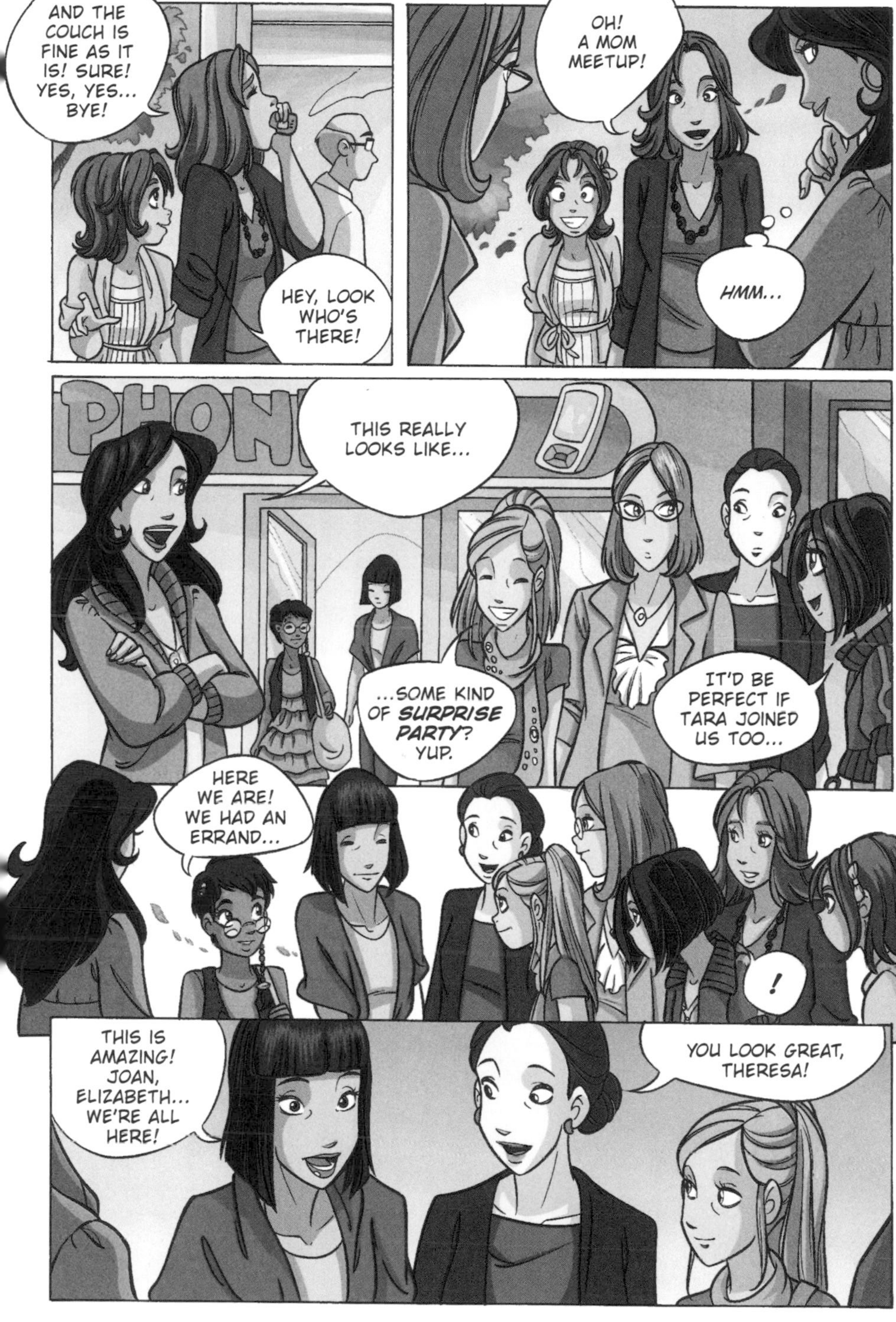
AND THE COUCH IS FINE AS IT IS! SURE! YES, YES... BYE!
HEY, LOOK WHO'S THERE!
OH! A MOM MEETUP!
HMM...
PHON
THIS REALLY LOOKS LIKE...
...SOME KIND OF SURPRISE PARTY? YUP.
IT'D BE PERFECT IF TARA JOINED US TOO...
HERE WE ARE! WE HAD AN ERRAND...
!
THIS IS AMAZING! JOAN, ELIZABETH... WE'RE ALL HERE!
YOU LOOK GREAT, THERESA!

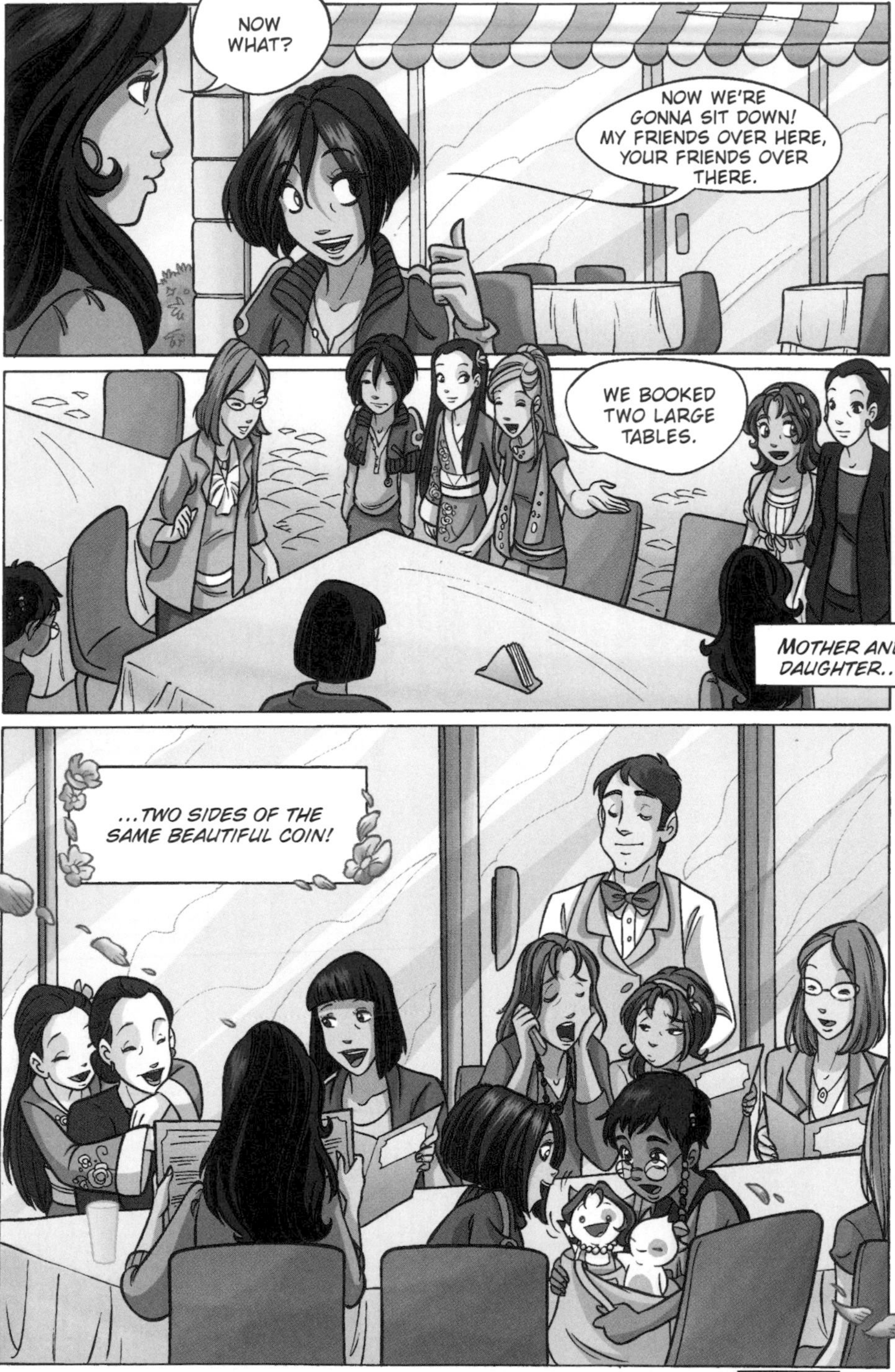
NOW WHAT?
NOW WE'RE GONNA SIT DOWN! MY FRIENDS OVER HERE, YOUR FRIENDS OVER THERE.
WE BOOKED TWO LARGE TABLES.
MOTHER AND DAUGHTER...
...TWO SIDES OF THE SAME BEAUTIFUL COIN!
END OF CHAPTER 110

Teamwork

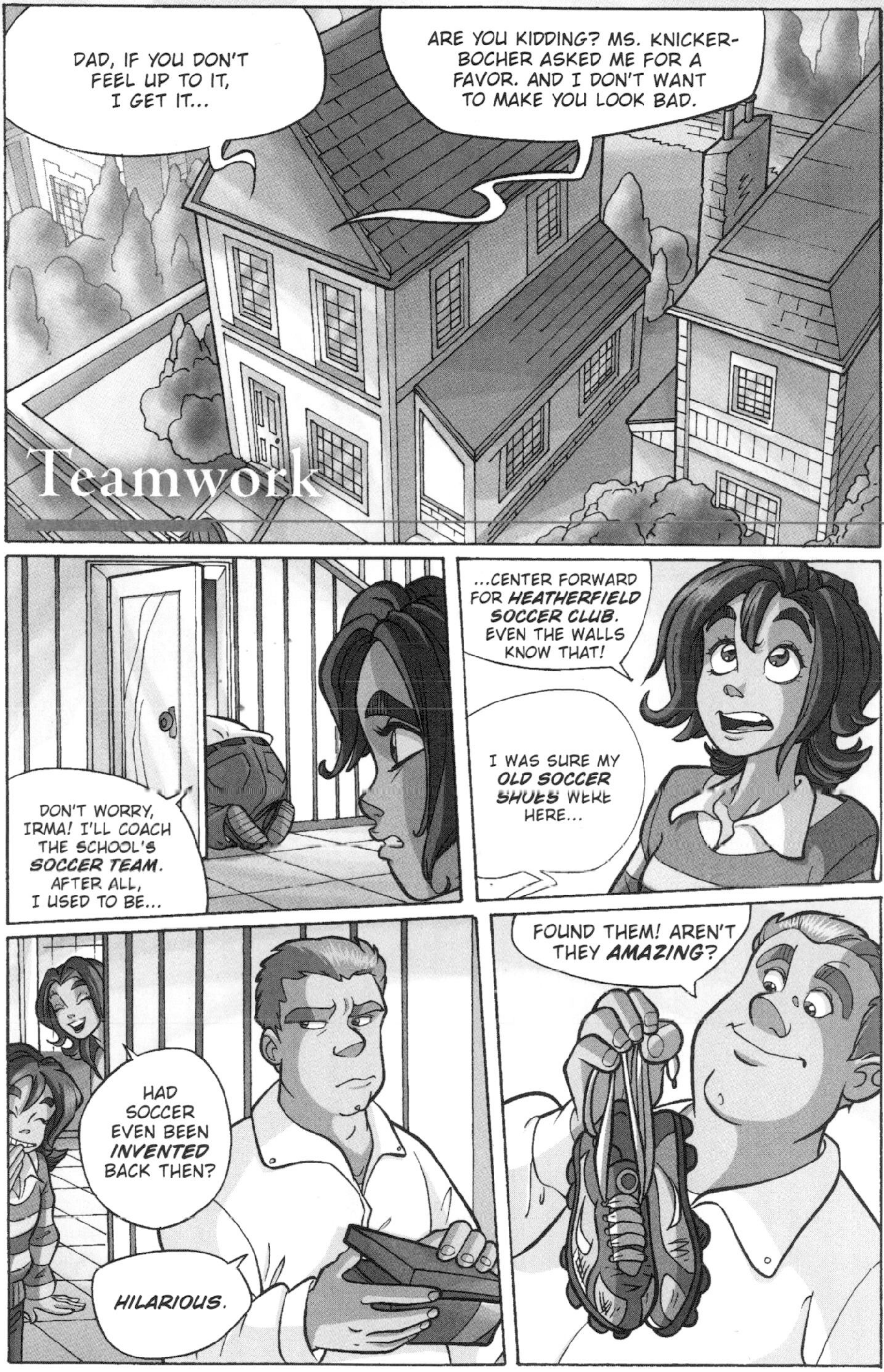
DAD, IF YOU DON'T FEEL UP TO IT, I GET IT...
ARE YOU KIDDING? MS. KNICKER-BOCHER ASKED ME FOR A FAVOR. AND I DON'T WANT TO MAKE YOU LOOK BAD.
DON'T WORRY, IRMA! I'LL COACH THE SCHOOL'S SOCCER TEAM. AFTER ALL, I USED TO BE...
...CENTER FORWARD FOR HEATHERFIELD SOCCER CLUB. EVEN THE WALLS KNOW THAT!
I WAS SURE MY OLD SOCCER SHOES WERE HERE...
HAD SOCCER EVEN BEEN INVENTED BACK THEN?
HILARIOUS.
FOUND THEM! AREN'T THEY AMAZING?

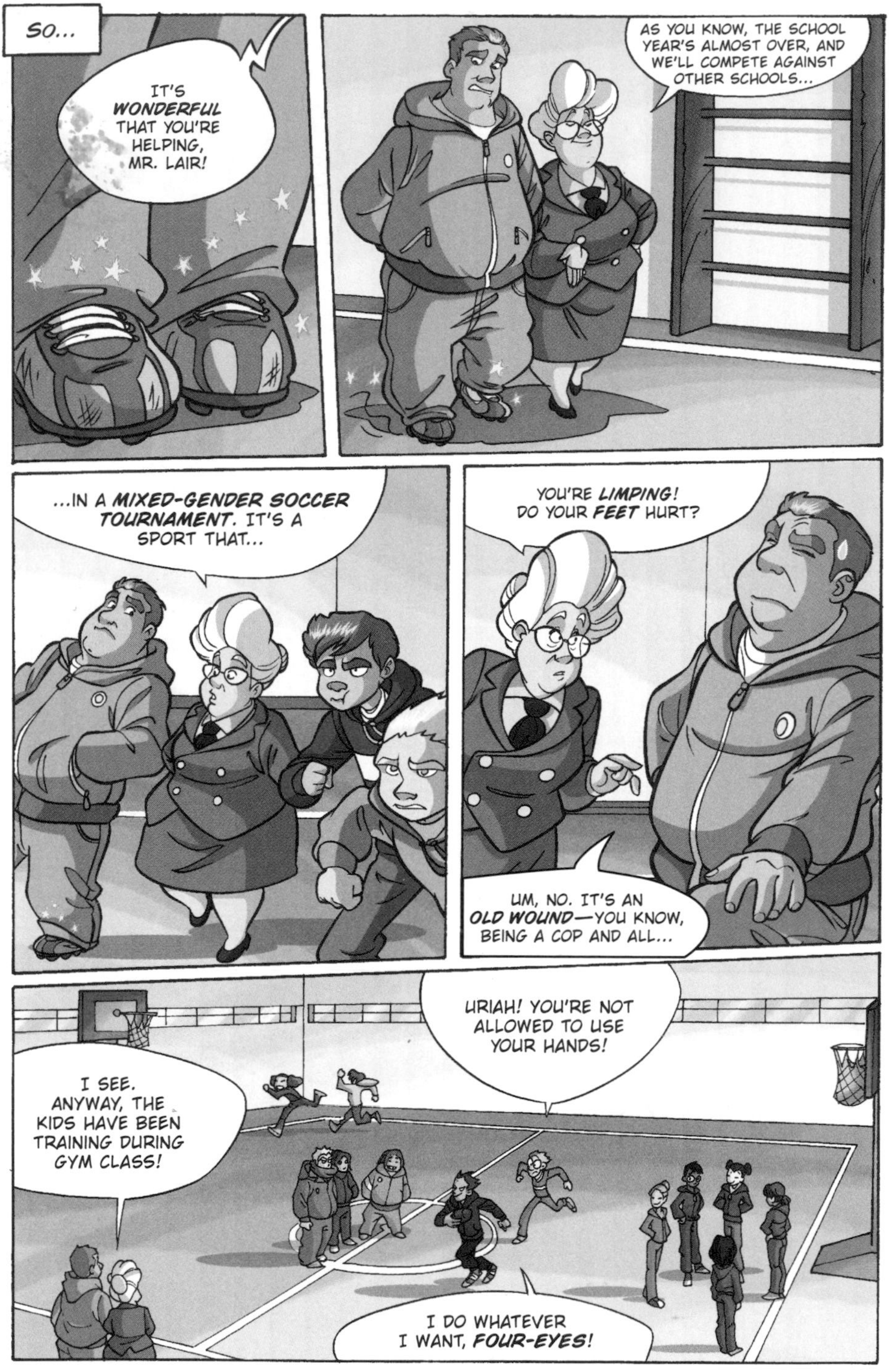
SO...
IT'S **WONDERFUL** THAT YOU'RE HELPING, MR. LAIR!
AS YOU KNOW, THE SCHOOL YEAR'S ALMOST OVER, AND WE'LL COMPETE AGAINST OTHER SCHOOLS...
...IN A ***MIXED-GENDER SOCCER TOURNAMENT***. IT'S A SPORT THAT...
YOU'RE ***LIMPING***! DO YOUR ***FEET*** HURT?
UM, NO. IT'S AN ***OLD WOUND***—YOU KNOW, BEING A COP AND ALL...
I SEE. ANYWAY, THE KIDS HAVE BEEN TRAINING DURING GYM CLASS!
URIAH! YOU'RE NOT ALLOWED TO USE YOUR HANDS!
I DO WHATEVER I WANT, ***FOUR-EYES***!

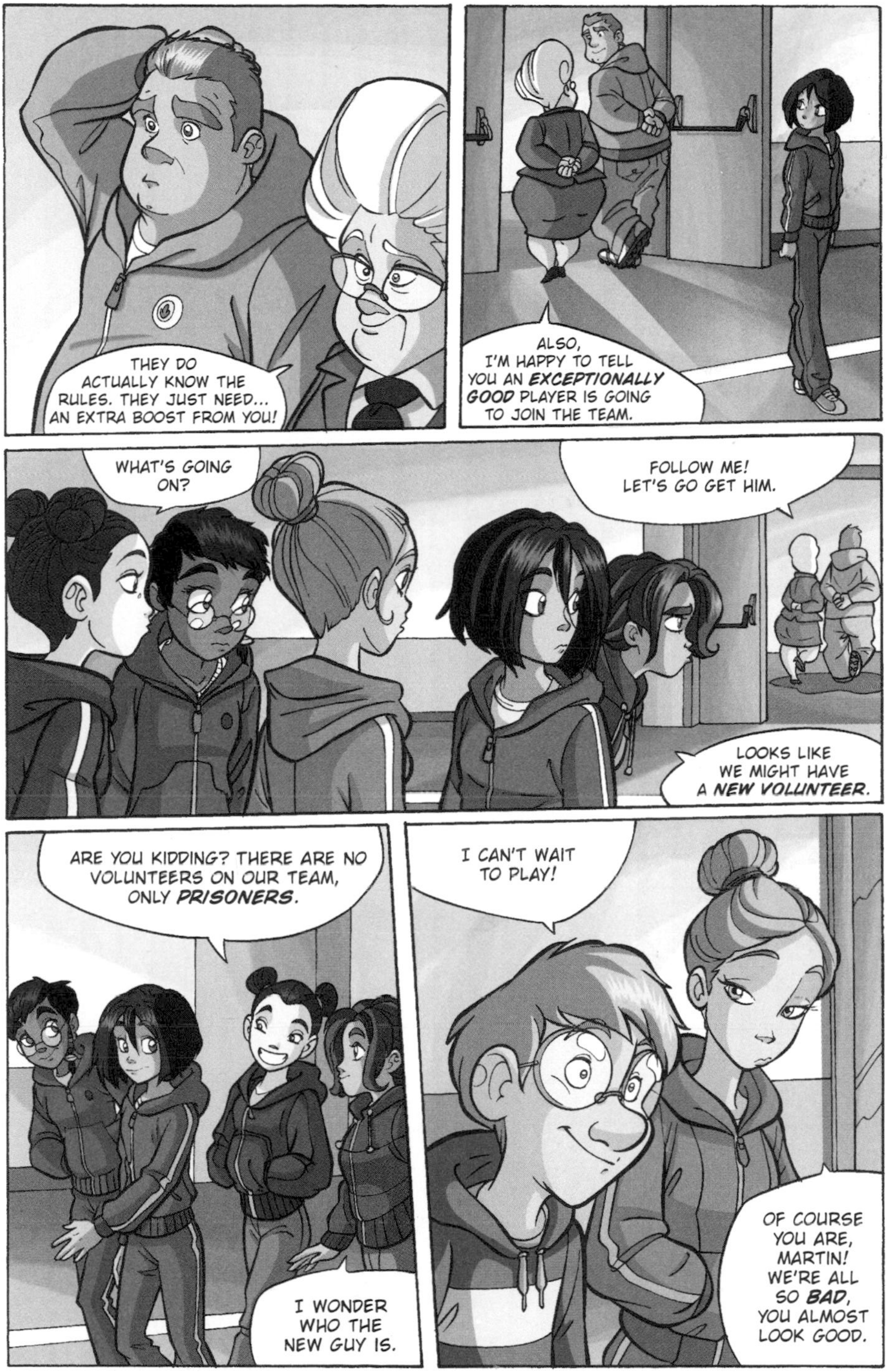
THEY DO ACTUALLY KNOW THE RULES. THEY JUST NEED... AN EXTRA BOOST FROM YOU!
ALSO, I'M HAPPY TO TELL YOU AN ***EXCEPTIONALLY GOOD*** PLAYER IS GOING TO JOIN THE TEAM.
WHAT'S GOING ON?
FOLLOW ME! LET'S GO GET HIM.
LOOKS LIKE WE MIGHT HAVE A ***NEW VOLUNTEER***.
ARE YOU KIDDING? THERE ARE NO VOLUNTEERS ON OUR TEAM, ONLY ***PRISONERS***.
I WONDER WHO THE NEW GUY IS.
I CAN'T WAIT TO PLAY!
OF COURSE YOU ARE, MARTIN! WE'RE ALL SO ***BAD***, YOU ALMOST LOOK GOOD.

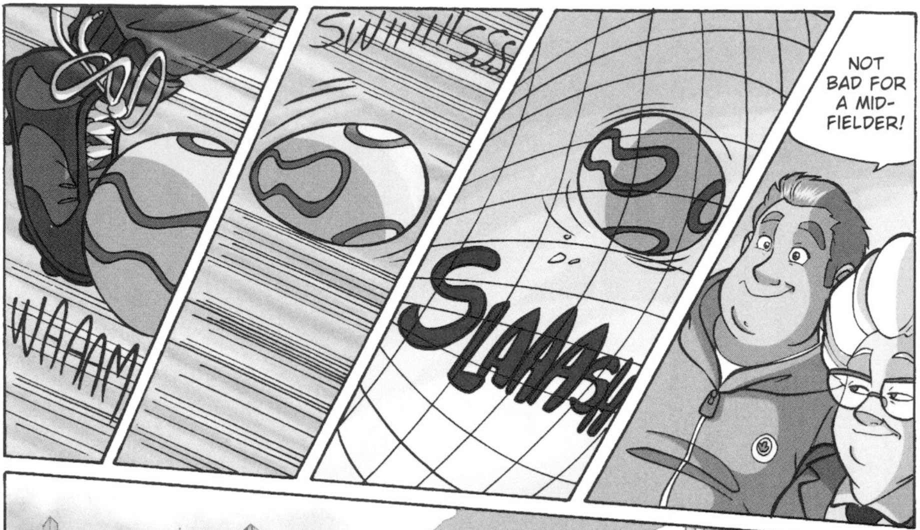
WHAAAM
SWIIIIISSS
SLAAASH
NOT BAD FOR A MID-FIELDER!

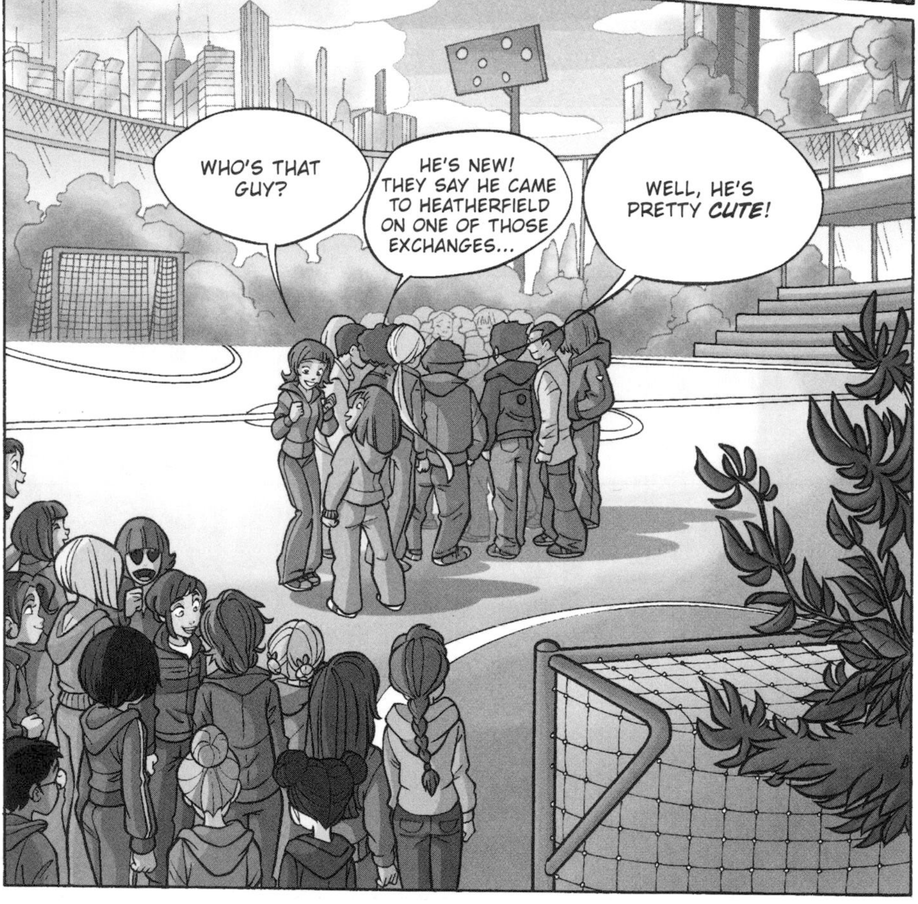
WHO'S THAT GUY?
HE'S NEW! THEY SAY HE CAME TO HEATHERFIELD ON ONE OF THOSE EXCHANGES...
WELL, HE'S PRETTY **CUTE**!

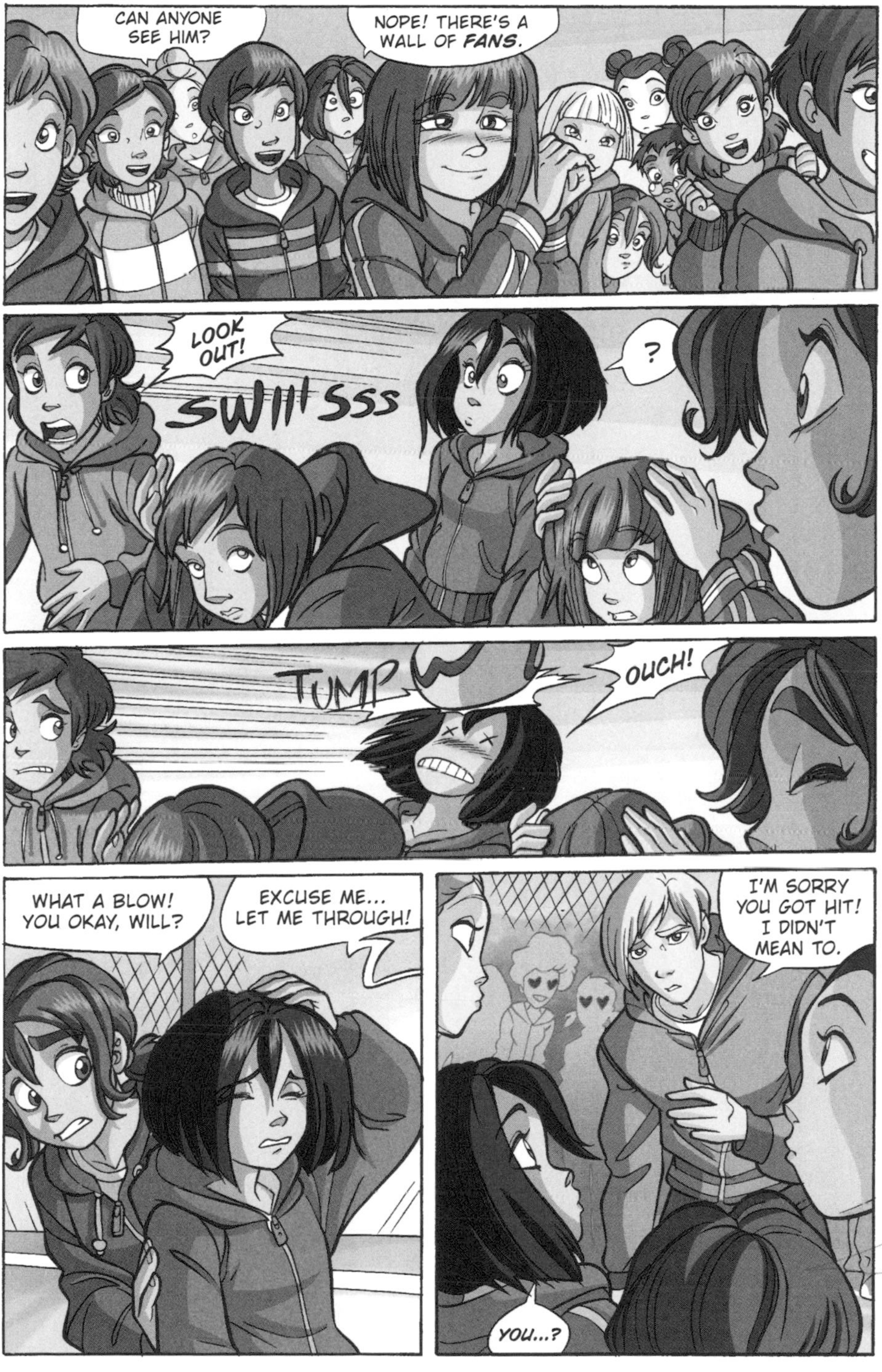
CAN ANYONE SEE HIM?
NOPE! THERE'S A WALL OF **FANS**.
LOOK OUT!
SWIIISSS
?
TUMP
OUCH!
WHAT A BLOW! YOU OKAY, WILL?
EXCUSE ME... LET ME THROUGH!
I'M SORRY YOU GOT HIT! I DIDN'T MEAN TO.
YOU...?

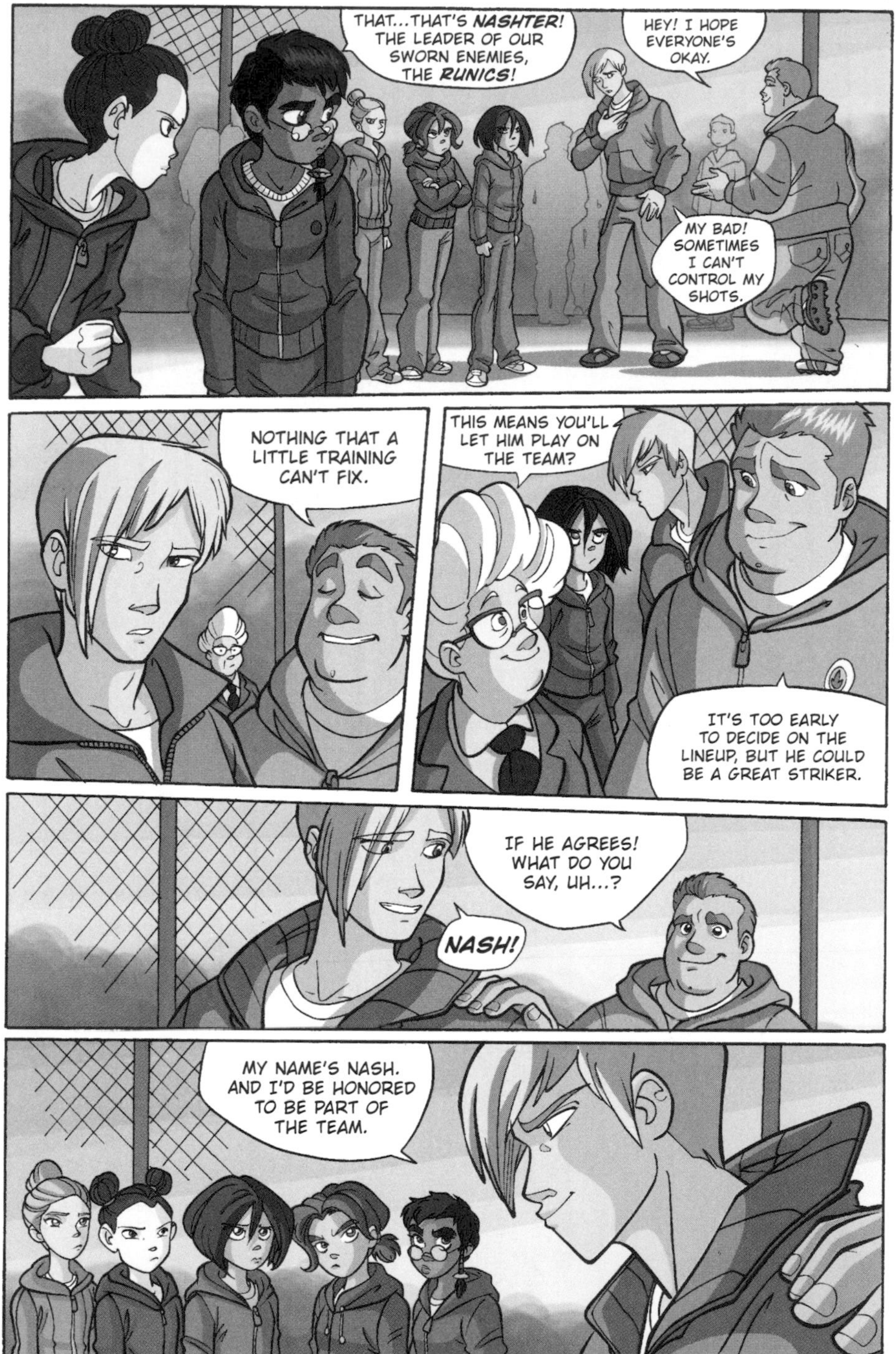
THAT...THAT'S **NASHTER**! THE LEADER OF OUR SWORN ENEMIES, THE **RUNICS**!
HEY! I HOPE EVERYONE'S OKAY.
MY BAD! SOMETIMES I CAN'T CONTROL MY SHOTS.
NOTHING THAT A LITTLE TRAINING CAN'T FIX.
THIS MEANS YOU'LL LET HIM PLAY ON THE TEAM?
IT'S TOO EARLY TO DECIDE ON THE LINEUP, BUT HE COULD BE A GREAT STRIKER.
IF HE AGREES! WHAT DO YOU SAY, UH...?
NASH!
MY NAME'S NASH. AND I'D BE HONORED TO BE PART OF THE TEAM.

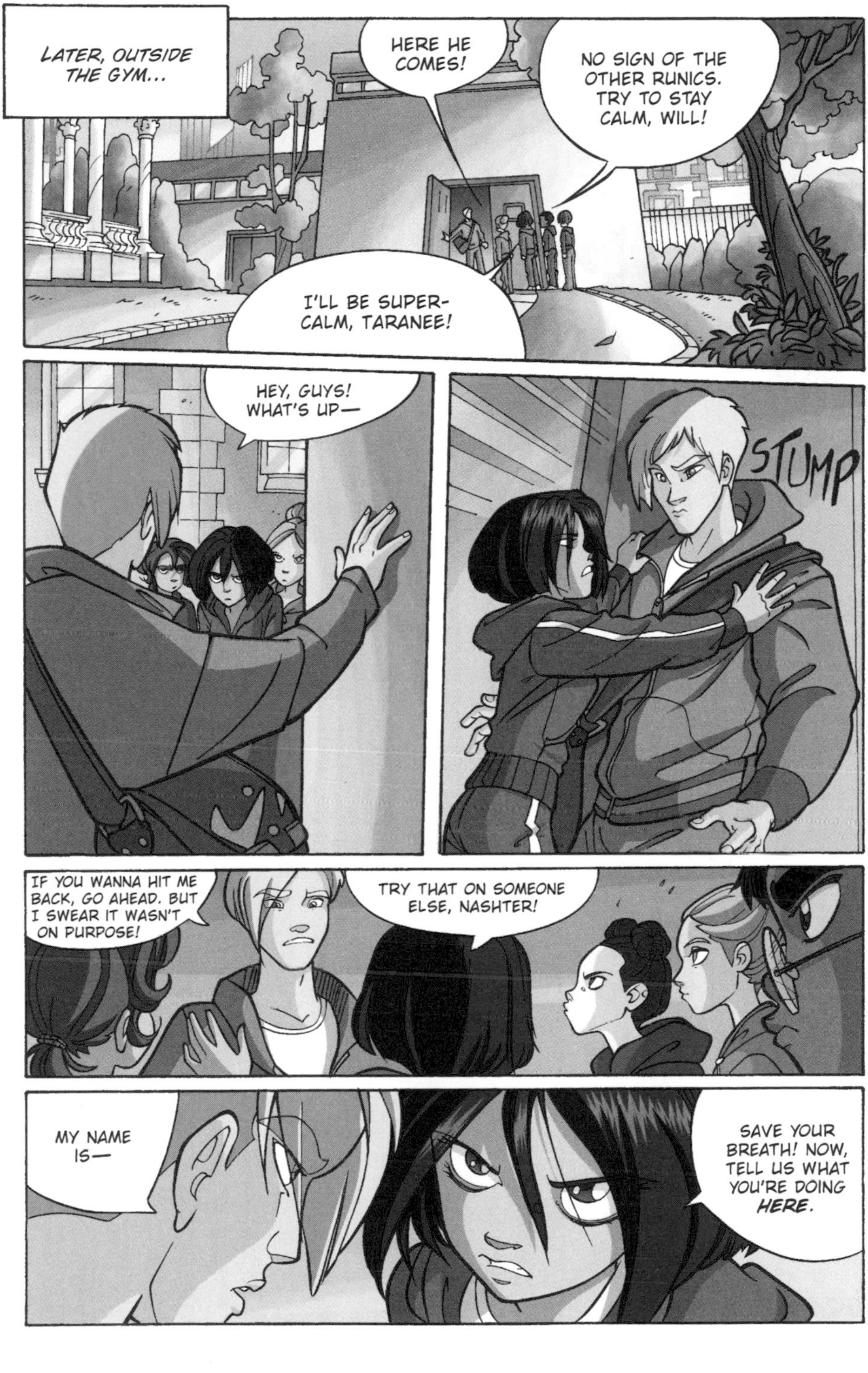
LATER, OUTSIDE THE GYM...
HERE HE COMES!
NO SIGN OF THE OTHER RUNICS. TRY TO STAY CALM, WILL!
I'LL BE SUPER-CALM, TARANEE!
HEY, GUYS! WHAT'S UP—
STUMP
IF YOU WANNA HIT ME BACK, GO AHEAD. BUT I SWEAR IT WASN'T ON PURPOSE!
TRY THAT ON SOMEONE ELSE, NASHTER!
MY NAME IS—
SAVE YOUR BREATH! NOW, TELL US WHAT YOU'RE DOING *HERE*.

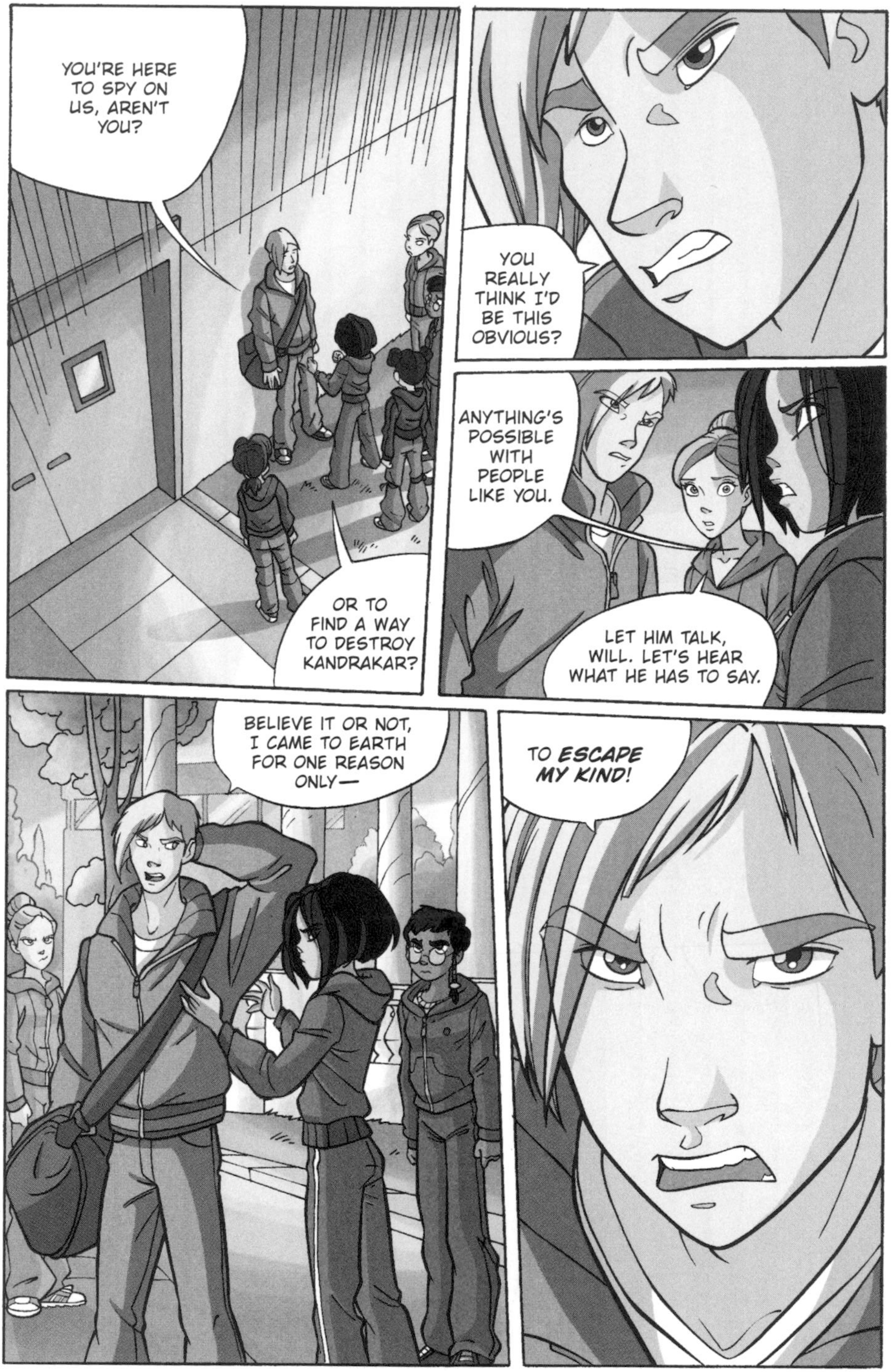
YOU'RE HERE TO SPY ON US, AREN'T YOU?
OR TO FIND A WAY TO DESTROY KANDRAKAR?
YOU REALLY THINK I'D BE THIS OBVIOUS?
ANYTHING'S POSSIBLE WITH PEOPLE LIKE YOU.
LET HIM TALK, WILL. LET'S HEAR WHAT HE HAS TO SAY.
BELIEVE IT OR NOT, I CAME TO EARTH FOR ONE REASON ONLY—
TO *ESCAPE MY KIND*!

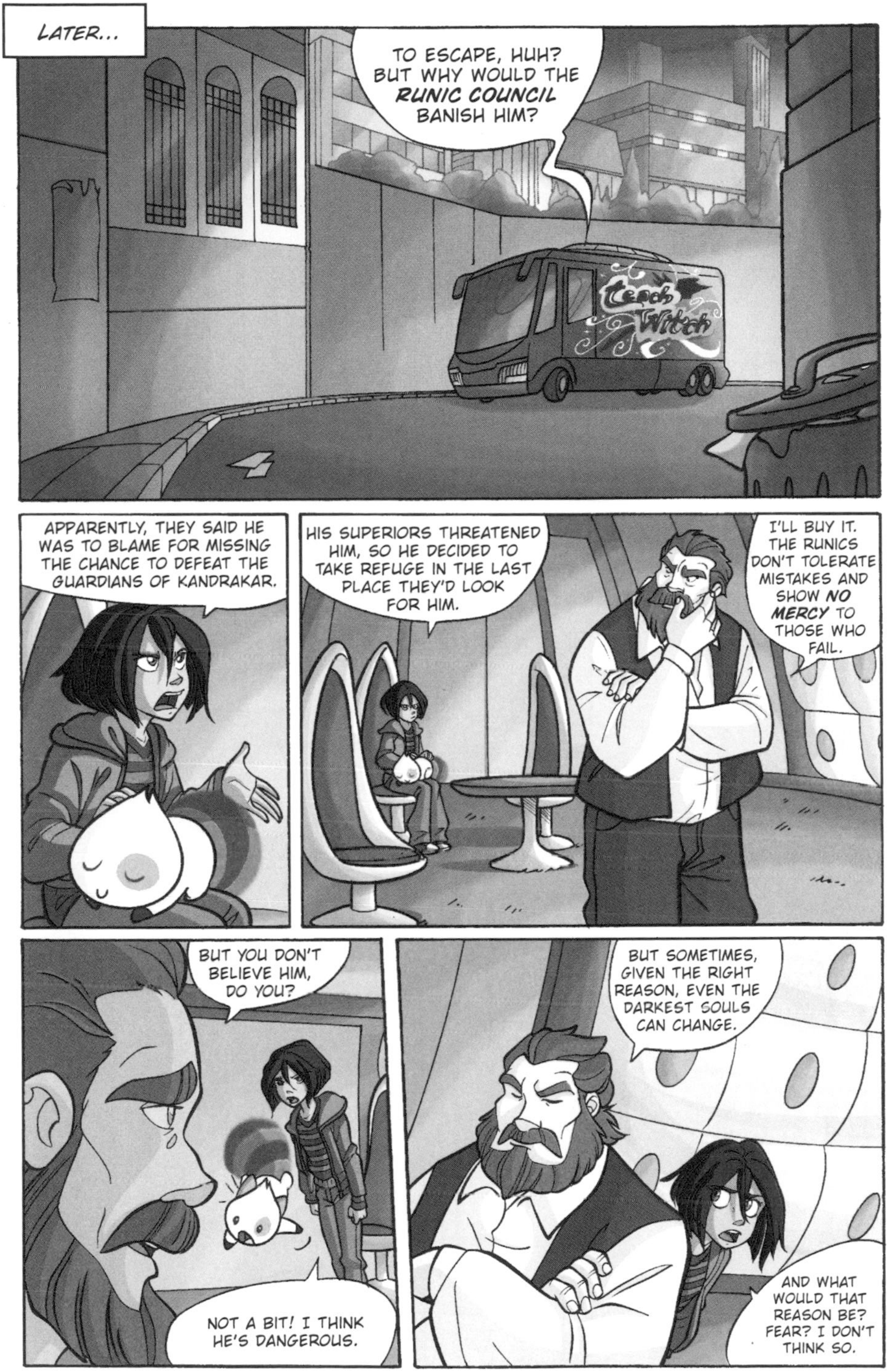
LATER...
TO ESCAPE, HUH? BUT WHY WOULD THE RUNIC COUNCIL BANISH HIM?
APPARENTLY, THEY SAID HE WAS TO BLAME FOR MISSING THE CHANCE TO DEFEAT THE GUARDIANS OF KANDRAKAR.
HIS SUPERIORS THREATENED HIM, SO HE DECIDED TO TAKE REFUGE IN THE LAST PLACE THEY'D LOOK FOR HIM.
I'LL BUY IT. THE RUNICS DON'T TOLERATE MISTAKES AND SHOW NO MERCY TO THOSE WHO FAIL.
BUT YOU DON'T BELIEVE HIM, DO YOU?
NOT A BIT! I THINK HE'S DANGEROUS.
BUT SOMETIMES, GIVEN THE RIGHT REASON, EVEN THE DARKEST SOULS CAN CHANGE.
AND WHAT WOULD THAT REASON BE? FEAR? I DON'T THINK SO.

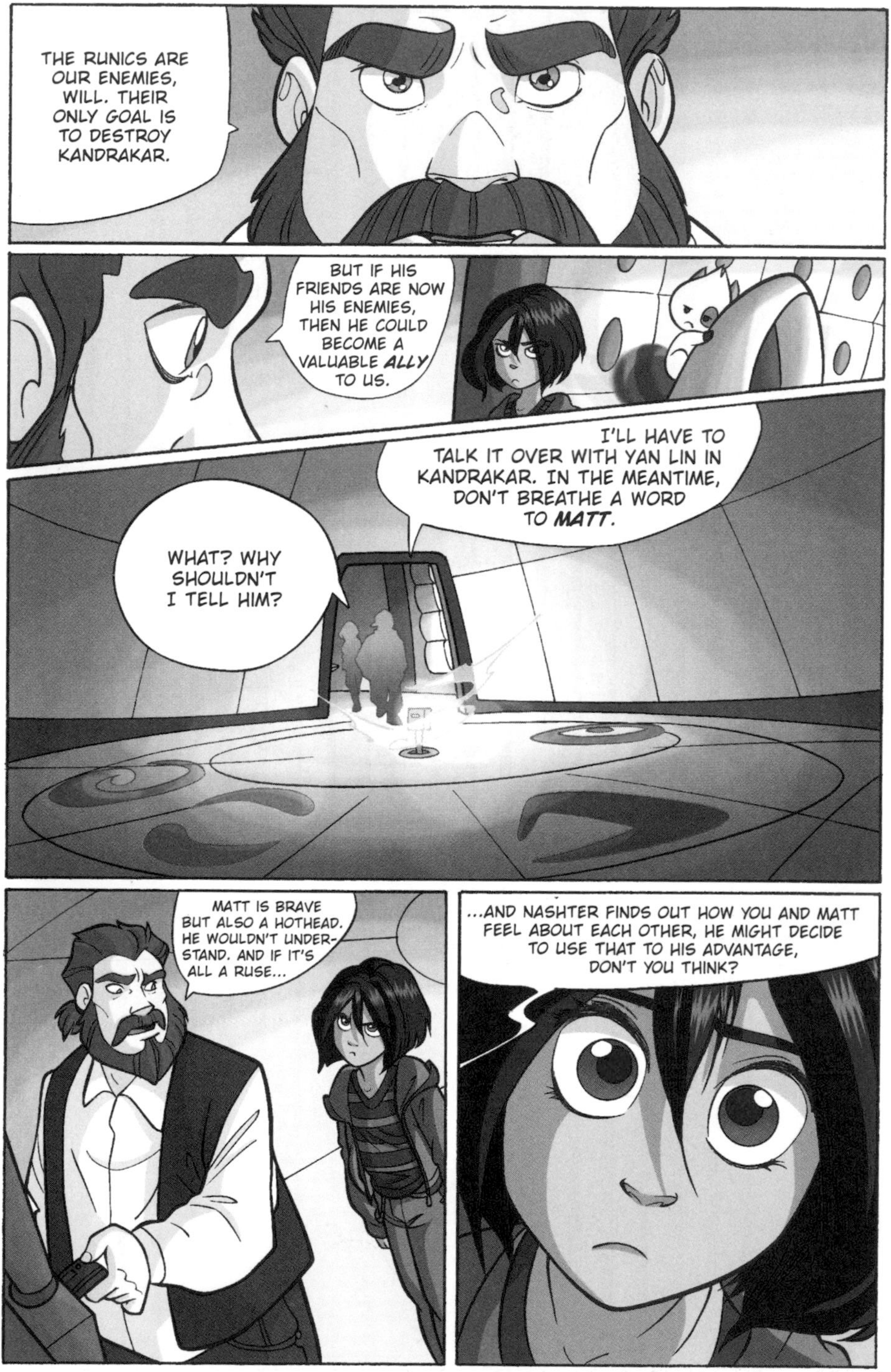
THE RUNICS ARE OUR ENEMIES, WILL. THEIR ONLY GOAL IS TO DESTROY KANDRAKAR.
BUT IF HIS FRIENDS ARE NOW HIS ENEMIES, THEN HE COULD BECOME A VALUABLE ALLY TO US.
I'LL HAVE TO TALK IT OVER WITH YAN LIN IN KANDRAKAR. IN THE MEANTIME, DON'T BREATHE A WORD TO MATT.
WHAT? WHY SHOULDN'T I TELL HIM?
MATT IS BRAVE BUT ALSO A HOTHEAD. HE WOULDN'T UNDER-STAND. AND IF IT'S ALL A RUSE...
...AND NASHTER FINDS OUT HOW YOU AND MATT FEEL ABOUT EACH OTHER, HE MIGHT DECIDE TO USE THAT TO HIS ADVANTAGE, DON'T YOU THINK?

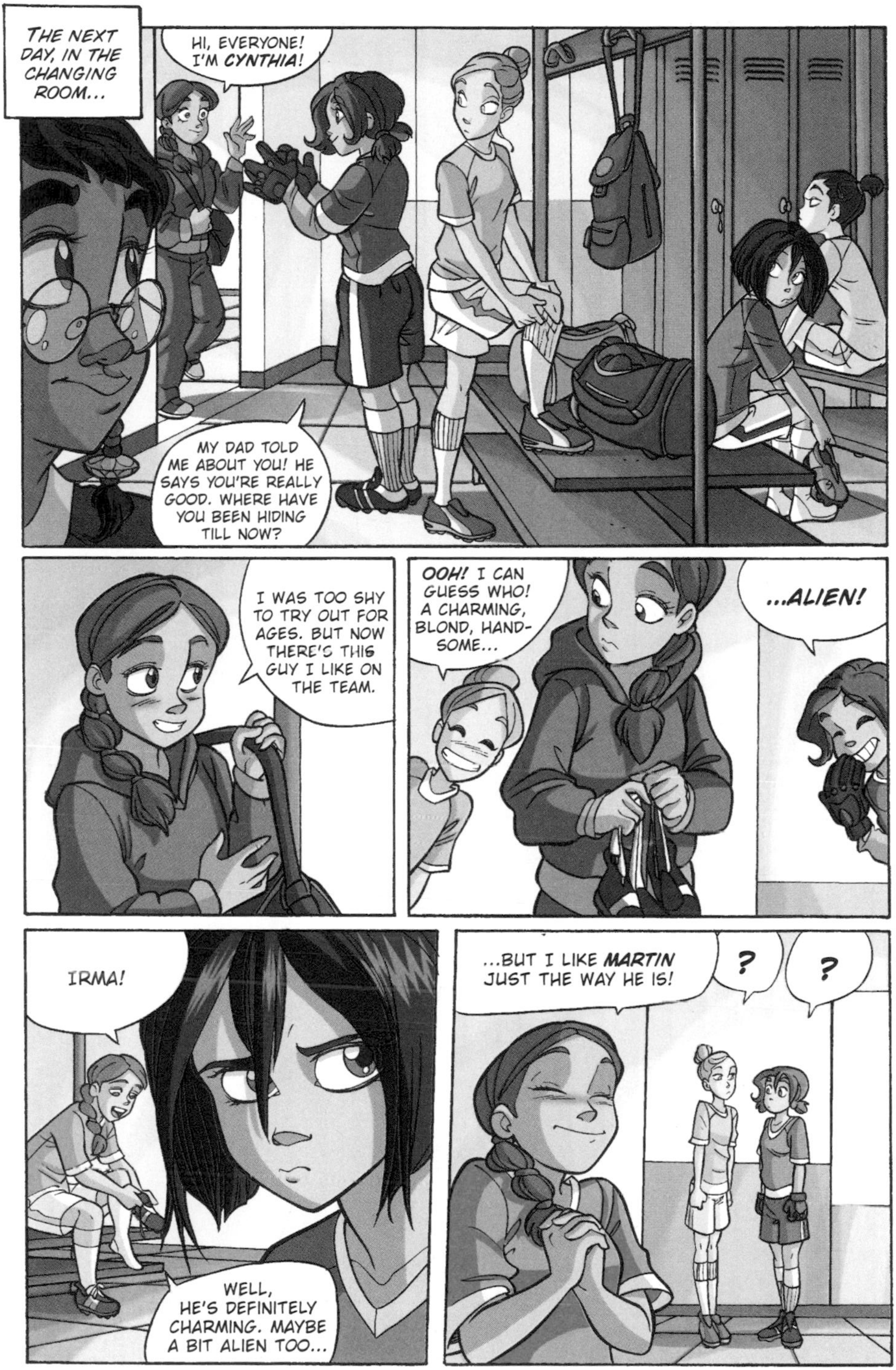

THE NEXT DAY, IN THE CHANGING ROOM...
HI, EVERYONE! I'M CYNTHIA!
MY DAD TOLD ME ABOUT YOU! HE SAYS YOU'RE REALLY GOOD. WHERE HAVE YOU BEEN HIDING TILL NOW?
I WAS TOO SHY TO TRY OUT FOR AGES. BUT NOW THERE'S THIS GUY I LIKE ON THE TEAM.
OOH! I CAN GUESS WHO! A CHARMING, BLOND, HAND-SOME...
...ALIEN!
IRMA!
WELL, HE'S DEFINITELY CHARMING. MAYBE A BIT ALIEN TOO...
...BUT I LIKE MARTIN JUST THE WAY HE IS!
?
?

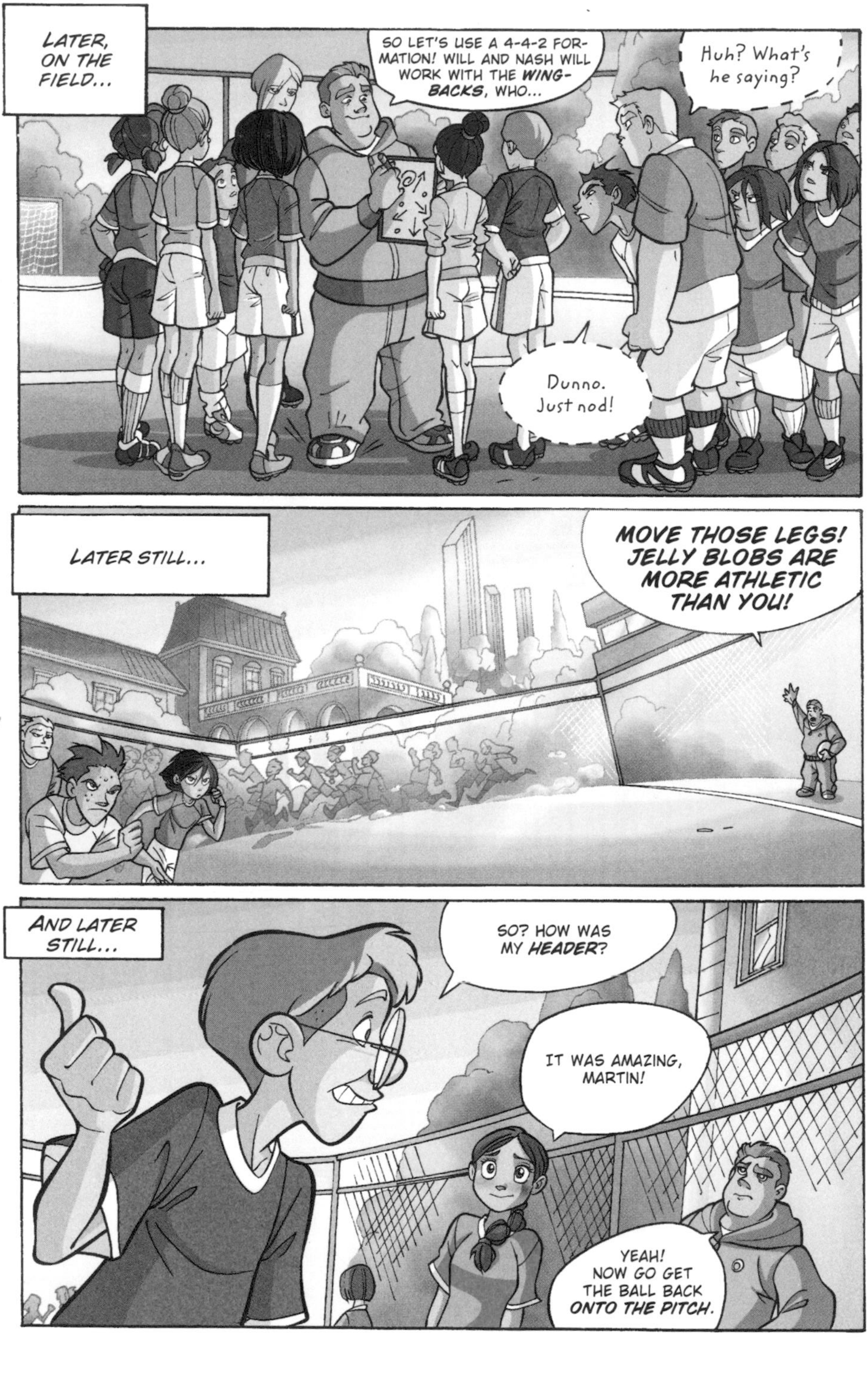
LATER, ON THE FIELD...
SO LET'S USE A 4-4-2 FORMATION! WILL AND NASH WILL WORK WITH THE WING-BACKS, WHO...
Huh? What's he saying?
Dunno. Just nod!
LATER STILL...
MOVE THOSE LEGS! JELLY BLOBS ARE MORE ATHLETIC THAN YOU!
AND LATER STILL...
SO? HOW WAS MY HEADER?
IT WAS AMAZING, MARTIN!
YEAH! NOW GO GET THE BALL BACK ONTO THE PITCH.

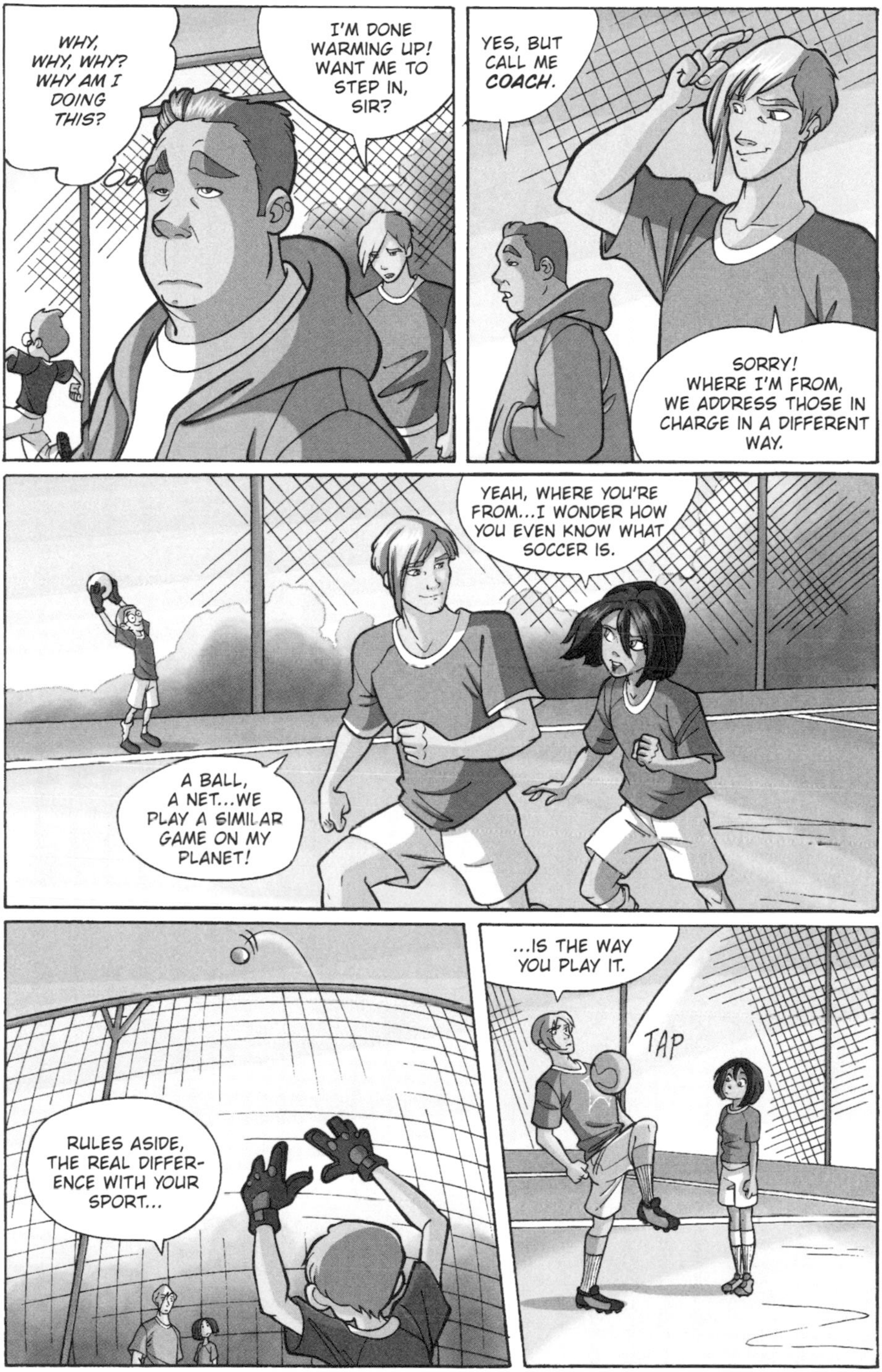
WHY, WHY, WHY? WHY AM I DOING THIS?
I'M DONE WARMING UP! WANT ME TO STEP IN, SIR?
YES, BUT CALL ME COACH.
SORRY! WHERE I'M FROM, WE ADDRESS THOSE IN CHARGE IN A DIFFERENT WAY.
YEAH, WHERE YOU'RE FROM...I WONDER HOW YOU EVEN KNOW WHAT SOCCER IS.
A BALL, A NET...WE PLAY A SIMILAR GAME ON MY PLANET!
RULES ASIDE, THE REAL DIFFERENCE WITH YOUR SPORT...
...IS THE WAY YOU PLAY IT.
TAP

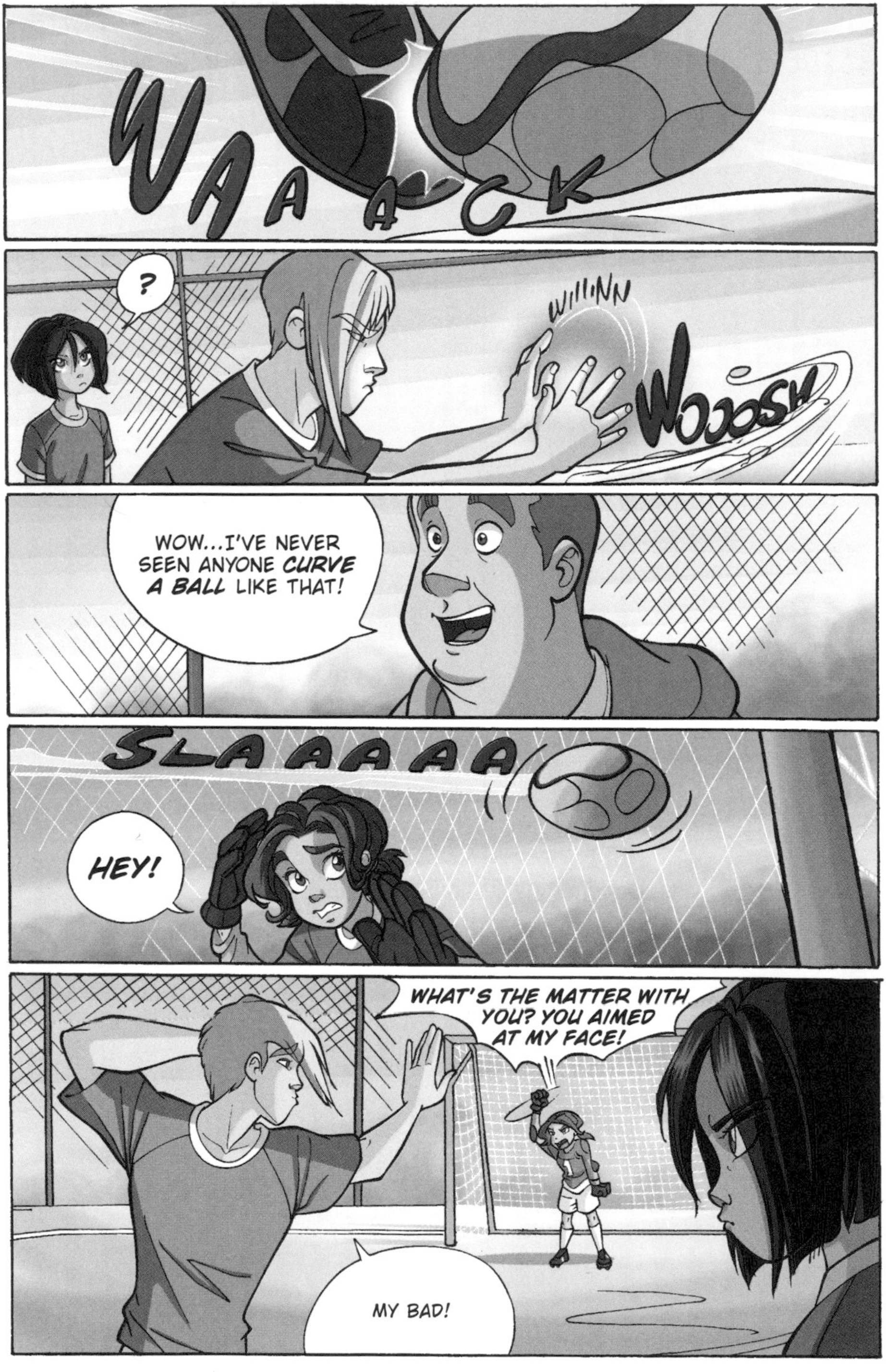
WAAACK
?
WHIINN
WOOOSH
WOW...I'VE NEVER SEEN ANYONE CURVE A BALL LIKE THAT!
SLAAAAA
HEY!
WHAT'S THE MATTER WITH YOU? YOU AIMED AT MY FACE!
MY BAD!

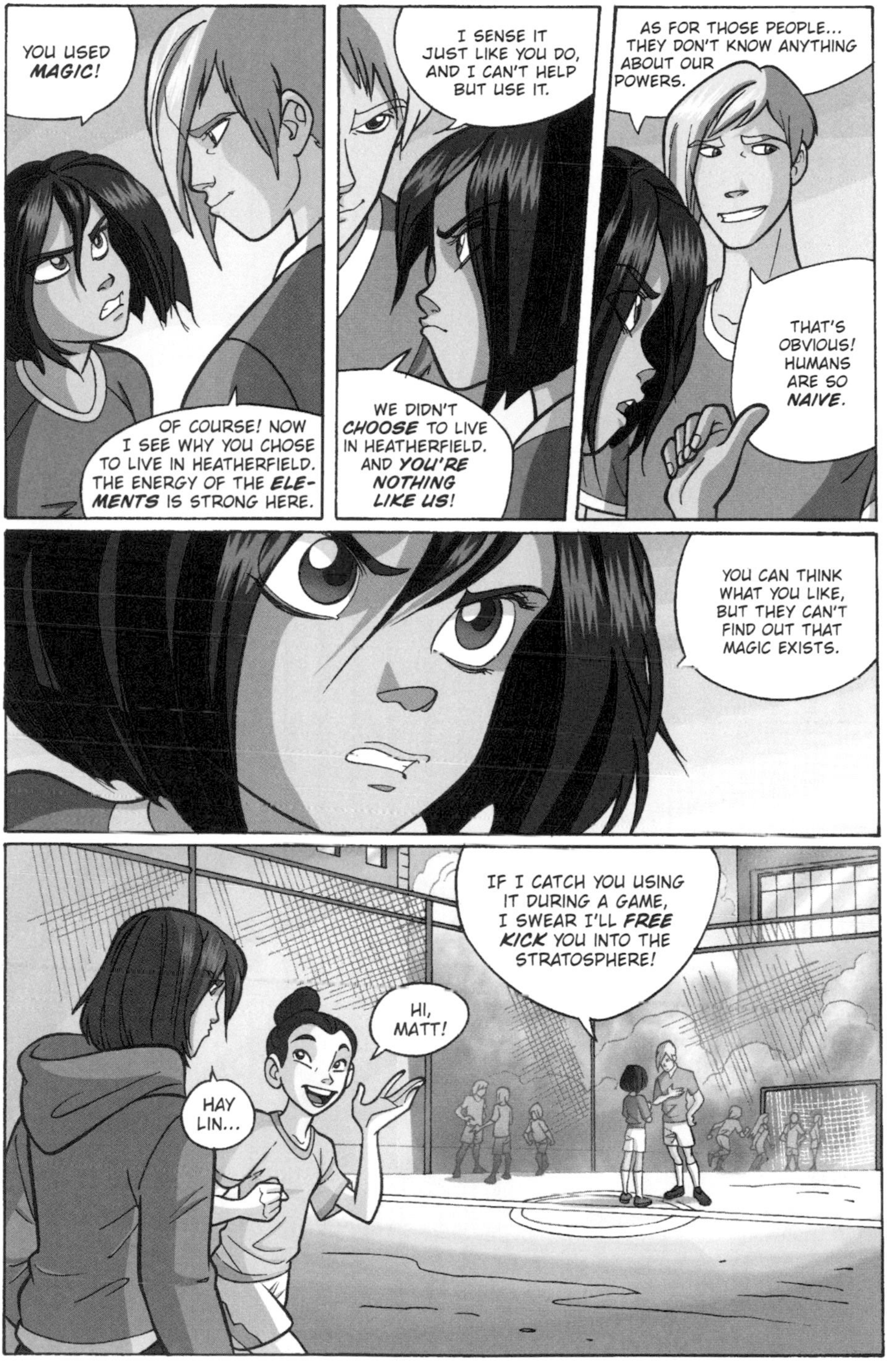
YOU USED MAGIC!
OF COURSE! NOW I SEE WHY YOU CHOSE TO LIVE IN HEATHERFIELD. THE ENERGY OF THE ELEMENTS IS STRONG HERE.
I SENSE IT JUST LIKE YOU DO, AND I CAN'T HELP BUT USE IT.
WE DIDN'T CHOOSE TO LIVE IN HEATHERFIELD. AND YOU'RE NOTHING LIKE US!
AS FOR THOSE PEOPLE... THEY DON'T KNOW ANYTHING ABOUT OUR POWERS.
THAT'S OBVIOUS! HUMANS ARE SO NAIVE.
YOU CAN THINK WHAT YOU LIKE, BUT THEY CAN'T FIND OUT THAT MAGIC EXISTS.
IF I CATCH YOU USING IT DURING A GAME, I SWEAR I'LL FREE KICK YOU INTO THE STRATOSPHERE!
HI, MATT!
HAY LIN...

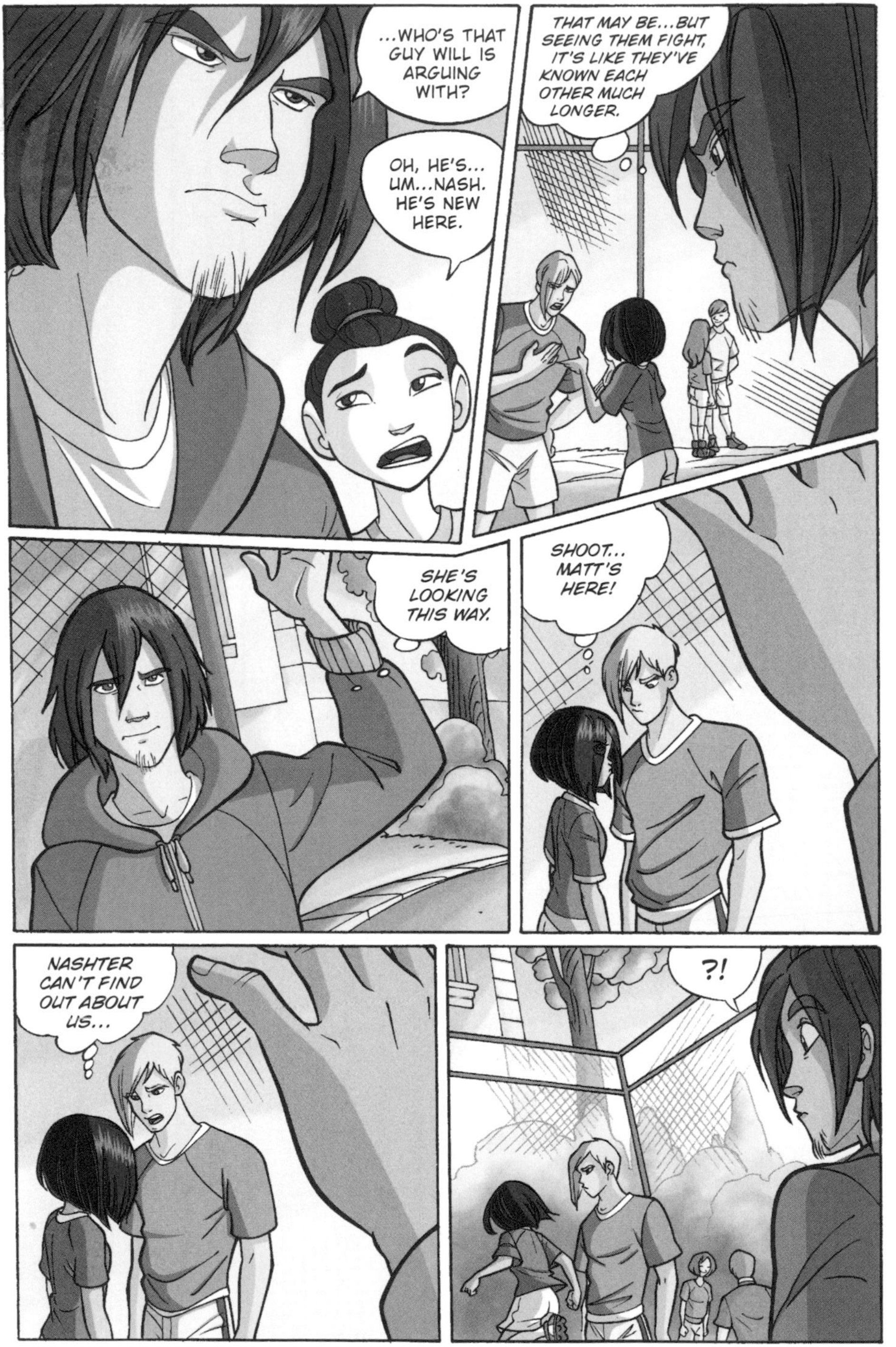
...WHO'S THAT GUY WILL IS ARGUING WITH?
OH, HE'S... UM...NASH. HE'S NEW HERE.
THAT MAY BE...BUT SEEING THEM FIGHT, IT'S LIKE THEY'VE KNOWN EACH OTHER MUCH LONGER.
SHE'S LOOKING THIS WAY.
SHOOT... MATT'S HERE!
NASHTER CAN'T FIND OUT ABOUT US...
?!

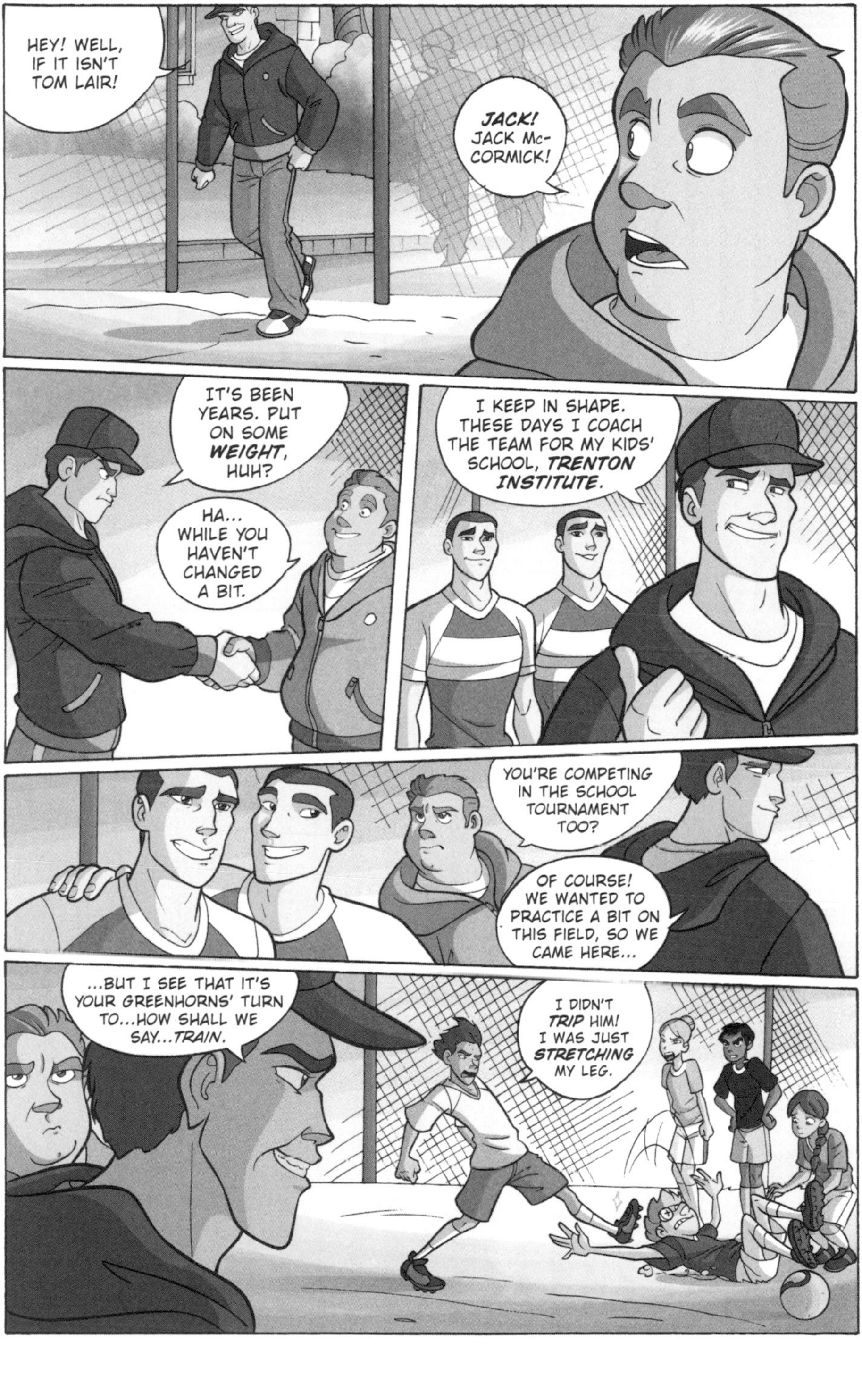
HEY! WELL, IF IT ISN'T TOM LAIR!
JACK! JACK McCORMICK!
IT'S BEEN YEARS. PUT ON SOME WEIGHT, HUH?
HA... WHILE YOU HAVEN'T CHANGED A BIT.
I KEEP IN SHAPE. THESE DAYS I COACH THE TEAM FOR MY KIDS' SCHOOL, TRENTON INSTITUTE.
YOU'RE COMPETING IN THE SCHOOL TOURNAMENT TOO?
OF COURSE! WE WANTED TO PRACTICE A BIT ON THIS FIELD, SO WE CAME HERE...
...BUT I SEE THAT IT'S YOUR GREENHORNS' TURN TO...HOW SHALL WE SAY...TRAIN.
I DIDN'T TRIP HIM! I WAS JUST STRETCHING MY LEG.

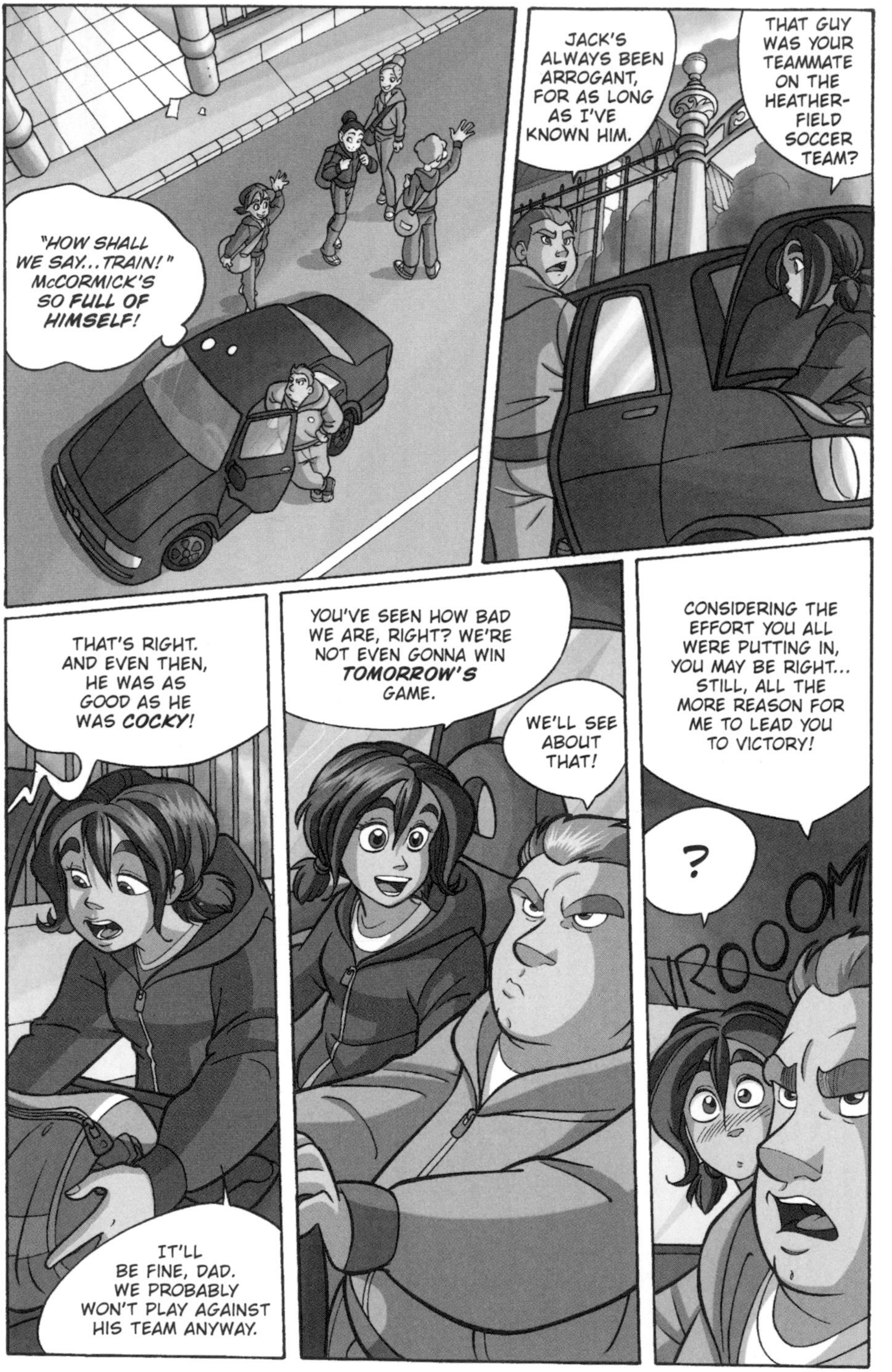
"HOW SHALL WE SAY...TRAIN!" McCORMICK'S SO **FULL OF HIMSELF**!
THAT GUY WAS YOUR TEAMMATE ON THE HEATHER-FIELD SOCCER TEAM?
JACK'S ALWAYS BEEN ARROGANT, FOR AS LONG AS I'VE KNOWN HIM.
THAT'S RIGHT. AND EVEN THEN, HE WAS AS GOOD AS HE WAS **COCKY**!
IT'LL BE FINE, DAD. WE PROBABLY WON'T PLAY AGAINST HIS TEAM ANYWAY.
YOU'VE SEEN HOW BAD WE ARE, RIGHT? WE'RE NOT EVEN GONNA WIN **TOMORROW'S** GAME.
WE'LL SEE ABOUT THAT!
CONSIDERING THE EFFORT YOU ALL WERE PUTTING IN, YOU MAY BE RIGHT... STILL, ALL THE MORE REASON FOR ME TO LEAD YOU TO VICTORY!
?
VROOOOM

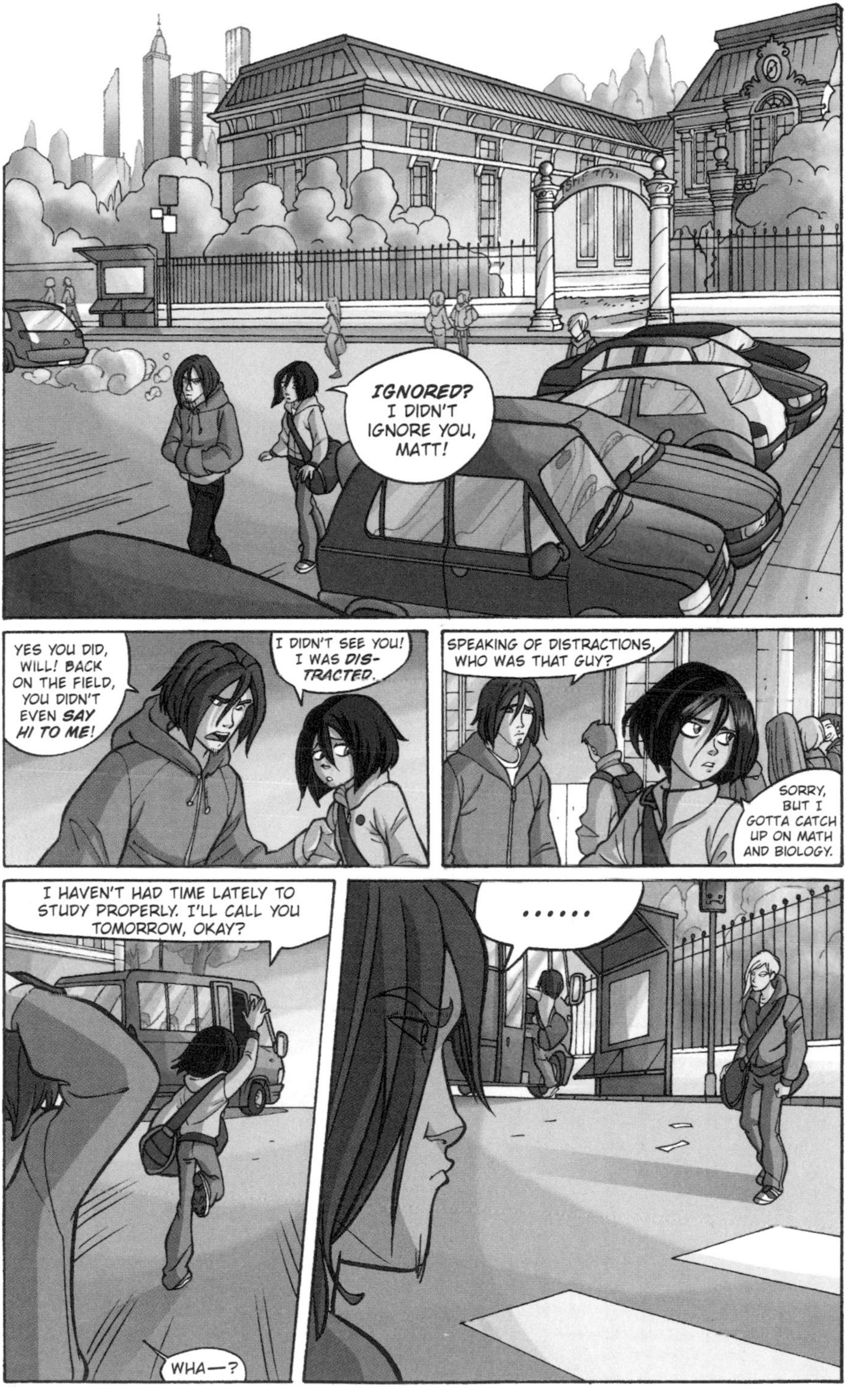
IGNORED? I DIDN'T IGNORE YOU, MATT!
YES YOU DID, WILL! BACK ON THE FIELD, YOU DIDN'T EVEN SAY HI TO ME!
I DIDN'T SEE YOU! I WAS DISTRACTED.
SPEAKING OF DISTRACTIONS, WHO WAS THAT GUY?
SORRY, BUT I GOTTA CATCH UP ON MATH AND BIOLOGY.
I HAVEN'T HAD TIME LATELY TO STUDY PROPERLY. I'LL CALL YOU TOMORROW, OKAY?
WHA—?
......

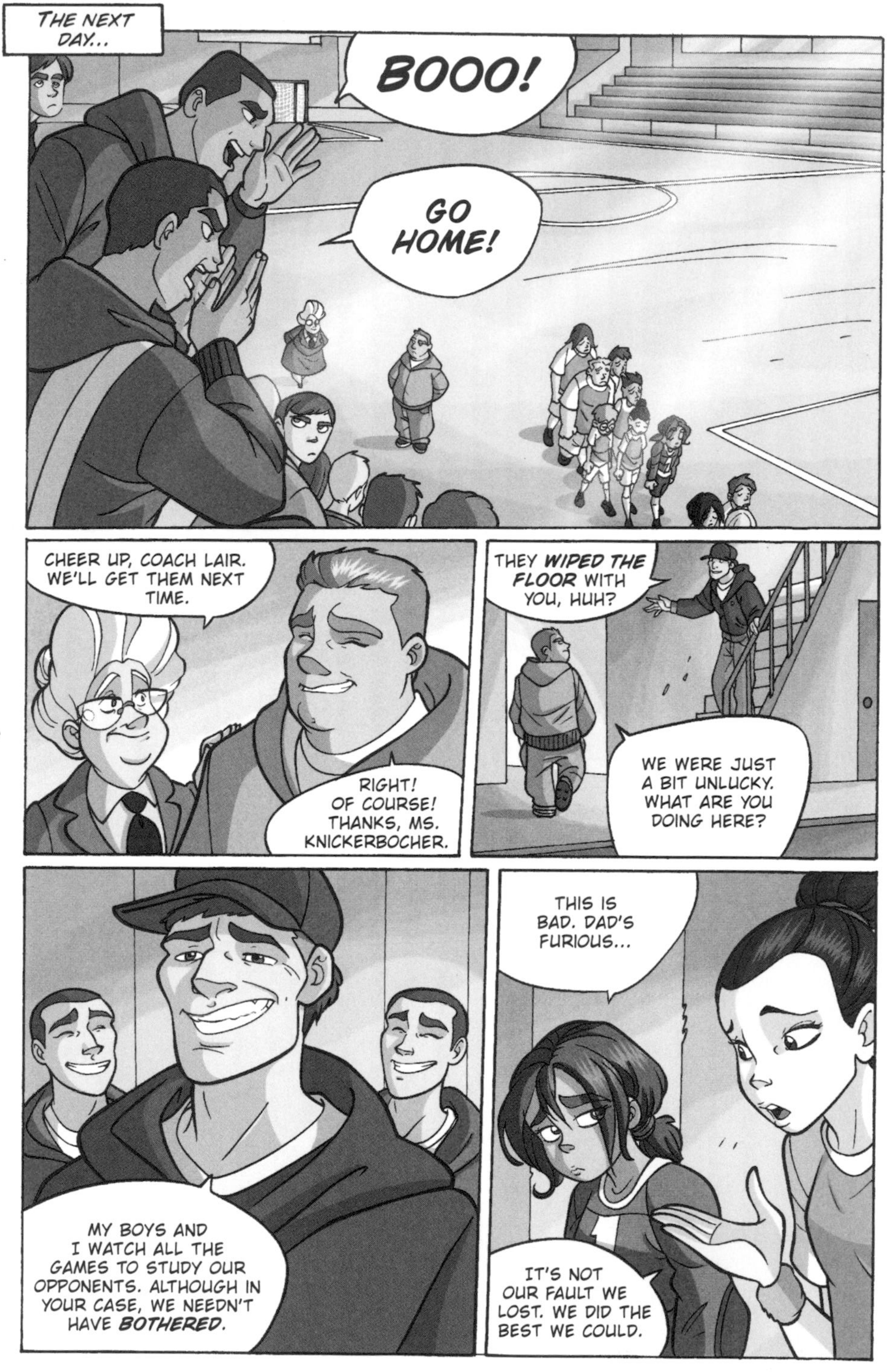
THE NEXT DAY...
BOOO!
GO HOME!
CHEER UP, COACH LAIR. WE'LL GET THEM NEXT TIME.
RIGHT! OF COURSE! THANKS, MS. KNICKERBOCHER.
THEY **WIPED THE FLOOR** WITH YOU, HUH?
WE WERE JUST A BIT UNLUCKY. WHAT ARE YOU DOING HERE?
MY BOYS AND I WATCH ALL THE GAMES TO STUDY OUR OPPONENTS. ALTHOUGH IN YOUR CASE, WE NEEDN'T HAVE **BOTHERED**.
THIS IS BAD. DAD'S FURIOUS...
IT'S NOT OUR FAULT WE LOST. WE DID THE BEST WE COULD.

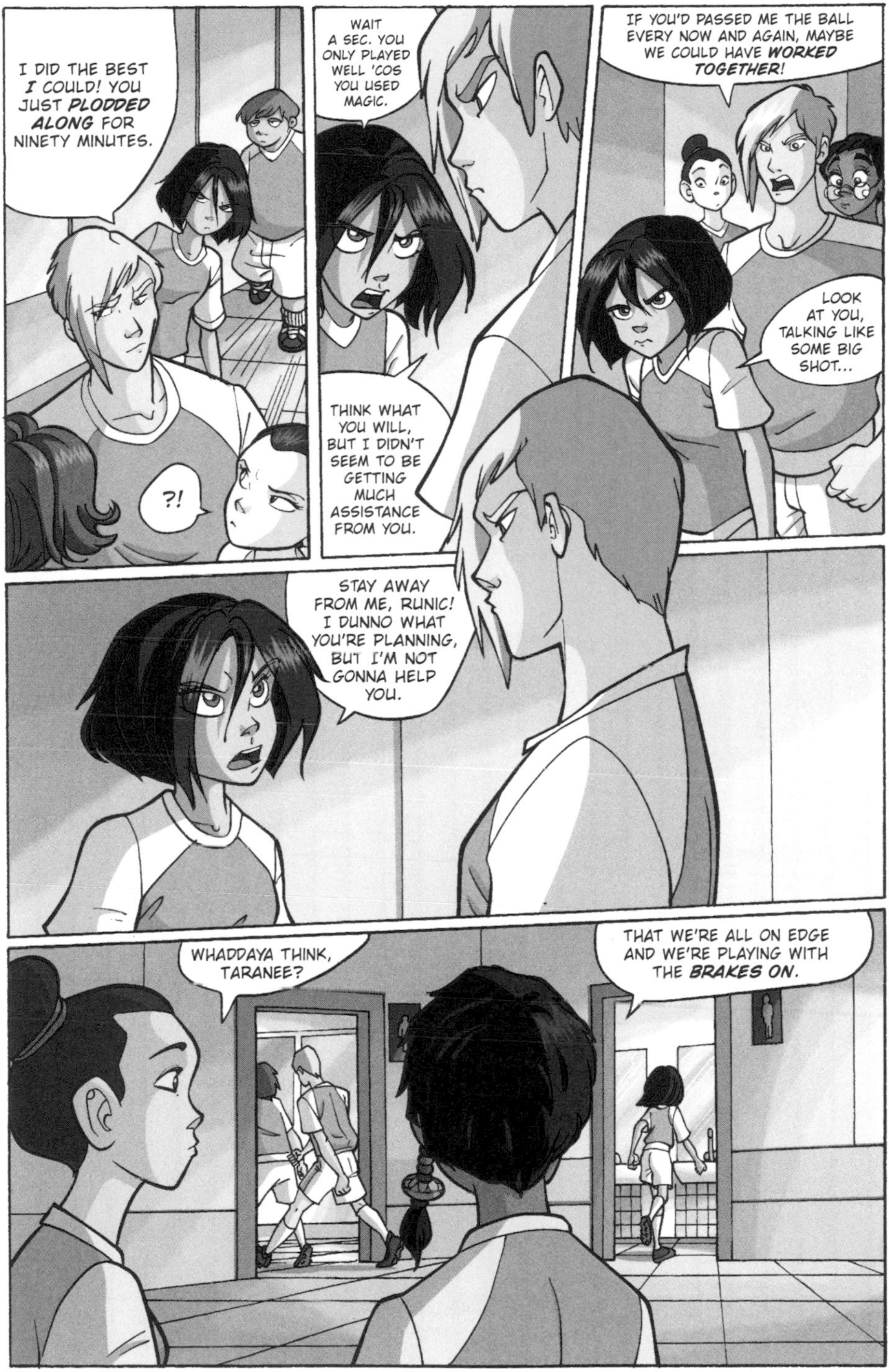
I DID THE BEST I COULD! YOU JUST PLODDED ALONG FOR NINETY MINUTES.
?!
WAIT A SEC. YOU ONLY PLAYED WELL 'COS YOU USED MAGIC.
THINK WHAT YOU WILL, BUT I DIDN'T SEEM TO BE GETTING MUCH ASSISTANCE FROM YOU.
IF YOU'D PASSED ME THE BALL EVERY NOW AND AGAIN, MAYBE WE COULD HAVE WORKED TOGETHER!
LOOK AT YOU, TALKING LIKE SOME BIG SHOT...
STAY AWAY FROM ME, RUNIC! I DUNNO WHAT YOU'RE PLANNING, BUT I'M NOT GONNA HELP YOU.
WHADDAYA THINK, TARANEE?
THAT WE'RE ALL ON EDGE AND WE'RE PLAYING WITH THE BRAKES ON.

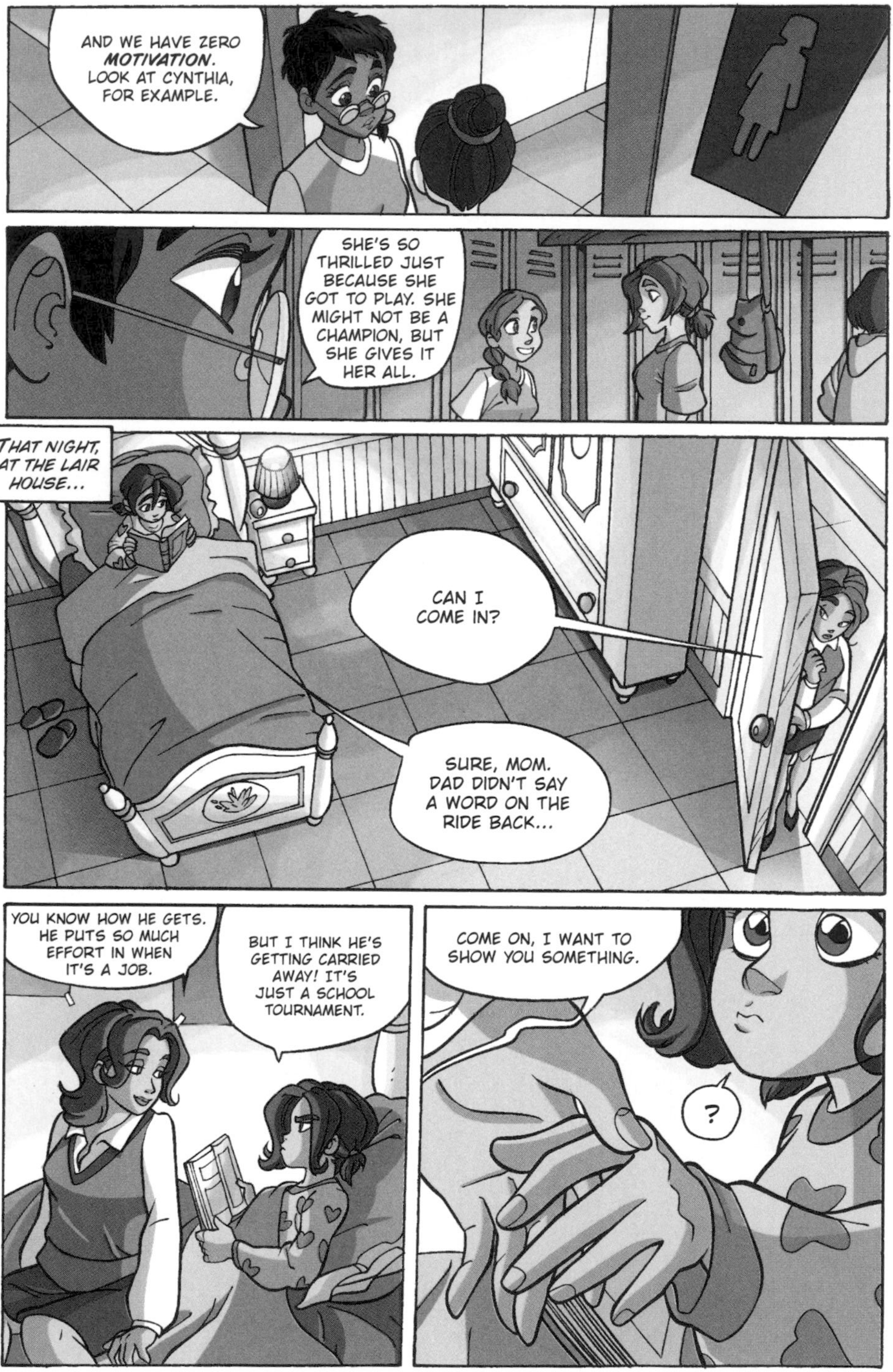
AND WE HAVE ZERO **MOTIVATION**. LOOK AT CYNTHIA, FOR EXAMPLE.
SHE'S SO THRILLED JUST BECAUSE SHE GOT TO PLAY. SHE MIGHT NOT BE A CHAMPION, BUT SHE GIVES IT HER ALL.
THAT NIGHT, AT THE LAIR HOUSE...
CAN I COME IN?
SURE, MOM. DAD DIDN'T SAY A WORD ON THE RIDE BACK...
YOU KNOW HOW HE GETS. HE PUTS SO MUCH EFFORT IN WHEN IT'S A JOB.
BUT I THINK HE'S GETTING CARRIED AWAY! IT'S JUST A SCHOOL TOURNAMENT.
COME ON, I WANT TO SHOW YOU SOMETHING.
?

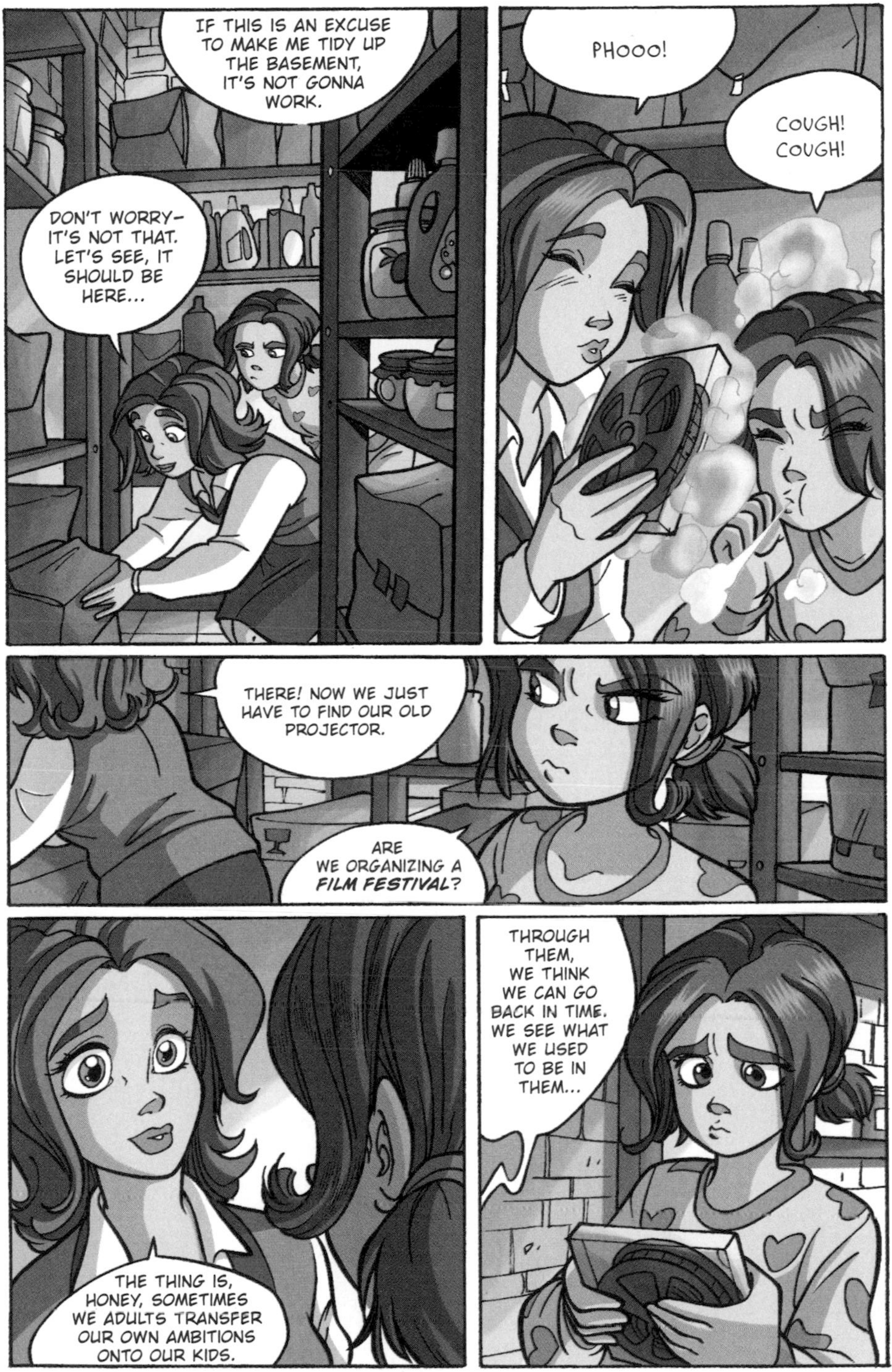
IF THIS IS AN EXCUSE TO MAKE ME TIDY UP THE BASEMENT, IT'S NOT GONNA WORK.
DON'T WORRY-IT'S NOT THAT. LET'S SEE, IT SHOULD BE HERE...
PHOOO!
COUGH! COUGH!
THERE! NOW WE JUST HAVE TO FIND OUR OLD PROJECTOR.
ARE WE ORGANIZING A *FILM FESTIVAL*?
THE THING IS, HONEY, SOMETIMES WE ADULTS TRANSFER OUR OWN AMBITIONS ONTO OUR KIDS.
THROUGH THEM, WE THINK WE CAN GO BACK IN TIME. WE SEE WHAT WE USED TO BE IN THEM...

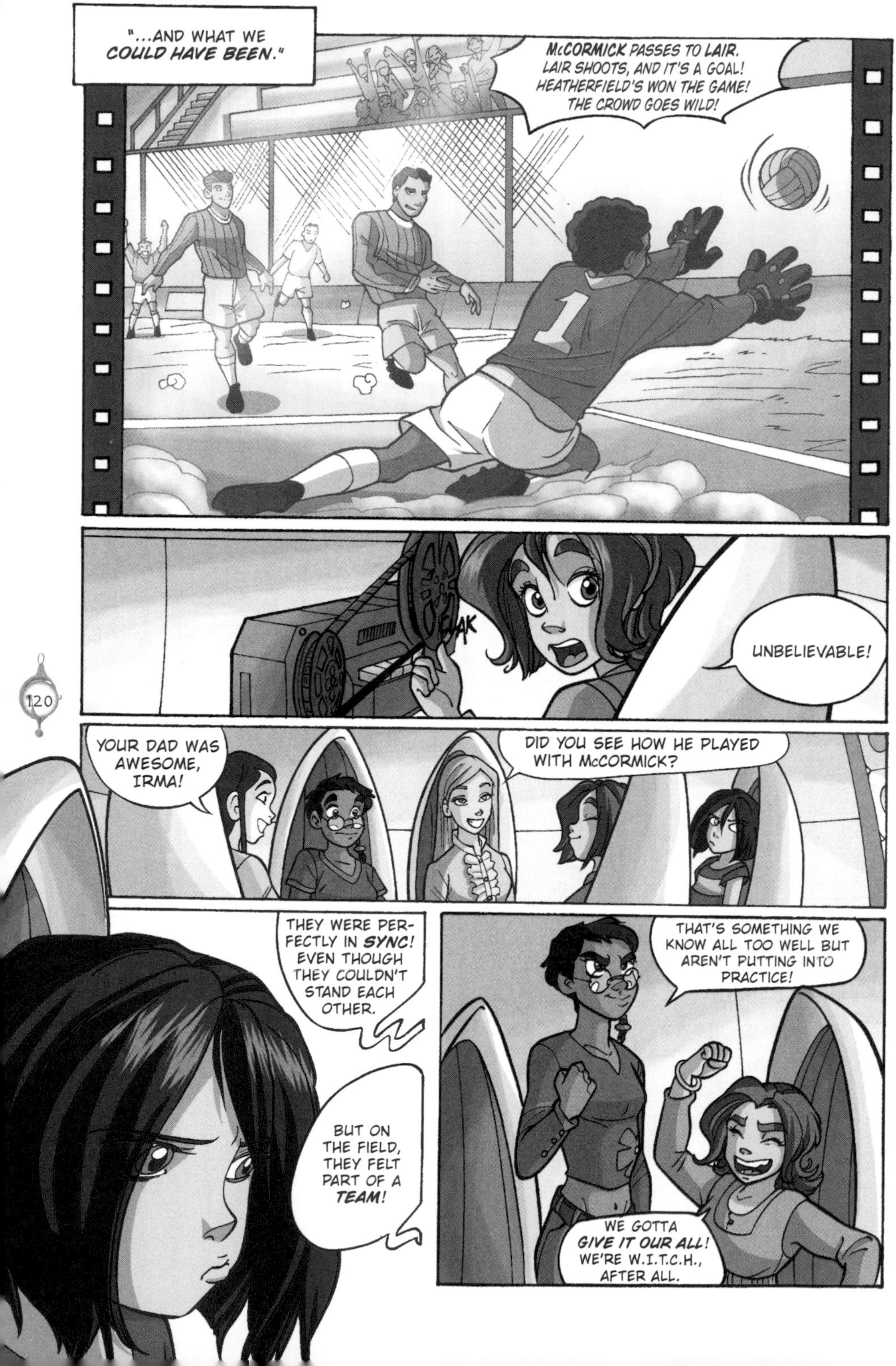
"...AND WHAT WE COULD HAVE BEEN."
McCORMICK PASSES TO LAIR. LAIR SHOOTS, AND IT'S A GOAL! HEATHERFIELD'S WON THE GAME! THE CROWD GOES WILD!
UNBELIEVABLE!
YOUR DAD WAS AWESOME, IRMA!
DID YOU SEE HOW HE PLAYED WITH McCORMICK?
THEY WERE PERFECTLY IN SYNC! EVEN THOUGH THEY COULDN'T STAND EACH OTHER.
BUT ON THE FIELD, THEY FELT PART OF A TEAM!
THAT'S SOMETHING WE KNOW ALL TOO WELL BUT AREN'T PUTTING INTO PRACTICE!
WE GOTTA GIVE IT OUR ALL! WE'RE W.I.T.C.H., AFTER ALL.

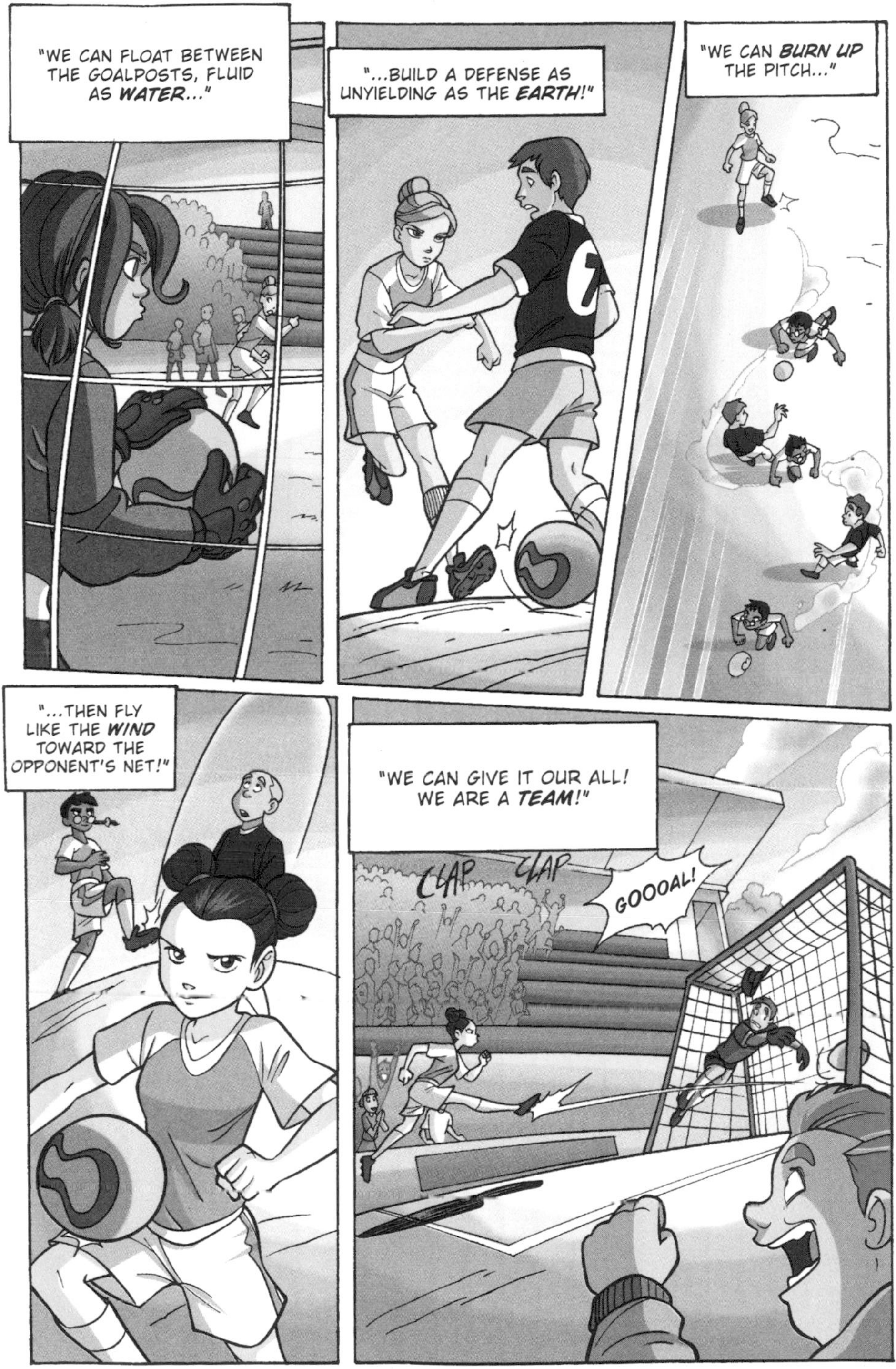
"WE CAN FLOAT BETWEEN THE GOALPOSTS, FLUID AS WATER..."
"...BUILD A DEFENSE AS UNYIELDING AS THE EARTH!"
"WE CAN BURN UP THE PITCH..."
"...THEN FLY LIKE THE WIND TOWARD THE OPPONENT'S NET!"
"WE CAN GIVE IT OUR ALL! WE ARE A TEAM!"
CLAP
CLAP
GOOOAL!

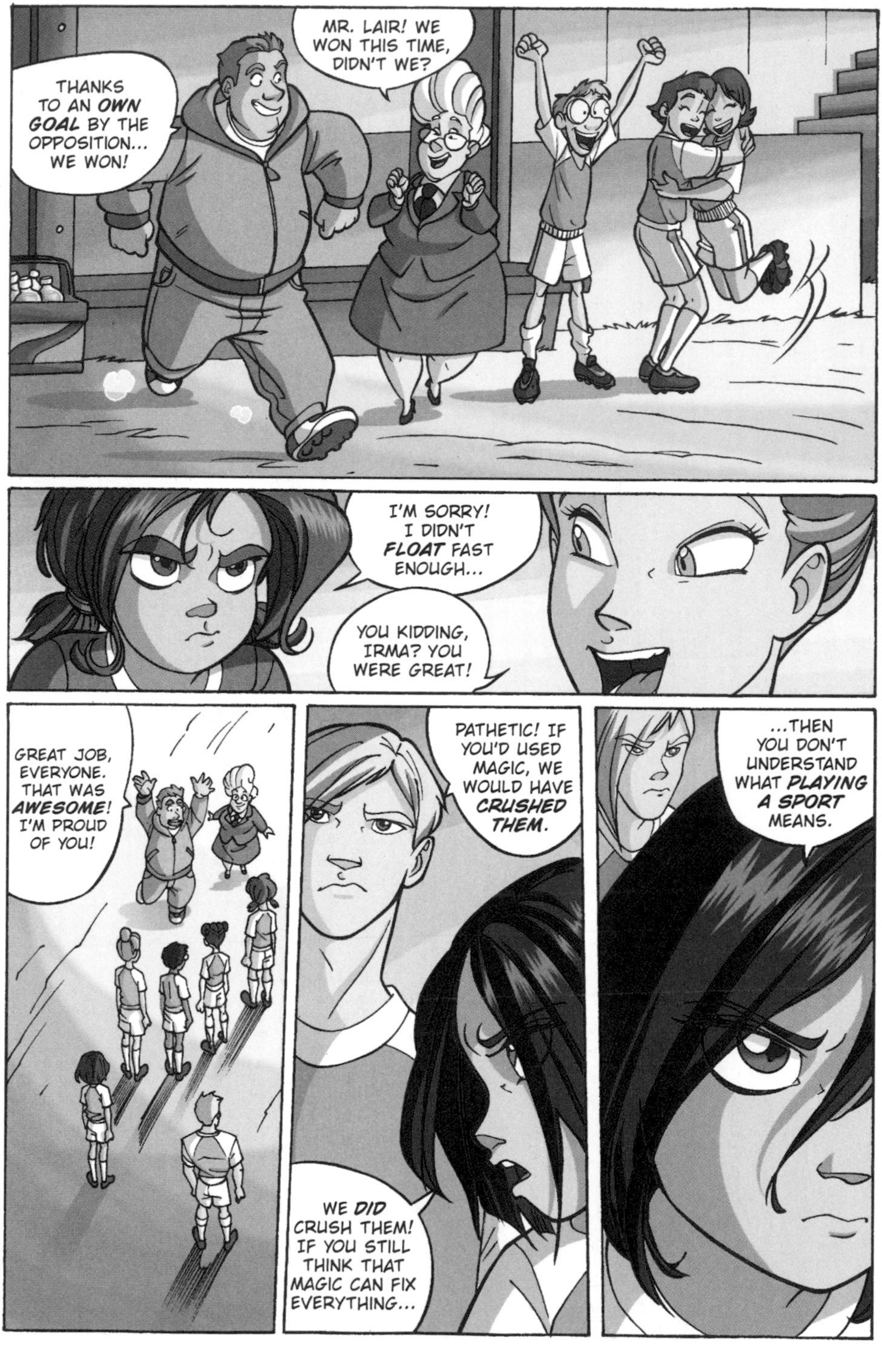

MR. LAIR! WE WON THIS TIME, DIDN'T WE?
THANKS TO AN ***OWN GOAL*** BY THE OPPOSITION... WE WON!
I'M SORRY! I DIDN'T ***FLOAT*** FAST ENOUGH...
YOU KIDDING, IRMA? YOU WERE GREAT!
GREAT JOB, EVERYONE. THAT WAS ***AWESOME***! I'M PROUD OF YOU!
PATHETIC! IF YOU'D USED MAGIC, WE WOULD HAVE ***CRUSHED THEM***.
WE ***DID*** CRUSH THEM! IF YOU STILL THINK THAT MAGIC CAN FIX EVERYTHING...
...THEN YOU DON'T UNDERSTAND WHAT ***PLAYING A SPORT*** MEANS.

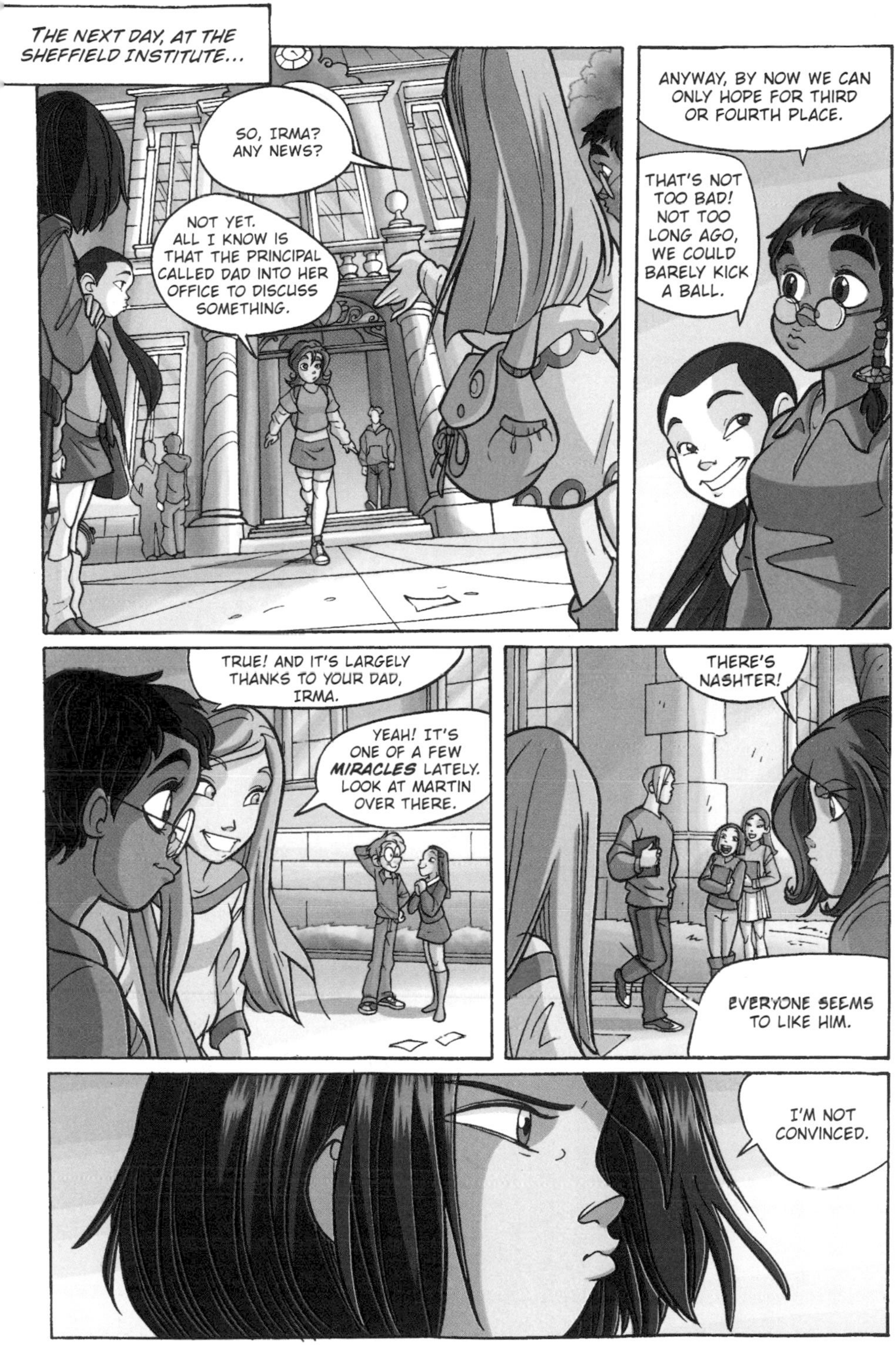

THE NEXT DAY, AT THE SHEFFIELD INSTITUTE...
SO, IRMA? ANY NEWS?
NOT YET. ALL I KNOW IS THAT THE PRINCIPAL CALLED DAD INTO HER OFFICE TO DISCUSS SOMETHING.
ANYWAY, BY NOW WE CAN ONLY HOPE FOR THIRD OR FOURTH PLACE.
THAT'S NOT TOO BAD! NOT TOO LONG AGO, WE COULD BARELY KICK A BALL.
TRUE! AND IT'S LARGELY THANKS TO YOUR DAD, IRMA.
YEAH! IT'S ONE OF A FEW MIRACLES LATELY. LOOK AT MARTIN OVER THERE.
THERE'S NASHTER!
EVERYONE SEEMS TO LIKE HIM.
I'M NOT CONVINCED.

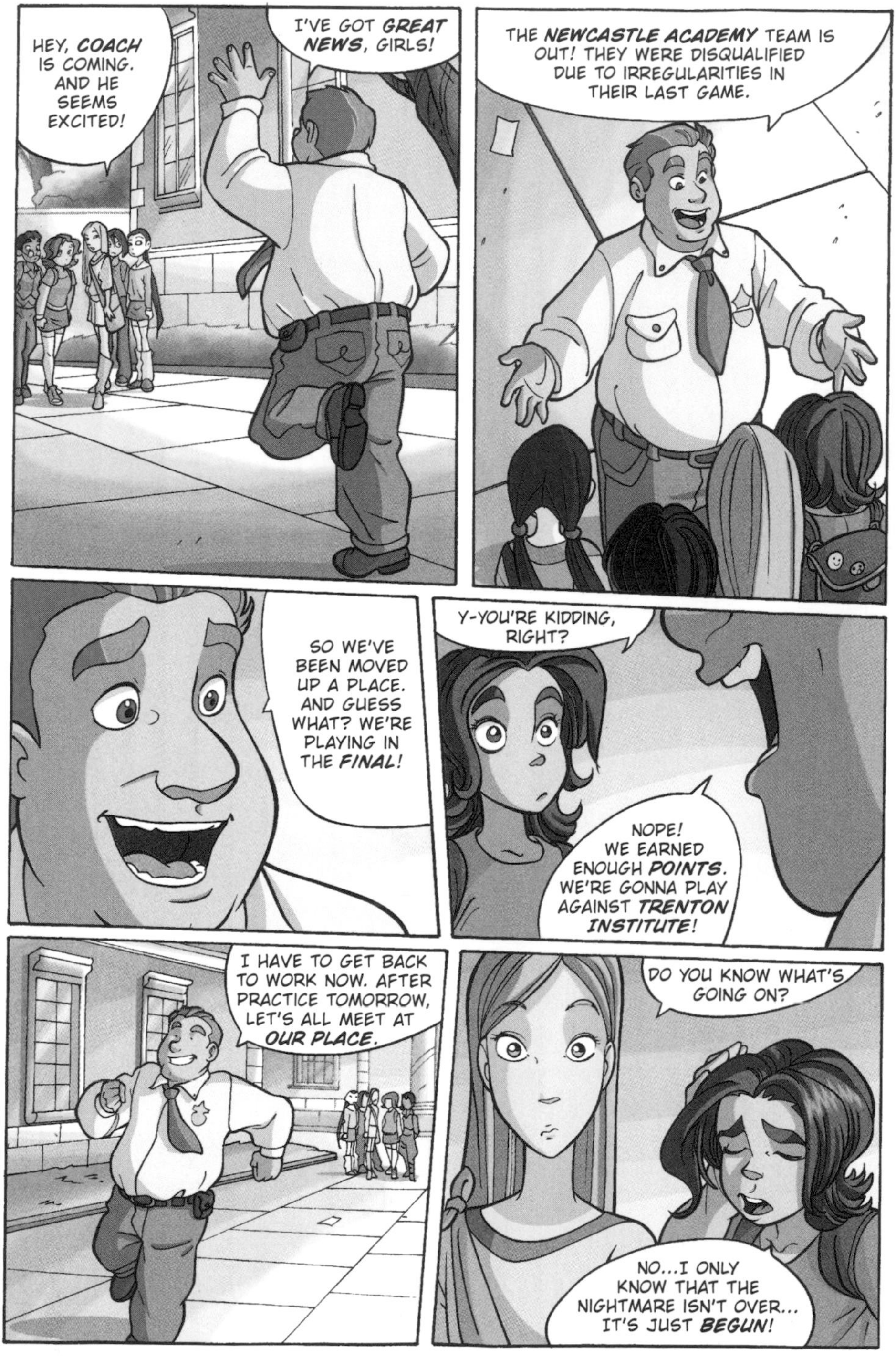
HEY, COACH IS COMING. AND HE SEEMS EXCITED!
I'VE GOT GREAT NEWS, GIRLS!
THE NEWCASTLE ACADEMY TEAM IS OUT! THEY WERE DISQUALIFIED DUE TO IRREGULARITIES IN THEIR LAST GAME.
SO WE'VE BEEN MOVED UP A PLACE. AND GUESS WHAT? WE'RE PLAYING IN THE FINAL!
Y-YOU'RE KIDDING, RIGHT?
NOPE! WE EARNED ENOUGH POINTS. WE'RE GONNA PLAY AGAINST TRENTON INSTITUTE!
I HAVE TO GET BACK TO WORK NOW. AFTER PRACTICE TOMORROW, LET'S ALL MEET AT OUR PLACE.
DO YOU KNOW WHAT'S GOING ON?
NO...I ONLY KNOW THAT THE NIGHTMARE ISN'T OVER... IT'S JUST BEGUN!

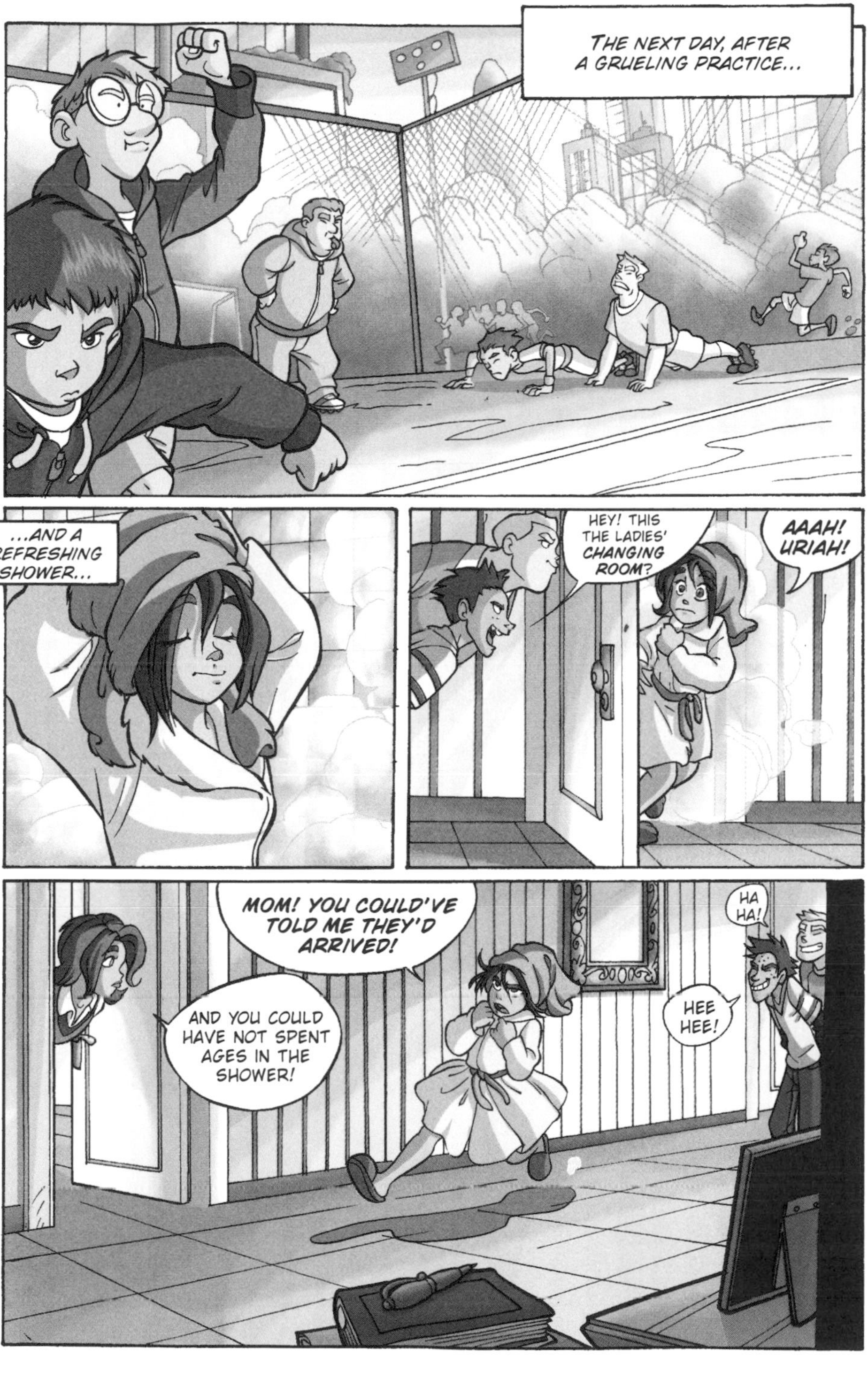
THE NEXT DAY, AFTER A GRUELING PRACTICE...
...AND A REFRESHING SHOWER...
HEY! THIS THE LADIES' CHANGING ROOM?
AAAH! URIAH!
MOM! YOU COULD'VE TOLD ME THEY'D ARRIVED!
AND YOU COULD HAVE NOT SPENT AGES IN THE SHOWER!
HA HA!
HEE HEE!

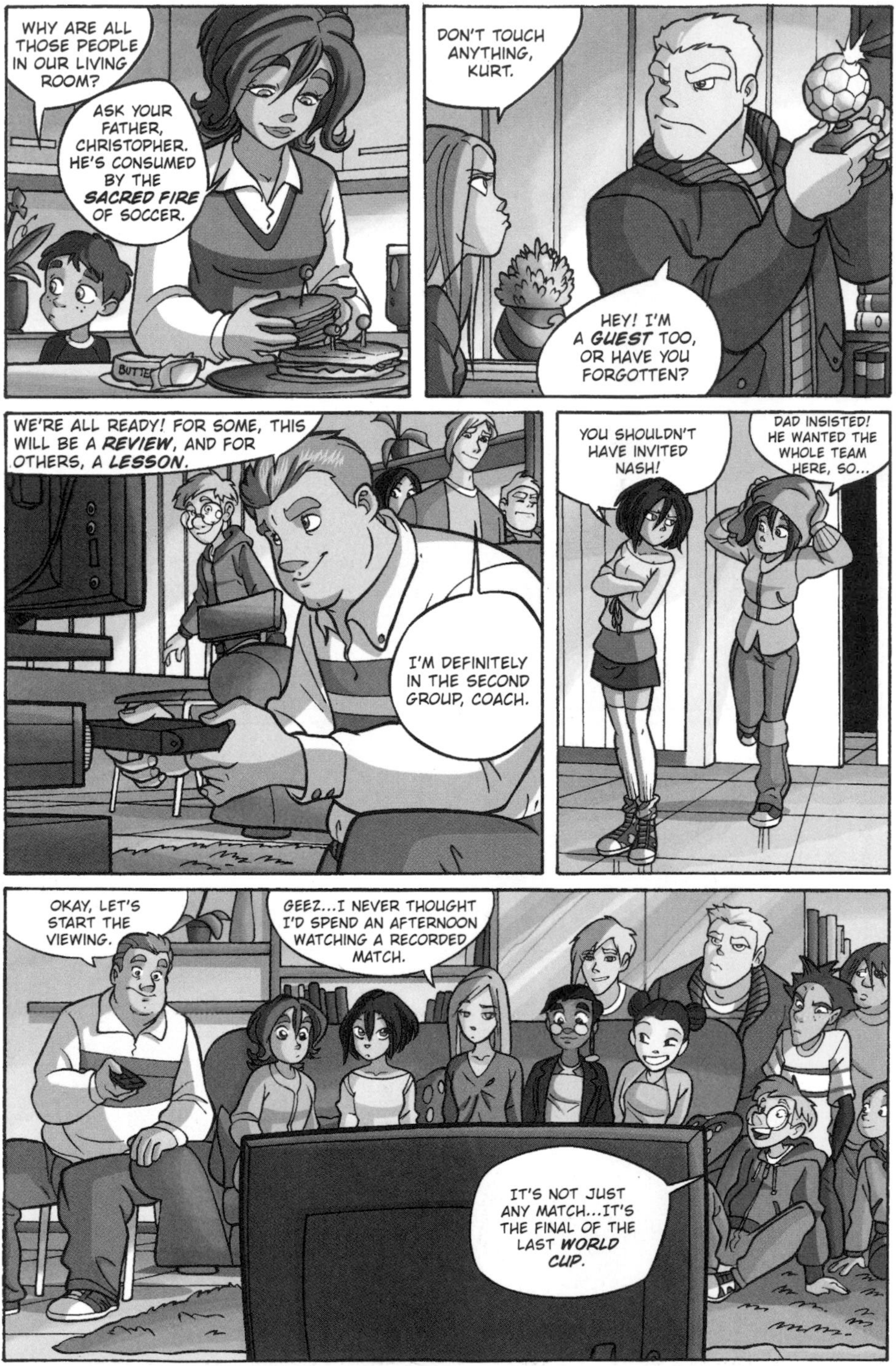
WHY ARE ALL THOSE PEOPLE IN OUR LIVING ROOM?
ASK YOUR FATHER, CHRISTOPHER. HE'S CONSUMED BY THE SACRED FIRE OF SOCCER.
BUTTE
DON'T TOUCH ANYTHING, KURT.
HEY! I'M A GUEST TOO, OR HAVE YOU FORGOTTEN?
WE'RE ALL READY! FOR SOME, THIS WILL BE A REVIEW, AND FOR OTHERS, A LESSON.
I'M DEFINITELY IN THE SECOND GROUP, COACH.
YOU SHOULDN'T HAVE INVITED NASH!
DAD INSISTED! HE WANTED THE WHOLE TEAM HERE, SO...
OKAY, LET'S START THE VIEWING.
GEEZ...I NEVER THOUGHT I'D SPEND AN AFTERNOON WATCHING A RECORDED MATCH.
IT'S NOT JUST ANY MATCH...IT'S THE FINAL OF THE LAST WORLD CUP.

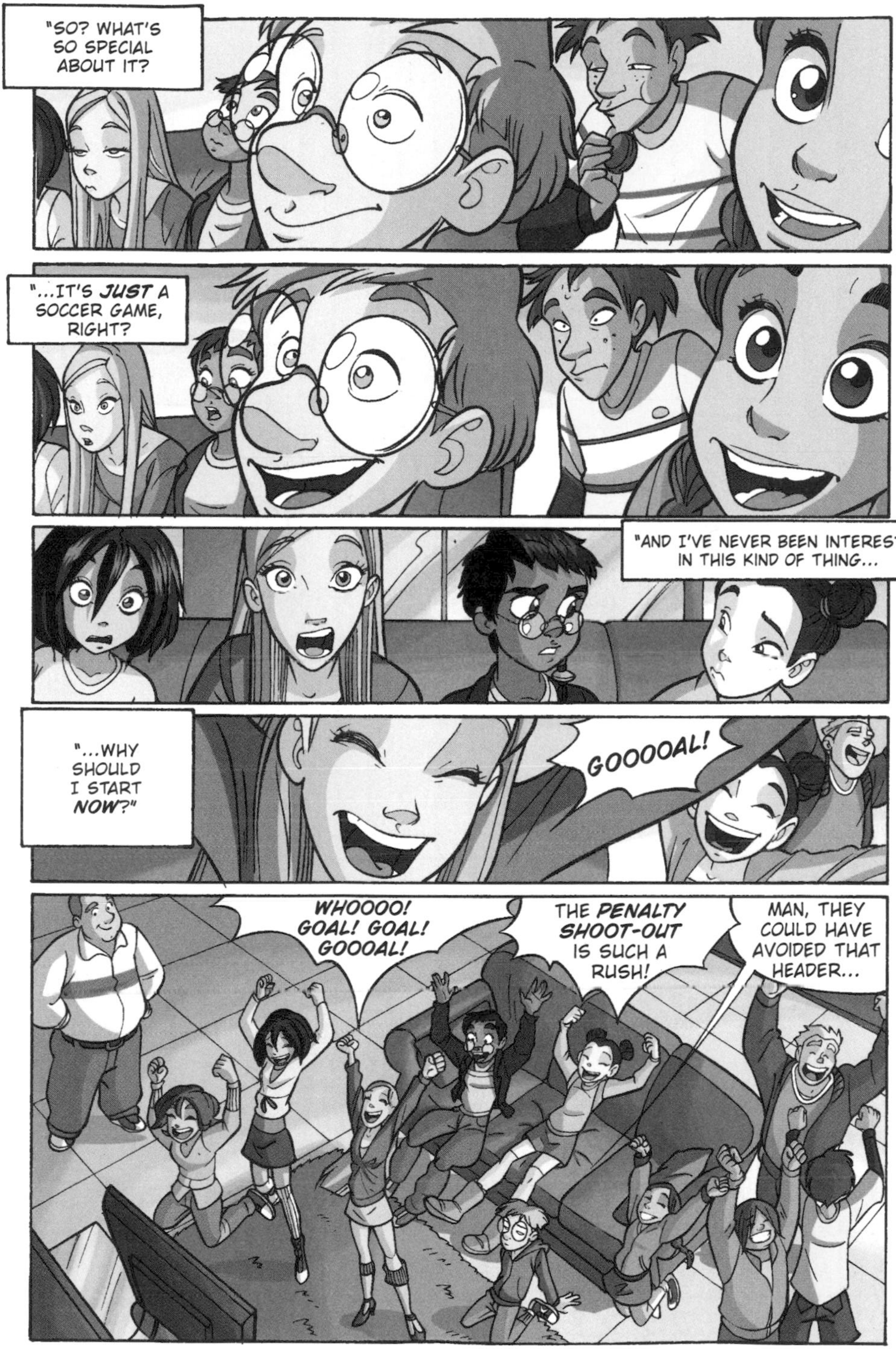
"SO? WHAT'S SO SPECIAL ABOUT IT?
"...IT'S JUST A SOCCER GAME, RIGHT?
"AND I'VE NEVER BEEN INTERESTED IN THIS KIND OF THING...
"...WHY SHOULD I START NOW?"
GOOOOAL!
WHOOOO! GOAL! GOAL! GOOOAL!
THE PENALTY SHOOT-OUT IS SUCH A RUSH!
MAN, THEY COULD HAVE AVOIDED THAT HEADER...

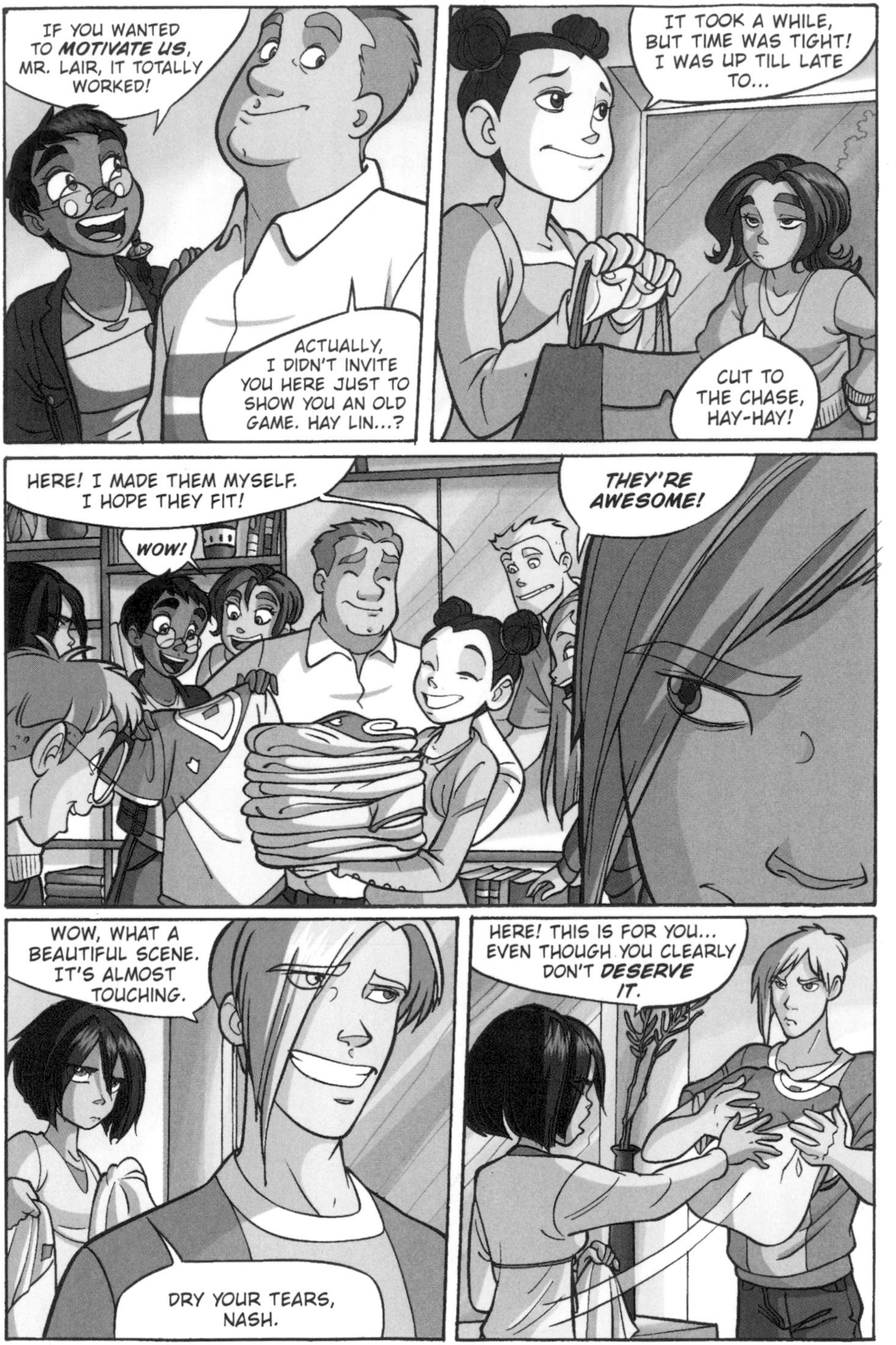

IF YOU WANTED TO **MOTIVATE US**, MR. LAIR, IT TOTALLY WORKED!
ACTUALLY, I DIDN'T INVITE YOU HERE JUST TO SHOW YOU AN OLD GAME. HAY LIN...?
IT TOOK A WHILE, BUT TIME WAS TIGHT! I WAS UP TILL LATE TO...
CUT TO THE CHASE, HAY-HAY!
HERE! I MADE THEM MYSELF. I HOPE THEY FIT!
WOW!
THEY'RE AWESOME!
WOW, WHAT A BEAUTIFUL SCENE. IT'S ALMOST TOUCHING.
DRY YOUR TEARS, NASH.
HERE! THIS IS FOR YOU... EVEN THOUGH YOU CLEARLY DON'T **DESERVE IT**.

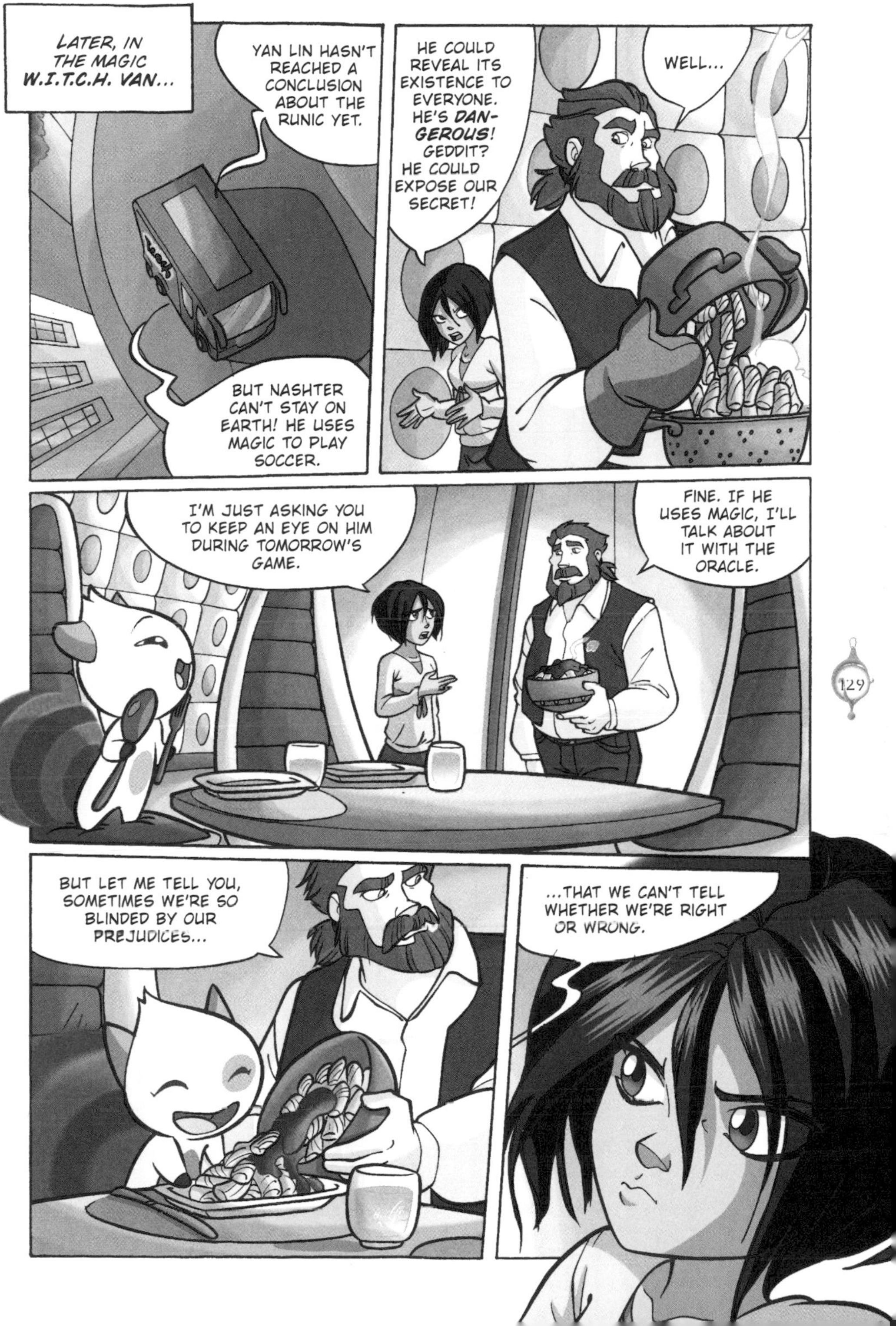

LATER, IN THE MAGIC W.I.T.C.H. VAN...
YAN LIN HASN'T REACHED A CONCLUSION ABOUT THE RUNIC YET.
BUT NASHTER CAN'T STAY ON EARTH! HE USES MAGIC TO PLAY SOCCER.
HE COULD REVEAL ITS EXISTENCE TO EVERYONE. HE'S DANGEROUS! GEDDIT? HE COULD EXPOSE OUR SECRET!
WELL...
I'M JUST ASKING YOU TO KEEP AN EYE ON HIM DURING TOMORROW'S GAME.
FINE. IF HE USES MAGIC, I'LL TALK ABOUT IT WITH THE ORACLE.
BUT LET ME TELL YOU, SOMETIMES WE'RE SO BLINDED BY OUR PREJUDICES...
...THAT WE CAN'T TELL WHETHER WE'RE RIGHT OR WRONG.

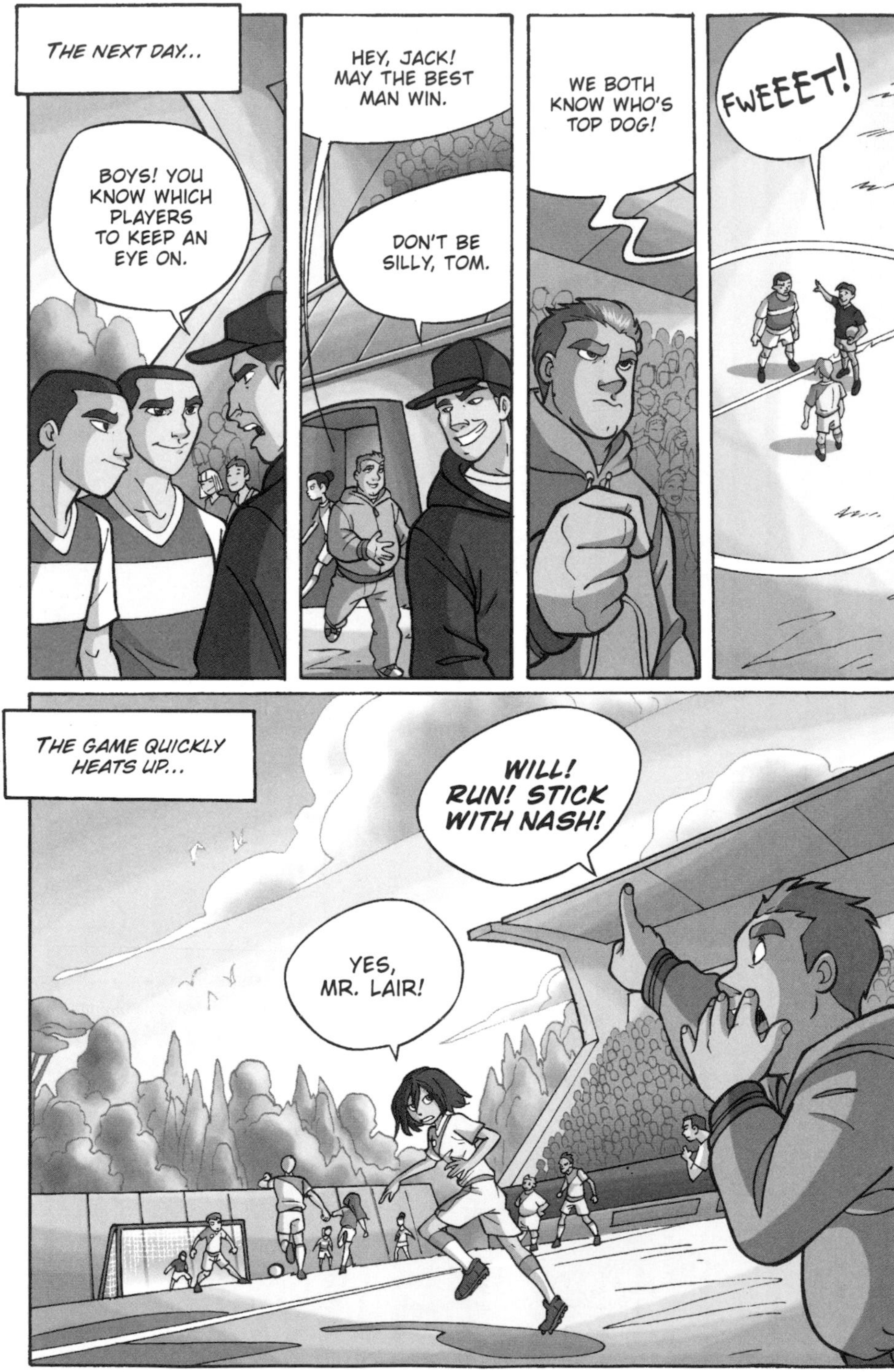
THE NEXT DAY...
BOYS! YOU KNOW WHICH PLAYERS TO KEEP AN EYE ON.
HEY, JACK! MAY THE BEST MAN WIN.
DON'T BE SILLY, TOM.
WE BOTH KNOW WHO'S TOP DOG!
FWEEET!
THE GAME QUICKLY HEATS UP...
WILL! RUN! STICK WITH NASH!
YES, MR. LAIR!

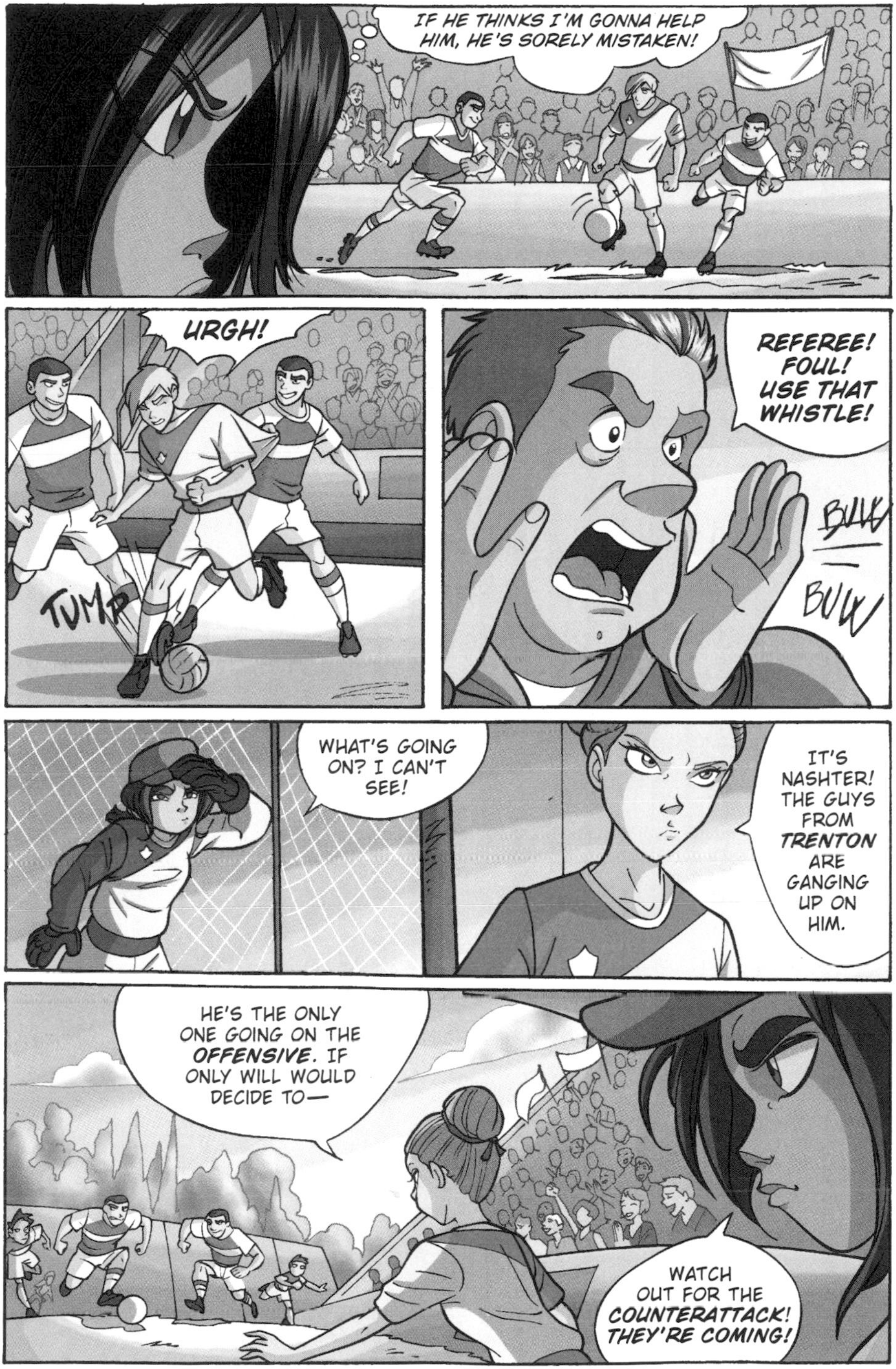
IF HE THINKS I'M GONNA HELP HIM, HE'S SORELY MISTAKEN!
URGH!
TUMP
REFEREE! FOUL! USE THAT WHISTLE!
BUW
BUW
WHAT'S GOING ON? I CAN'T SEE!
IT'S NASHTER! THE GUYS FROM TRENTON ARE GANGING UP ON HIM.
HE'S THE ONLY ONE GOING ON THE OFFENSIVE. IF ONLY WILL WOULD DECIDE TO—
WATCH OUT FOR THE COUNTERATTACK! THEY'RE COMING!

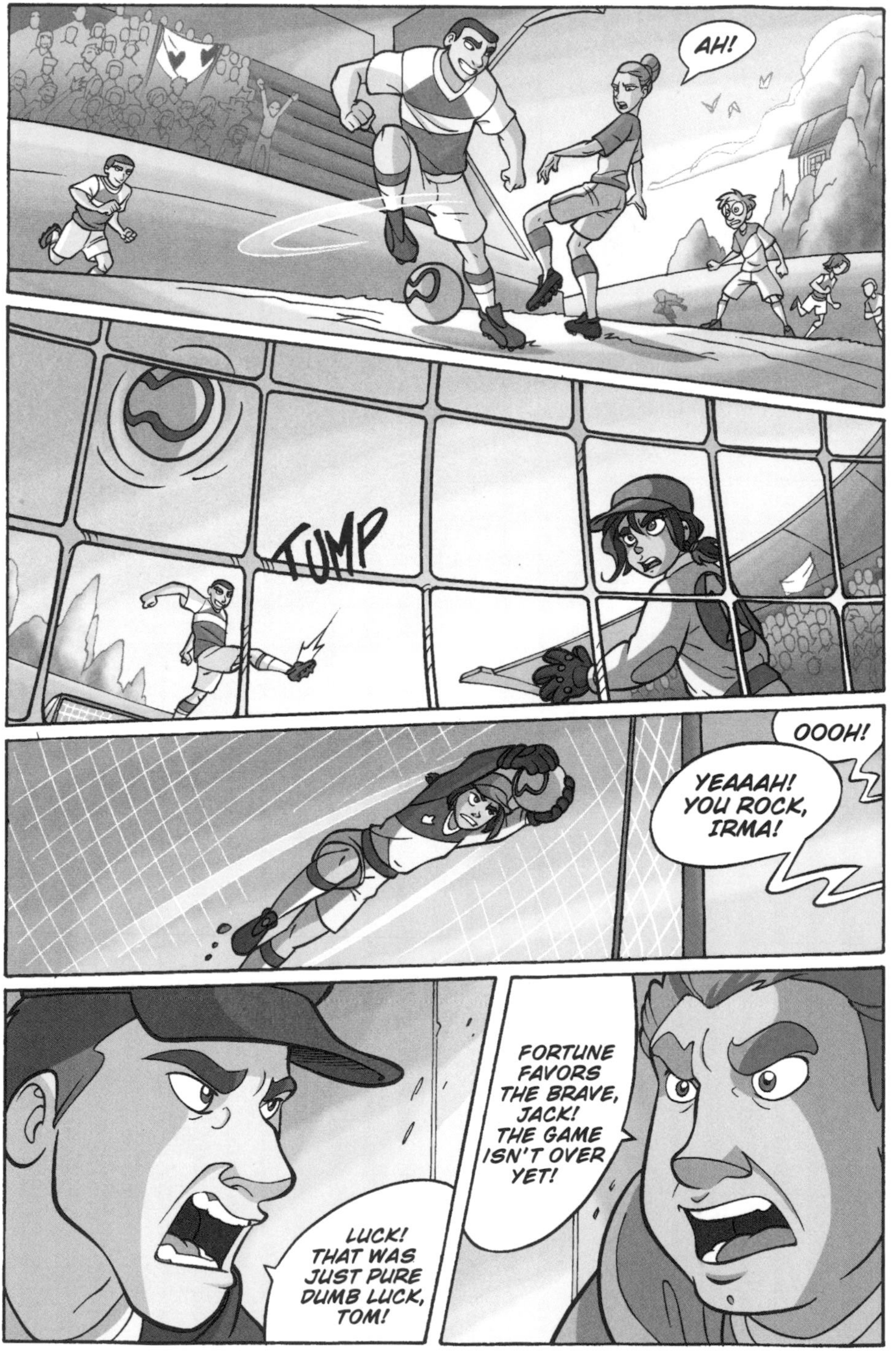
AH!
TUMP
OOOH!
YEAAAH! YOU ROCK, IRMA!
LUCK! THAT WAS JUST PURE DUMB LUCK, TOM!
FORTUNE FAVORS THE BRAVE, JACK! THE GAME ISN'T OVER YET!

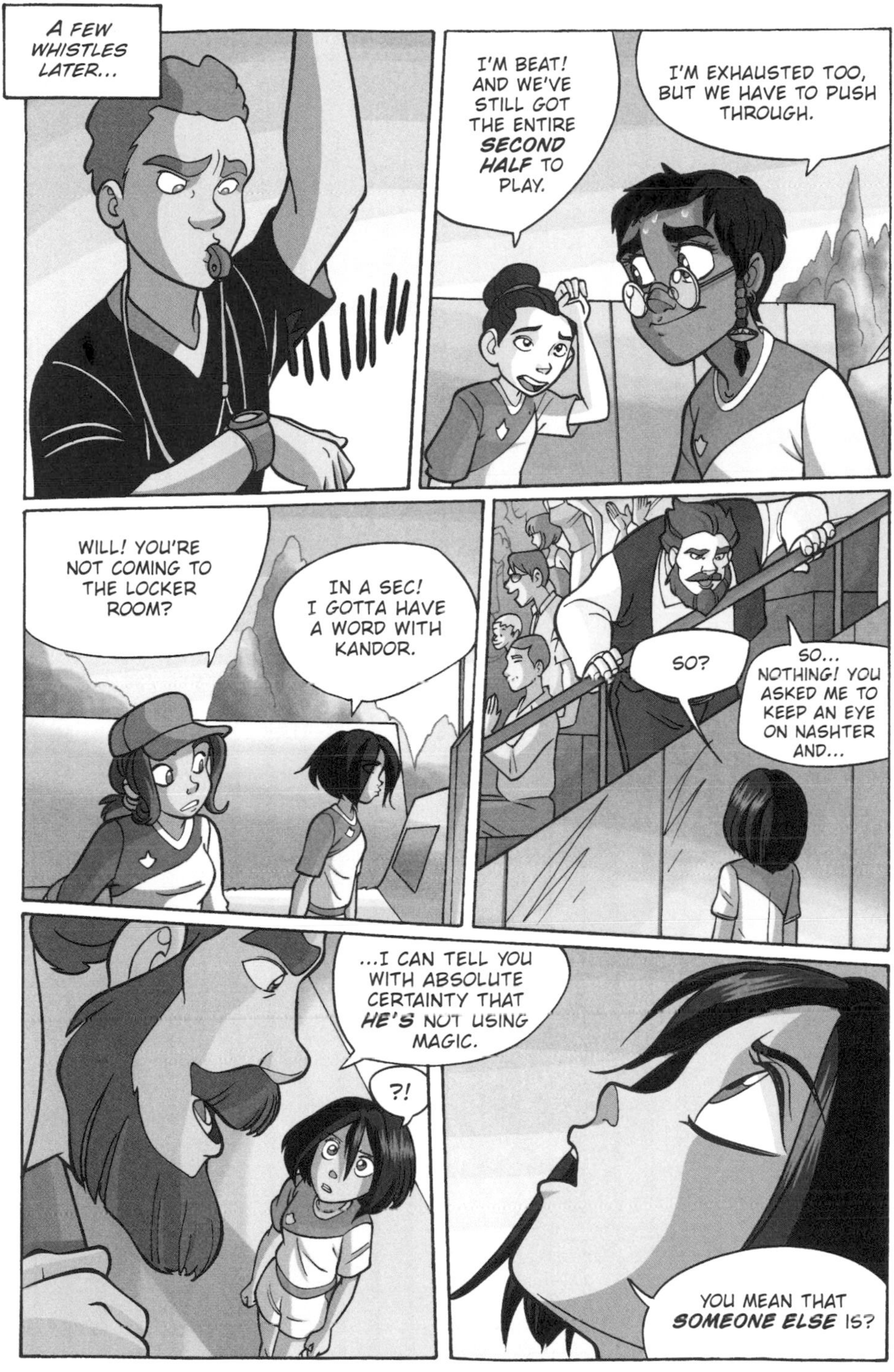
A FEW WHISTLES LATER...
I'M BEAT! AND WE'VE STILL GOT THE ENTIRE SECOND HALF TO PLAY.
I'M EXHAUSTED TOO, BUT WE HAVE TO PUSH THROUGH.
WILL! YOU'RE NOT COMING TO THE LOCKER ROOM?
IN A SEC! I GOTTA HAVE A WORD WITH KANDOR.
SO?
SO... NOTHING! YOU ASKED ME TO KEEP AN EYE ON NASHTER AND...
...I CAN TELL YOU WITH ABSOLUTE CERTAINTY THAT HE'S NOT USING MAGIC.
?!
YOU MEAN THAT SOMEONE ELSE IS?

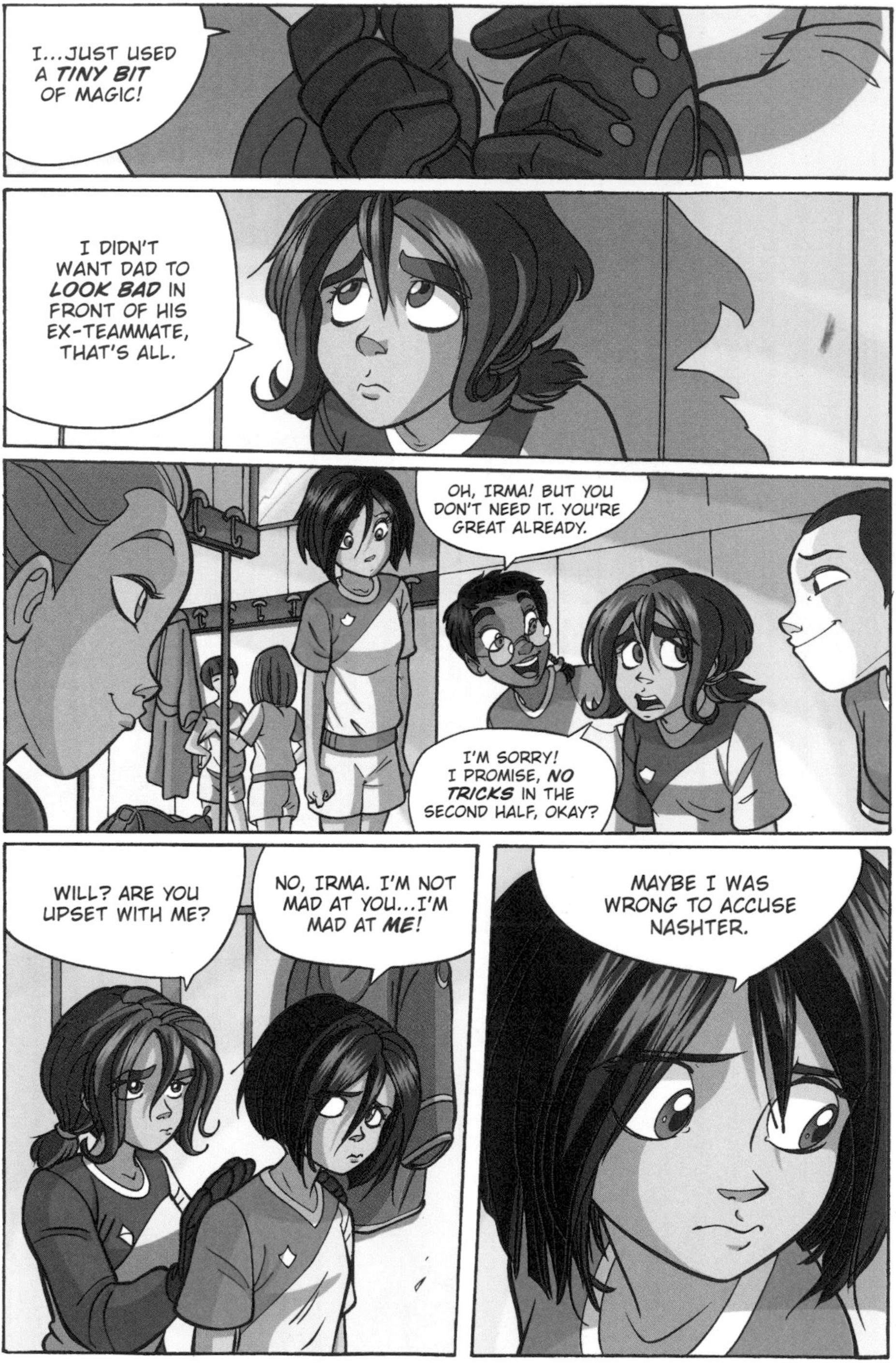
I...JUST USED A TINY BIT OF MAGIC!
I DIDN'T WANT DAD TO LOOK BAD IN FRONT OF HIS EX-TEAMMATE, THAT'S ALL.
OH, IRMA! BUT YOU DON'T NEED IT. YOU'RE GREAT ALREADY.
I'M SORRY! I PROMISE, NO TRICKS IN THE SECOND HALF, OKAY?
WILL? ARE YOU UPSET WITH ME?
NO, IRMA. I'M NOT MAD AT YOU...I'M MAD AT ME!
MAYBE I WAS WRONG TO ACCUSE NASHTER.

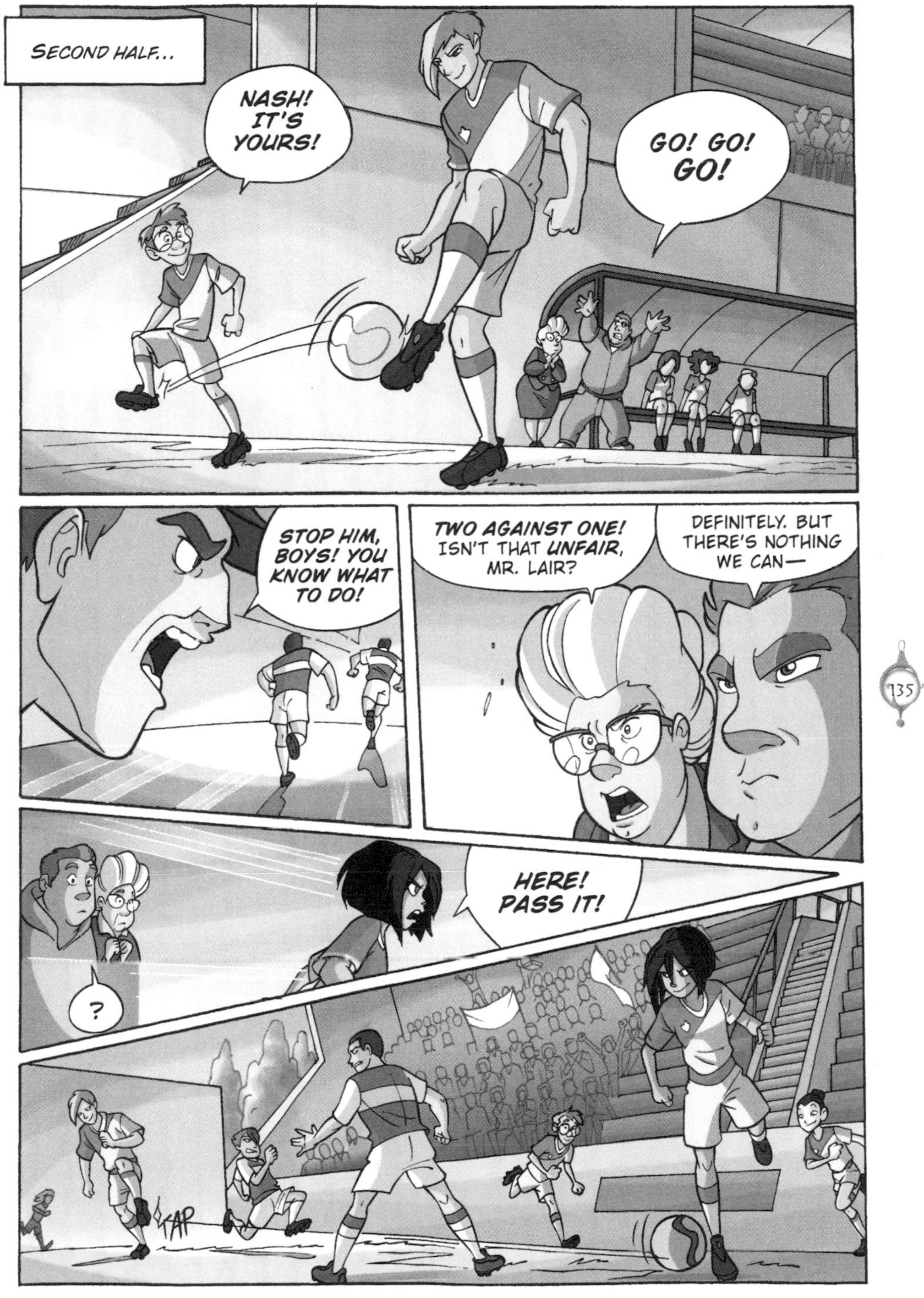
SECOND HALF...
NASH! IT'S YOURS!
GO! GO! GO!
STOP HIM, BOYS! YOU KNOW WHAT TO DO!
TWO AGAINST ONE! ISN'T THAT UNFAIR, MR. LAIR?
DEFINITELY. BUT THERE'S NOTHING WE CAN—
?
HERE! PASS IT!
TAP

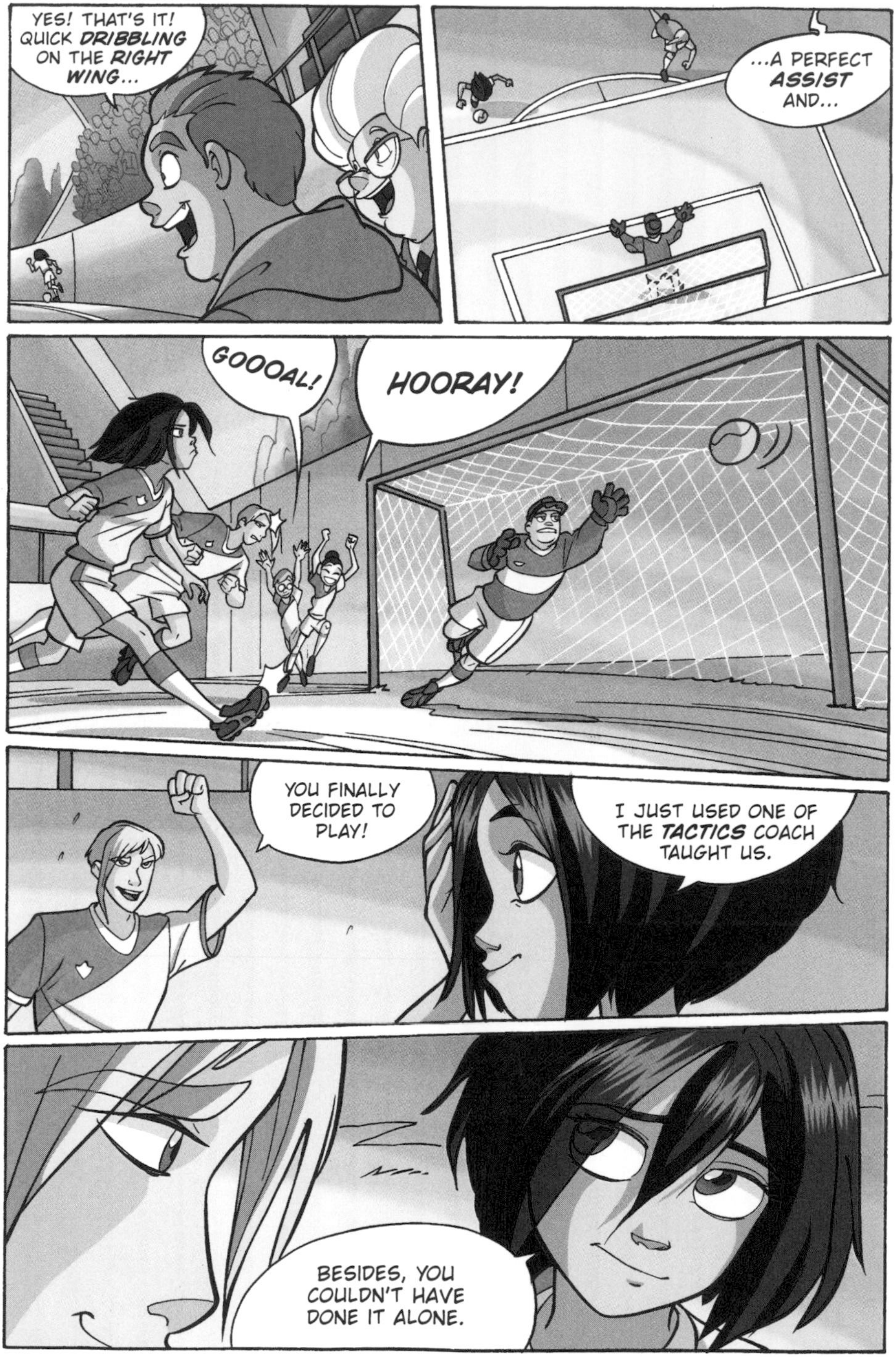
YES! THAT'S IT! QUICK DRIBBLING ON THE RIGHT WING...
...A PERFECT ASSIST AND...
GOOOAL!
HOORAY!
YOU FINALLY DECIDED TO PLAY!
I JUST USED ONE OF THE TACTICS COACH TAUGHT US.
BESIDES, YOU COULDN'T HAVE DONE IT ALONE.

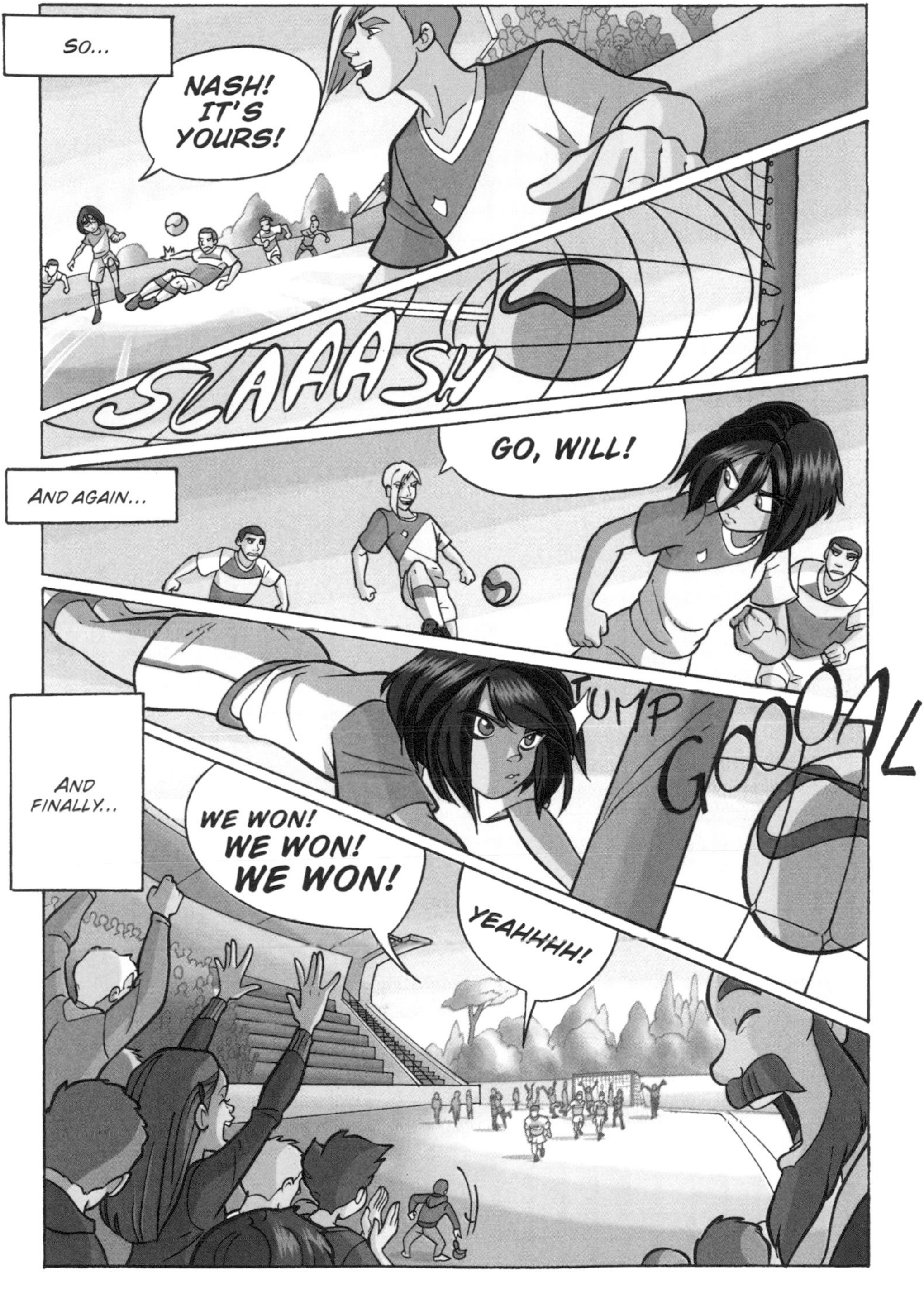
SO...
NASH! IT'S YOURS!
SLAAASH
AND AGAIN...
GO, WILL!
TUMP
GOOOAL
AND FINALLY...
WE WON! WE WON! WE WON!
YEAHHHH!

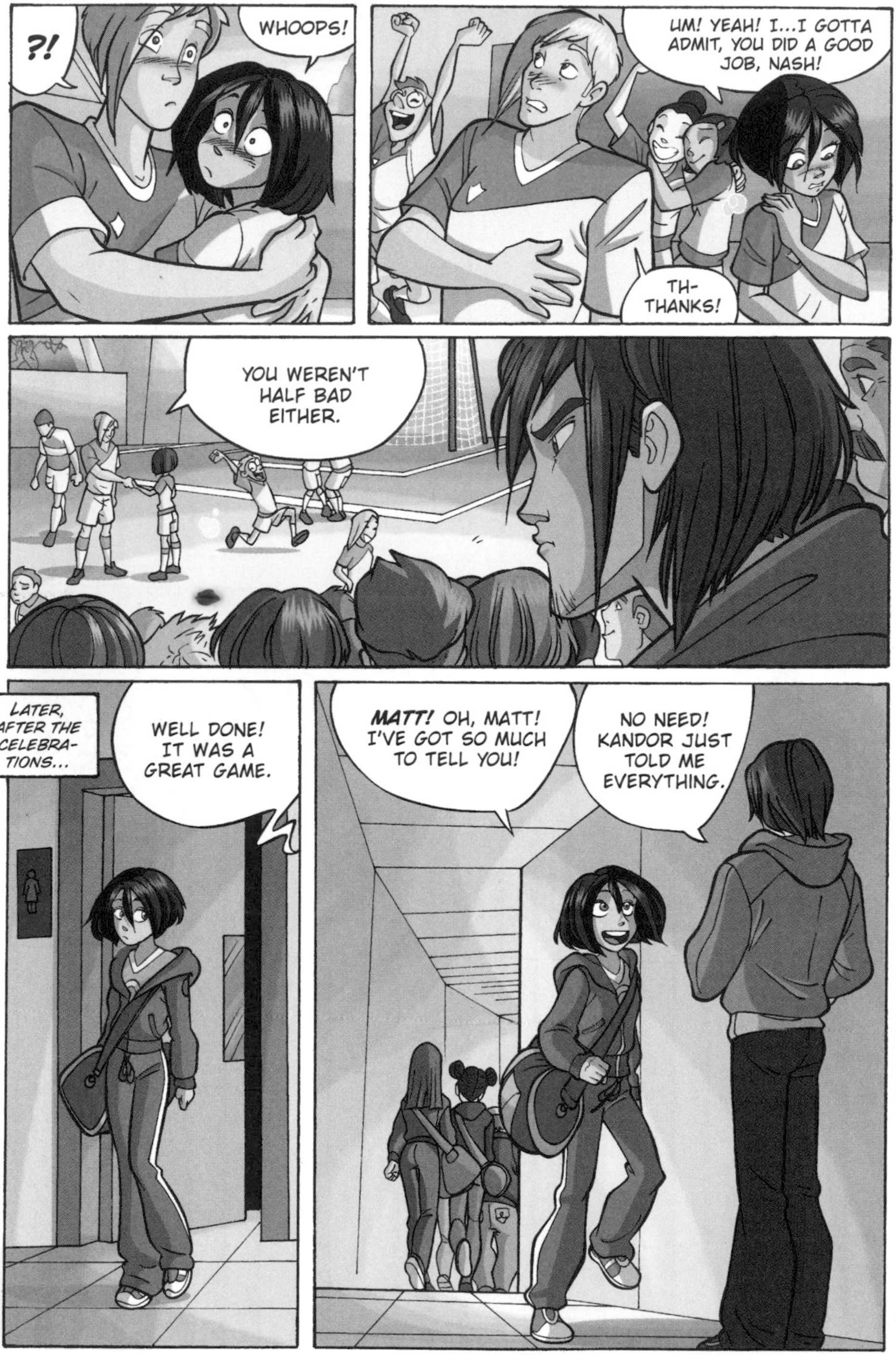
?!
WHOOPS!
UM! YEAH! I...I GOTTA ADMIT, YOU DID A GOOD JOB, NASH!
TH- THANKS!
YOU WEREN'T HALF BAD EITHER.
LATER, AFTER THE CELEBRATIONS...
WELL DONE! IT WAS A GREAT GAME.
MATT! OH, MATT! I'VE GOT SO MUCH TO TELL YOU!
NO NEED! KANDOR JUST TOLD ME EVERYTHING.

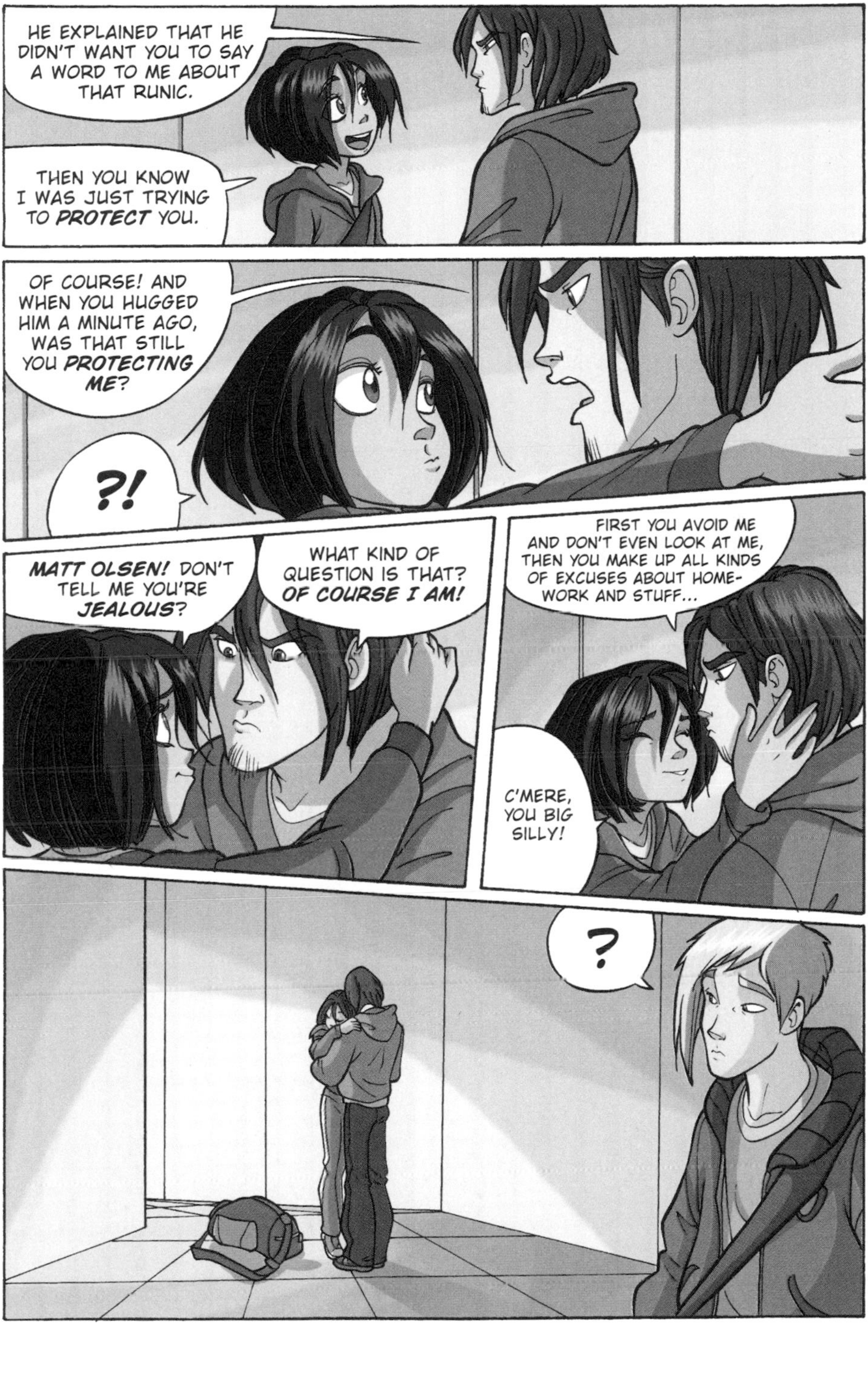
HE EXPLAINED THAT HE DIDN'T WANT YOU TO SAY A WORD TO ME ABOUT THAT RUNIC.
THEN YOU KNOW I WAS JUST TRYING TO PROTECT YOU.
OF COURSE! AND WHEN YOU HUGGED HIM A MINUTE AGO, WAS THAT STILL YOU PROTECTING ME?
?!
MATT OLSEN! DON'T TELL ME YOU'RE JEALOUS?
WHAT KIND OF QUESTION IS THAT? OF COURSE I AM!
FIRST YOU AVOID ME AND DON'T EVEN LOOK AT ME, THEN YOU MAKE UP ALL KINDS OF EXCUSES ABOUT HOME-WORK AND STUFF...
C'MERE, YOU BIG SILLY!
?

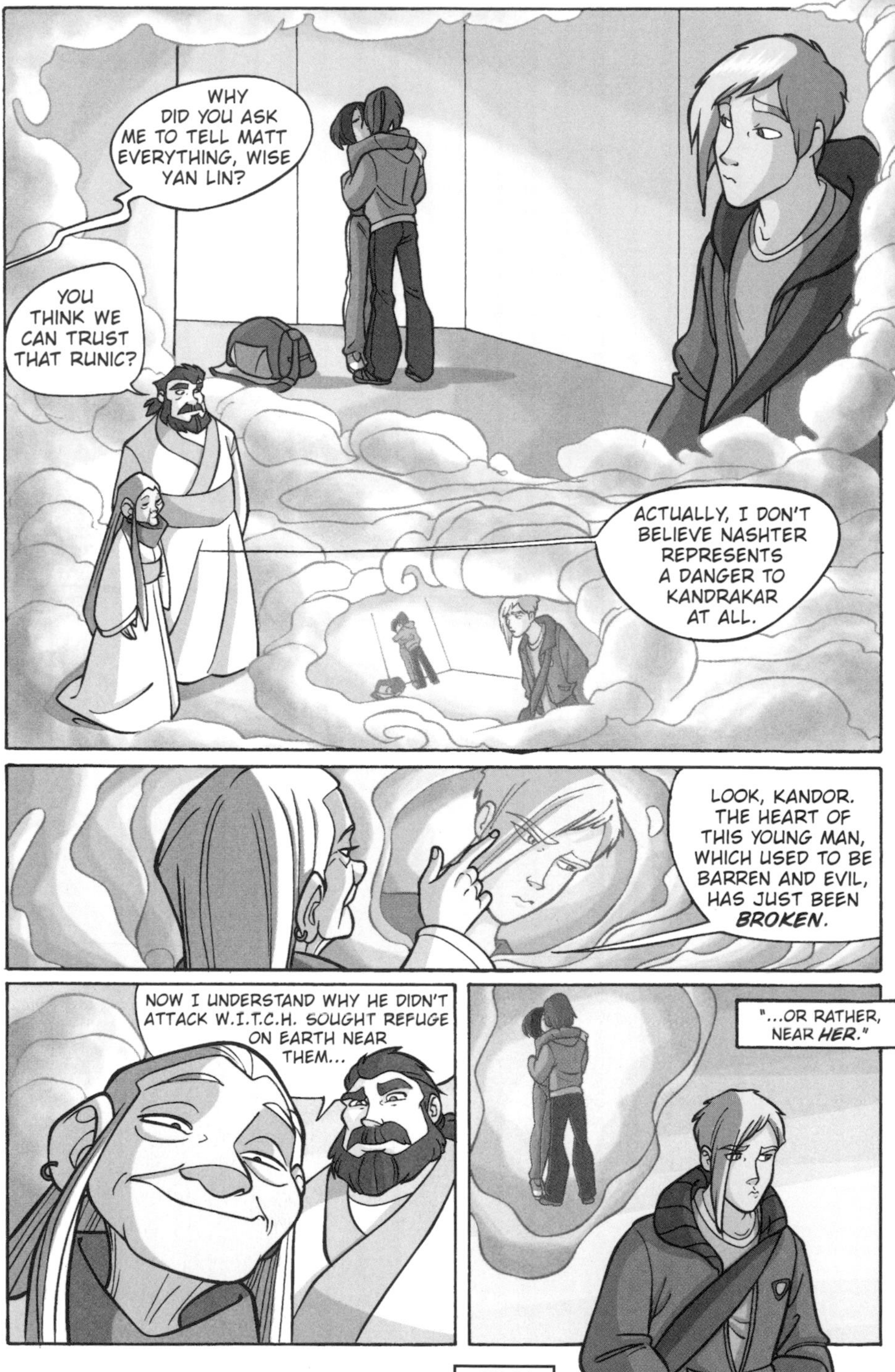
WHY DID YOU ASK ME TO TELL MATT EVERYTHING, WISE YAN LIN?
YOU THINK WE CAN TRUST THAT RUNIC?
ACTUALLY, I DON'T BELIEVE NASHTER REPRESENTS A DANGER TO KANDRAKAR AT ALL.
LOOK, KANDOR. THE HEART OF THIS YOUNG MAN, WHICH USED TO BE BARREN AND EVIL, HAS JUST BEEN **BROKEN**.
NOW I UNDERSTAND WHY HE DIDN'T ATTACK W.I.T.C.H. SOUGHT REFUGE ON EARTH NEAR THEM...
"...OR RATHER, NEAR *HER*."
END OF CHAPTER 111

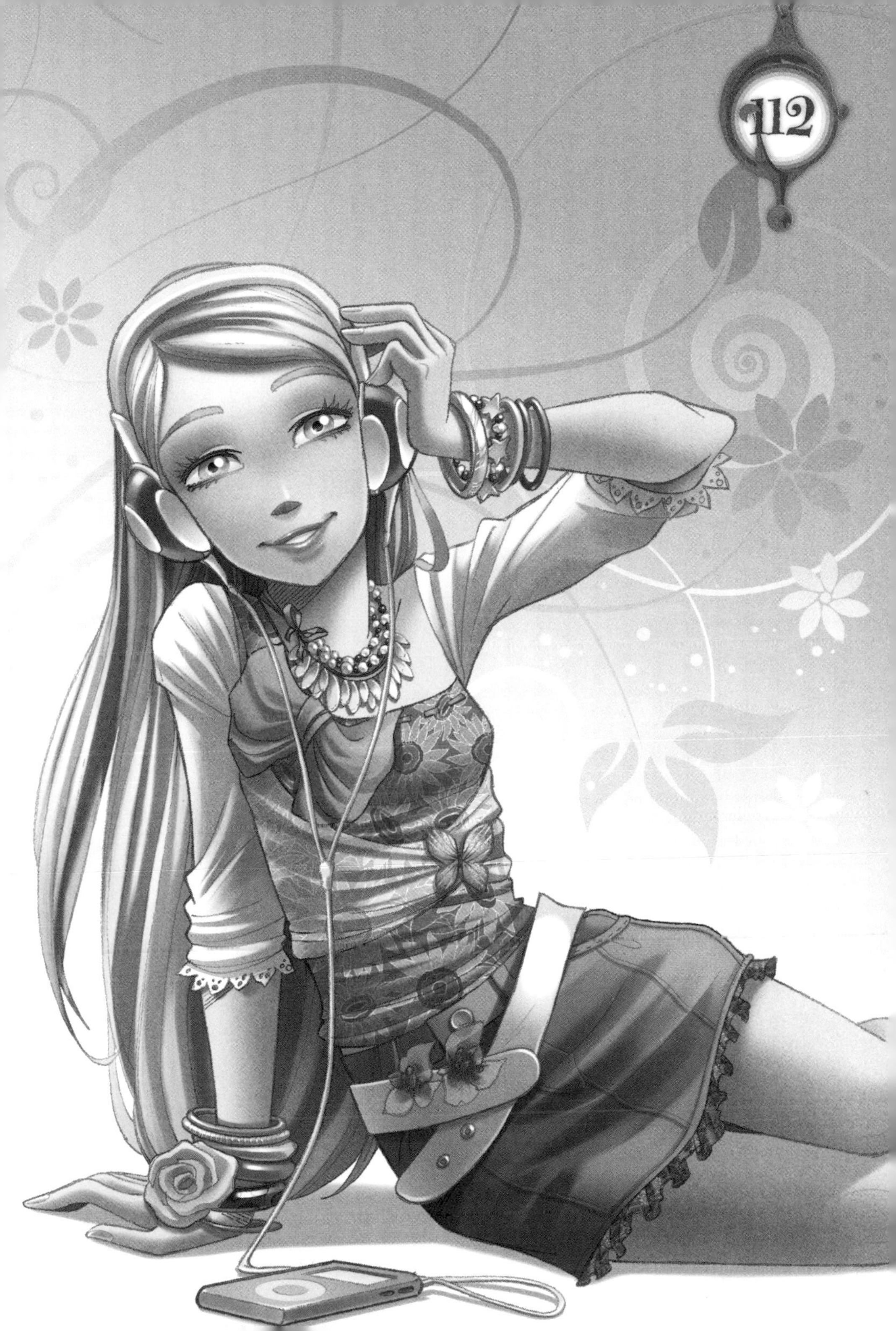

W.i.t.c.h.

Will Irma Taranee Cornelia Hay Lin

First Days

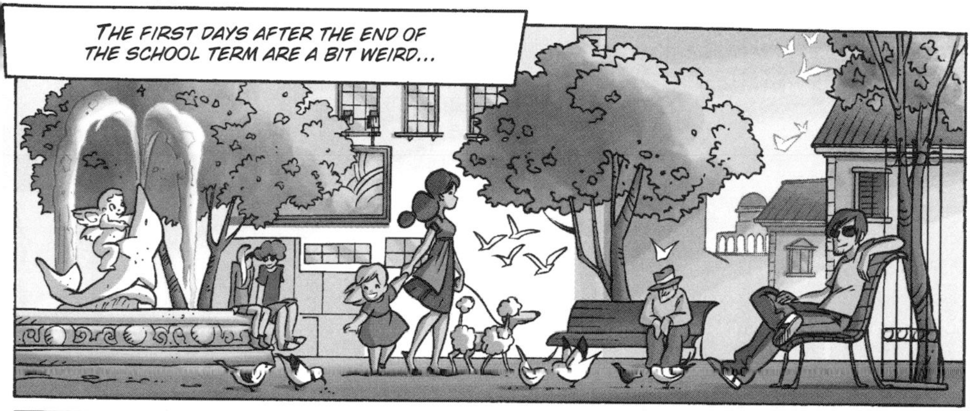
THE FIRST DAYS AFTER THE END OF THE SCHOOL TERM ARE A BIT WEIRD...

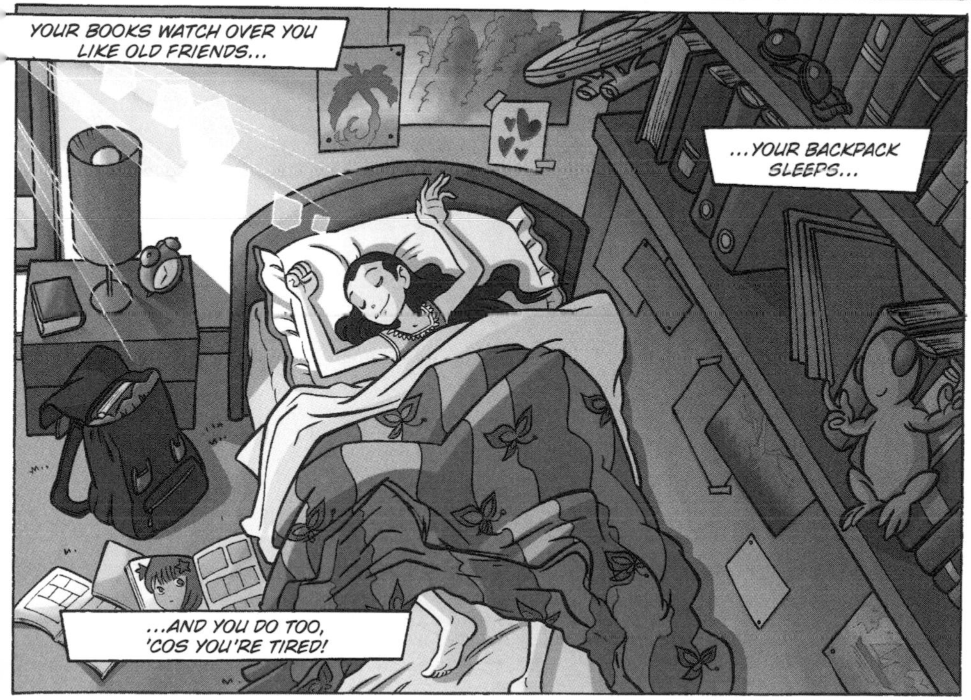
YOUR BOOKS WATCH OVER YOU LIKE OLD FRIENDS...
...YOUR BACKPACK SLEEPS...
...AND YOU DO TOO, 'COS YOU'RE TIRED!

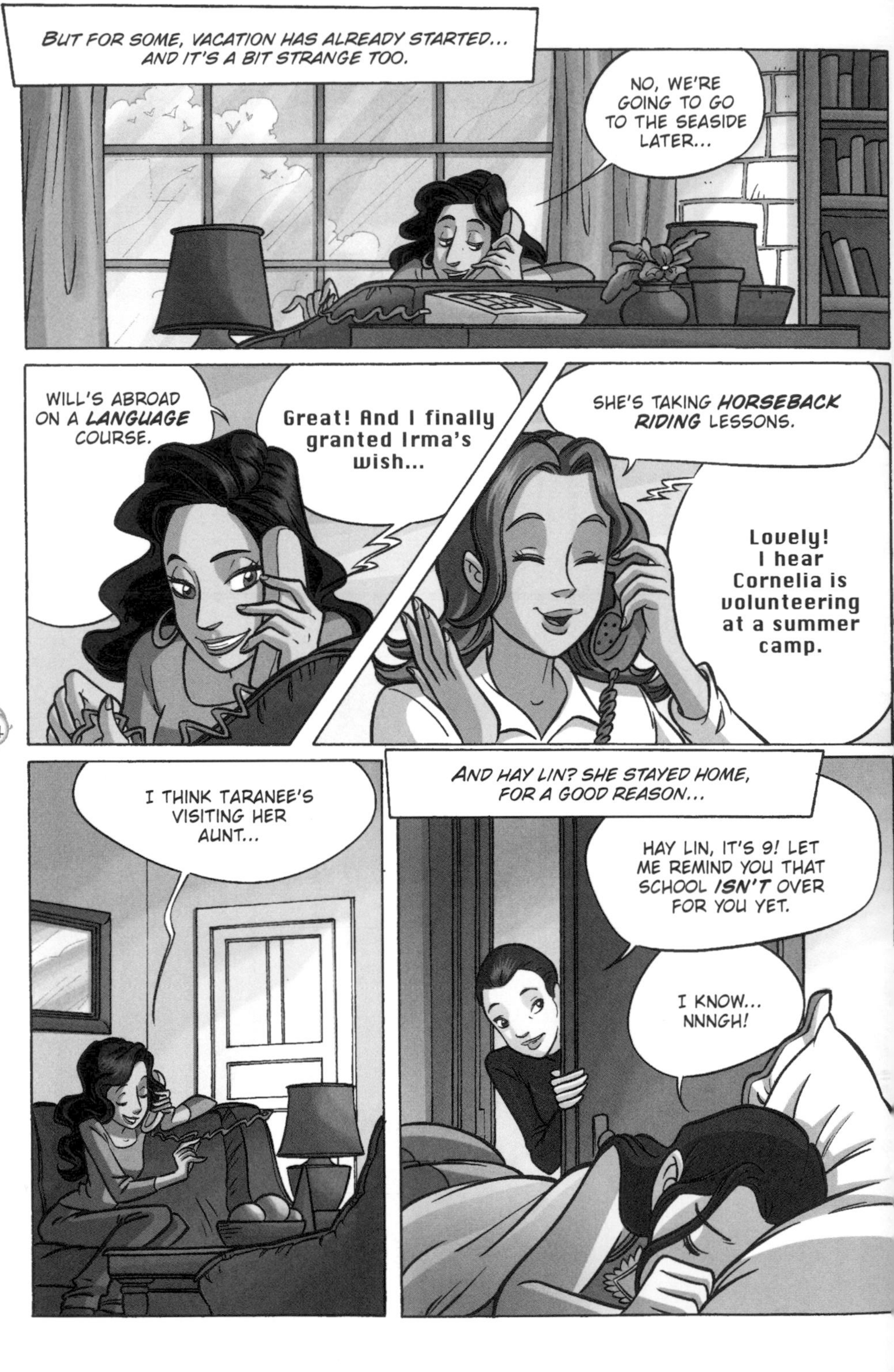
BUT FOR SOME, VACATION HAS ALREADY STARTED... AND IT'S A BIT STRANGE TOO.
NO, WE'RE GOING TO GO TO THE SEASIDE LATER...
WILL'S ABROAD ON A LANGUAGE COURSE.
Great! And I finally granted Irma's wish...
SHE'S TAKING HORSEBACK RIDING LESSONS.
Lovely! I hear Cornelia is volunteering at a summer camp.
I THINK TARANEE'S VISITING HER AUNT...
AND HAY LIN? SHE STAYED HOME, FOR A GOOD REASON...
HAY LIN, IT'S 9! LET ME REMIND YOU THAT SCHOOL ISN'T OVER FOR YOU YET.
I KNOW... NNNGH!

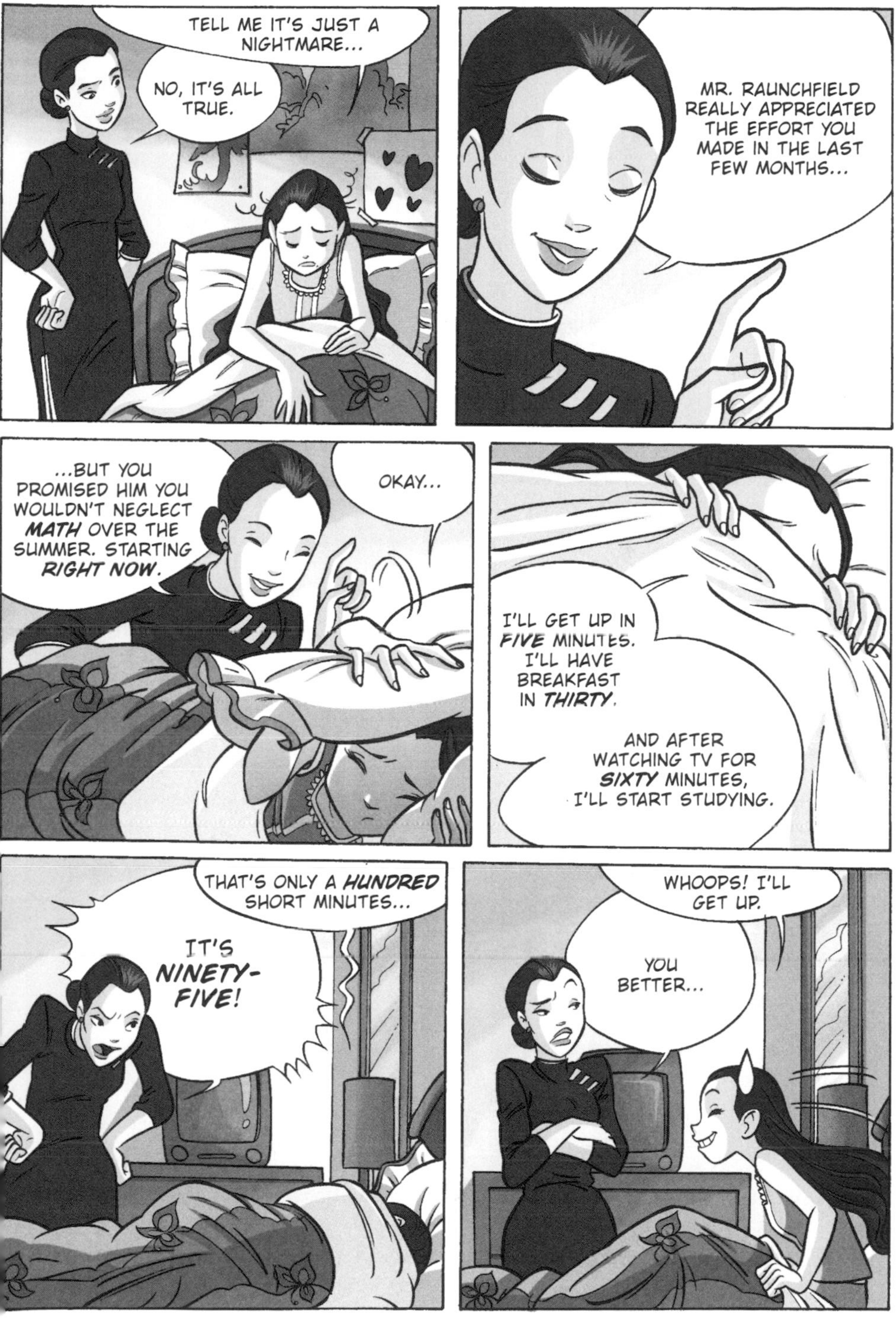
TELL ME IT'S JUST A NIGHTMARE...
NO, IT'S ALL TRUE.
MR. RAUNCHFIELD REALLY APPRECIATED THE EFFORT YOU MADE IN THE LAST FEW MONTHS...
...BUT YOU PROMISED HIM YOU WOULDN'T NEGLECT MATH OVER THE SUMMER. STARTING RIGHT NOW.
OKAY...
I'LL GET UP IN FIVE MINUTES. I'LL HAVE BREAKFAST IN THIRTY.
AND AFTER WATCHING TV FOR SIXTY MINUTES, I'LL START STUDYING.
THAT'S ONLY A HUNDRED SHORT MINUTES...
IT'S NINETY-FIVE!
WHOOPS! I'LL GET UP.
YOU BETTER...

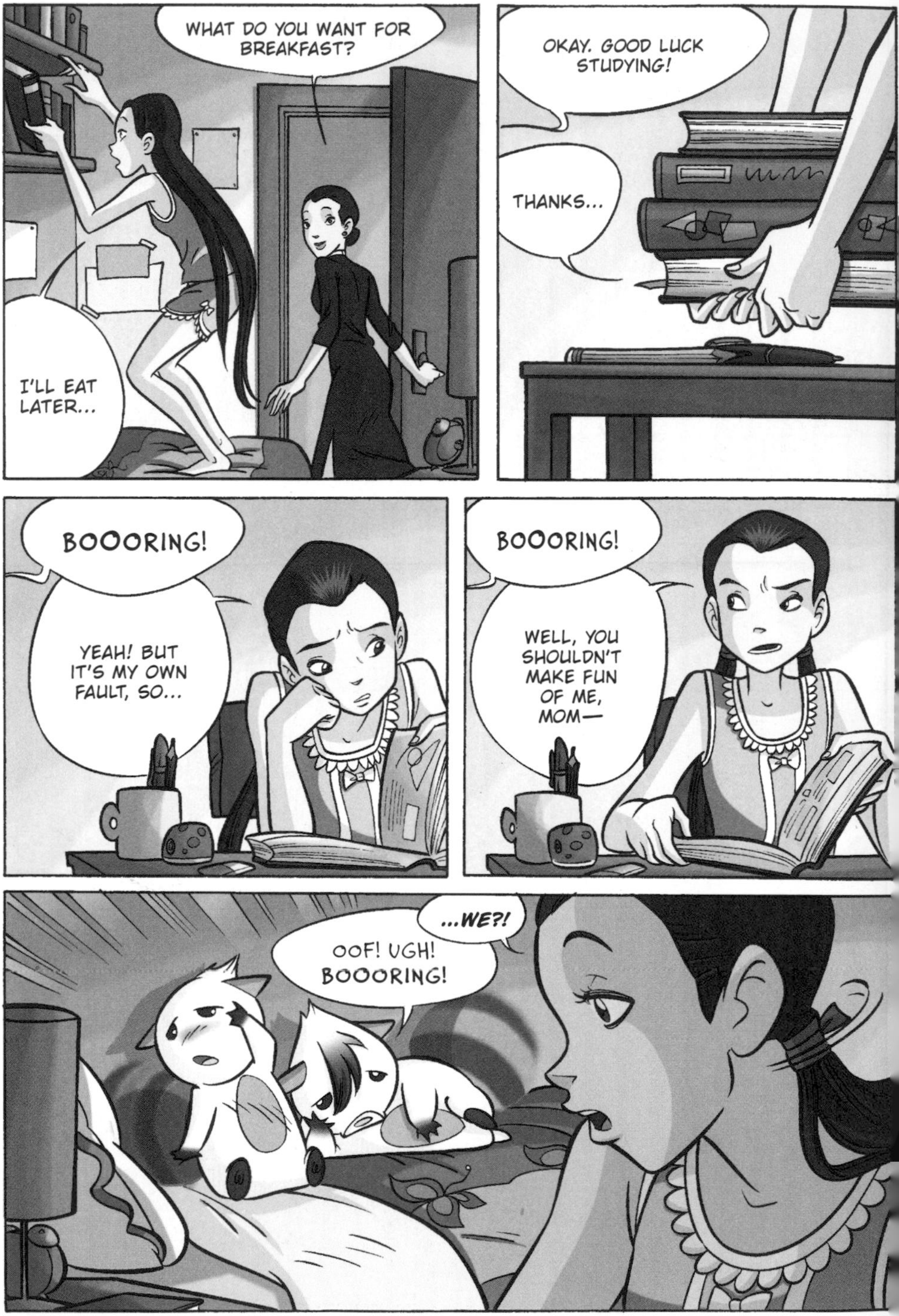
WHAT DO YOU WANT FOR BREAKFAST?
I'LL EAT LATER...
OKAY. GOOD LUCK STUDYING!
THANKS...
BOOORING!
YEAH! BUT IT'S MY OWN FAULT, SO...
BOOORING!
WELL, YOU SHOULDN'T MAKE FUN OF ME, MOM—
OOF! UGH! BOOORING!
...WE?!

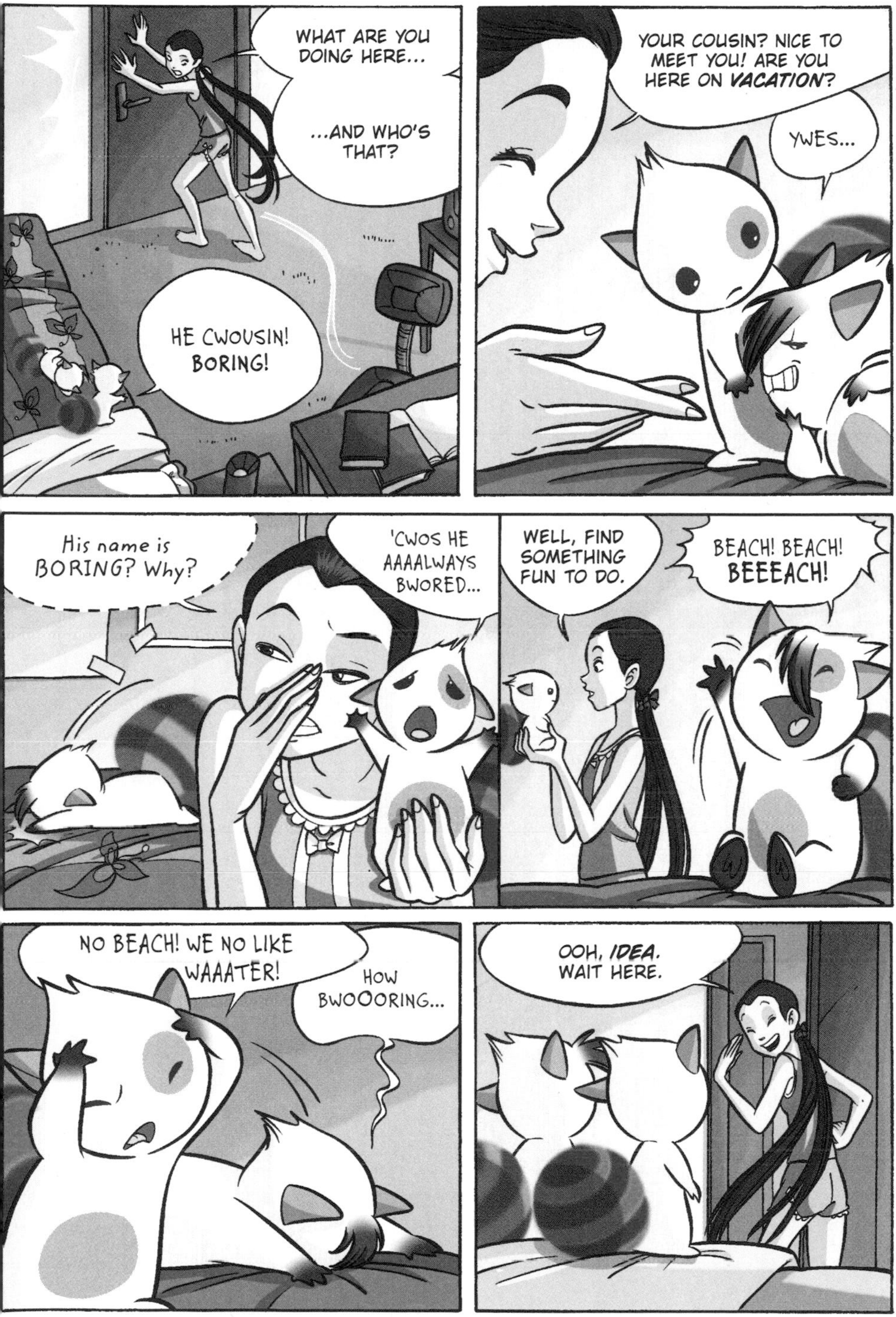
WHAT ARE YOU DOING HERE...
...AND WHO'S THAT?
HE CWOUSIN! BORING!
YOUR COUSIN? NICE TO MEET YOU! ARE YOU HERE ON *VACATION*?
YWES...
His name is BORING? Why?
'CWOS HE AAAALWAYS BWORED...
WELL, FIND SOMETHING FUN TO DO.
BEACH! BEACH! BEEEACH!
NO BEACH! WE NO LIKE WAAATER!
HOW BWOOORING...
OOH, *IDEA*. WAIT HERE.

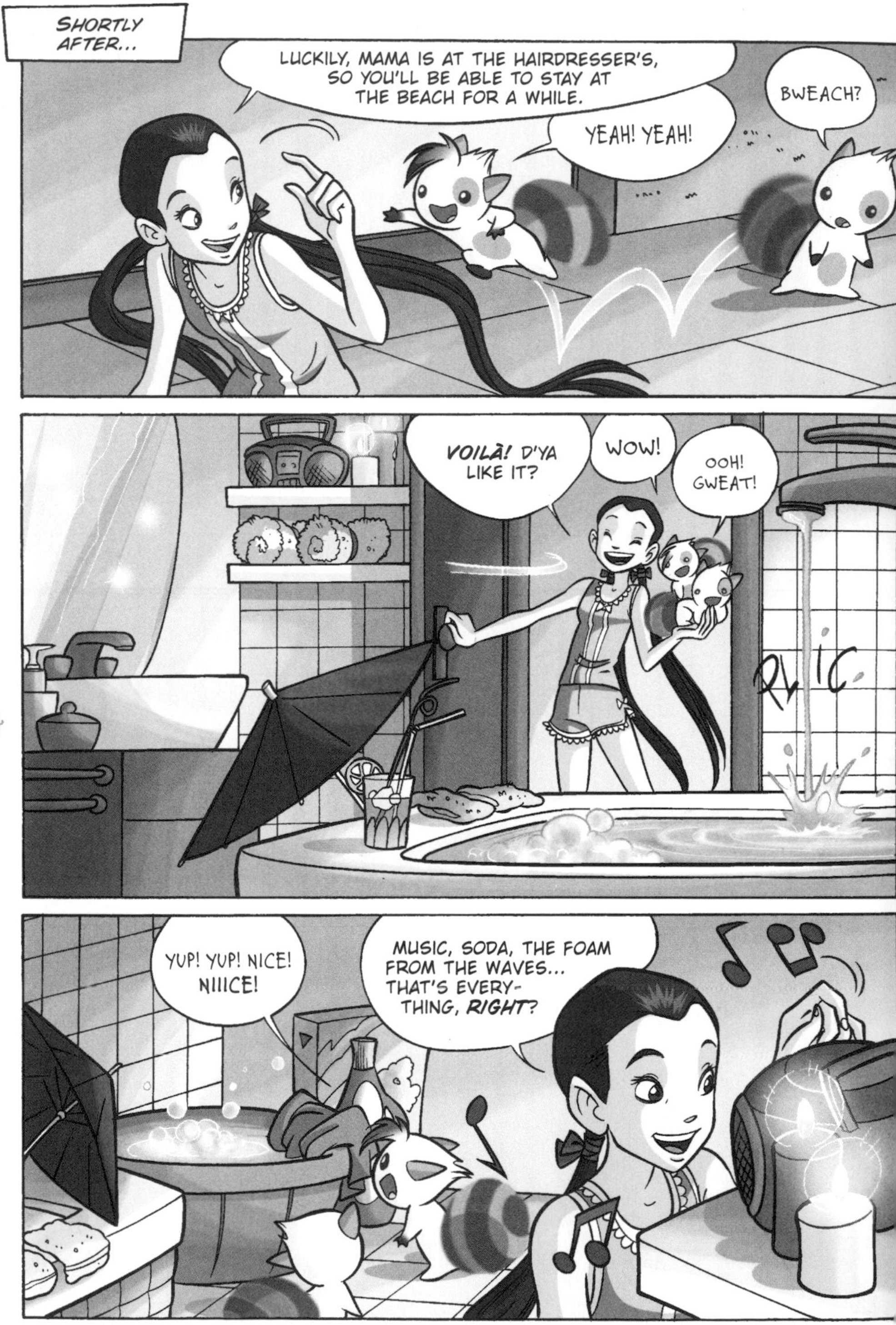
SHORTLY AFTER...
LUCKILY, MAMA IS AT THE HAIRDRESSER'S, SO YOU'LL BE ABLE TO STAY AT THE BEACH FOR A WHILE.
YEAH! YEAH!
BWEACH?
VOILÀ! D'YA LIKE IT?
WOW!
OOH! GWEAT!
YUP! YUP! NICE! NIIICE!
MUSIC, SODA, THE FOAM FROM THE WAVES... THAT'S EVERY-THING, RIGHT?

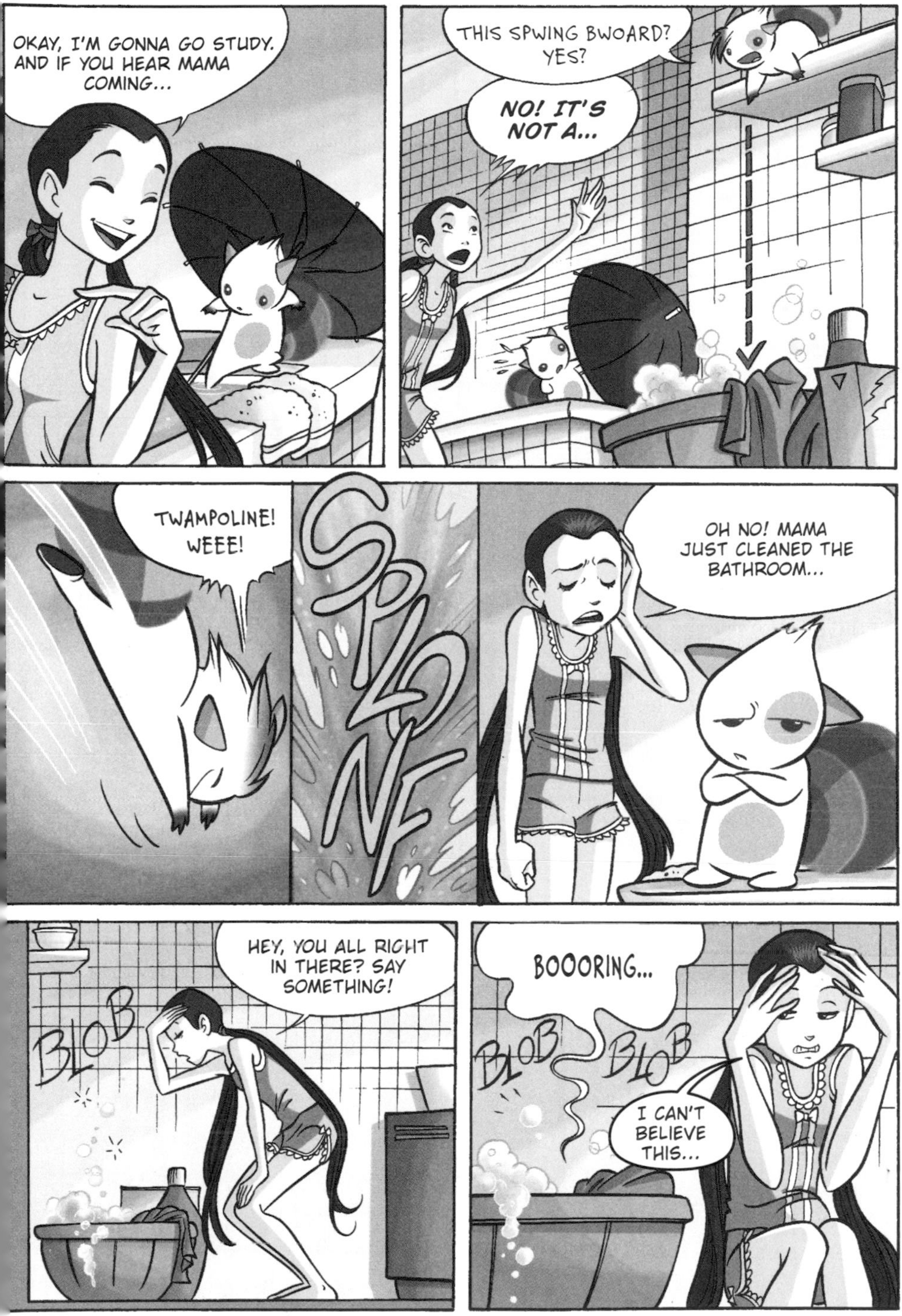
OKAY, I'M GONNA GO STUDY. AND IF YOU HEAR MAMA COMING...
THIS SPWING BWOARD? YES?
NO! IT'S NOT A...
TWAMPOLINE! WEEE!
SPLOOF
OH NO! MAMA JUST CLEANED THE BATHROOM...
BLOB
HEY, YOU ALL RIGHT IN THERE? SAY SOMETHING!
BOOORING...
BLOB BLOB
I CAN'T BELIEVE THIS...

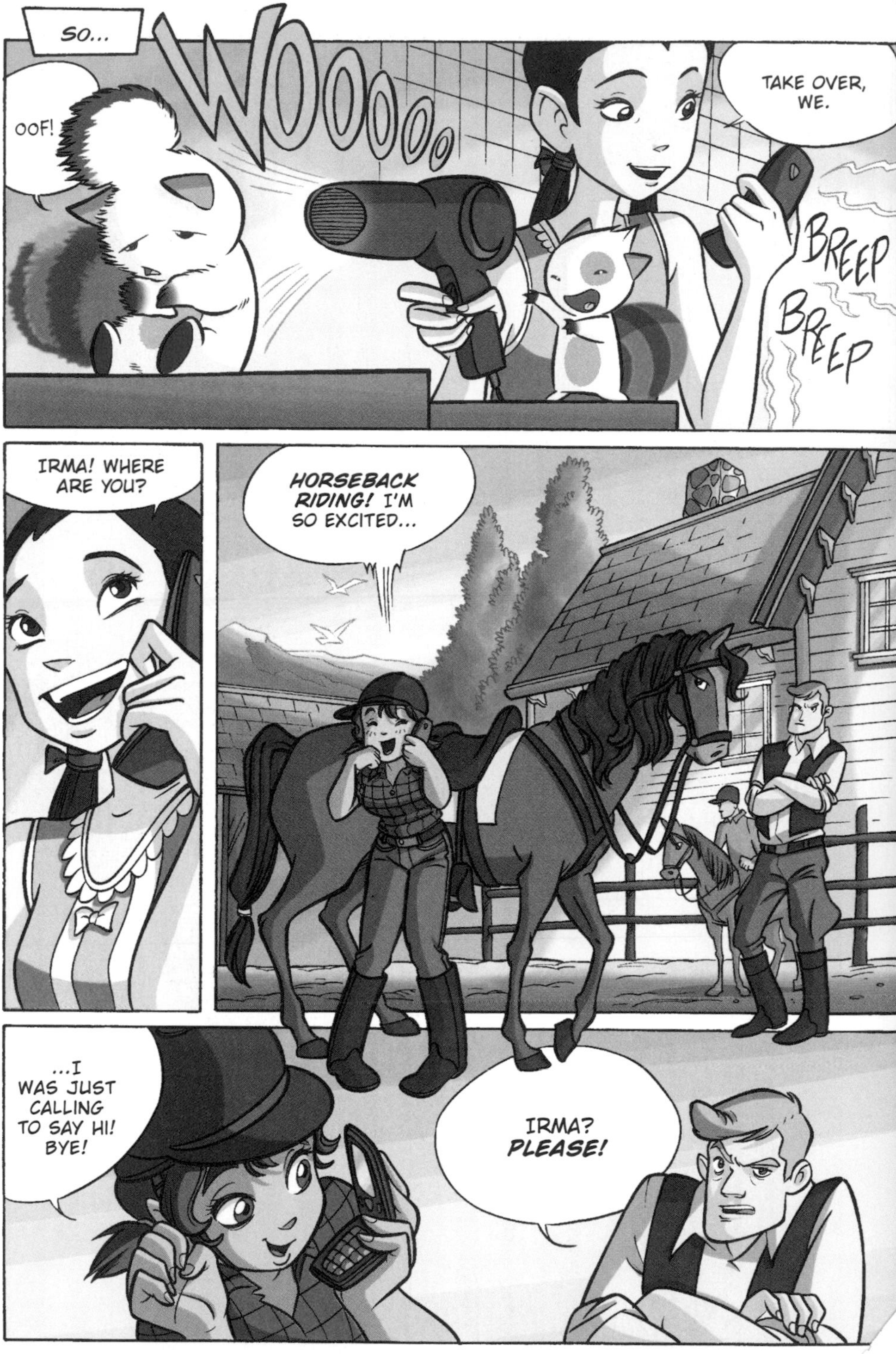

SO...
OOF!
WOOOOOo
TAKE OVER, WE.
BREEP BREEP
IRMA! WHERE ARE YOU?
HORSEBACK RIDING! I'M SO EXCITED...
...I WAS JUST CALLING TO SAY HI! BYE!
IRMA? ***PLEASE!***

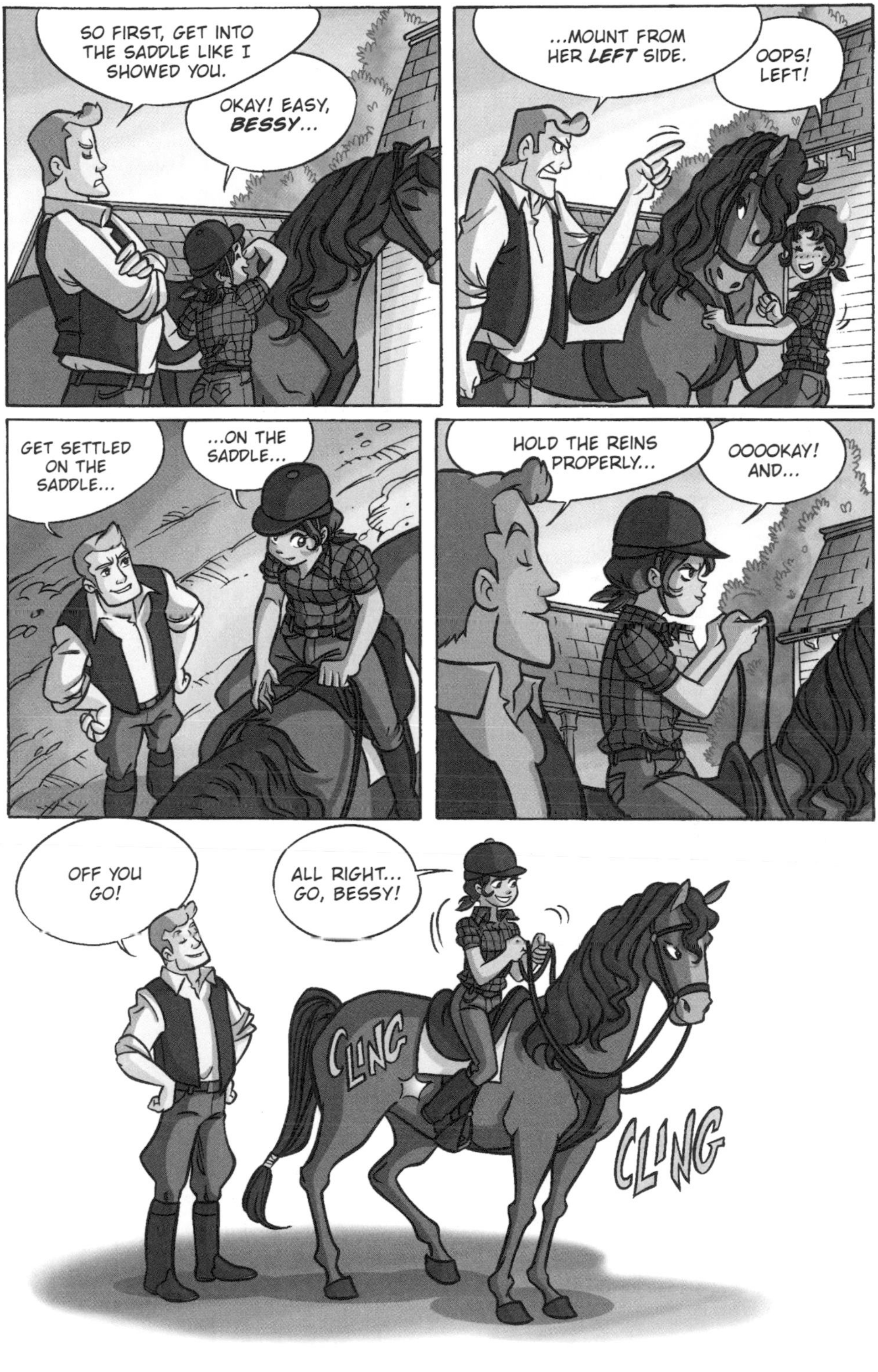
SO FIRST, GET INTO THE SADDLE LIKE I SHOWED YOU.
OKAY! EASY, BESSY...
...MOUNT FROM HER LEFT SIDE.
OOPS! LEFT!
GET SETTLED ON THE SADDLE...
...ON THE SADDLE...
HOLD THE REINS PROPERLY...
OOOOKAY! AND...
OFF YOU GO!
ALL RIGHT... GO, BESSY!
CLING
CLING

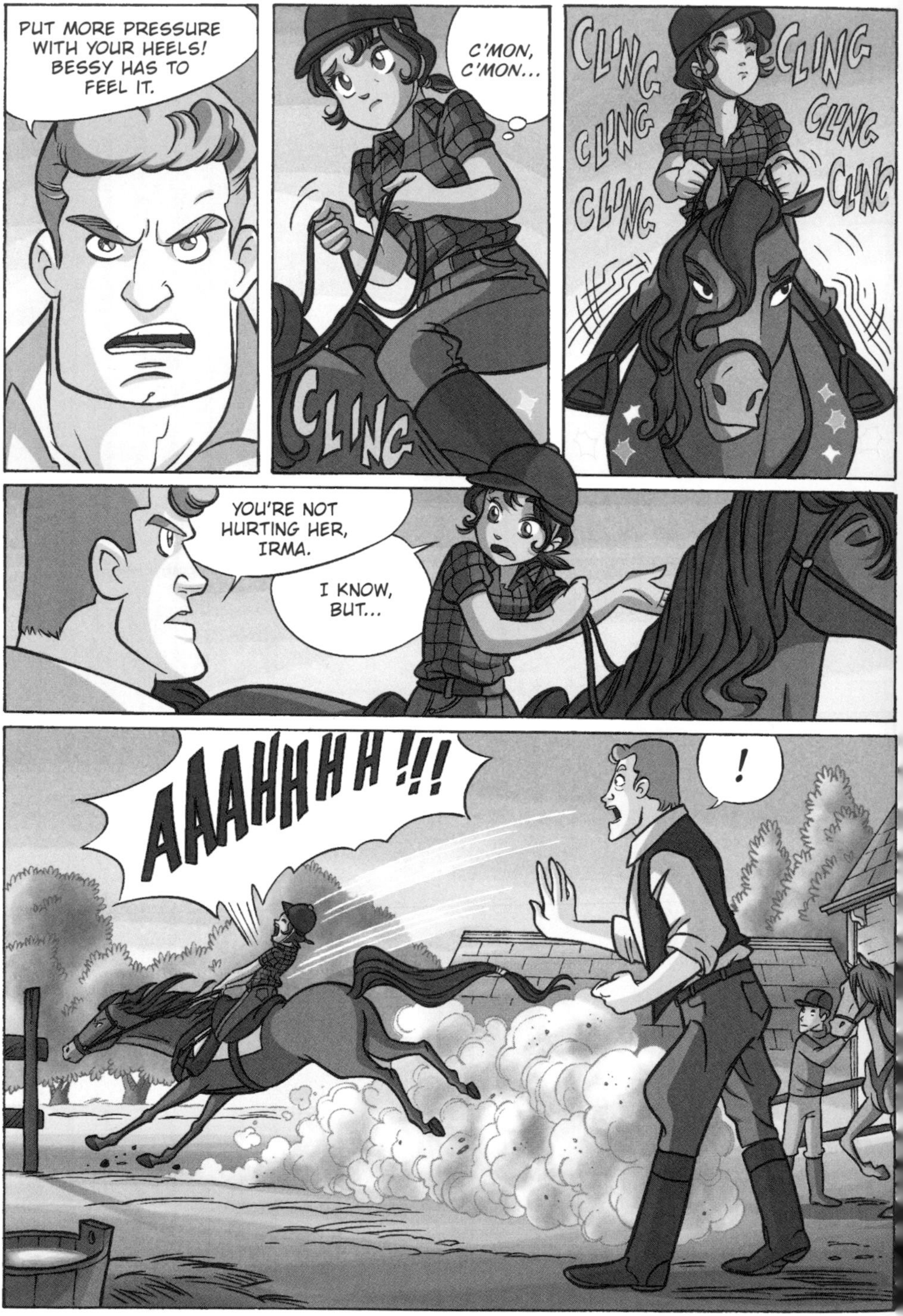
PUT MORE PRESSURE WITH YOUR HEELS! BESSY HAS TO FEEL IT.
C'MON, C'MON...
CLINC
CLING
CLING
CLING
CLING
CLING
CLINC
YOU'RE NOT HURTING HER, IRMA.
I KNOW, BUT...
AAAHHHH!!!
!

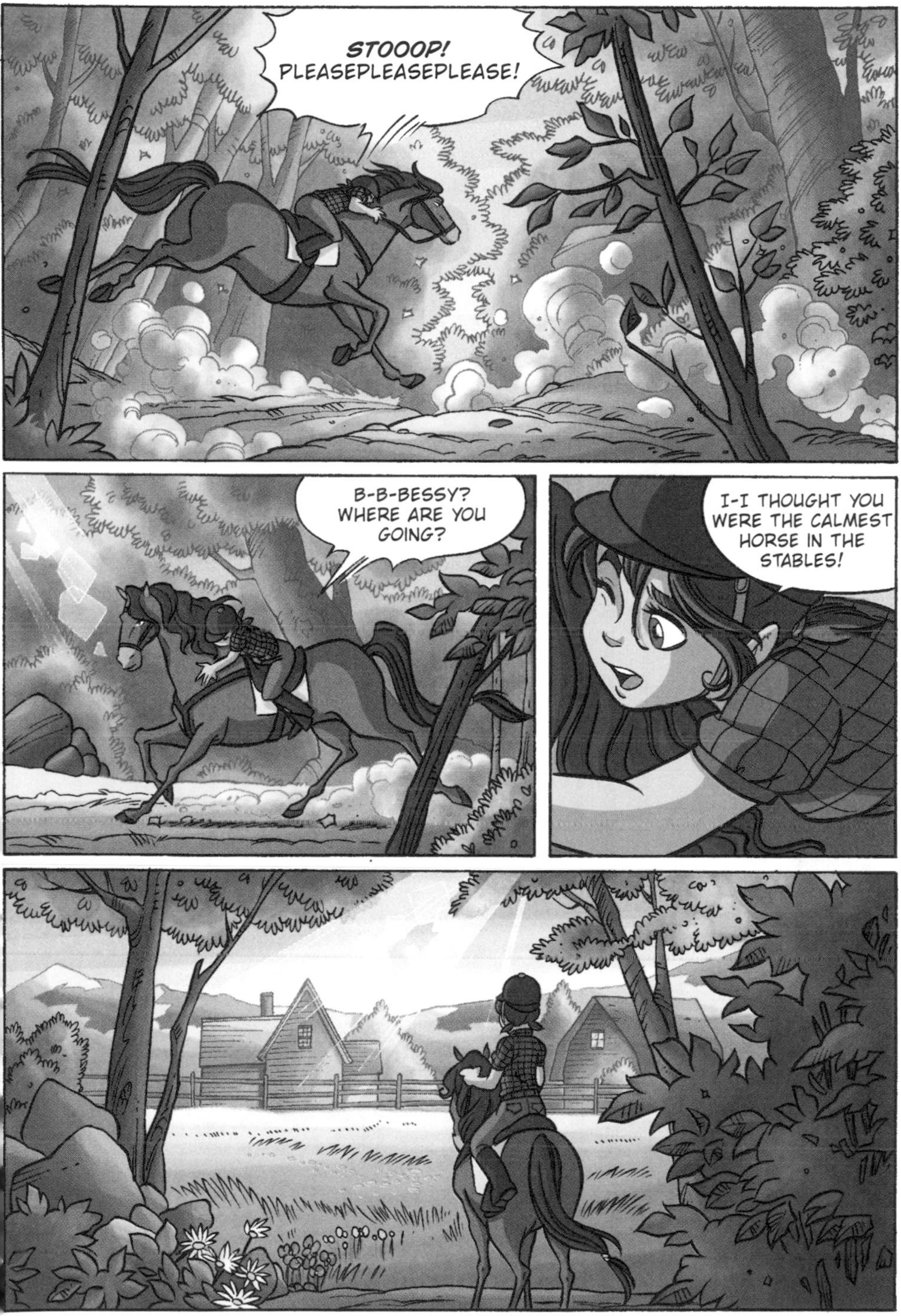
STOOOP!
PLEASEPLEASEPLEASE!
B-B-BESSY? WHERE ARE YOU GOING?
I-I THOUGHT YOU WERE THE CALMEST HORSE IN THE STABLES!

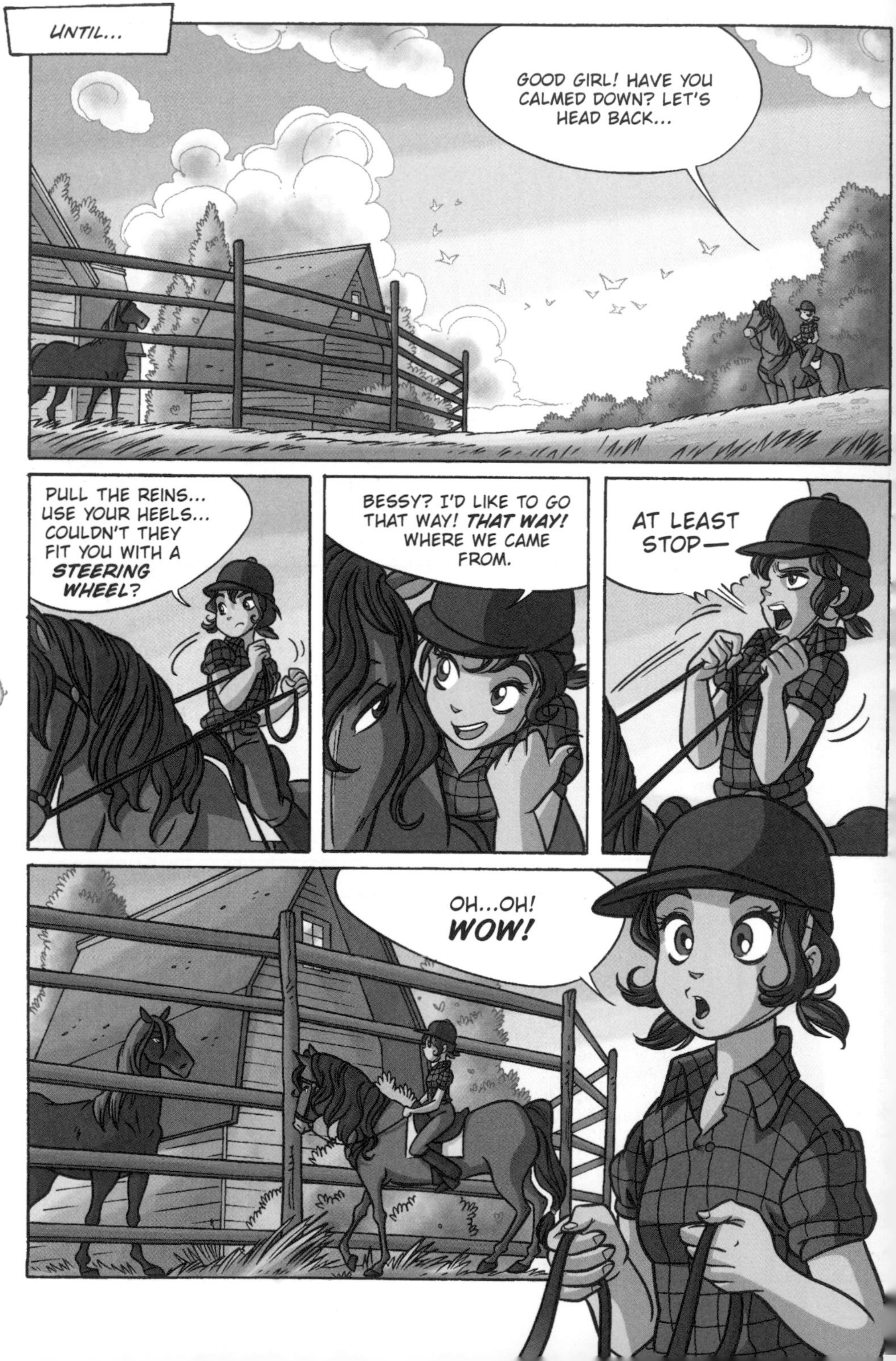

UNTIL...
GOOD GIRL! HAVE YOU CALMED DOWN? LET'S HEAD BACK...
PULL THE REINS... USE YOUR HEELS... COULDN'T THEY FIT YOU WITH A STEERING WHEEL?
BESSY? I'D LIKE TO GO THAT WAY! THAT WAY! WHERE WE CAME FROM.
AT LEAST STOP—
OH...OH! WOW!

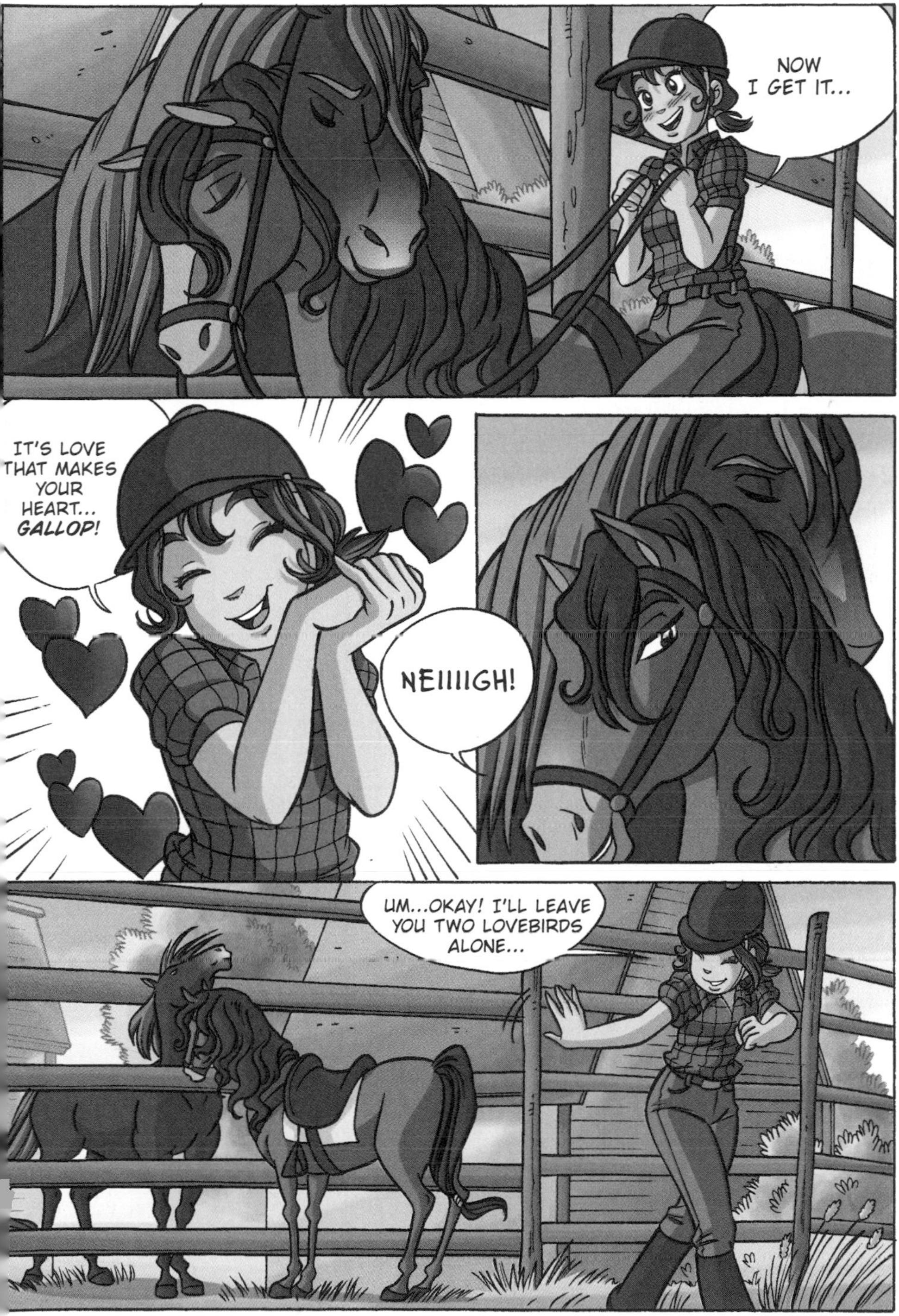
NOW I GET IT...
IT'S LOVE THAT MAKES YOUR HEART... *GALLOP*!
NEIIIIGH!
UM...OKAY! I'LL LEAVE YOU TWO LOVEBIRDS ALONE...

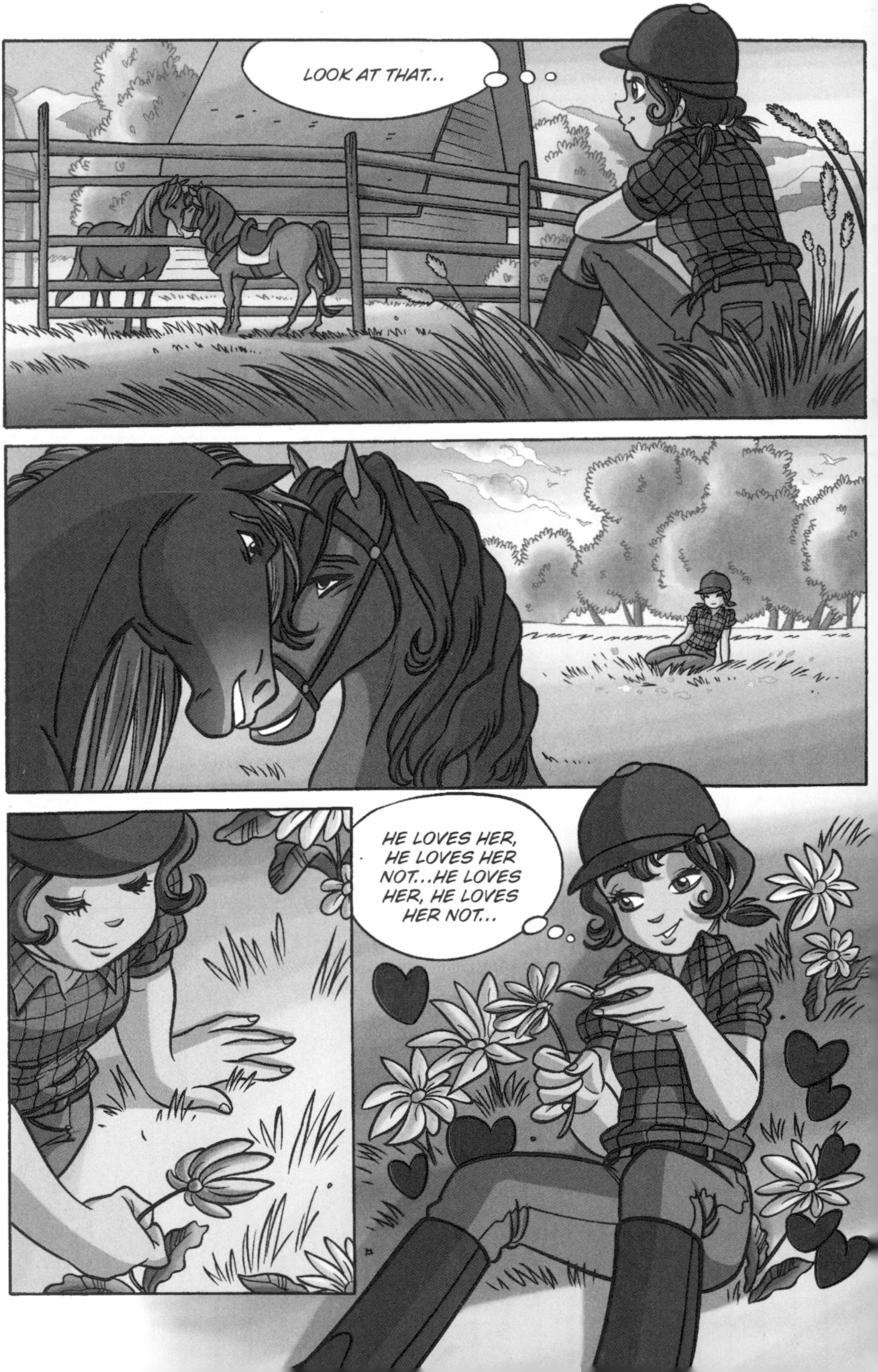
LOOK AT THAT...
HE LOVES HER, HE LOVES HER NOT...HE LOVES HER, HE LOVES HER NOT...

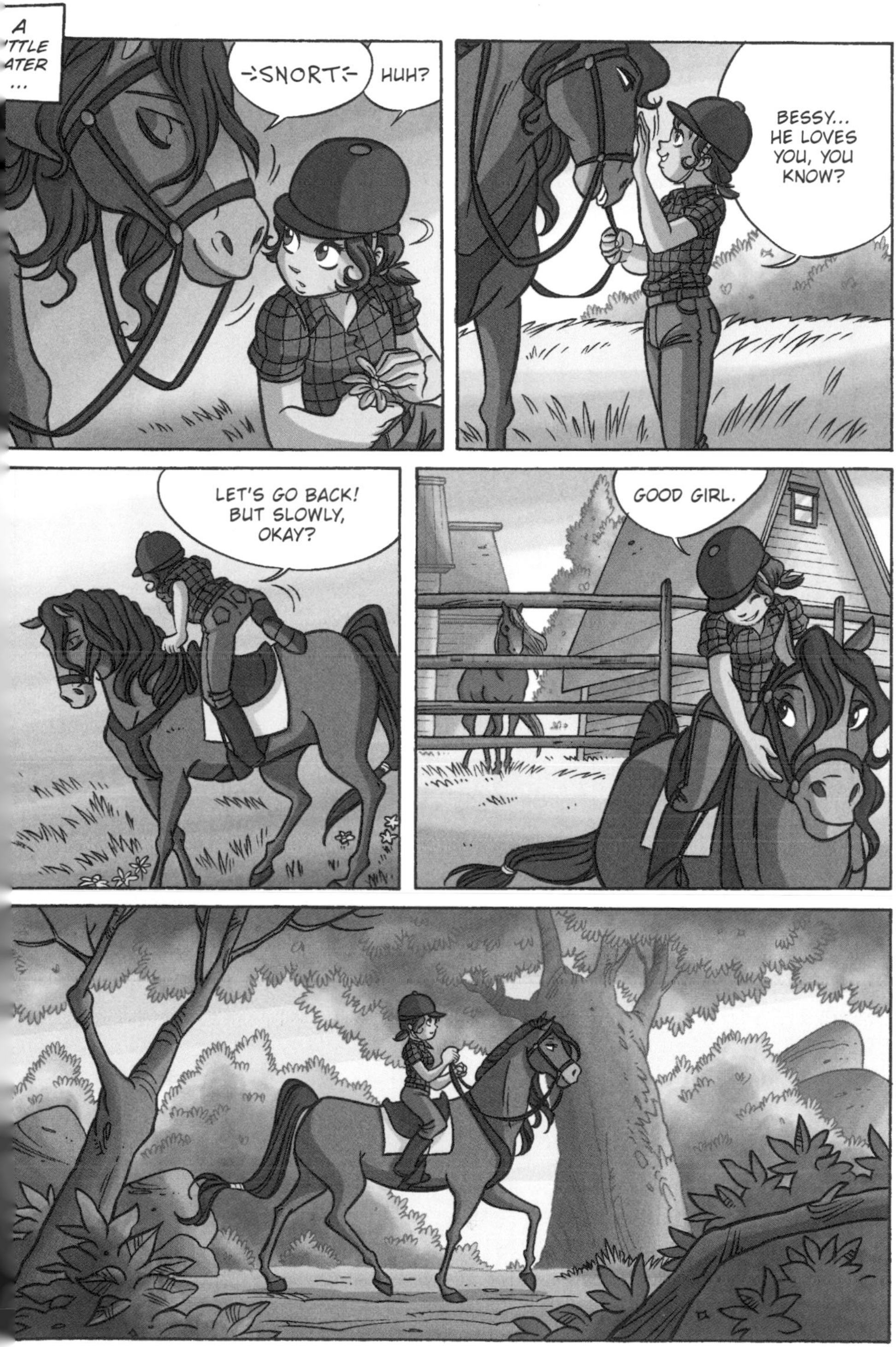
A
TTLE
ATER
...
-SNORT-
HUH?
BESSY... HE LOVES YOU, YOU KNOW?
LET'S GO BACK! BUT SLOWLY, OKAY?
GOOD GIRL.

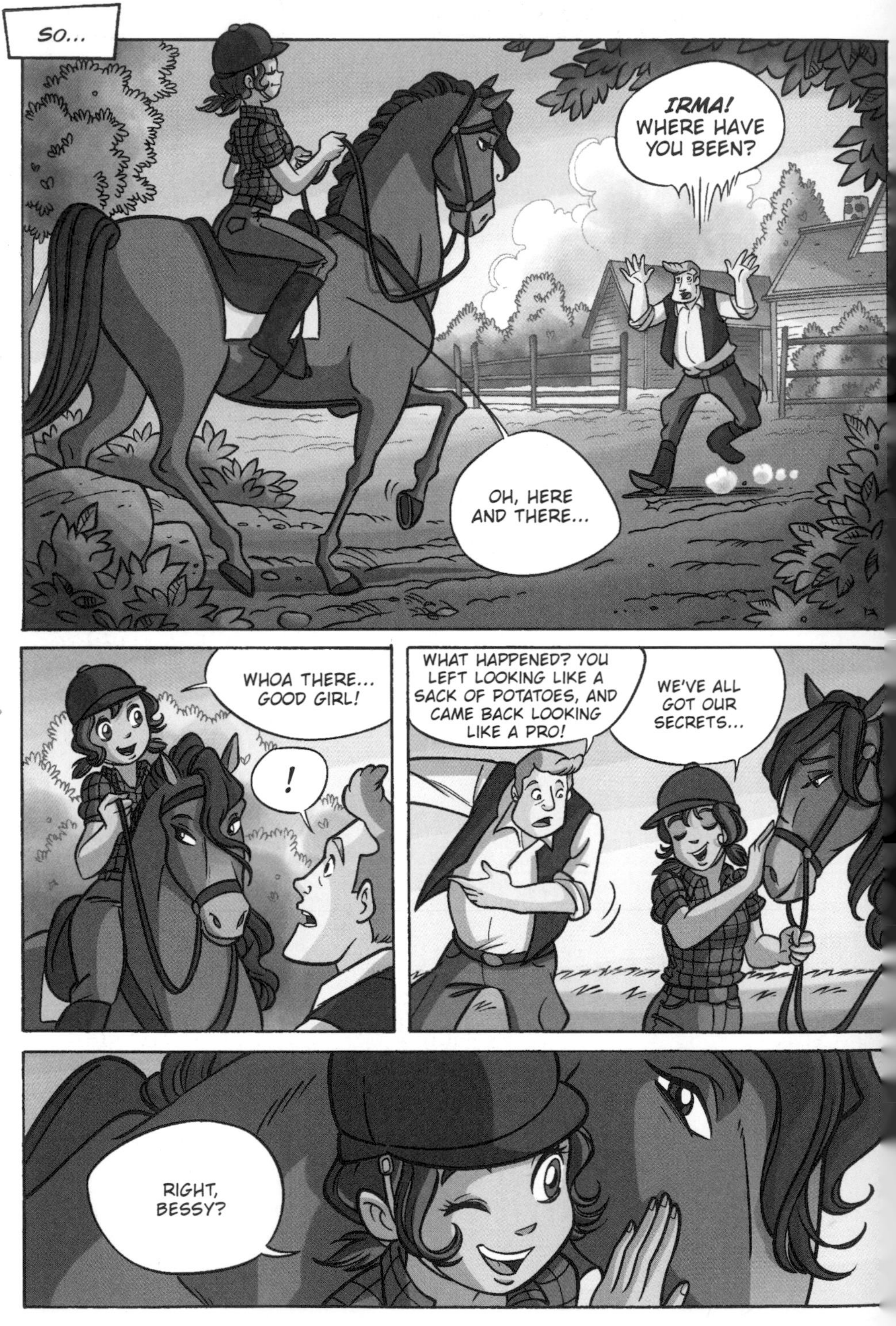
SO...
IRMA! WHERE HAVE YOU BEEN?
OH, HERE AND THERE...
WHOA THERE... GOOD GIRL!
!
WHAT HAPPENED? YOU LEFT LOOKING LIKE A SACK OF POTATOES, AND CAME BACK LOOKING LIKE A PRO!
WE'VE ALL GOT OUR SECRETS...
RIGHT, BESSY?

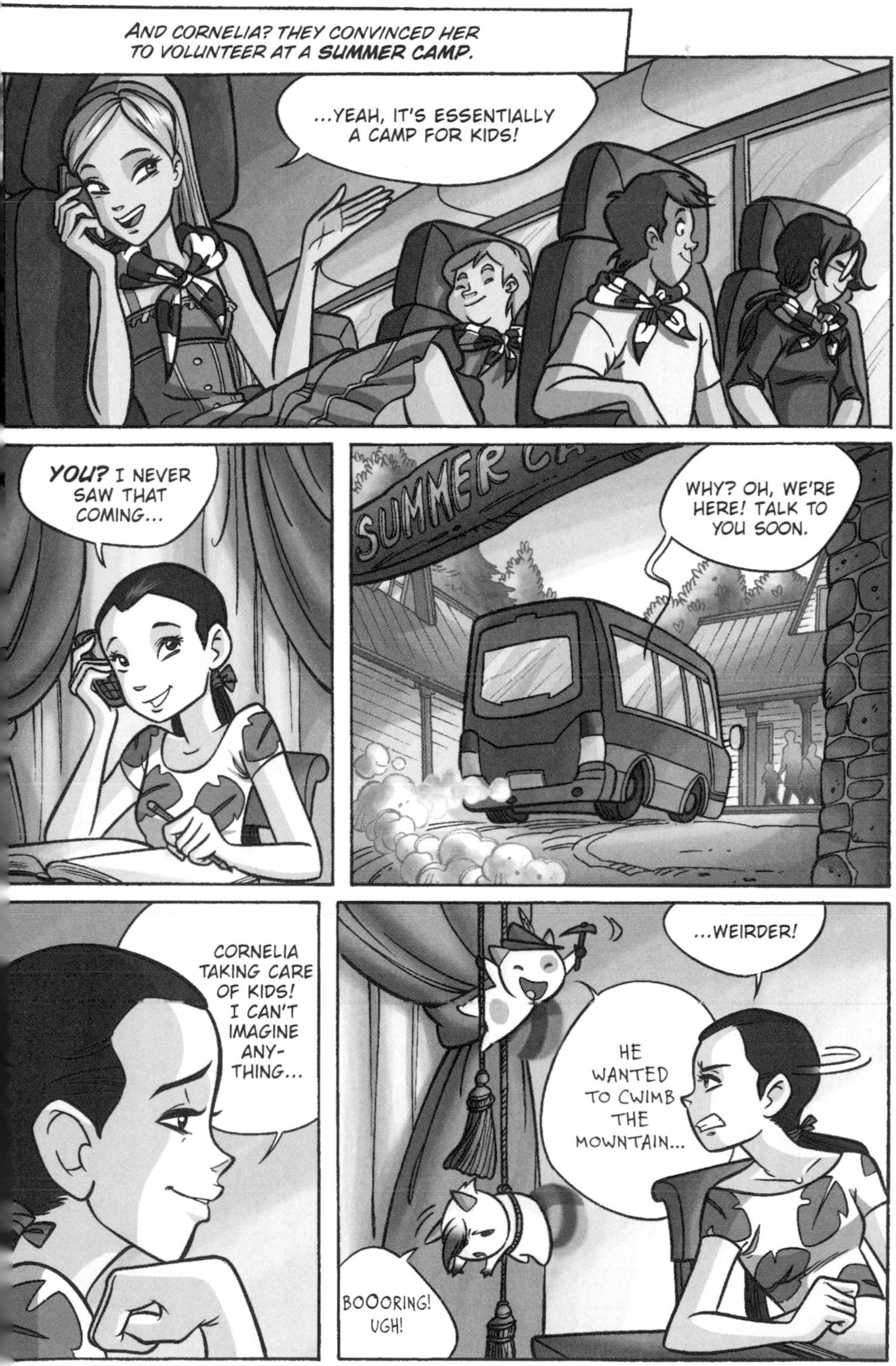
AND CORNELIA? THEY CONVINCED HER TO VOLUNTEER AT A SUMMER CAMP.
...YEAH, IT'S ESSENTIALLY A CAMP FOR KIDS!
YOU? I NEVER SAW THAT COMING...
SUMMER CA
WHY? OH, WE'RE HERE! TALK TO YOU SOON.
CORNELIA TAKING CARE OF KIDS! I CAN'T IMAGINE ANY-THING...
...WEIRDER!
HE WANTED TO CWIMB THE MOWNTAIN...
BOOORING! UGH!

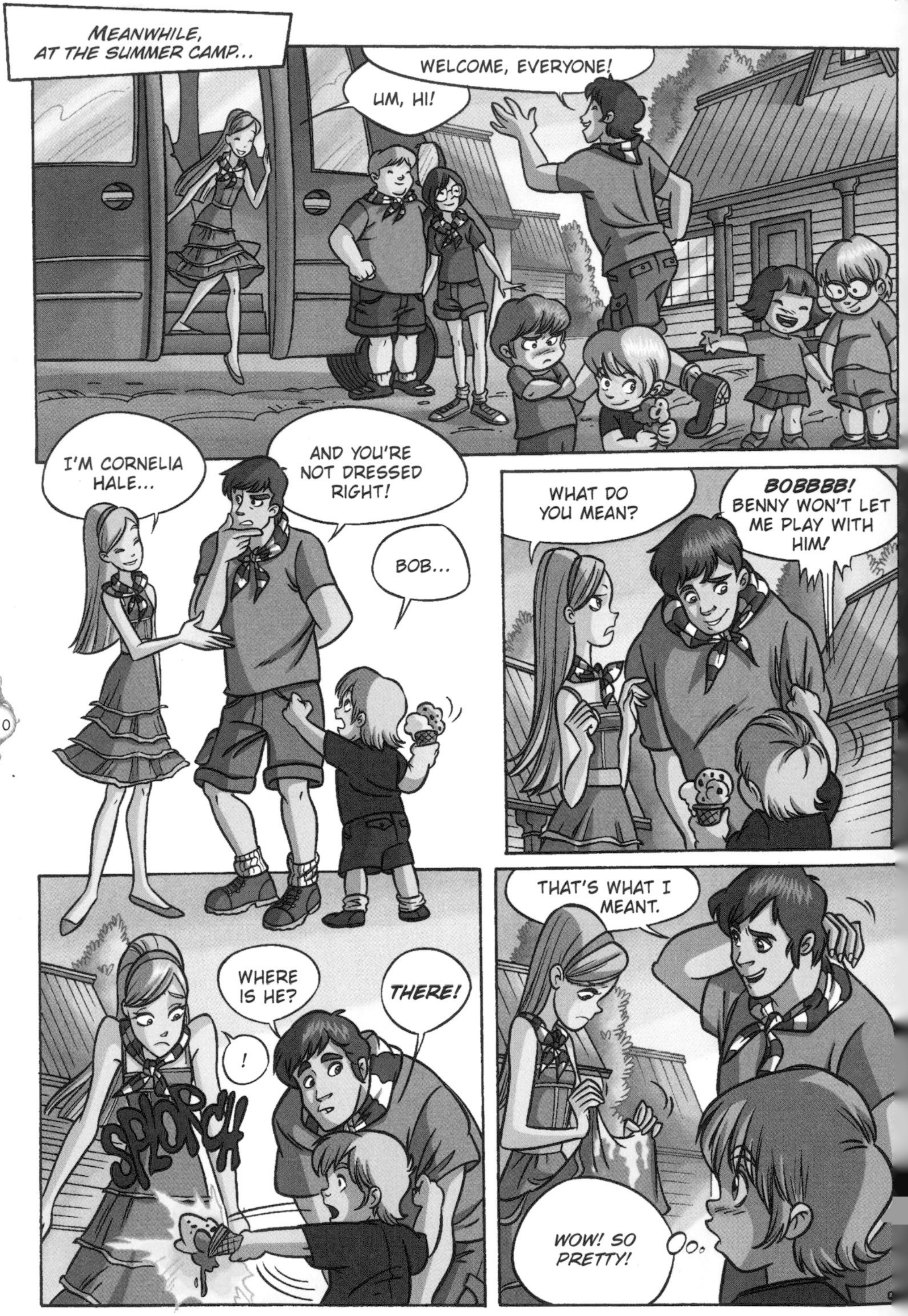
MEANWHILE, AT THE SUMMER CAMP...
WELCOME, EVERYONE!
UM, HI!
I'M CORNELIA HALE...
AND YOU'RE NOT DRESSED RIGHT!
BOB...
WHAT DO YOU MEAN?
BOBBBB! BENNY WON'T LET ME PLAY WITH HIM!
WHERE IS HE?
THERE!
!
SPLORCH
THAT'S WHAT I MEANT.
WOW! SO PRETTY!
Ooo

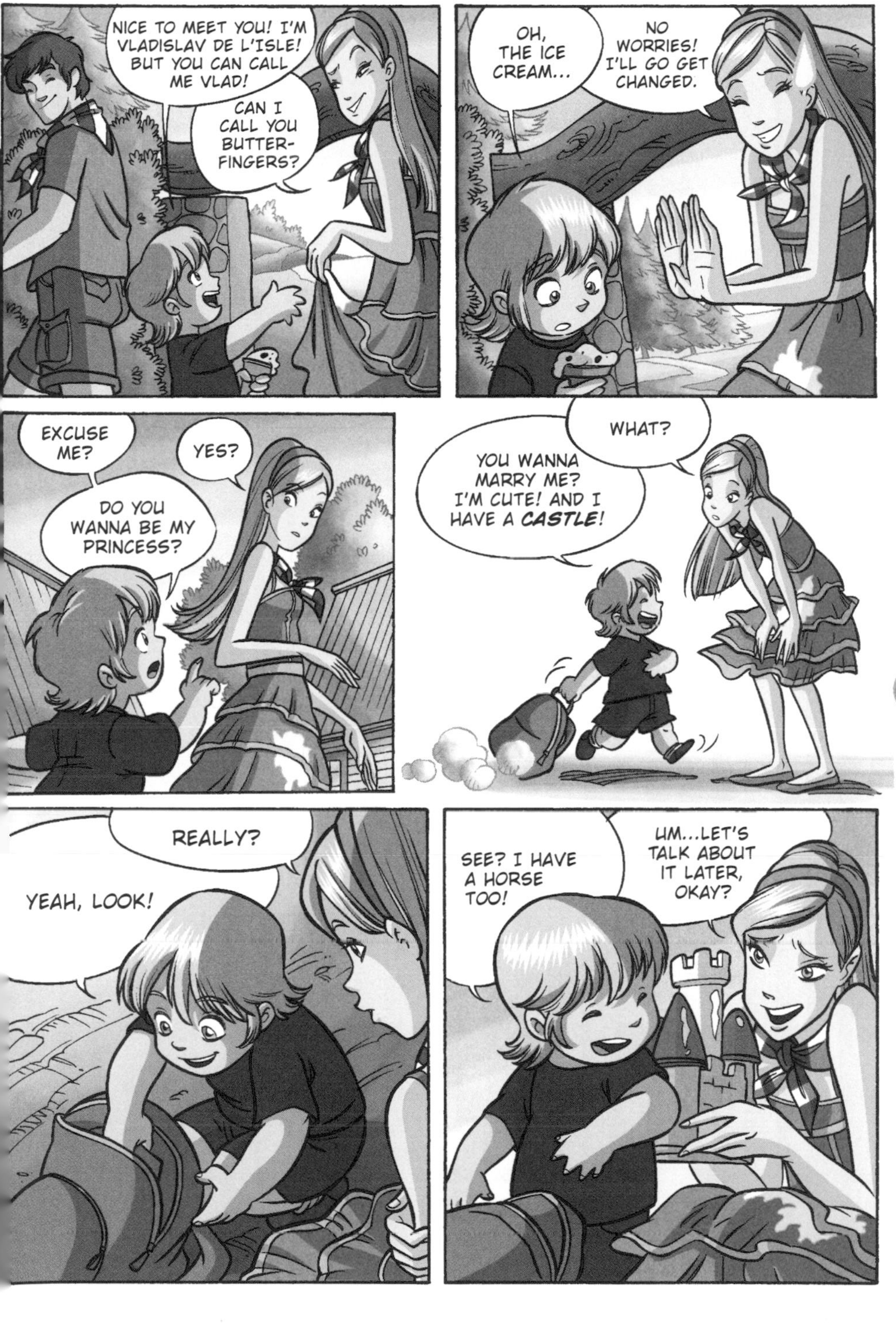

NICE TO MEET YOU! I'M VLADISLAV DE L'ISLE! BUT YOU CAN CALL ME VLAD!
CAN I CALL YOU BUTTER-FINGERS?
OH, THE ICE CREAM...
NO WORRIES! I'LL GO GET CHANGED.
EXCUSE ME?
YES?
DO YOU WANNA BE MY PRINCESS?
YOU WANNA MARRY ME? I'M CUTE! AND I HAVE A CASTLE!
WHAT?
REALLY?
YEAH, LOOK!
SEE? I HAVE A HORSE TOO!
UM...LET'S TALK ABOUT IT LATER, OKAY?

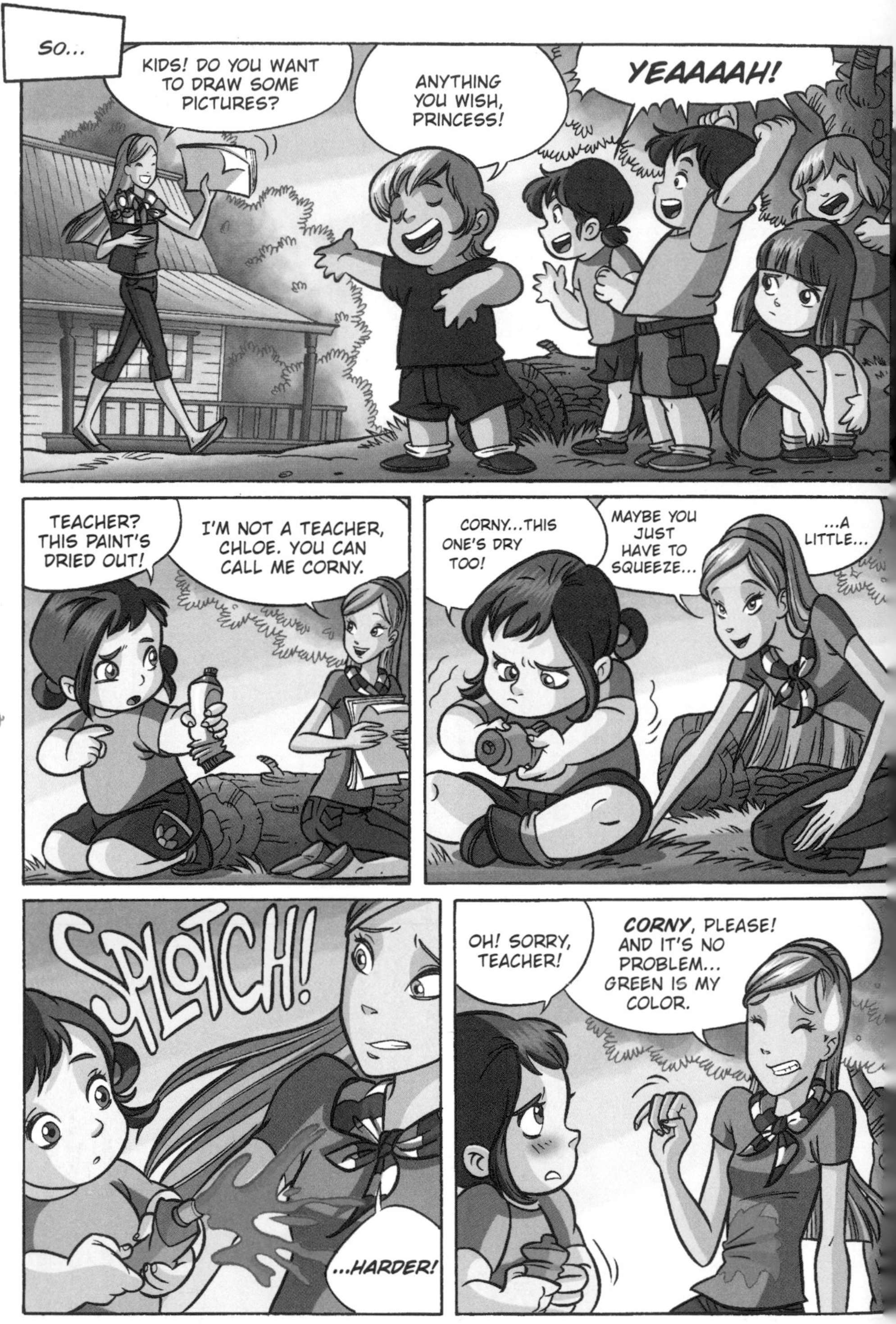
SO...
KIDS! DO YOU WANT TO DRAW SOME PICTURES?
ANYTHING YOU WISH, PRINCESS!
YEAAAAH!
TEACHER? THIS PAINT'S DRIED OUT!
I'M NOT A TEACHER, CHLOE. YOU CAN CALL ME CORNY.
CORNY...THIS ONE'S DRY TOO!
MAYBE YOU JUST HAVE TO SQUEEZE...
...A LITTLE...
SPLOTCH!
...HARDER!
OH! SORRY, TEACHER!
CORNY, PLEASE! AND IT'S NO PROBLEM... GREEN IS MY COLOR.

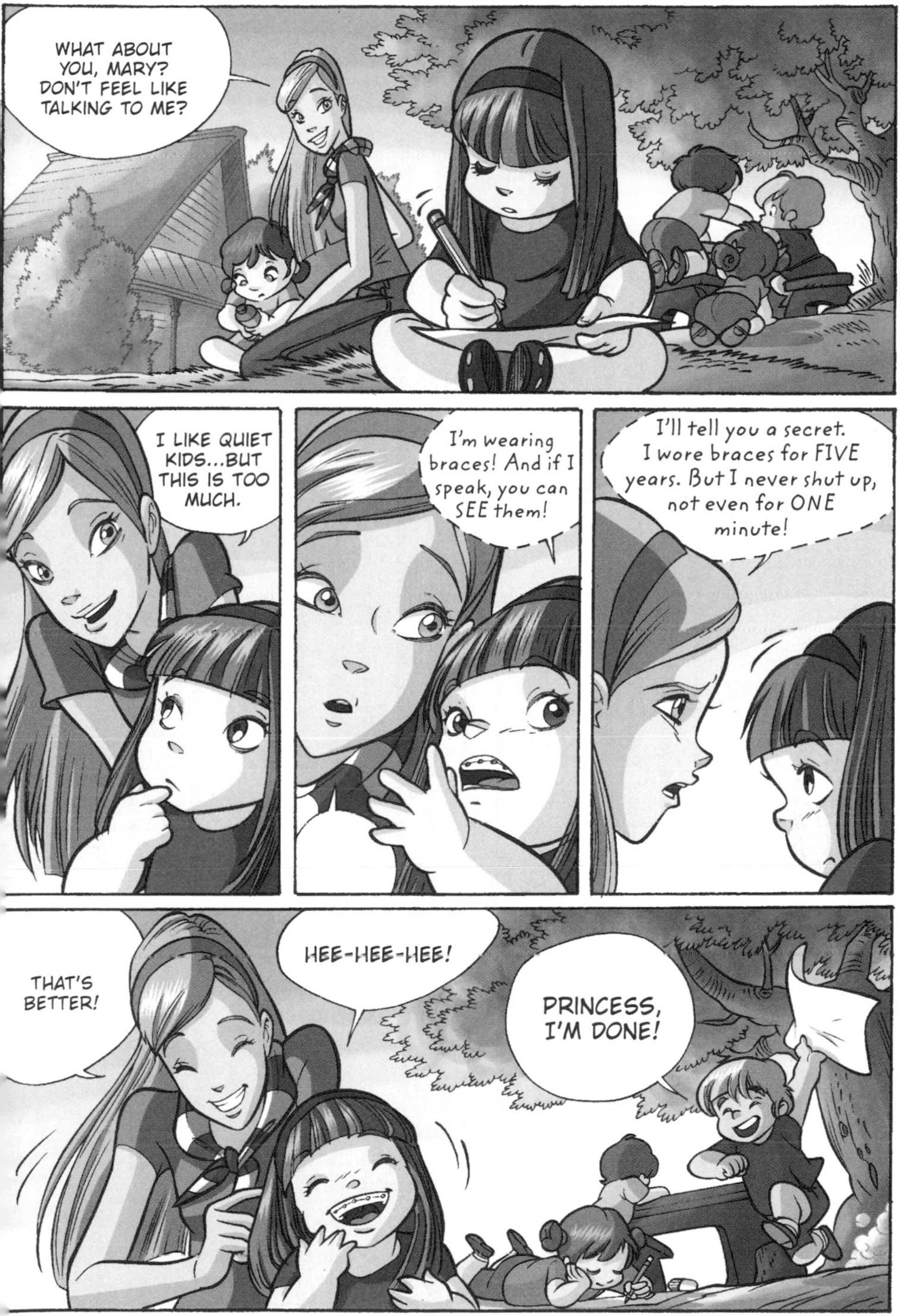
WHAT ABOUT YOU, MARY? DON'T FEEL LIKE TALKING TO ME?
I LIKE QUIET KIDS...BUT THIS IS TOO MUCH.
I'm wearing braces! And if I speak, you can SEE them!
I'll tell you a secret. I wore braces for FIVE years. But I never shut up, not even for ONE minute!
THAT'S BETTER!
HEE-HEE-HEE!
PRINCESS, I'M DONE!

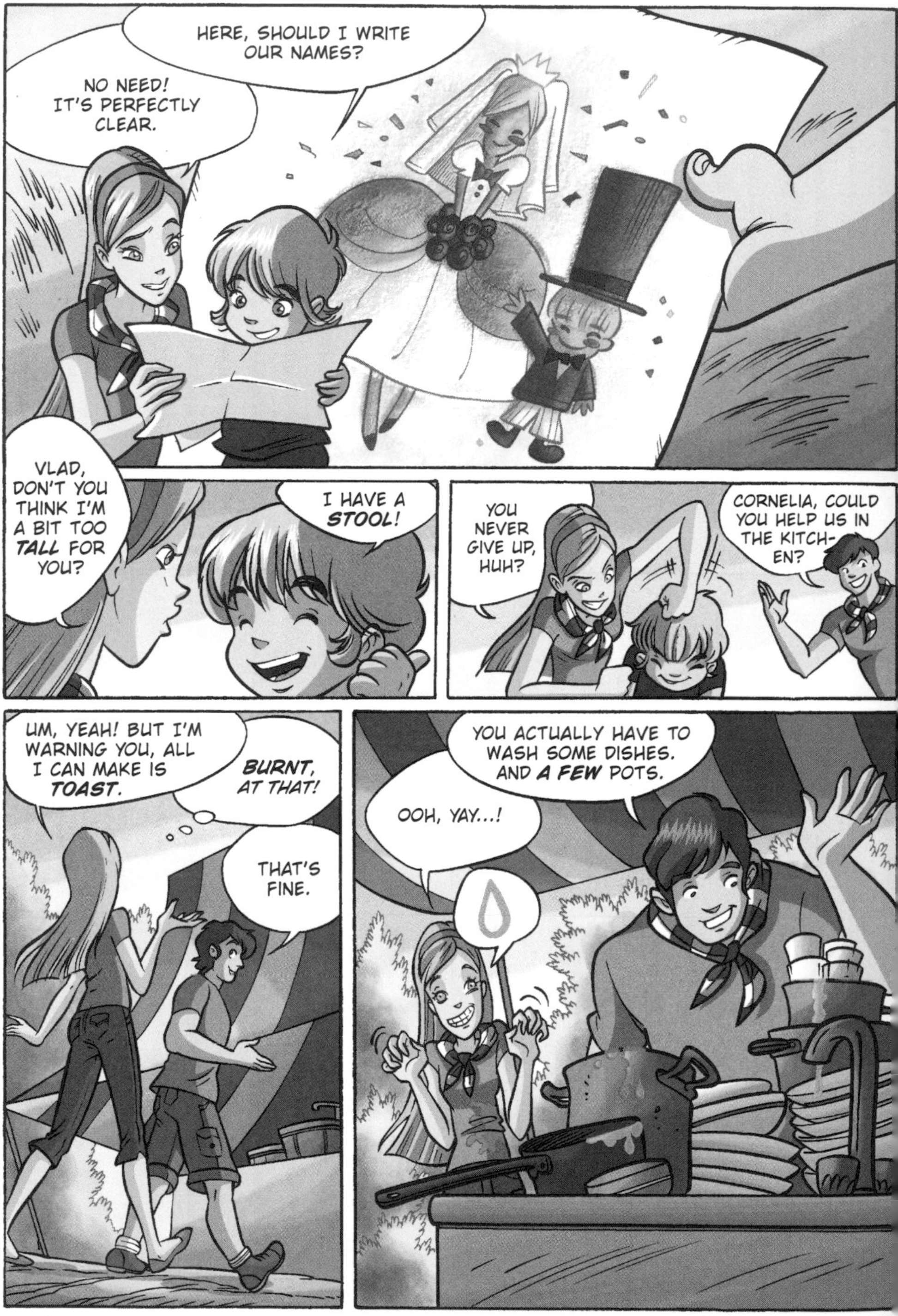
HERE, SHOULD I WRITE OUR NAMES?
NO NEED! IT'S PERFECTLY CLEAR.
VLAD, DON'T YOU THINK I'M A BIT TOO TALL FOR YOU?
I HAVE A STOOL!
YOU NEVER GIVE UP, HUH?
CORNELIA, COULD YOU HELP US IN THE KITCH- EN?
UM, YEAH! BUT I'M WARNING YOU, ALL I CAN MAKE IS TOAST.
BURNT, AT THAT!
THAT'S FINE.
YOU ACTUALLY HAVE TO WASH SOME DISHES. AND A FEW POTS.
OOH, YAY...!

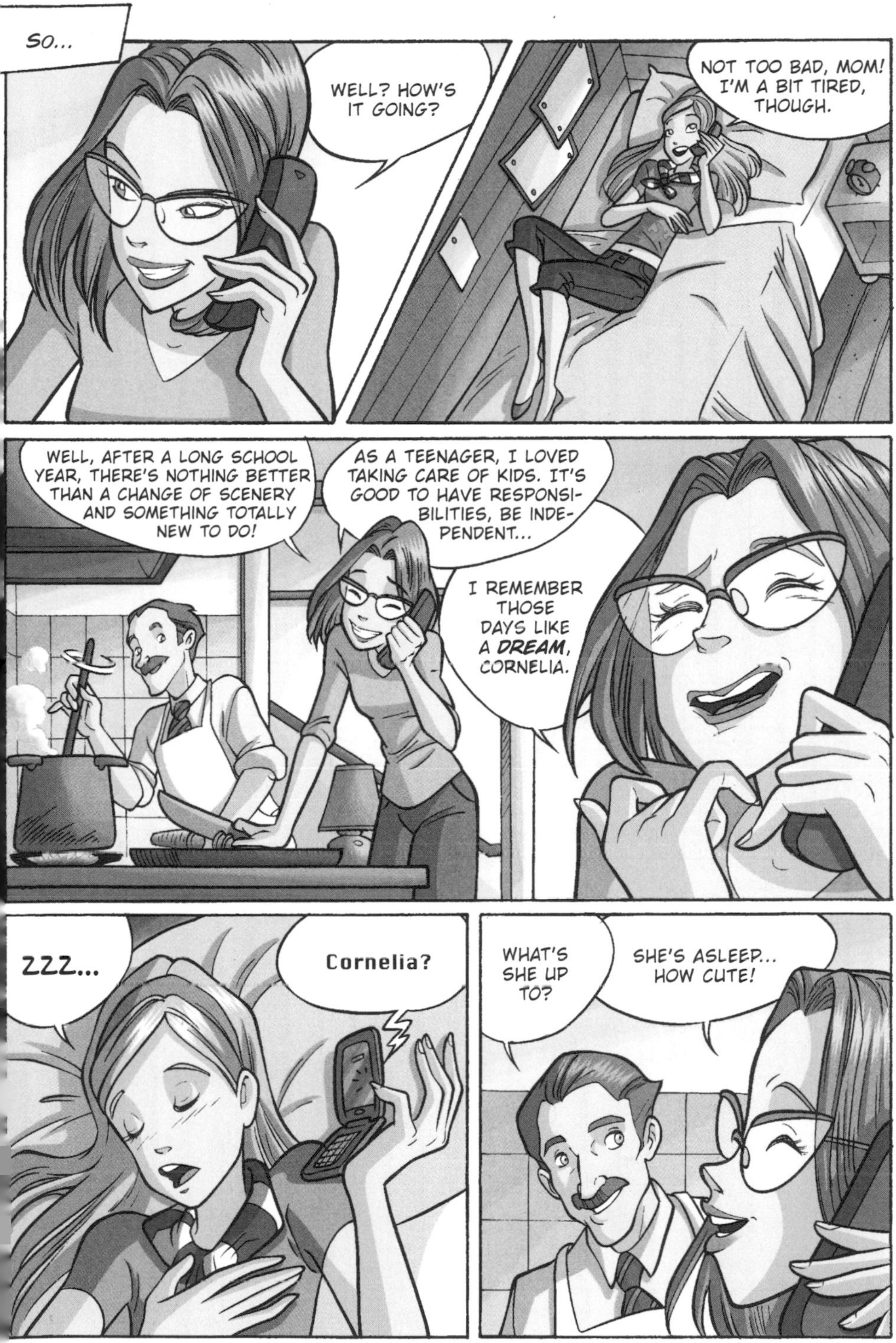
SO...
WELL? HOW'S IT GOING?
NOT TOO BAD, MOM! I'M A BIT TIRED, THOUGH.
WELL, AFTER A LONG SCHOOL YEAR, THERE'S NOTHING BETTER THAN A CHANGE OF SCENERY AND SOMETHING TOTALLY NEW TO DO!
AS A TEENAGER, I LOVED TAKING CARE OF KIDS. IT'S GOOD TO HAVE RESPONSIBILITIES, BE INDEPENDENT...
I REMEMBER THOSE DAYS LIKE A **DREAM**, CORNELIA.
ZZZ...
Cornelia?
WHAT'S SHE UP TO?
SHE'S ASLEEP... HOW CUTE!

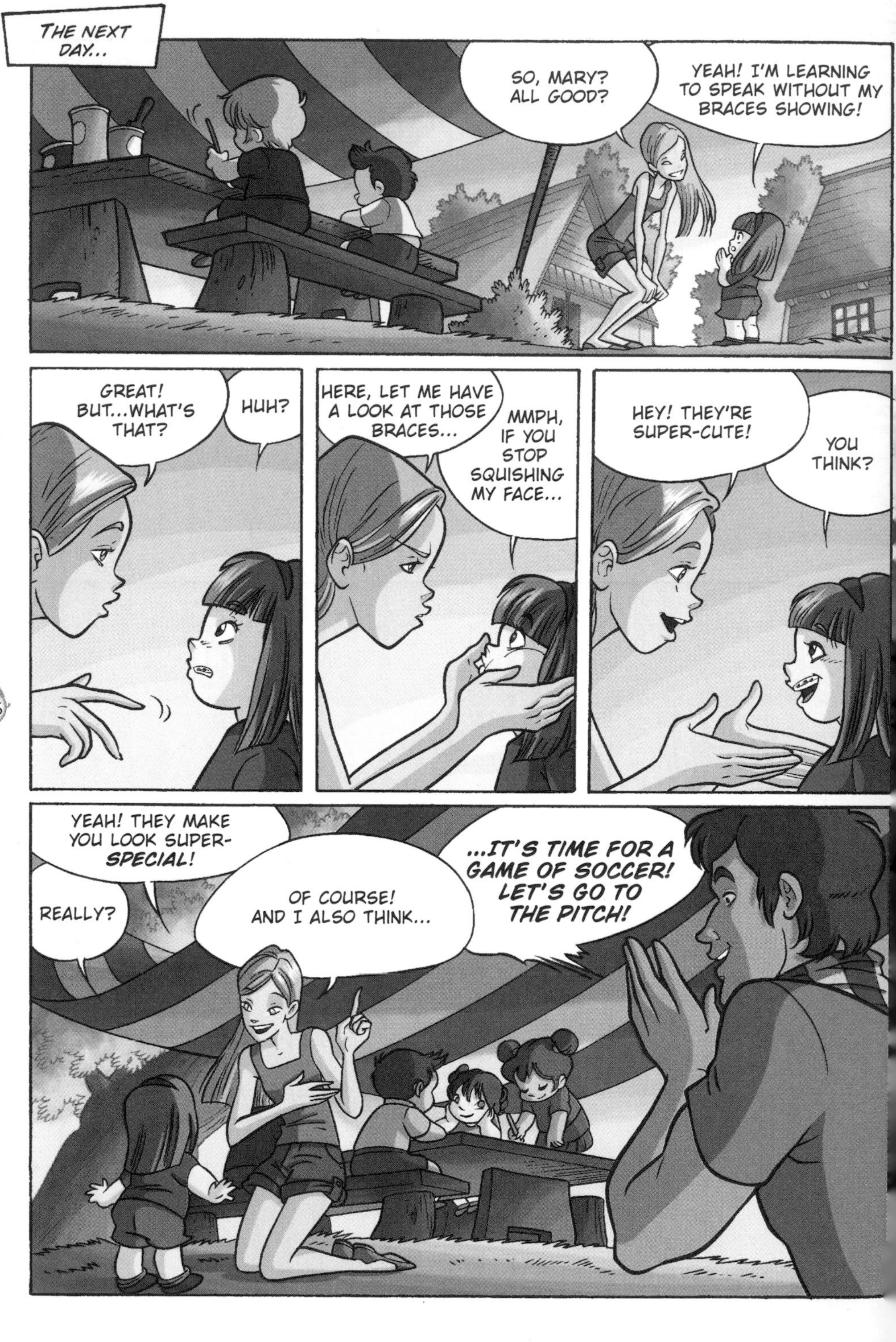

THE NEXT DAY...
SO, MARY? ALL GOOD?
YEAH! I'M LEARNING TO SPEAK WITHOUT MY BRACES SHOWING!
GREAT! BUT...WHAT'S THAT?
HUH?
HERE, LET ME HAVE A LOOK AT THOSE BRACES...
MMPH, IF YOU STOP SQUISHING MY FACE...
HEY! THEY'RE SUPER-CUTE!
YOU THINK?
YEAH! THEY MAKE YOU LOOK SUPER-SPECIAL!
REALLY?
OF COURSE! AND I ALSO THINK...
...IT'S TIME FOR A GAME OF SOCCER! LET'S GO TO THE PITCH!

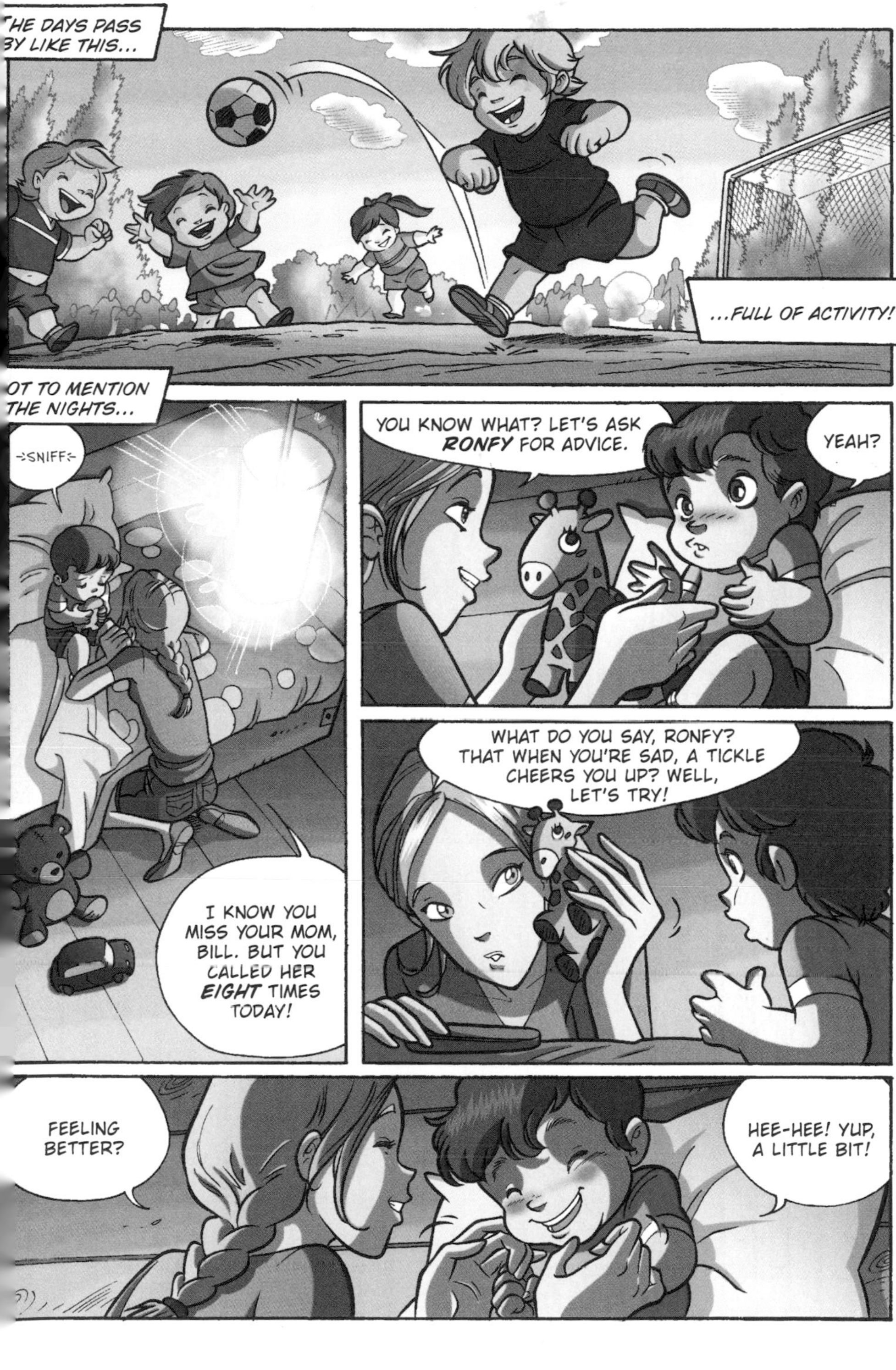
HE DAYS PASS
BY LIKE THIS...
...FULL OF ACTIVITY!
OT TO MENTION
THE NIGHTS...
SNIFF
I KNOW YOU MISS YOUR MOM, BILL. BUT YOU CALLED HER *EIGHT* TIMES TODAY!
YOU KNOW WHAT? LET'S ASK *RONFY* FOR ADVICE.
YEAH?
WHAT DO YOU SAY, RONFY? THAT WHEN YOU'RE SAD, A TICKLE CHEERS YOU UP? WELL, LET'S TRY!
FEELING BETTER?
HEE-HEE! YUP, A LITTLE BIT!

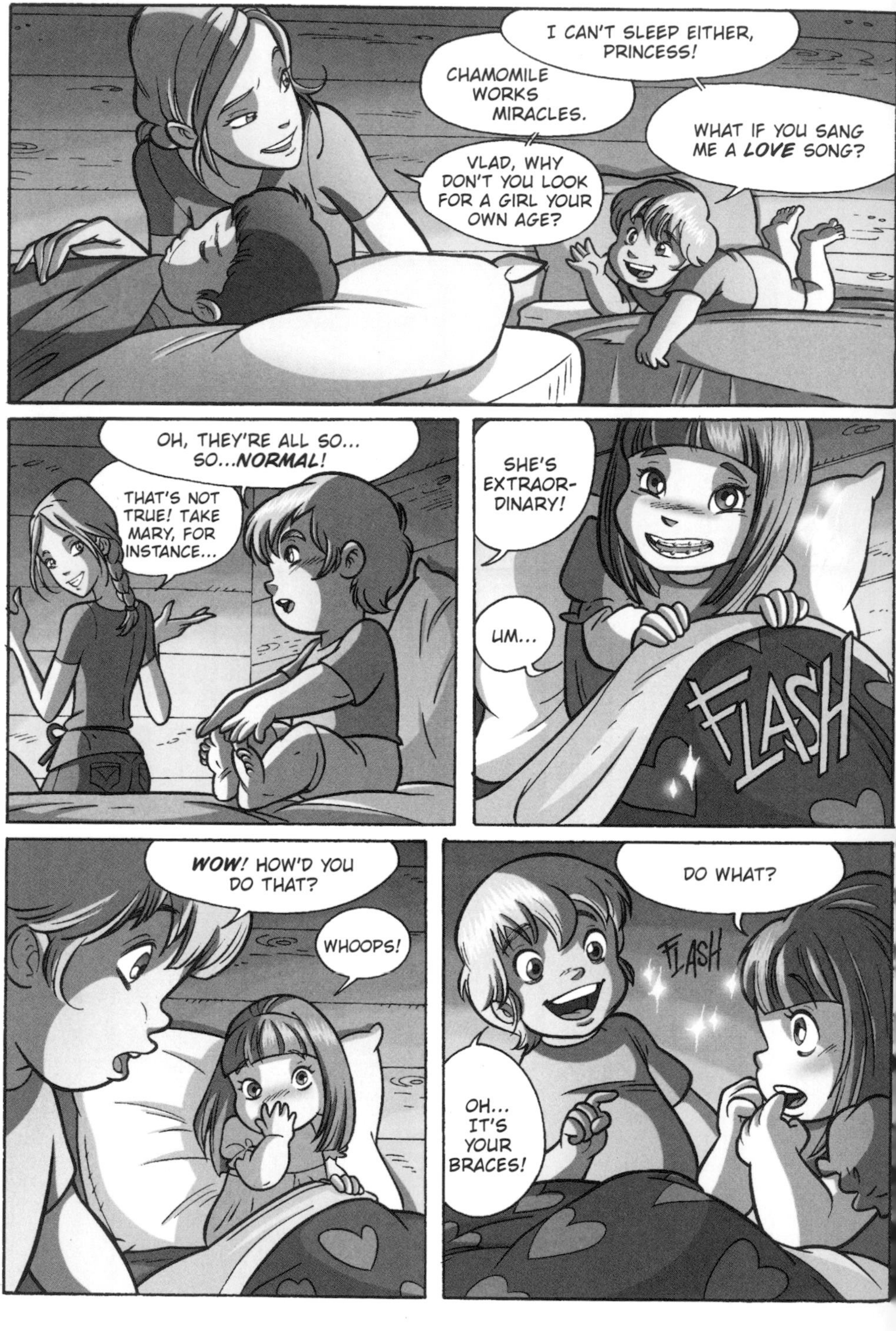

I CAN'T SLEEP EITHER, PRINCESS!
CHAMOMILE WORKS MIRACLES.
WHAT IF YOU SANG ME A **LOVE** SONG?
VLAD, WHY DON'T YOU LOOK FOR A GIRL YOUR OWN AGE?
OH, THEY'RE ALL SO... SO...**NORMAL**!
THAT'S NOT TRUE! TAKE MARY, FOR INSTANCE...
SHE'S EXTRAOR-DINARY!
UM...
FLASH
WOW! HOW'D YOU DO THAT?
WHOOPS!
DO WHAT?
FLASH
OH... IT'S YOUR BRACES!

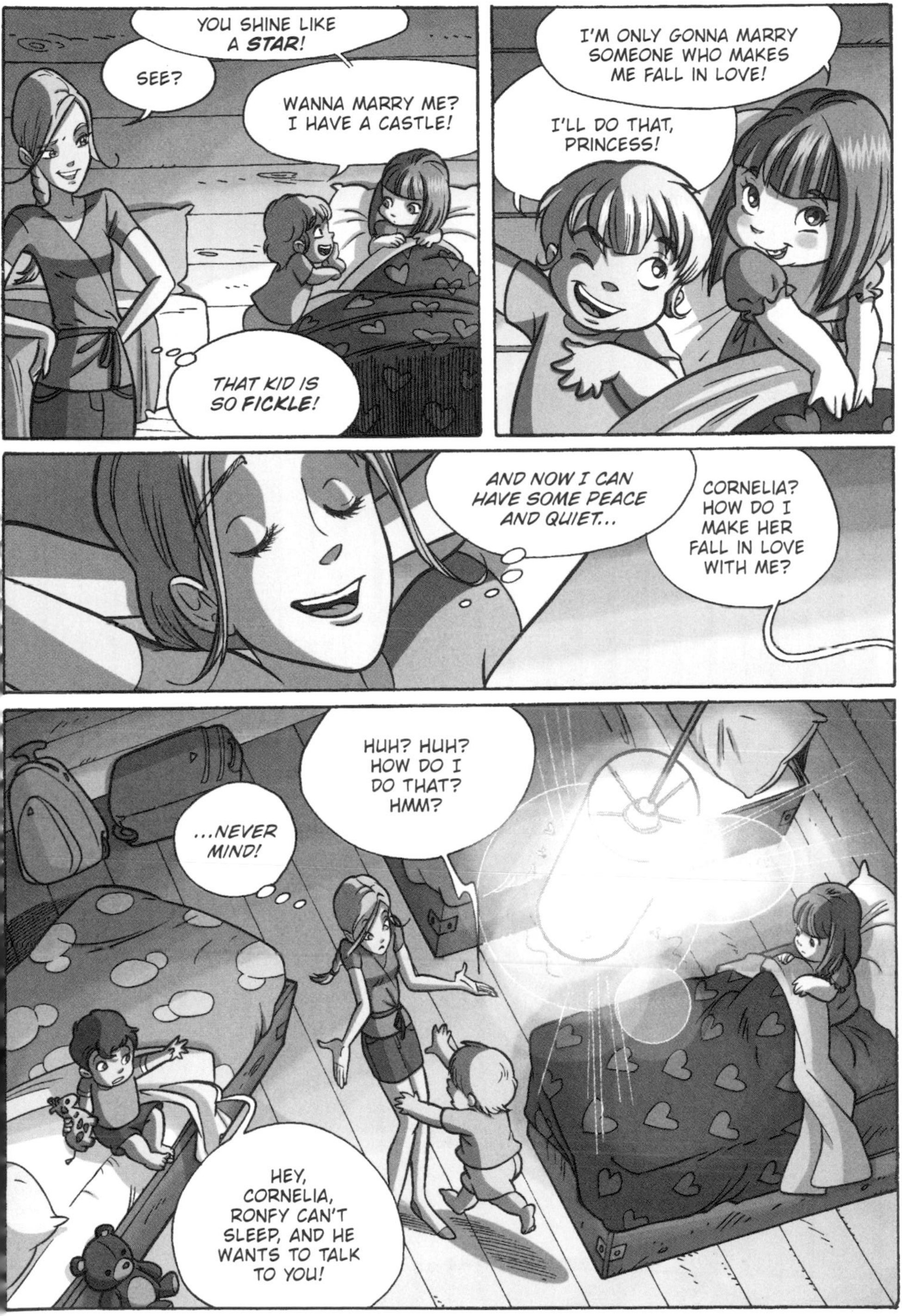

SEE?
YOU SHINE LIKE A STAR!
WANNA MARRY ME? I HAVE A CASTLE!
THAT KID IS SO FICKLE!
I'M ONLY GONNA MARRY SOMEONE WHO MAKES ME FALL IN LOVE!
I'LL DO THAT, PRINCESS!
AND NOW I CAN HAVE SOME PEACE AND QUIET...
CORNELIA? HOW DO I MAKE HER FALL IN LOVE WITH ME?
HUH? HUH? HOW DO I DO THAT? HMM?
...NEVER MIND!
HEY, CORNELIA, RONFY CAN'T SLEEP, AND HE WANTS TO TALK TO YOU!

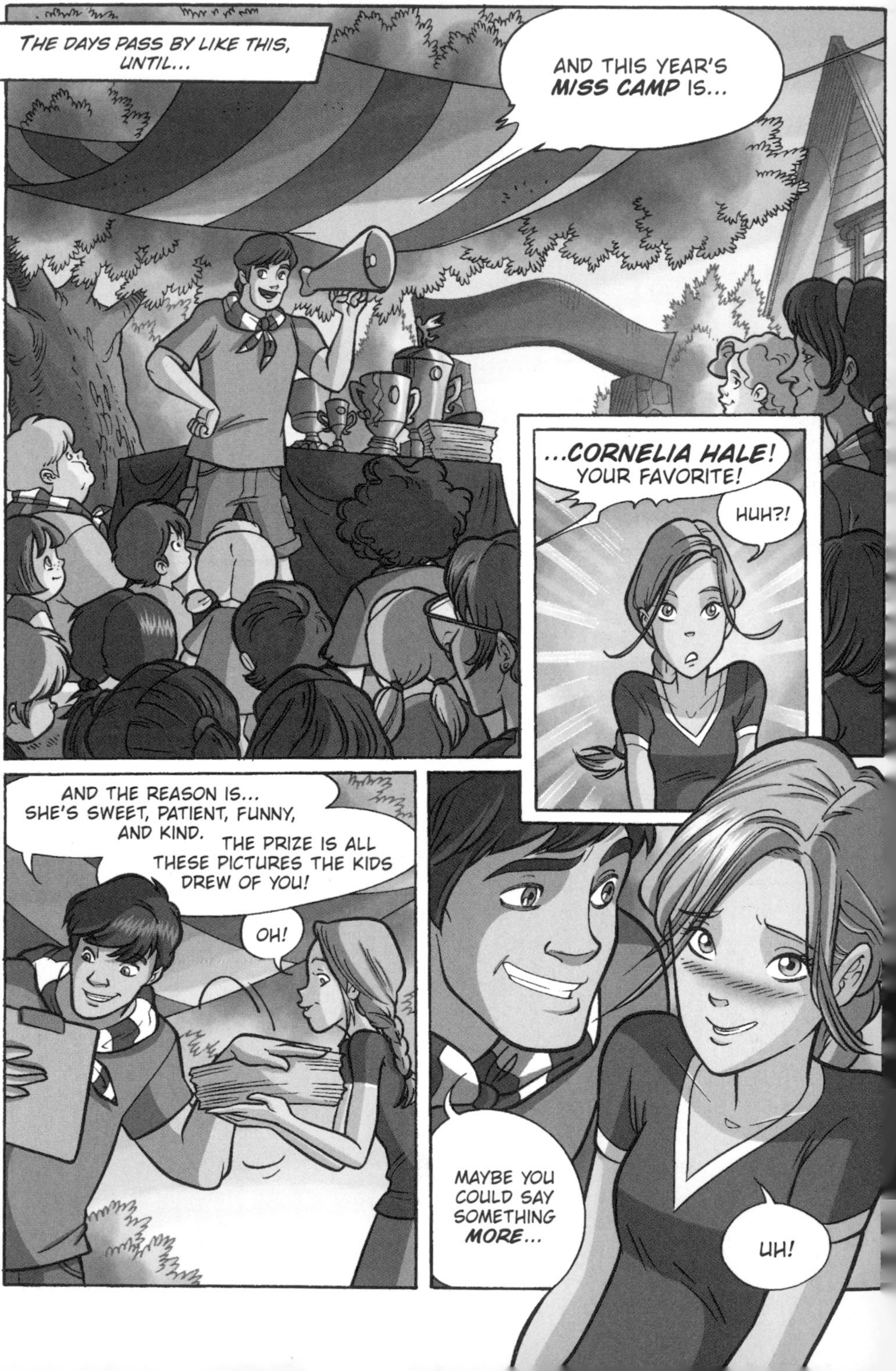
THE DAYS PASS BY LIKE THIS, UNTIL...
AND THIS YEAR'S MISS CAMP IS...
...CORNELIA HALE! YOUR FAVORITE!
HUH?!
AND THE REASON IS... SHE'S SWEET, PATIENT, FUNNY, AND KIND.
THE PRIZE IS ALL THESE PICTURES THE KIDS DREW OF YOU!
OH!
MAYBE YOU COULD SAY SOMETHING MORE...
UH!

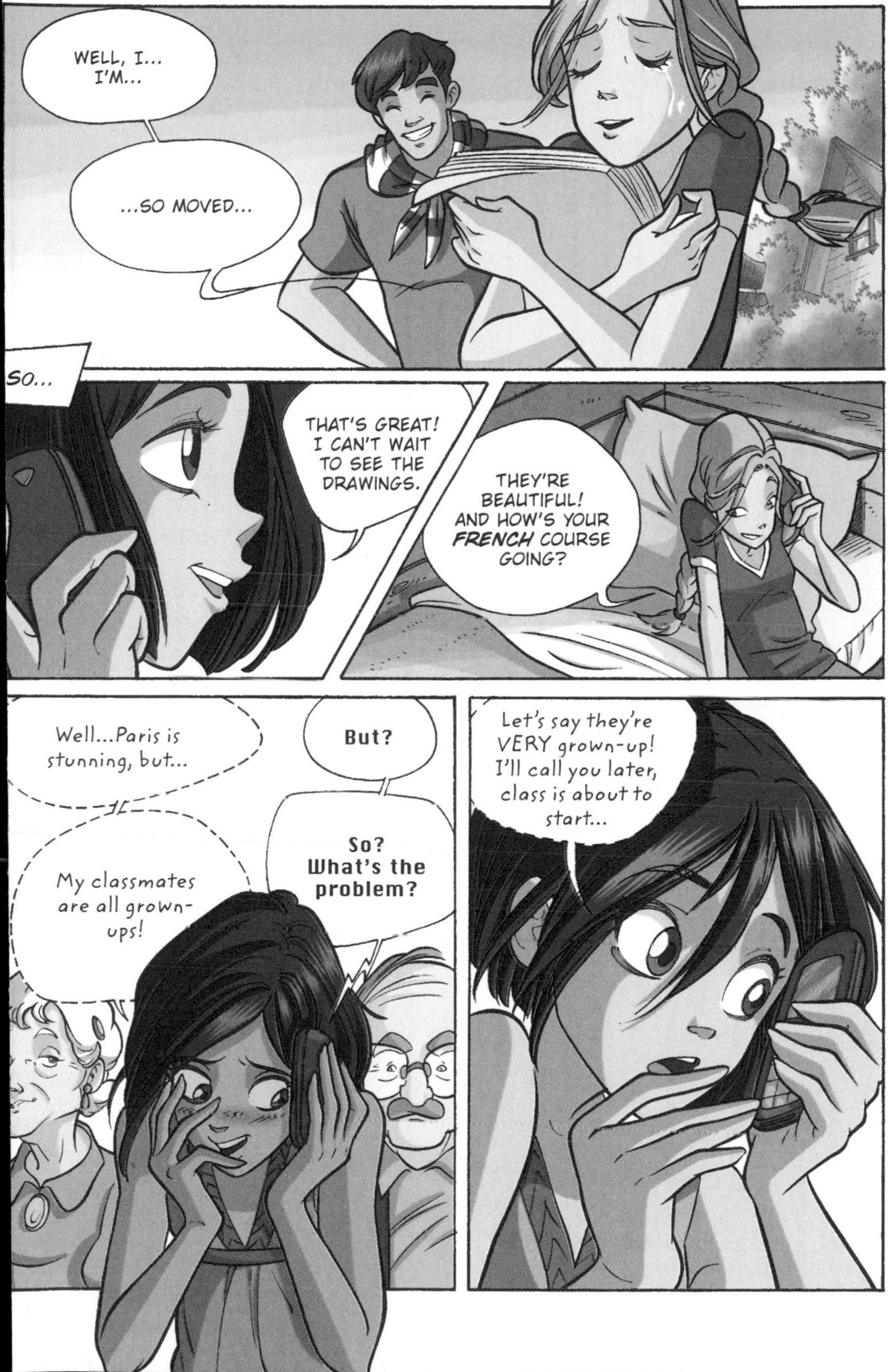

WELL, I... I'M...
...SO MOVED...
SO...
THAT'S GREAT! I CAN'T WAIT TO SEE THE DRAWINGS.
THEY'RE BEAUTIFUL! AND HOW'S YOUR *FRENCH* COURSE GOING?
Well...Paris is stunning, but...
But?
My classmates are all grown-ups!
So? What's the problem?
Let's say they're VERY grown-up! I'll call you later, class is about to start...

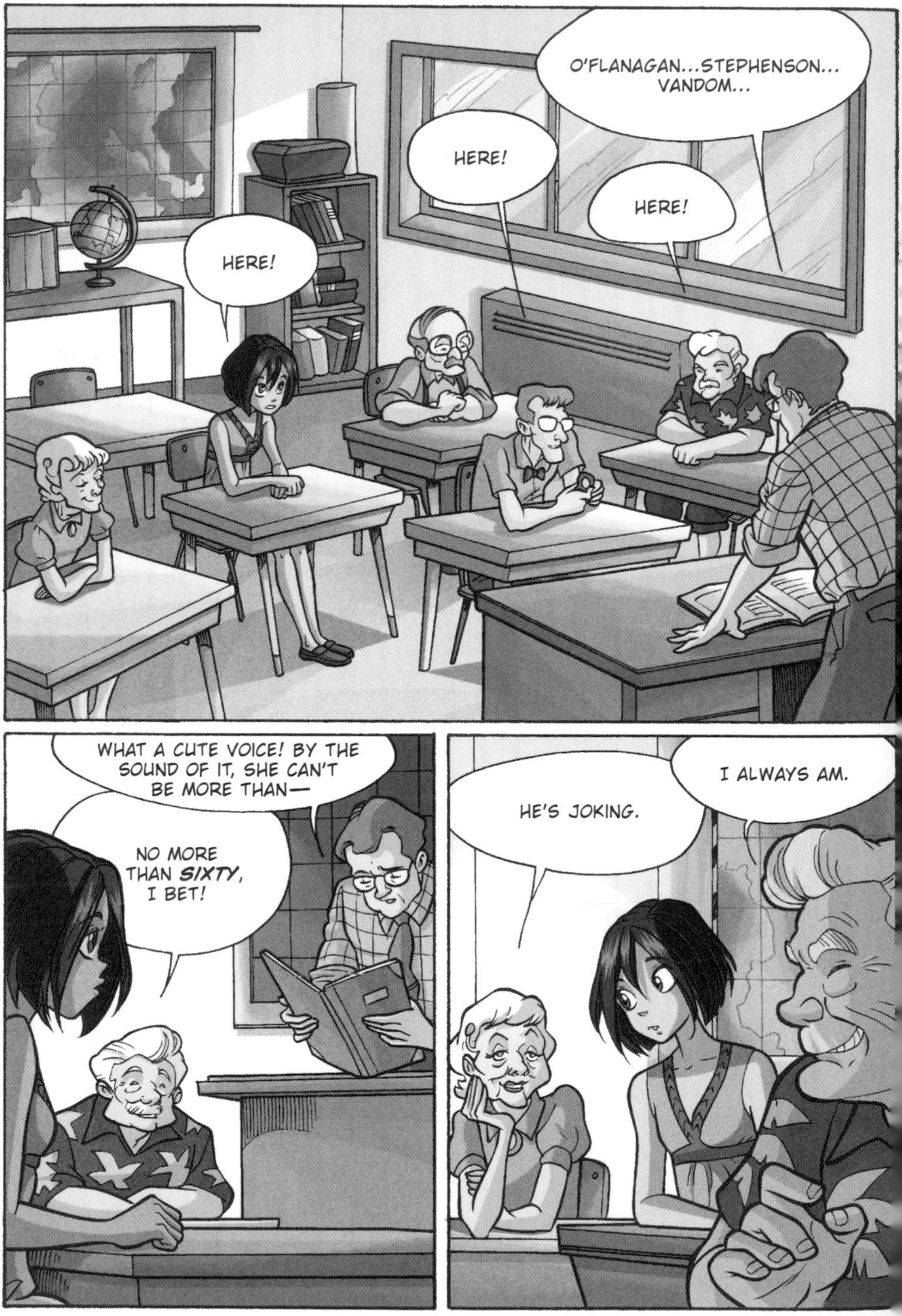
O'FLANAGAN...STEPHENSON... VANDOM...
HERE!
HERE!
HERE!
WHAT A CUTE VOICE! BY THE SOUND OF IT, SHE CAN'T BE MORE THAN—
NO MORE THAN *SIXTY*, I BET!
HE'S JOKING.
I ALWAYS AM.

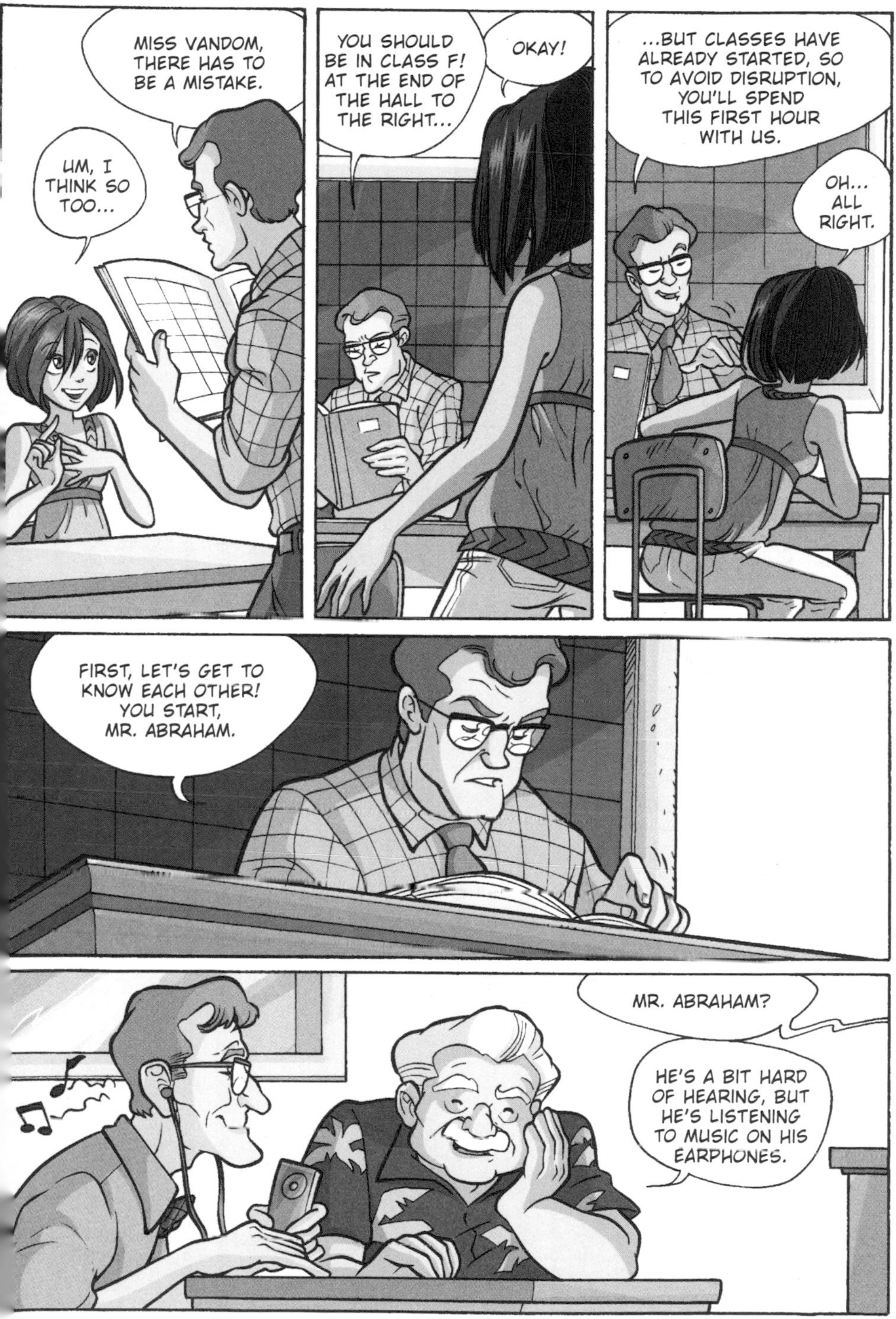
MISS VANDOM, THERE HAS TO BE A MISTAKE.
UM, I THINK SO TOO...
YOU SHOULD BE IN CLASS F! AT THE END OF THE HALL TO THE RIGHT...
OKAY!
...BUT CLASSES HAVE ALREADY STARTED, SO TO AVOID DISRUPTION, YOU'LL SPEND THIS FIRST HOUR WITH US.
OH... ALL RIGHT.
FIRST, LET'S GET TO KNOW EACH OTHER! YOU START, MR. ABRAHAM.
MR. ABRAHAM?
HE'S A BIT HARD OF HEARING, BUT HE'S LISTENING TO MUSIC ON HIS EARPHONES.

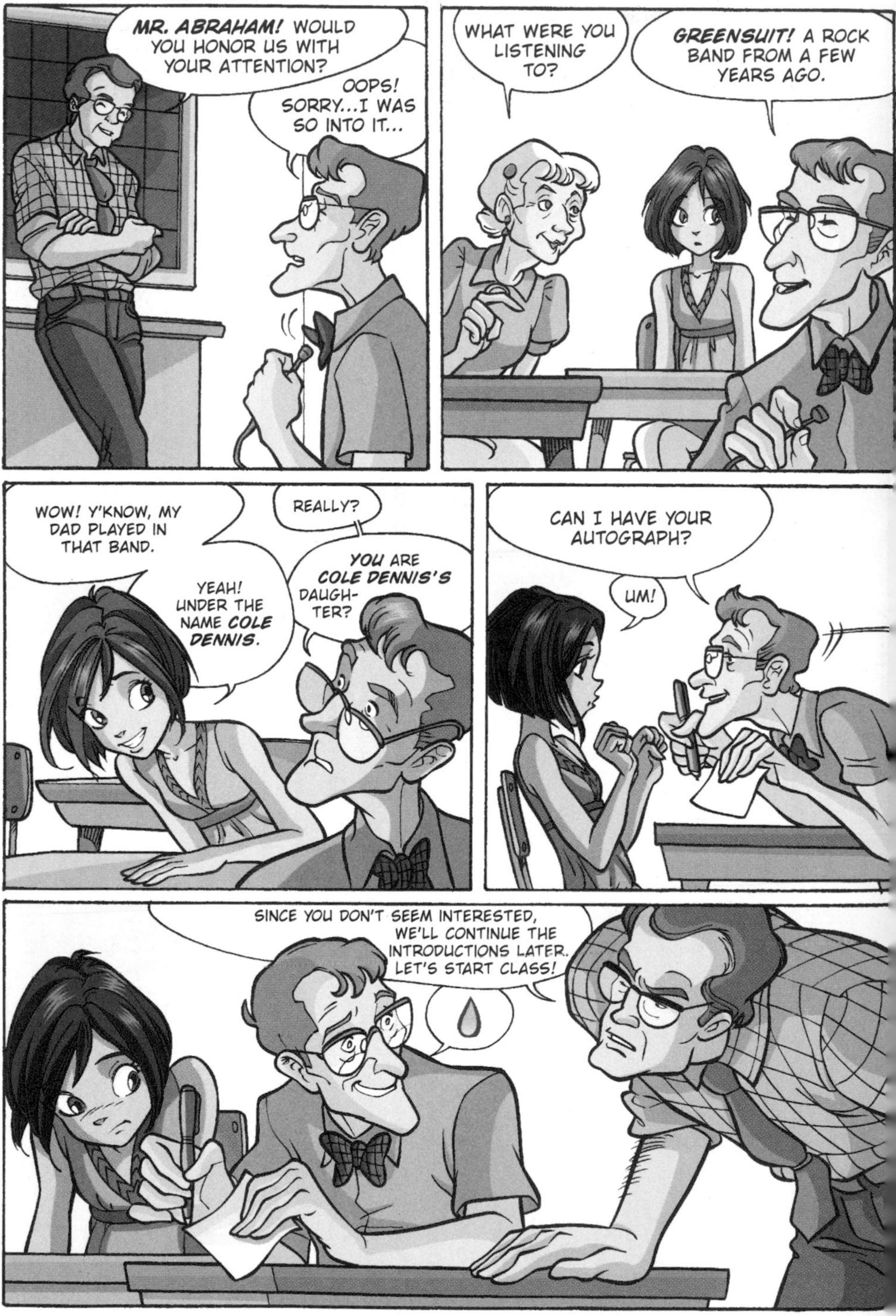

MR. ABRAHAM! WOULD YOU HONOR US WITH YOUR ATTENTION?
OOPS! SORRY...I WAS SO INTO IT...
WHAT WERE YOU LISTENING TO?
GREENSUIT! A ROCK BAND FROM A FEW YEARS AGO.
WOW! Y'KNOW, MY DAD PLAYED IN THAT BAND.
REALLY?
YEAH! UNDER THE NAME COLE DENNIS.
YOU ARE COLE DENNIS'S DAUGHTER?
CAN I HAVE YOUR AUTOGRAPH?
UM!
SINCE YOU DON'T SEEM INTERESTED, WE'LL CONTINUE THE INTRODUCTIONS LATER. LET'S START CLASS!

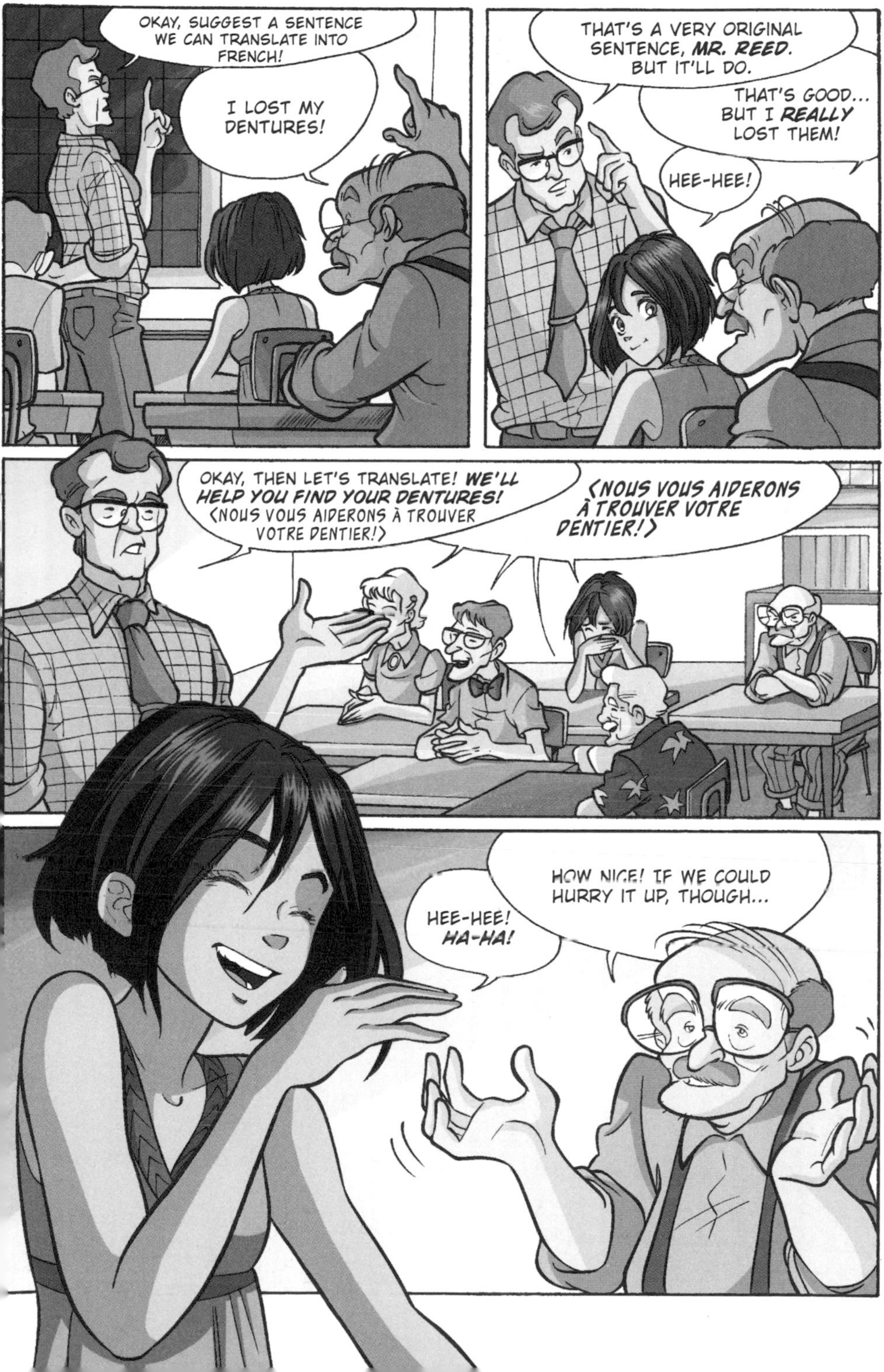

OKAY, SUGGEST A SENTENCE WE CAN TRANSLATE INTO FRENCH!
I LOST MY DENTURES!
THAT'S A VERY ORIGINAL SENTENCE, ***MR. REED.*** BUT IT'LL DO.
THAT'S GOOD... BUT I ***REALLY*** LOST THEM!
HEE-HEE!
OKAY, THEN LET'S TRANSLATE! ***WE'LL HELP YOU FIND YOUR DENTURES!***
<NOUS VOUS AIDERONS À TROUVER VOTRE DENTIER!>
<NOUS VOUS AIDERONS À TROUVER VOTRE DENTIER!>
HEE-HEE! ***HA-HA!***
HOW NICE! IF WE COULD HURRY IT UP, THOUGH...

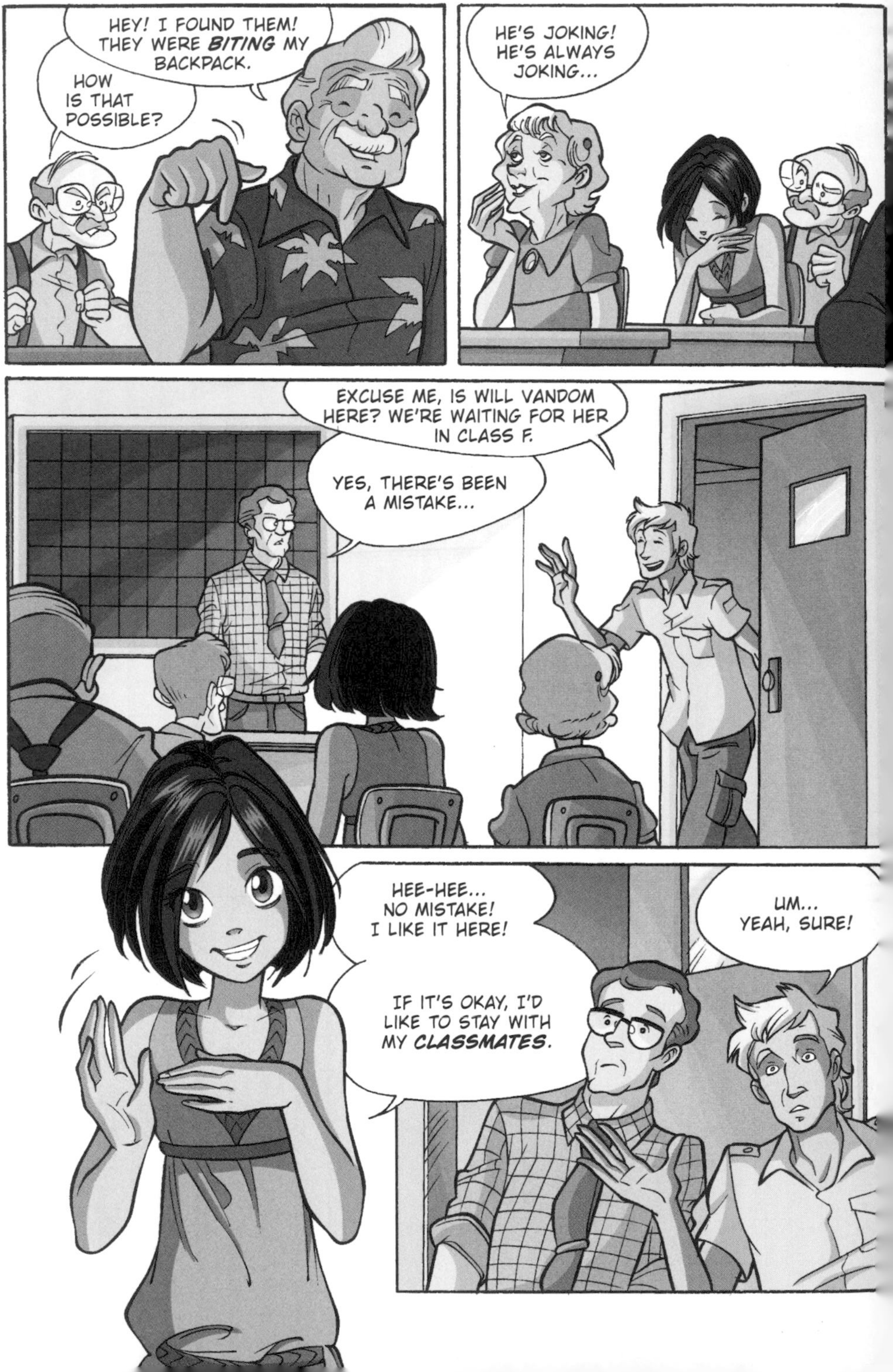
HEY! I FOUND THEM! THEY WERE BITING MY BACKPACK.
HOW IS THAT POSSIBLE?
HE'S JOKING! HE'S ALWAYS JOKING...
EXCUSE ME, IS WILL VANDOM HERE? WE'RE WAITING FOR HER IN CLASS F.
YES, THERE'S BEEN A MISTAKE...
HEE-HEE... NO MISTAKE! I LIKE IT HERE!
IF IT'S OKAY, I'D LIKE TO STAY WITH MY CLASSMATES.
UM... YEAH, SURE!

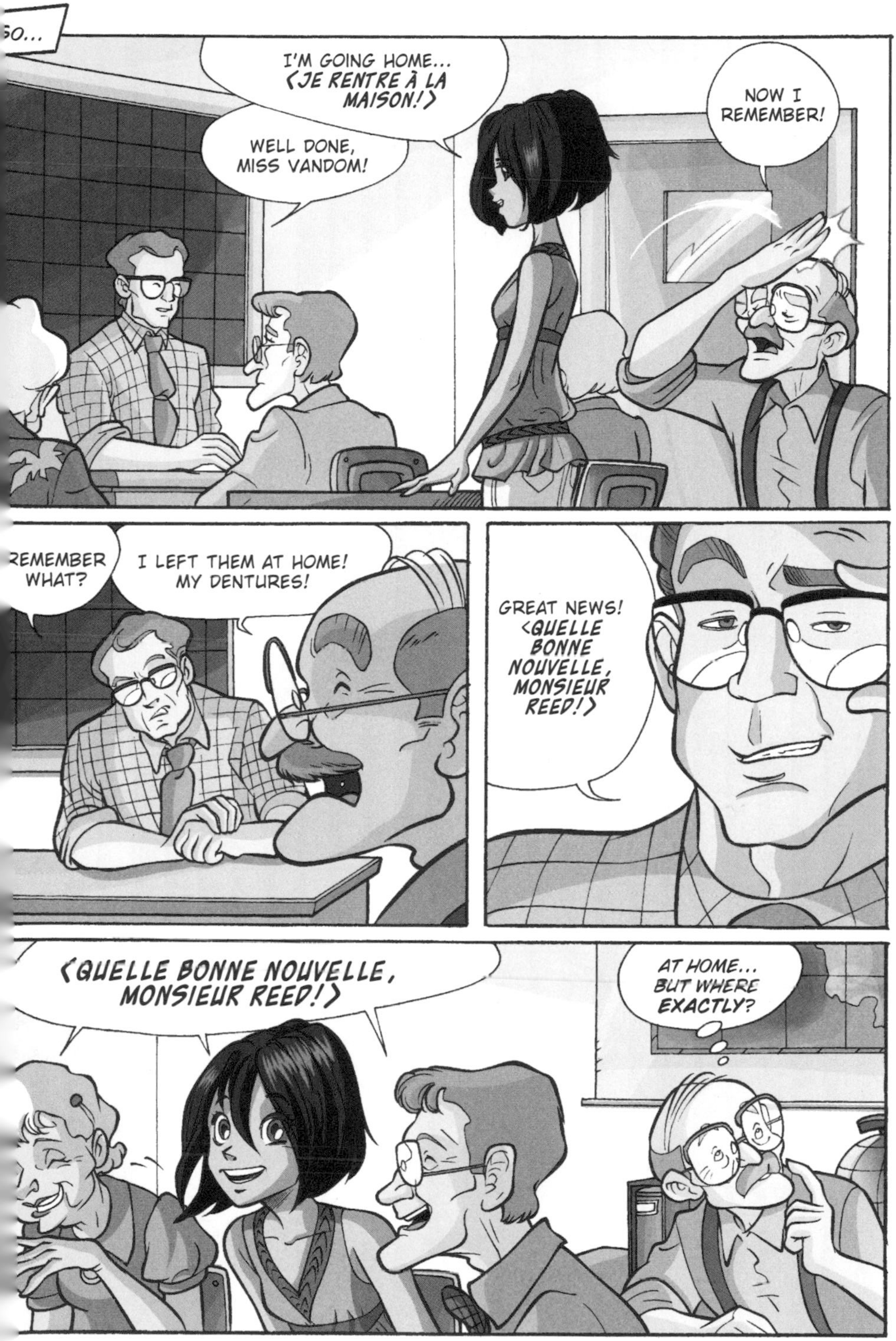
SO...
I'M GOING HOME... <JE RENTRE À LA MAISON!>
WELL DONE, MISS VANDOM!
NOW I REMEMBER!
REMEMBER WHAT?
I LEFT THEM AT HOME! MY DENTURES!
GREAT NEWS! <QUELLE BONNE NOUVELLE, MONSIEUR REED!>
<QUELLE BONNE NOUVELLE, MONSIEUR REED!>
AT HOME... BUT WHERE EXACTLY?

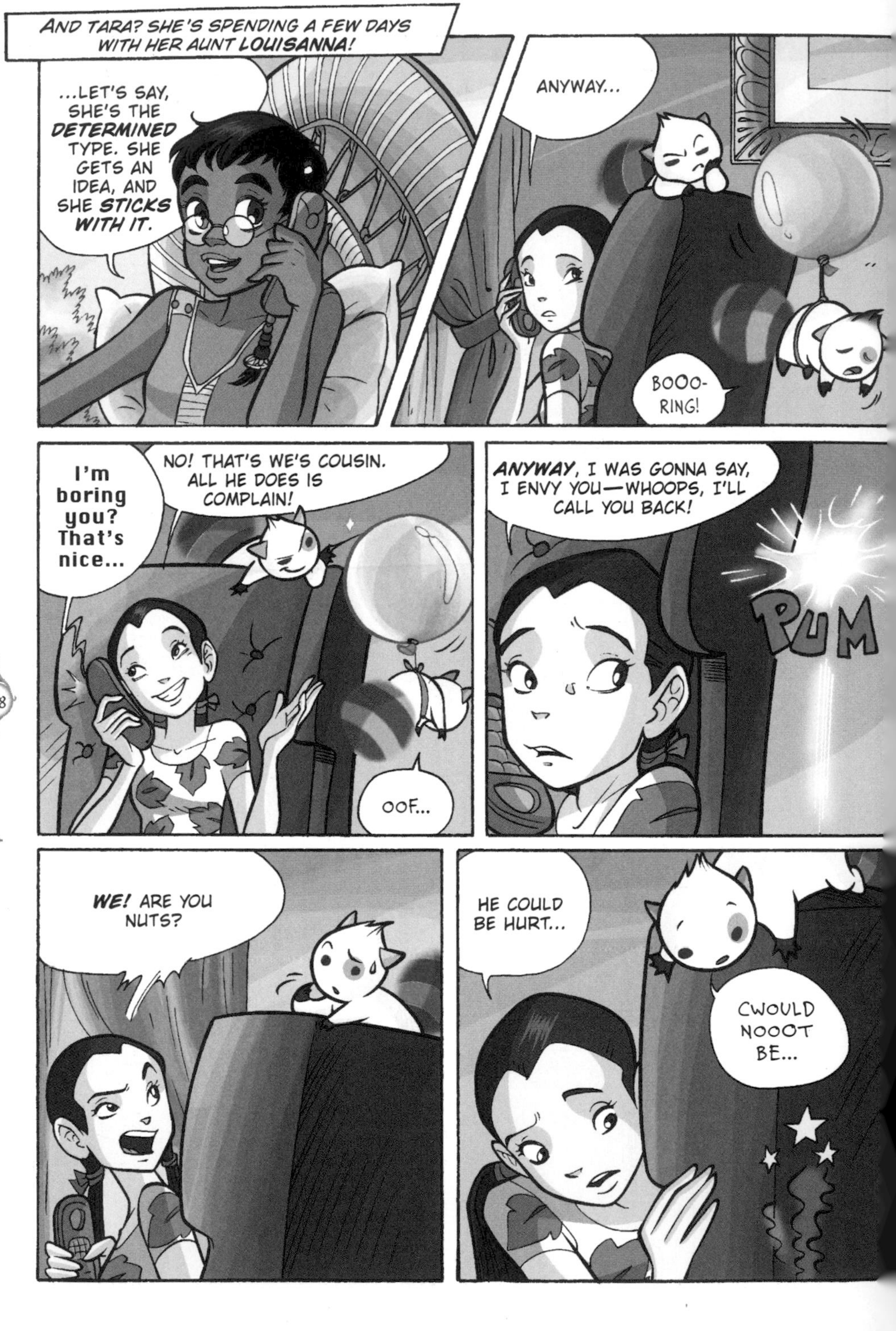
AND TARA? SHE'S SPENDING A FEW DAYS WITH HER AUNT LOUISANNA!
...LET'S SAY, SHE'S THE DETERMINED TYPE. SHE GETS AN IDEA, AND SHE STICKS WITH IT.
ANYWAY...
BOOO-RING!
I'm boring you? That's nice...
NO! THAT'S WE'S COUSIN. ALL HE DOES IS COMPLAIN!
OOF...
ANYWAY, I WAS GONNA SAY, I ENVY YOU—WHOOPS, I'LL CALL YOU BACK!
PUM
WE! ARE YOU NUTS?
HE COULD BE HURT...
CWOULD NOOOT BE...

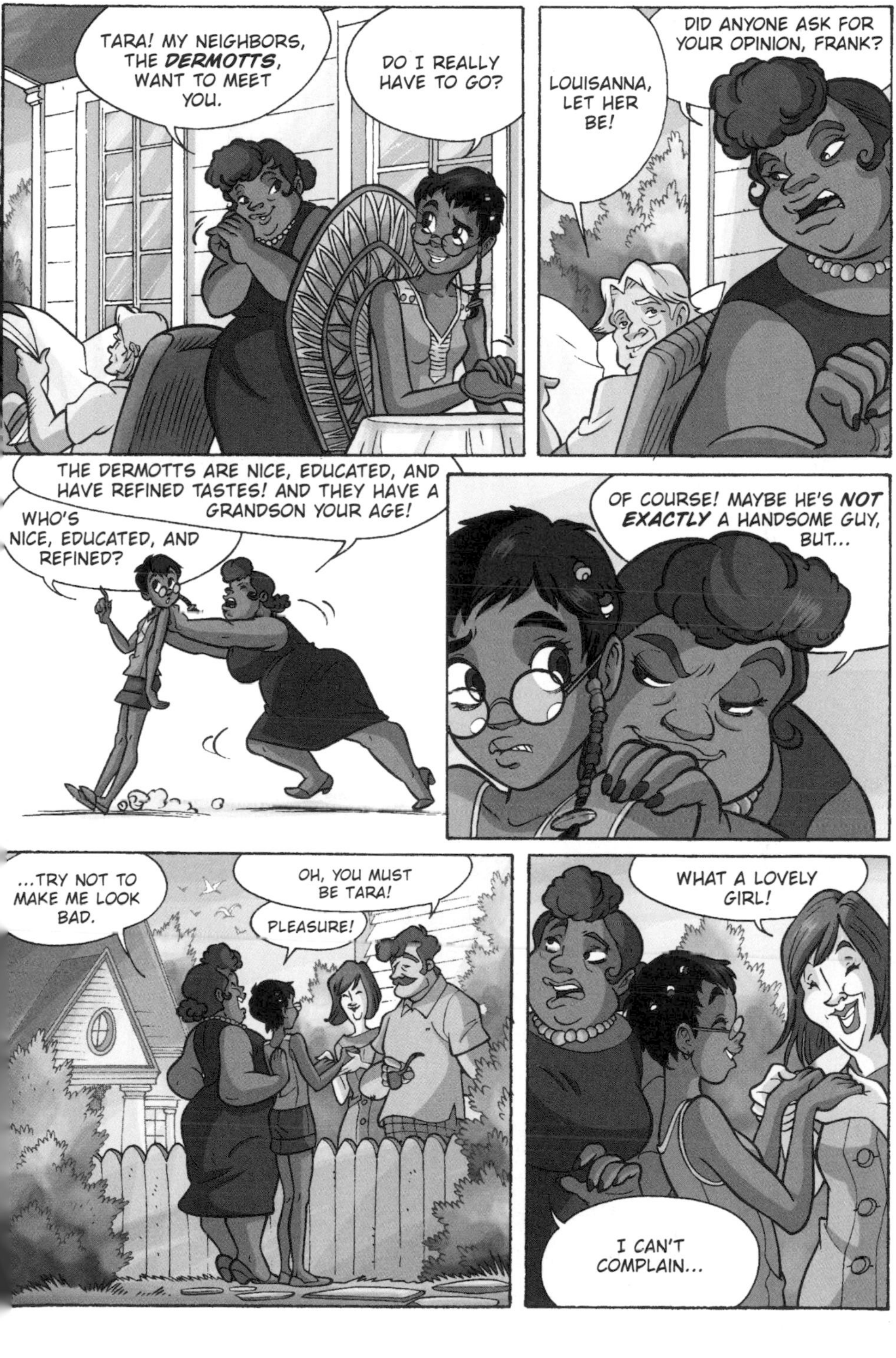
TARA! MY NEIGHBORS, THE **DERMOTTS**, WANT TO MEET YOU.
DO I REALLY HAVE TO GO?
LOUISANNA, LET HER BE!
DID ANYONE ASK FOR YOUR OPINION, FRANK?
THE DERMOTTS ARE NICE, EDUCATED, AND HAVE REFINED TASTES! AND THEY HAVE A GRANDSON YOUR AGE!
WHO'S NICE, EDUCATED, AND REFINED?
OF COURSE! MAYBE HE'S ***NOT EXACTLY*** A HANDSOME GUY, BUT...
...TRY NOT TO MAKE ME LOOK BAD.
OH, YOU MUST BE TARA!
PLEASURE!
WHAT A LOVELY GIRL!
I CAN'T COMPLAIN...

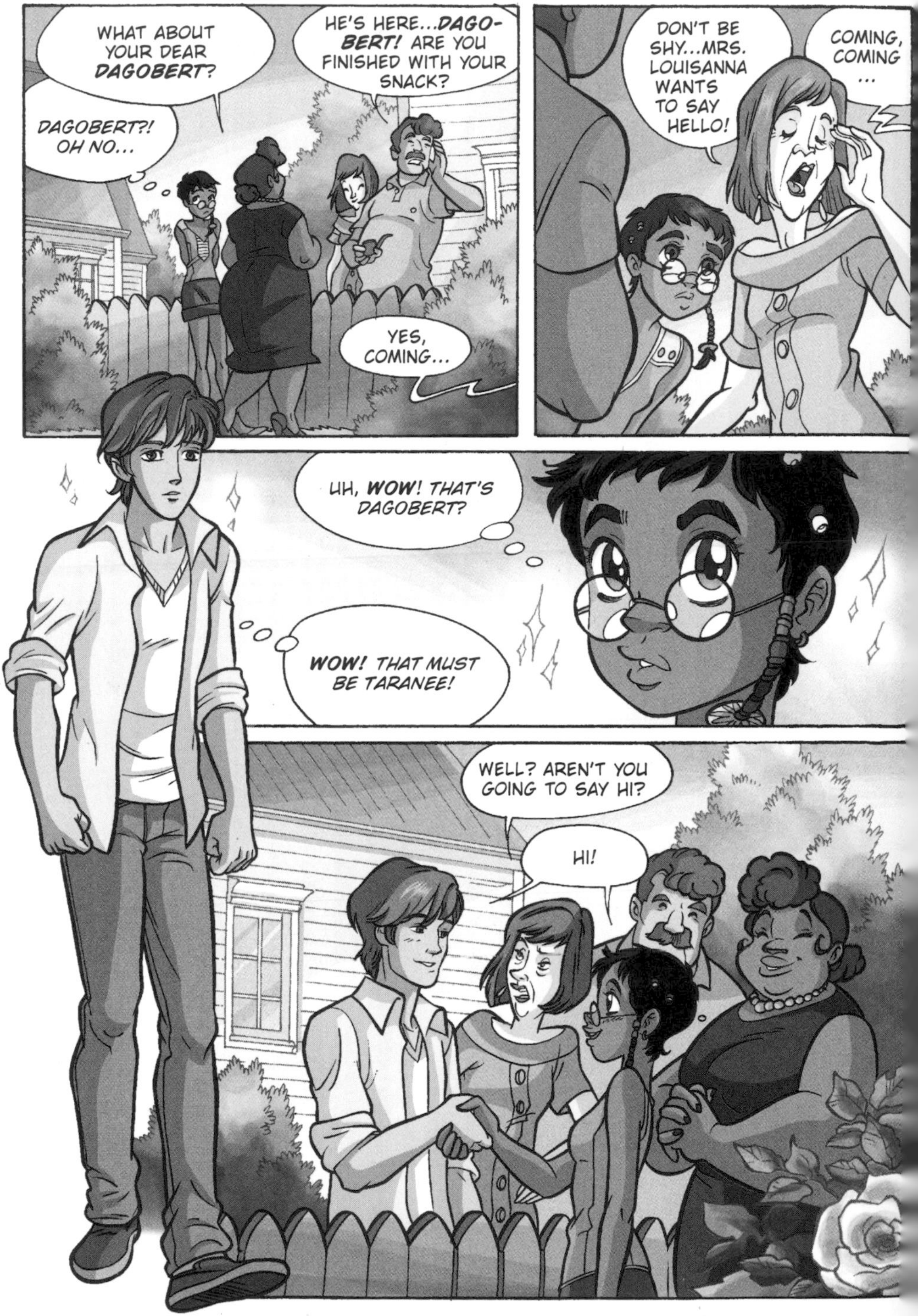
WHAT ABOUT YOUR DEAR DAGOBERT?
DAGOBERT?! OH NO...
HE'S HERE...DAGOBERT! ARE YOU FINISHED WITH YOUR SNACK?
YES, COMING...
DON'T BE SHY...MRS. LOUISANNA WANTS TO SAY HELLO!
COMING, COMING ...
UH, WOW! THAT'S DAGOBERT?
WOW! THAT MUST BE TARANEE!
WELL? AREN'T YOU GOING TO SAY HI?
HI!

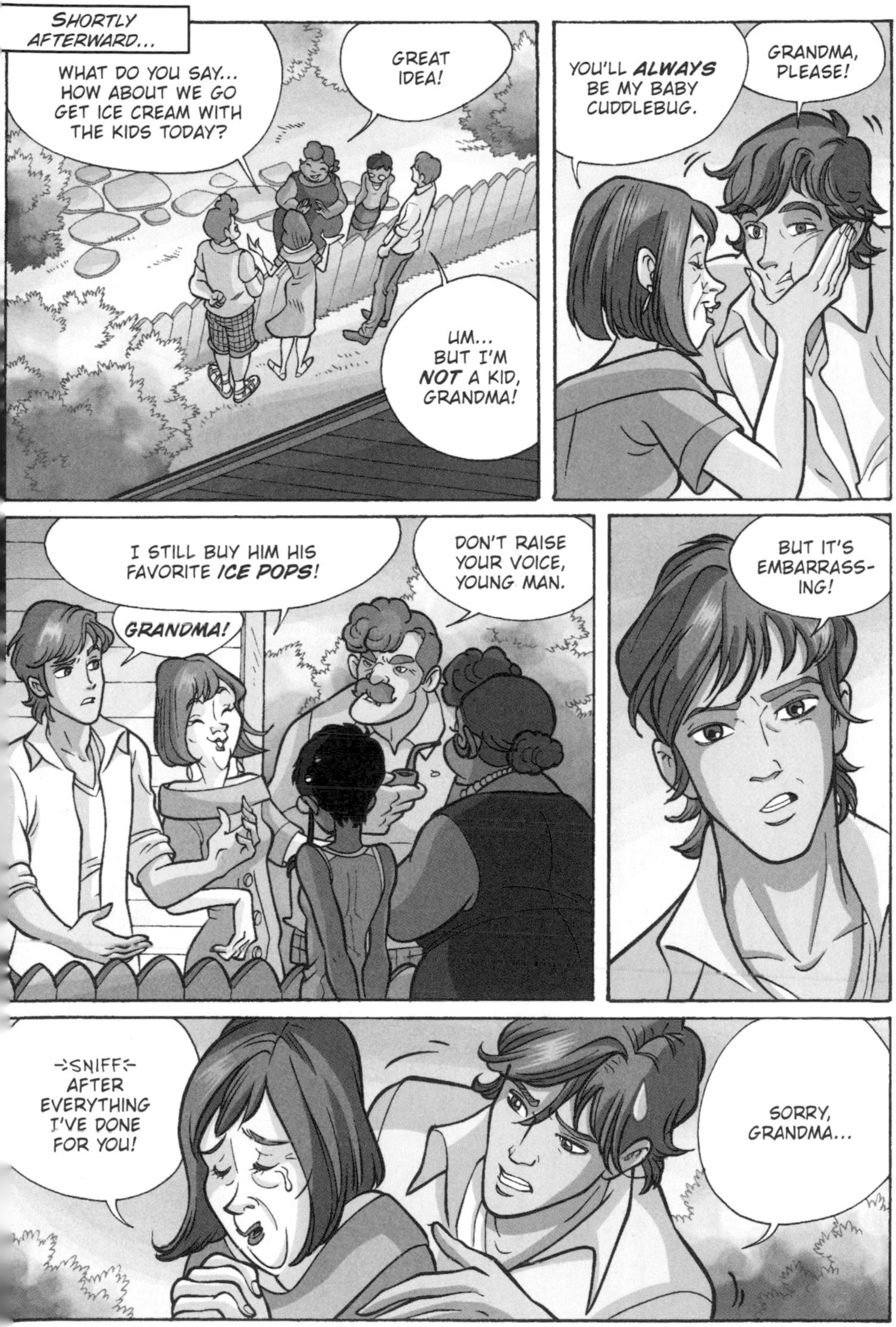
SHORTLY AFTERWARD...
WHAT DO YOU SAY... HOW ABOUT WE GO GET ICE CREAM WITH THE KIDS TODAY?
GREAT IDEA!
UM... BUT I'M NOT A KID, GRANDMA!
YOU'LL ALWAYS BE MY BABY CUDDLEBUG.
GRANDMA, PLEASE!
I STILL BUY HIM HIS FAVORITE ICE POPS!
GRANDMA!
DON'T RAISE YOUR VOICE, YOUNG MAN.
BUT IT'S EMBARRASS-ING!
-SNIFF- AFTER EVERYTHING I'VE DONE FOR YOU!
SORRY, GRANDMA...

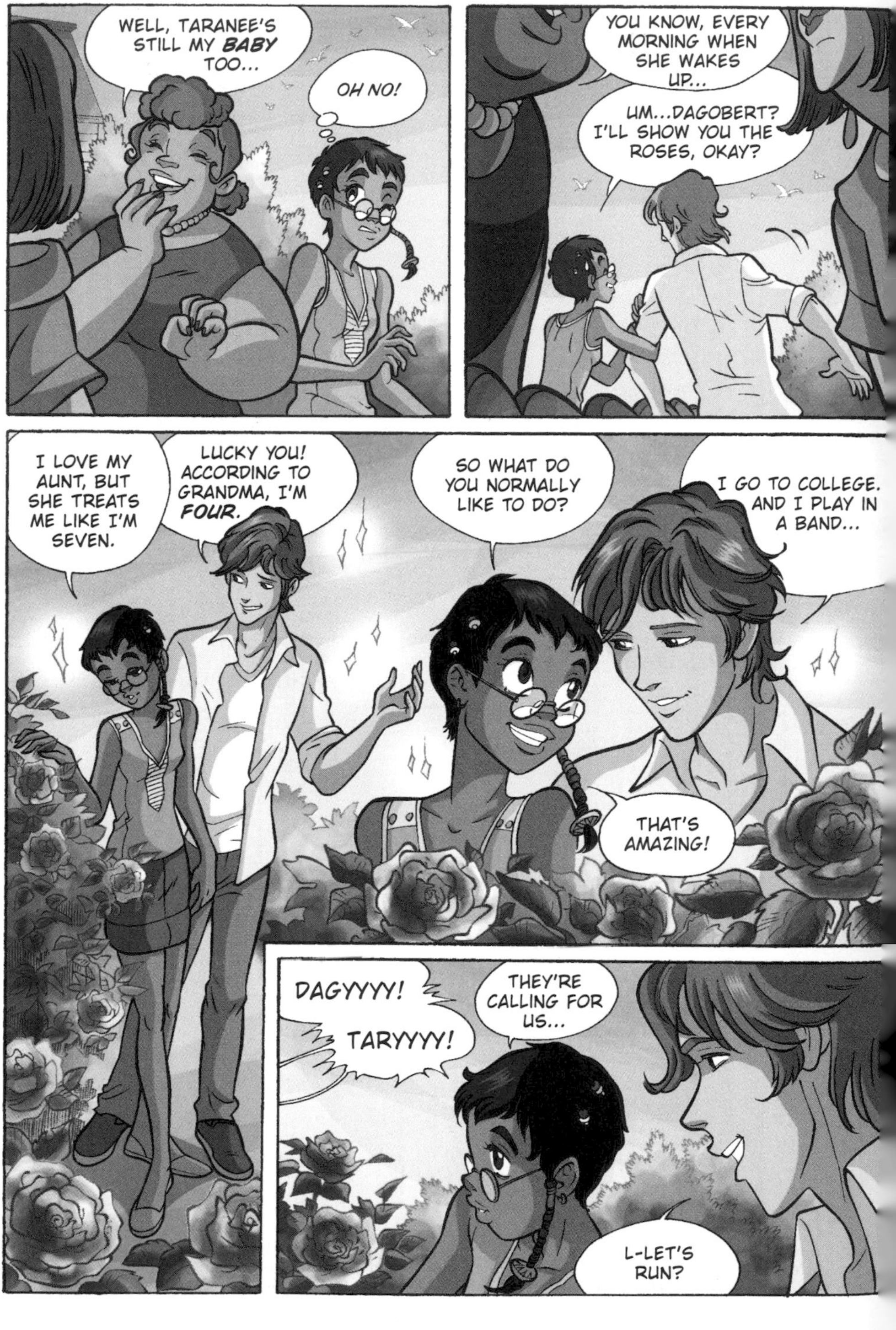
WELL, TARANEE'S STILL MY BABY TOO...
OH NO!
YOU KNOW, EVERY MORNING WHEN SHE WAKES UP...
UM...DAGOBERT? I'LL SHOW YOU THE ROSES, OKAY?
I LOVE MY AUNT, BUT SHE TREATS ME LIKE I'M SEVEN.
LUCKY YOU! ACCORDING TO GRANDMA, I'M FOUR.
SO WHAT DO YOU NORMALLY LIKE TO DO?
I GO TO COLLEGE. AND I PLAY IN A BAND...
THAT'S AMAZING!
DAGYYYY!
TARYYYY!
THEY'RE CALLING FOR US...
L-LET'S RUN?

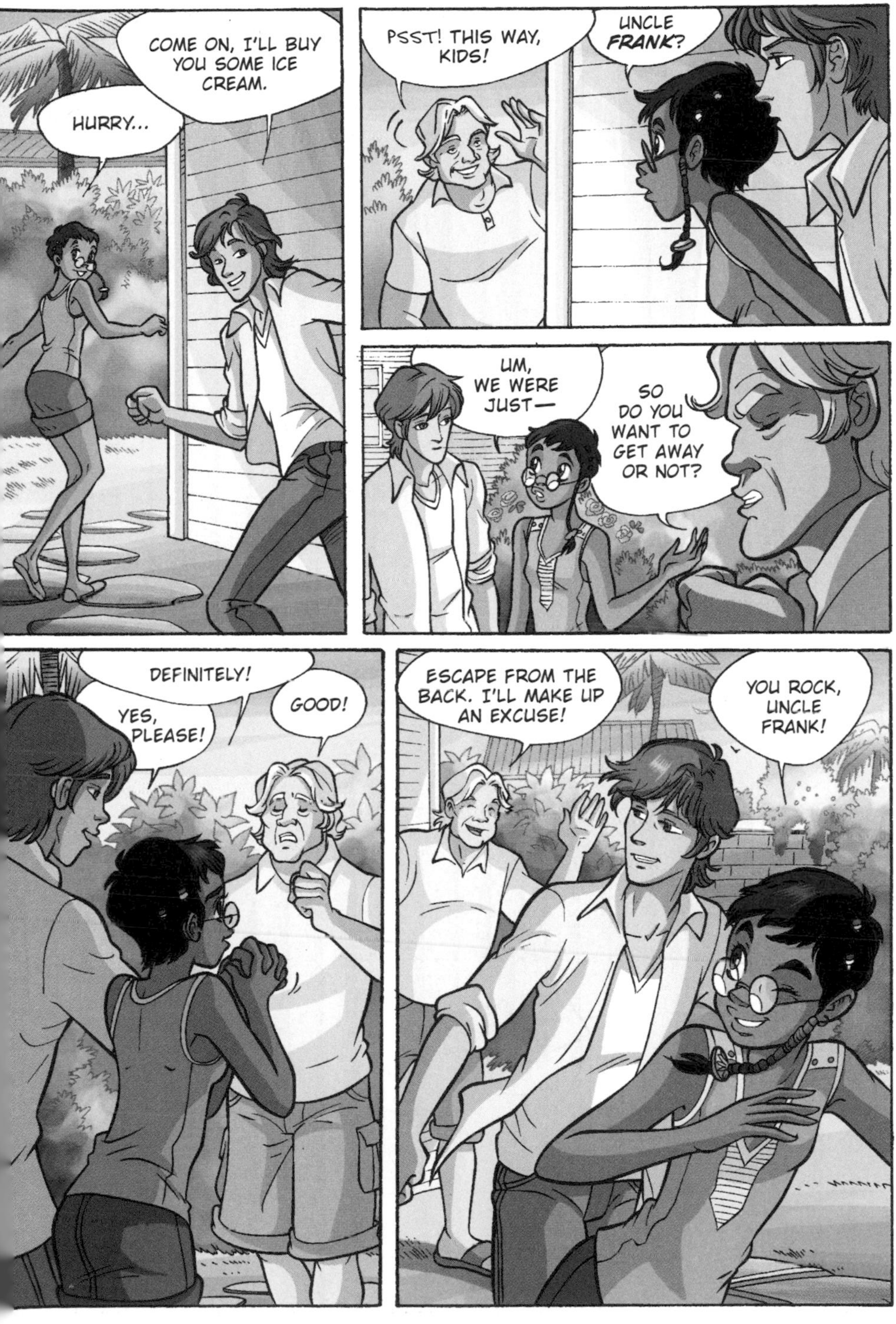

HURRY...
COME ON, I'LL BUY YOU SOME ICE CREAM.
PSST! THIS WAY, KIDS!
UNCLE FRANK?
UM, WE WERE JUST—
SO DO YOU WANT TO GET AWAY OR NOT?
DEFINITELY!
YES, PLEASE!
GOOD!
ESCAPE FROM THE BACK. I'LL MAKE UP AN EXCUSE!
YOU ROCK, UNCLE FRANK!

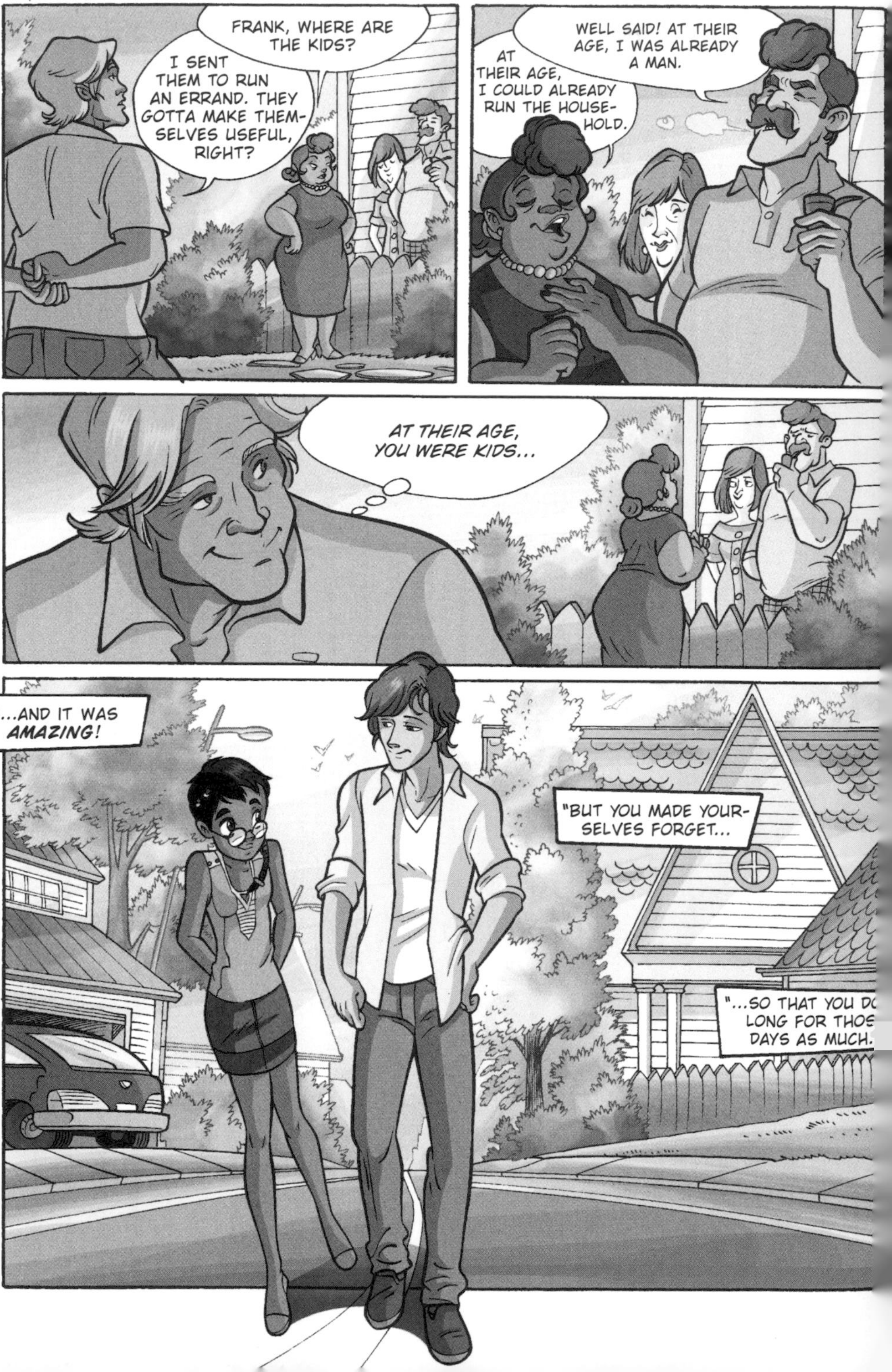
FRANK, WHERE ARE THE KIDS?
I SENT THEM TO RUN AN ERRAND. THEY GOTTA MAKE THEM-SELVES USEFUL, RIGHT?
AT THEIR AGE, I COULD ALREADY RUN THE HOUSE-HOLD.
WELL SAID! AT THEIR AGE, I WAS ALREADY A MAN.
AT THEIR AGE, YOU WERE KIDS...
"...AND IT WAS AMAZING!
"BUT YOU MADE YOUR-SELVES FORGET...
"...SO THAT YOU DO LONG FOR THOS DAYS AS MUCH.

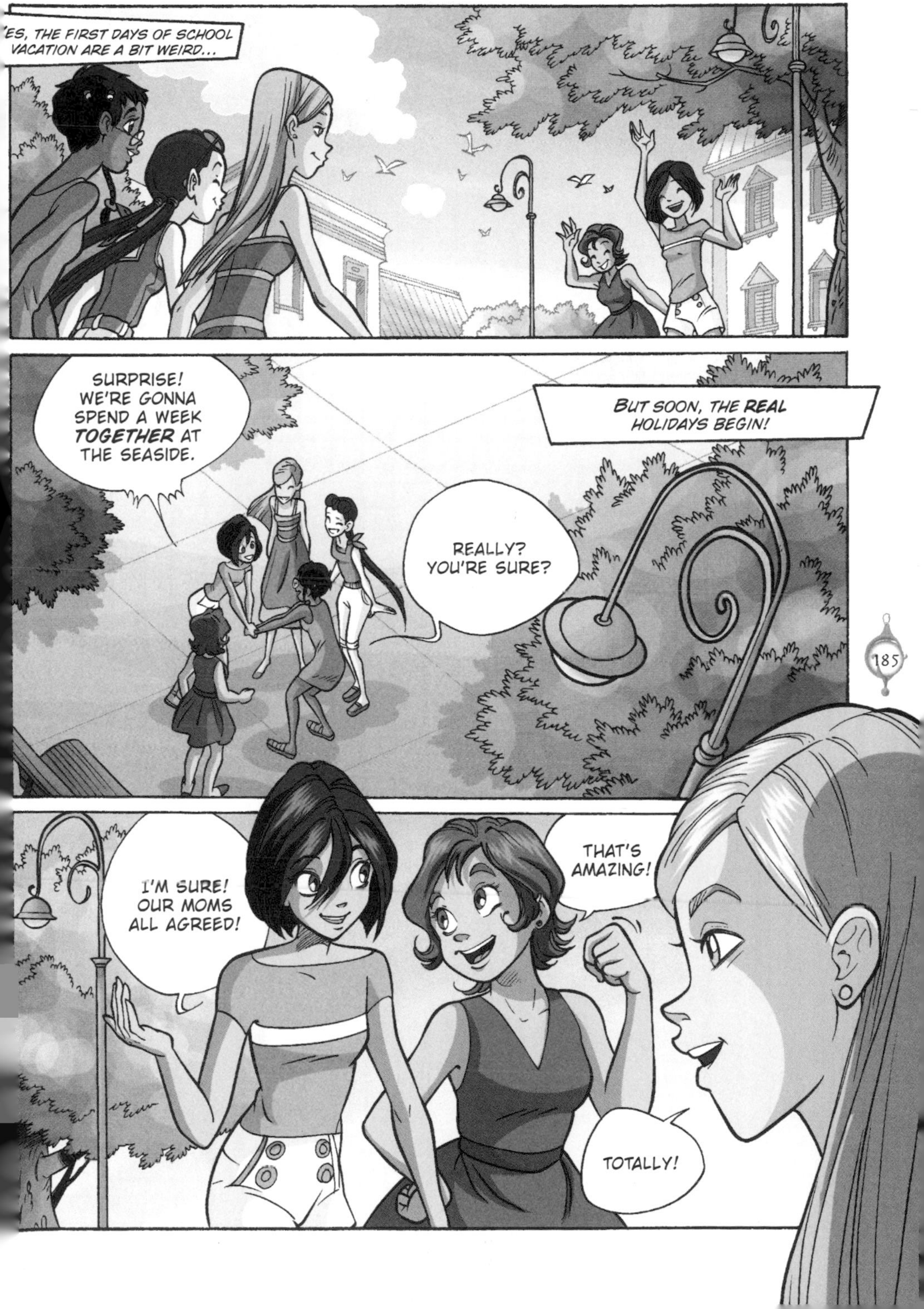
'ES, THE FIRST DAYS OF SCHOOL VACATION ARE A BIT WEIRD...
SURPRISE! WE'RE GONNA SPEND A WEEK TOGETHER AT THE SEASIDE.
BUT SOON, THE REAL HOLIDAYS BEGIN!
REALLY? YOU'RE SURE?
I'M SURE! OUR MOMS ALL AGREED!
THAT'S AMAZING!
TOTALLY!

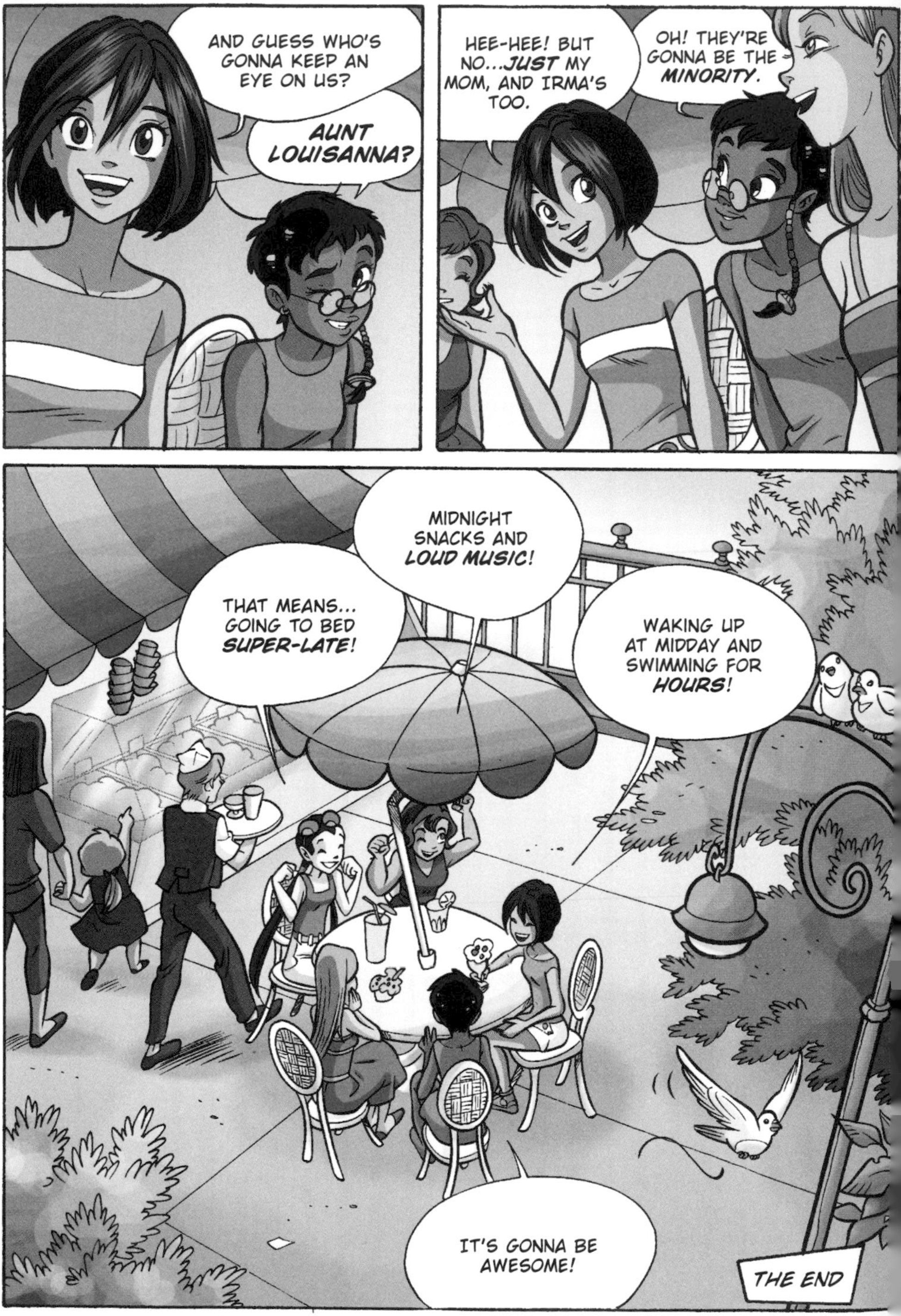
AND GUESS WHO'S GONNA KEEP AN EYE ON US?
AUNT LOUISANNA?
HEE-HEE! BUT NO...JUST MY MOM, AND IRMA'S TOO.
OH! THEY'RE GONNA BE THE MINORITY.
THAT MEANS... GOING TO BED SUPER-LATE!
MIDNIGHT SNACKS AND LOUD MUSIC!
WAKING UP AT MIDDAY AND SWIMMING FOR HOURS!
IT'S GONNA BE AWESOME!
THE END

W.i.t.c.h.

Will Irma Taranee Cornelia Hay Lin

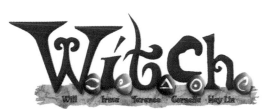

W.i.t.c.h.

Will Irma Taranee Cornelia Hay Lin

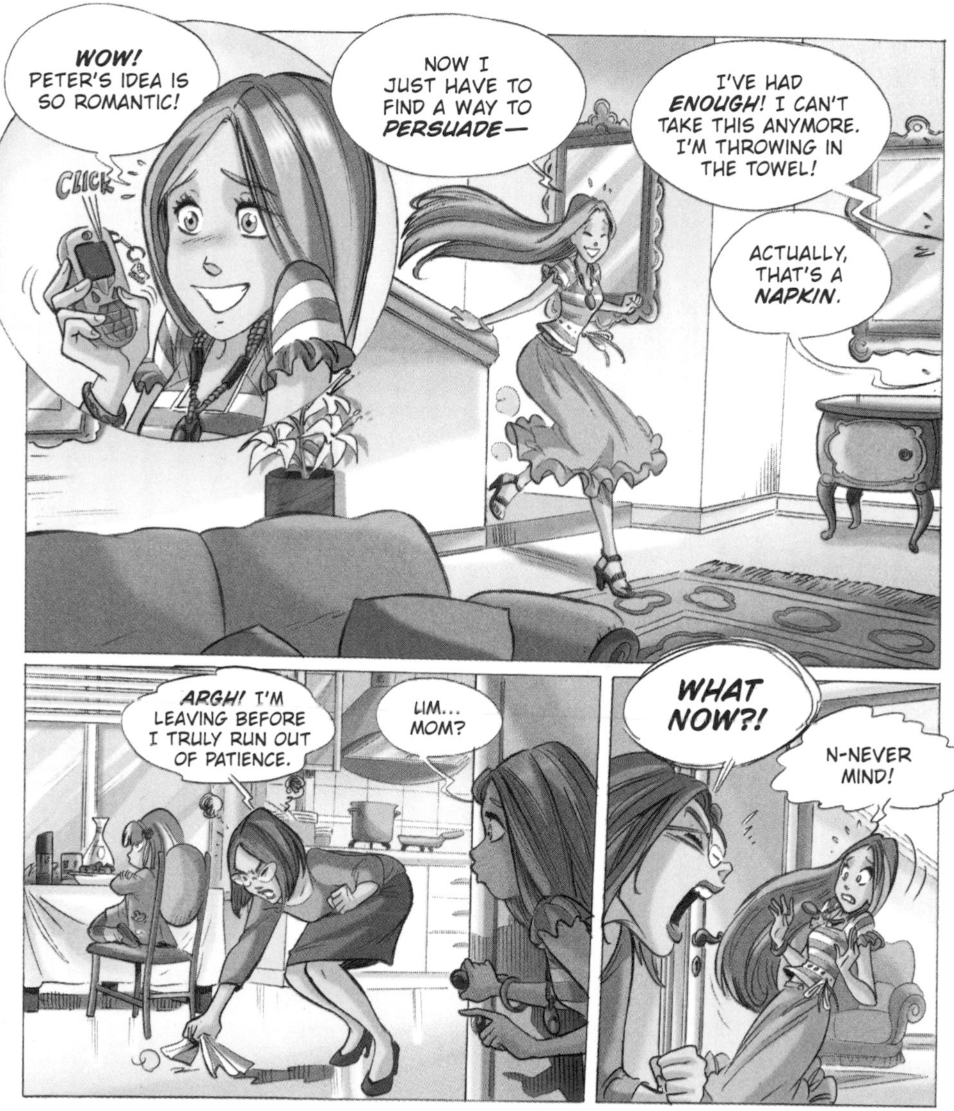
WOW! PETER'S IDEA IS SO ROMANTIC!
CLICK
NOW I JUST HAVE TO FIND A WAY TO PERSUADE—
I'VE HAD ENOUGH! I CAN'T TAKE THIS ANYMORE. I'M THROWING IN THE TOWEL!
ACTUALLY, THAT'S A NAPKIN.
ARGH! I'M LEAVING BEFORE I TRULY RUN OUT OF PATIENCE.
UM... MOM?
WHAT NOW?!
N-NEVER MIND!

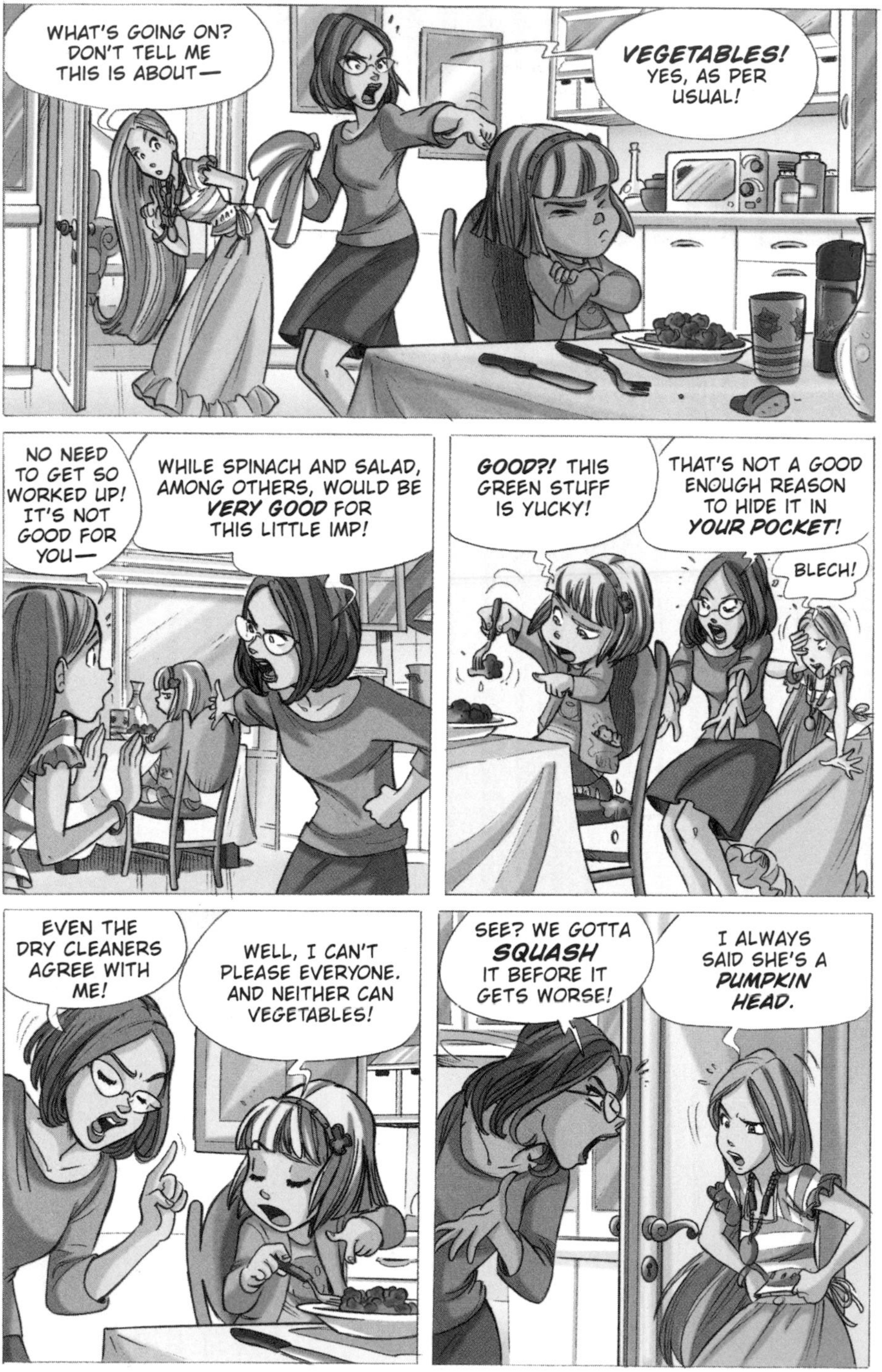
WHAT'S GOING ON? DON'T TELL ME THIS IS ABOUT—
VEGETABLES! YES, AS PER USUAL!
NO NEED TO GET SO WORKED UP! IT'S NOT GOOD FOR YOU—
WHILE SPINACH AND SALAD, AMONG OTHERS, WOULD BE VERY GOOD FOR THIS LITTLE IMP!
GOOD?! THIS GREEN STUFF IS YUCKY!
THAT'S NOT A GOOD ENOUGH REASON TO HIDE IT IN YOUR POCKET!
BLECH!
EVEN THE DRY CLEANERS AGREE WITH ME!
WELL, I CAN'T PLEASE EVERYONE. AND NEITHER CAN VEGETABLES!
SEE? WE GOTTA SQUASH IT BEFORE IT GETS WORSE!
I ALWAYS SAID SHE'S A PUMPKIN HEAD.

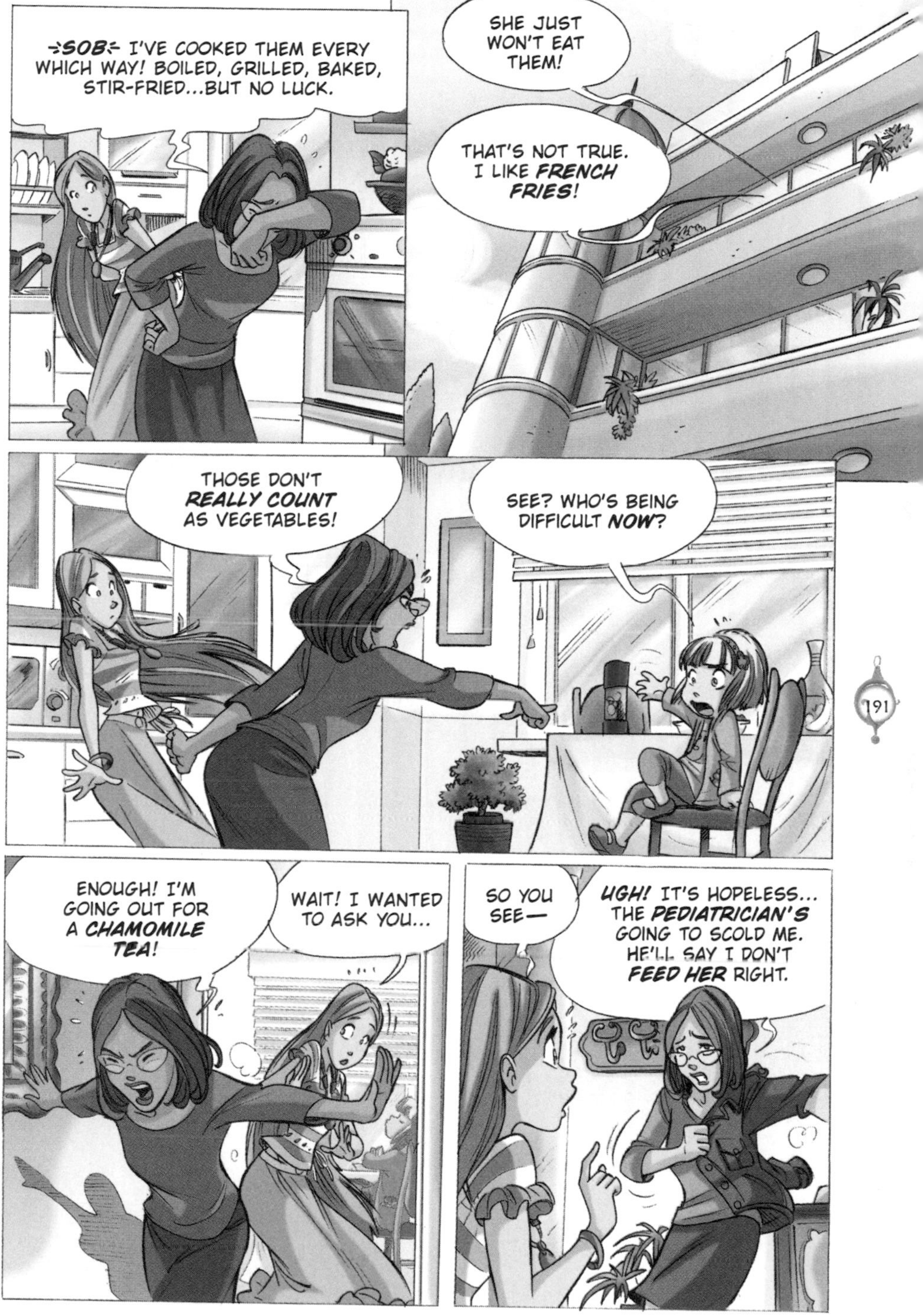

SOB I'VE COOKED THEM EVERY WHICH WAY! BOILED, GRILLED, BAKED, STIR-FRIED...BUT NO LUCK.
SHE JUST WON'T EAT THEM!
THAT'S NOT TRUE. I LIKE FRENCH FRIES!
THOSE DON'T REALLY COUNT AS VEGETABLES!
SEE? WHO'S BEING DIFFICULT NOW?
ENOUGH! I'M GOING OUT FOR A CHAMOMILE TEA!
WAIT! I WANTED TO ASK YOU...
SO YOU SEE—
UGH! IT'S HOPELESS... THE PEDIATRICIAN'S GOING TO SCOLD ME. HE'LL SAY I DON'T FEED HER RIGHT.

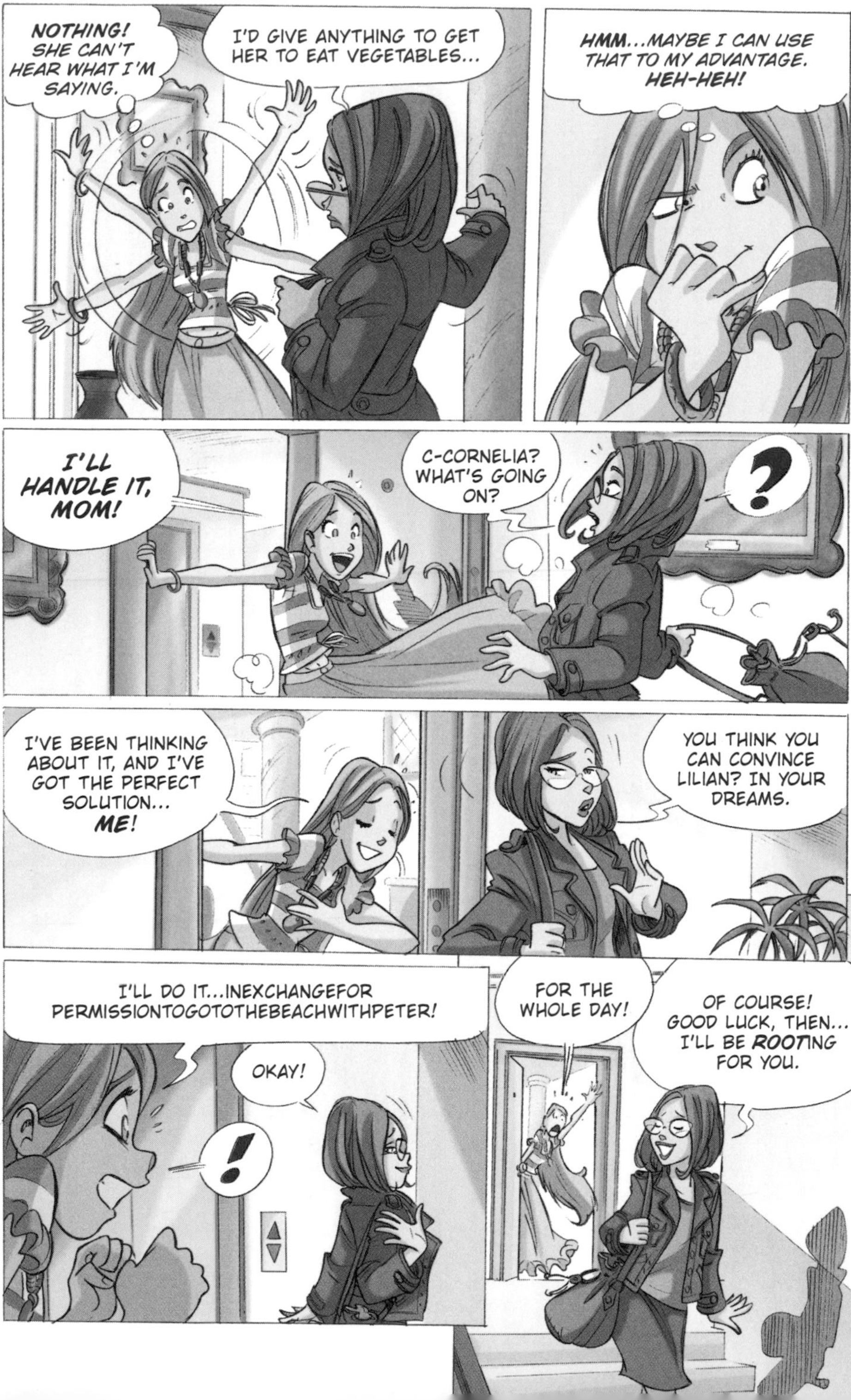
NOTHING! SHE CAN'T HEAR WHAT I'M SAYING.
I'D GIVE ANYTHING TO GET HER TO EAT VEGETABLES...
HMM...MAYBE I CAN USE THAT TO MY ADVANTAGE. HEH-HEH!
I'LL HANDLE IT, MOM!
C-CORNELIA? WHAT'S GOING ON?
?
I'VE BEEN THINKING ABOUT IT, AND I'VE GOT THE PERFECT SOLUTION... ME!
YOU THINK YOU CAN CONVINCE LILIAN? IN YOUR DREAMS.
I'LL DO IT...INEXCHANGEFOR PERMISSIONTOGOTOTHEBEACHWITHPETER!
OKAY!
!
FOR THE WHOLE DAY!
OF COURSE! GOOD LUCK, THEN... I'LL BE ROOTING FOR YOU.

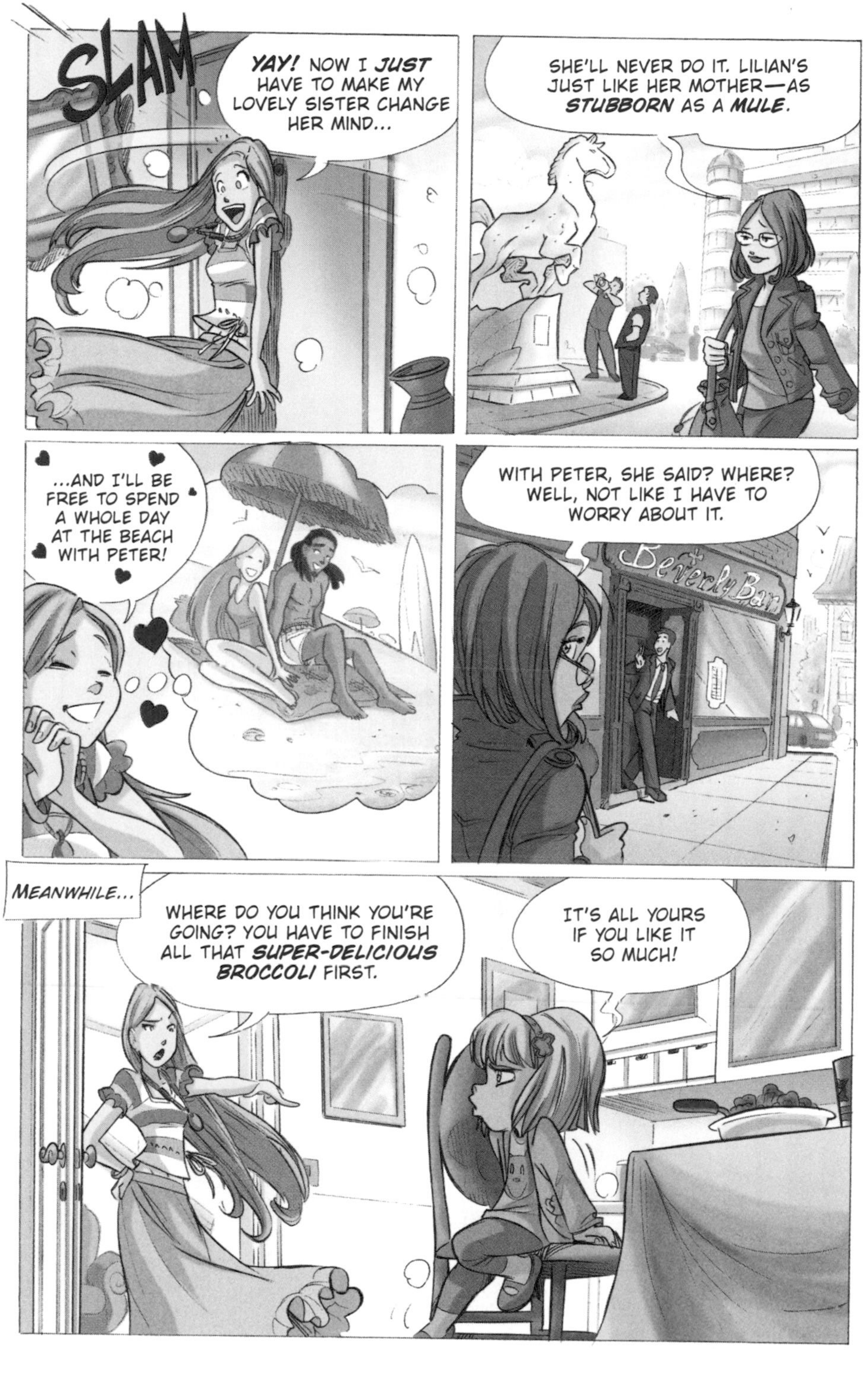

SLAM
YAY! NOW I JUST HAVE TO MAKE MY LOVELY SISTER CHANGE HER MIND...
SHE'LL NEVER DO IT. LILIAN'S JUST LIKE HER MOTHER—AS STUBBORN AS A MULE.
...AND I'LL BE FREE TO SPEND A WHOLE DAY AT THE BEACH WITH PETER!
WITH PETER, SHE SAID? WHERE? WELL, NOT LIKE I HAVE TO WORRY ABOUT IT.
Beverly Bar
MEANWHILE...
WHERE DO YOU THINK YOU'RE GOING? YOU HAVE TO FINISH ALL THAT SUPER-DELICIOUS BROCCOLI FIRST.
IT'S ALL YOURS IF YOU LIKE IT SO MUCH!

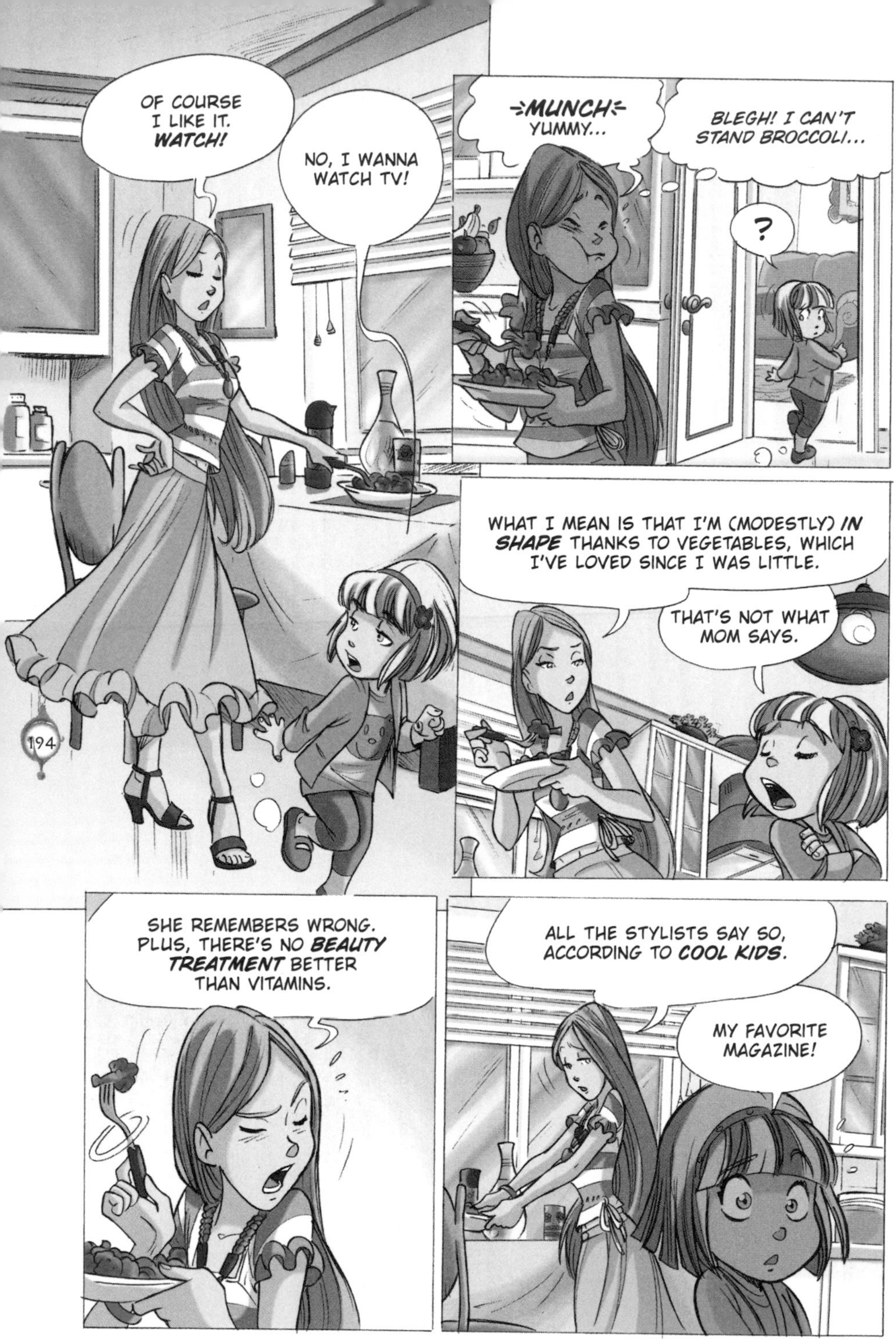
OF COURSE I LIKE IT. WATCH!
NO, I WANNA WATCH TV!
MUNCH YUMMY...
BLEGH! I CAN'T STAND BROCCOLI...
?
WHAT I MEAN IS THAT I'M (MODESTLY) IN SHAPE THANKS TO VEGETABLES, WHICH I'VE LOVED SINCE I WAS LITTLE.
THAT'S NOT WHAT MOM SAYS.
SHE REMEMBERS WRONG. PLUS, THERE'S NO BEAUTY TREATMENT BETTER THAN VITAMINS.
ALL THE STYLISTS SAY SO, ACCORDING TO COOL KIDS.
MY FAVORITE MAGAZINE!

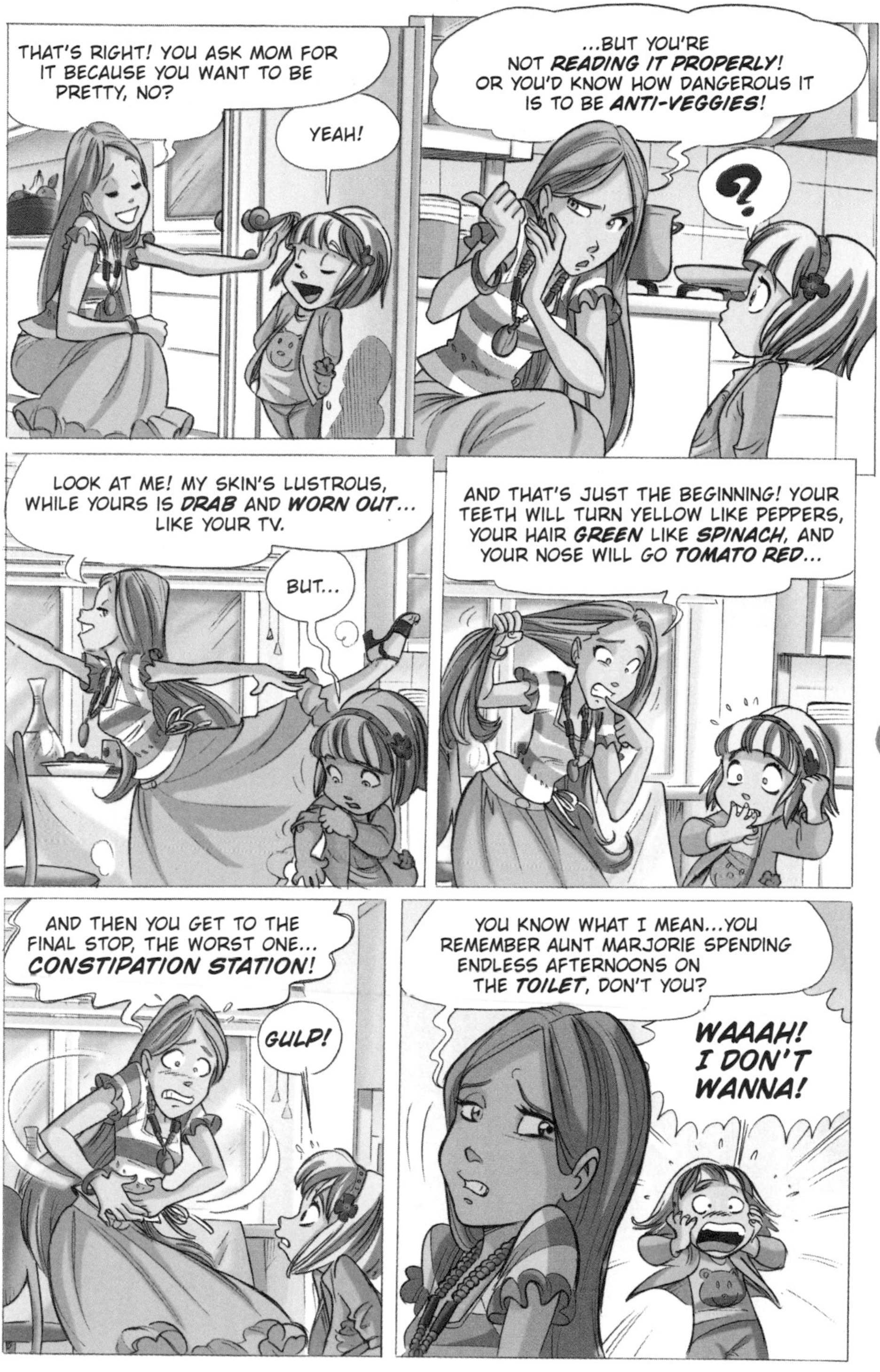
THAT'S RIGHT! YOU ASK MOM FOR IT BECAUSE YOU WANT TO BE PRETTY, NO?
YEAH!
...BUT YOU'RE NOT *READING IT PROPERLY*! OR YOU'D KNOW HOW DANGEROUS IT IS TO BE *ANTI-VEGGIES*!
?
LOOK AT ME! MY SKIN'S LUSTROUS, WHILE YOURS IS *DRAB* AND *WORN OUT*... LIKE YOUR TV.
BUT...
AND THAT'S JUST THE BEGINNING! YOUR TEETH WILL TURN YELLOW LIKE PEPPERS, YOUR HAIR *GREEN* LIKE *SPINACH*, AND YOUR NOSE WILL GO *TOMATO RED*...
AND THEN YOU GET TO THE FINAL STOP, THE WORST ONE... *CONSTIPATION STATION*!
GULP!
YOU KNOW WHAT I MEAN...YOU REMEMBER AUNT MARJORIE SPENDING ENDLESS AFTERNOONS ON THE *TOILET*, DON'T YOU?
WAAAH! I DON'T WANNA!

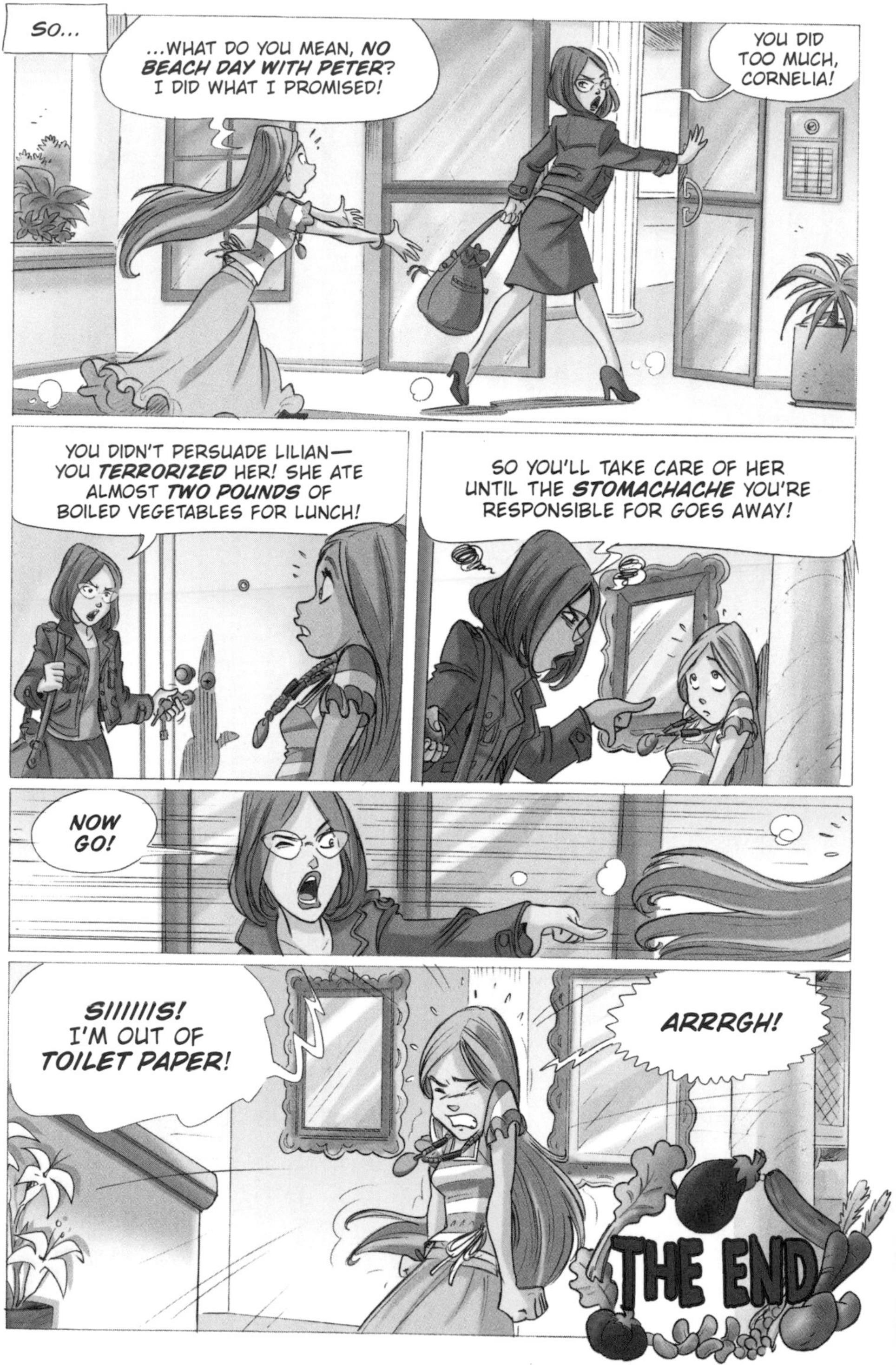
SO...
...WHAT DO YOU MEAN, NO BEACH DAY WITH PETER? I DID WHAT I PROMISED!
YOU DID TOO MUCH, CORNELIA!
YOU DIDN'T PERSUADE LILIAN—YOU TERRORIZED HER! SHE ATE ALMOST TWO POUNDS OF BOILED VEGETABLES FOR LUNCH!
SO YOU'LL TAKE CARE OF HER UNTIL THE STOMACHACHE YOU'RE RESPONSIBLE FOR GOES AWAY!
NOW GO!
SIIIIIIS! I'M OUT OF TOILET PAPER!
ARRRGH!
THE END

What's Truly Lucky

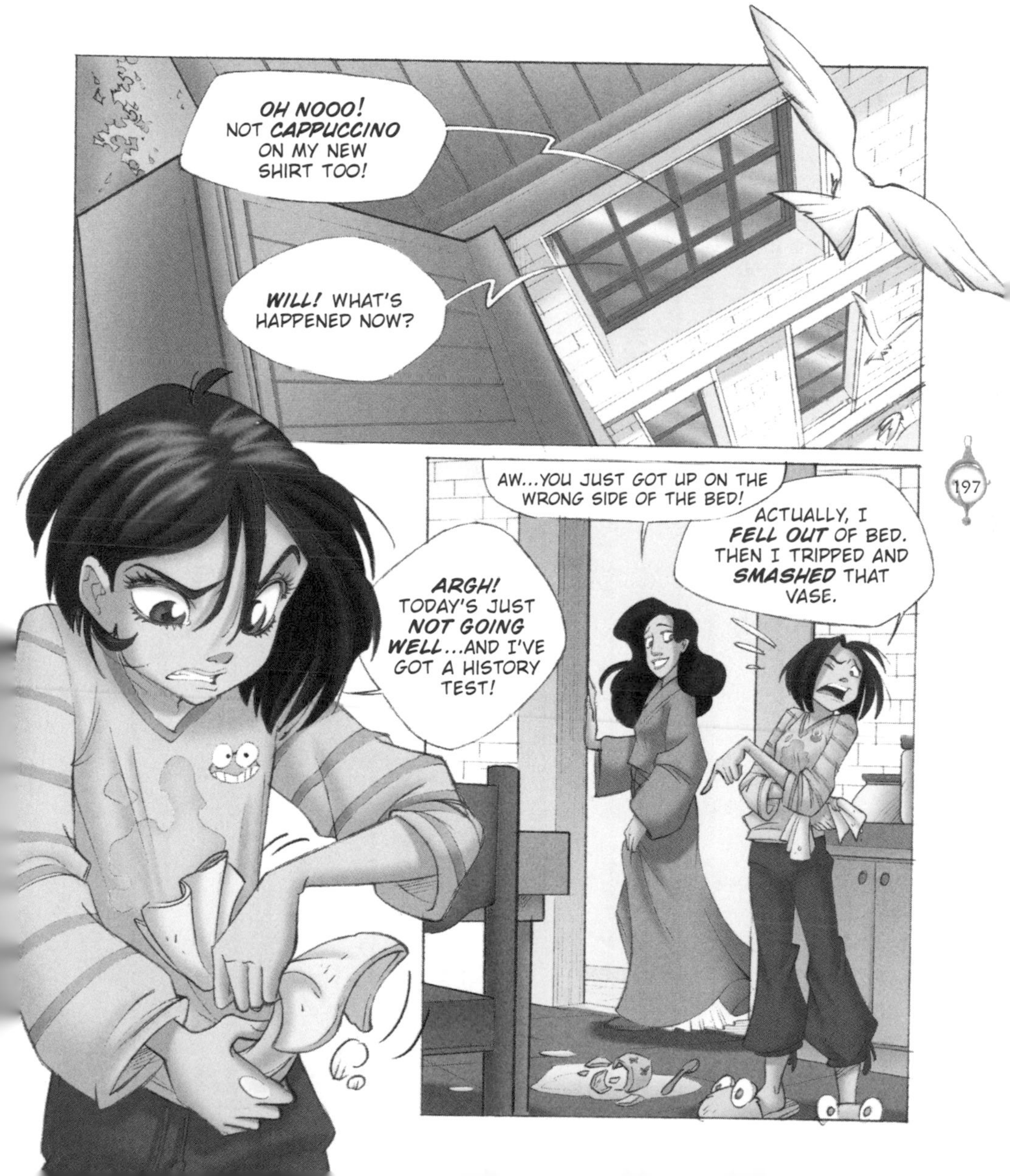
OH NOOO! NOT CAPPUCCINO ON MY NEW SHIRT TOO!
WILL! WHAT'S HAPPENED NOW?
ARGH! TODAY'S JUST NOT GOING WELL...AND I'VE GOT A HISTORY TEST!
AW...YOU JUST GOT UP ON THE WRONG SIDE OF THE BED!
ACTUALLY, I FELL OUT OF BED. THEN I TRIPPED AND SMASHED THAT VASE.

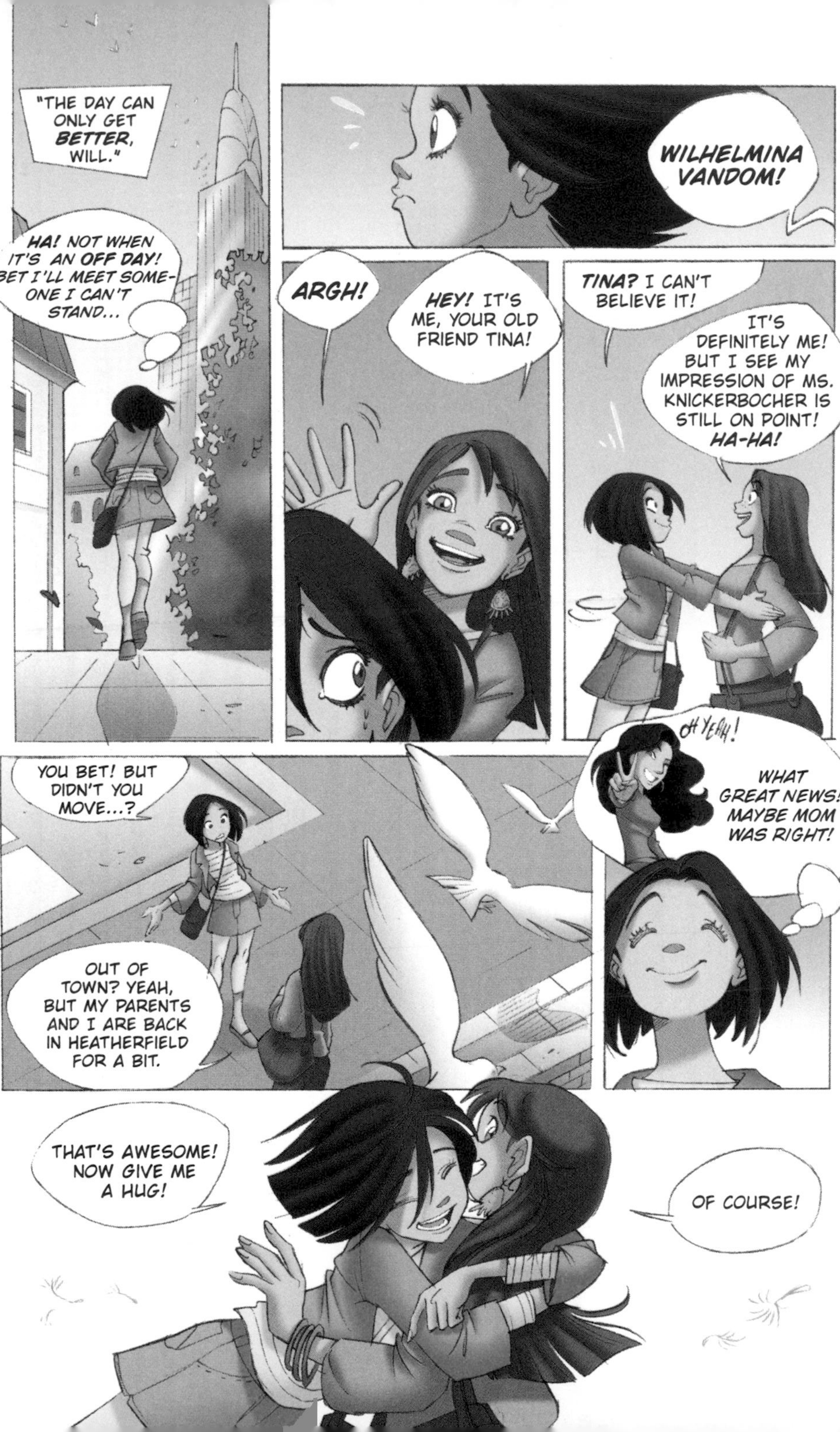
"THE DAY CAN ONLY GET BETTER, WILL."
HA! NOT WHEN IT'S AN OFF DAY! BET I'LL MEET SOME-ONE I CAN'T STAND...
WILHELMINA VANDOM!
ARGH!
HEY! IT'S ME, YOUR OLD FRIEND TINA!
TINA? I CAN'T BELIEVE IT!
IT'S DEFINITELY ME! BUT I SEE MY IMPRESSION OF MS. KNICKERBOCHER IS STILL ON POINT! HA-HA!
YOU BET! BUT DIDN'T YOU MOVE...?
OUT OF TOWN? YEAH, BUT MY PARENTS AND I ARE BACK IN HEATHERFIELD FOR A BIT.
OH YEAH!
WHAT GREAT NEWS! MAYBE MOM WAS RIGHT!
THAT'S AWESOME! NOW GIVE ME A HUG!
OF COURSE!

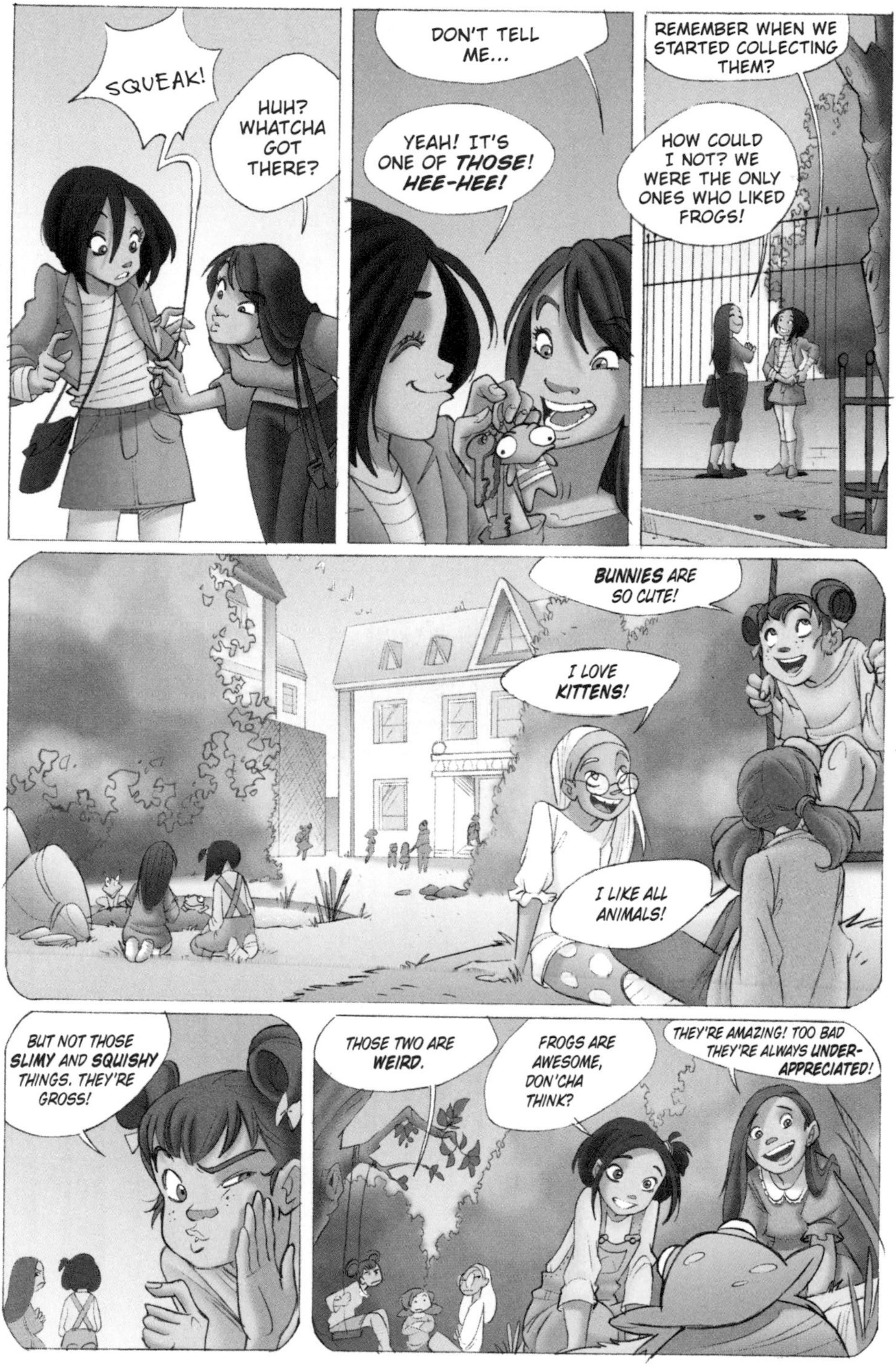
SQUEAK!
HUH? WHATCHA GOT THERE?
DON'T TELL ME...
YEAH! IT'S ONE OF **THOSE**! **HEE-HEE!**
REMEMBER WHEN WE STARTED COLLECTING THEM?
HOW COULD I NOT? WE WERE THE ONLY ONES WHO LIKED FROGS!
BUNNIES ARE SO CUTE!
I LOVE **KITTENS**!
I LIKE ALL ANIMALS!
BUT NOT THOSE **SLIMY** AND **SQUISHY** THINGS. THEY'RE GROSS!
THOSE TWO ARE **WEIRD**.
FROGS ARE AWESOME, DON'CHA THINK?
THEY'RE AMAZING! TOO BAD THEY'RE ALWAYS **UNDER-APPRECIATED**!

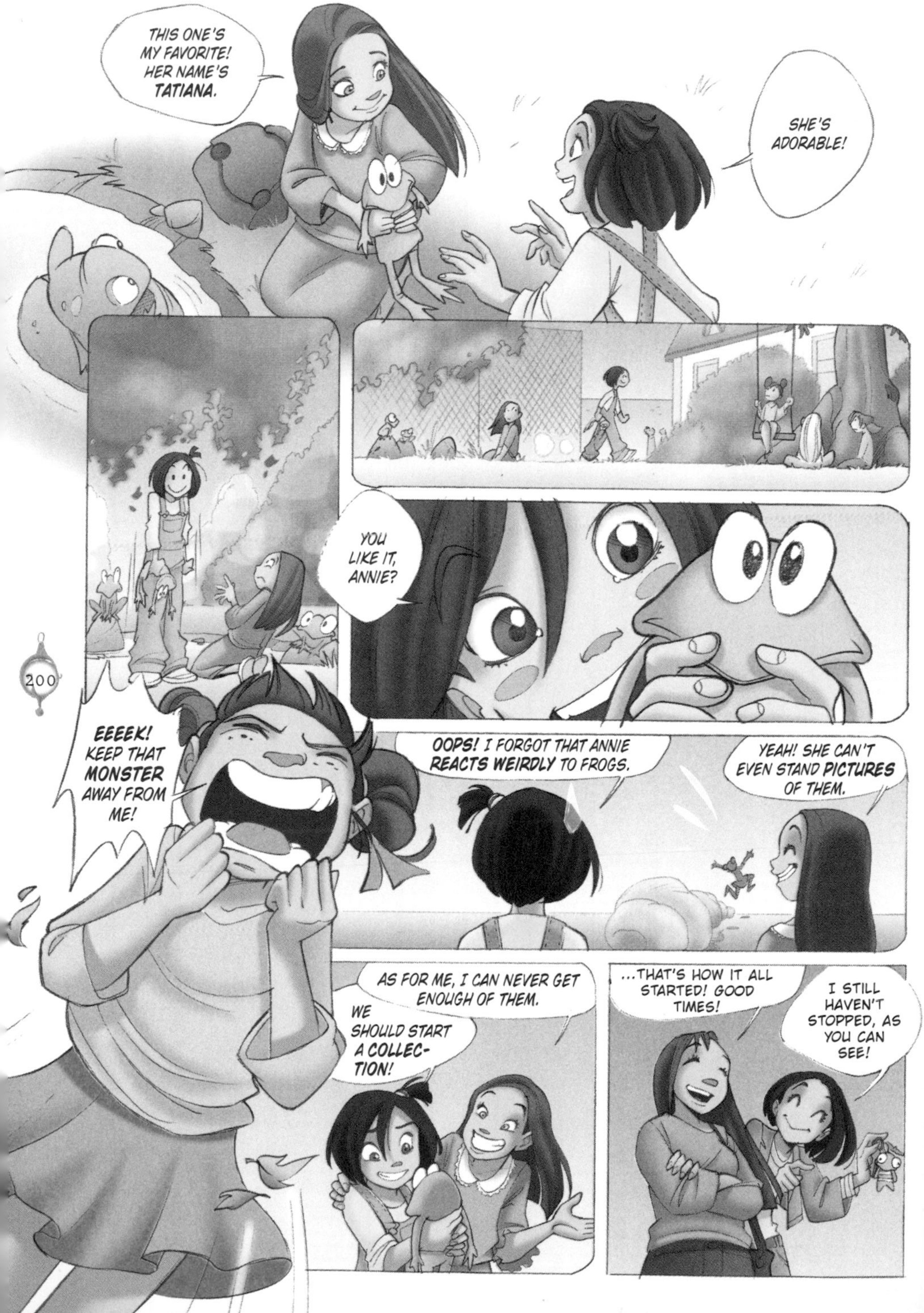

THIS ONE'S MY FAVORITE! HER NAME'S TATIANA.
SHE'S ADORABLE!
YOU LIKE IT, ANNIE?
EEEEK! KEEP THAT MONSTER AWAY FROM ME!
OOPS! I FORGOT THAT ANNIE REACTS WEIRDLY TO FROGS.
YEAH! SHE CAN'T EVEN STAND PICTURES OF THEM.
AS FOR ME, I CAN NEVER GET ENOUGH OF THEM.
WE SHOULD START A COLLEC-TION!
...THAT'S HOW IT ALL STARTED! GOOD TIMES!
I STILL HAVEN'T STOPPED, AS YOU CAN SEE!

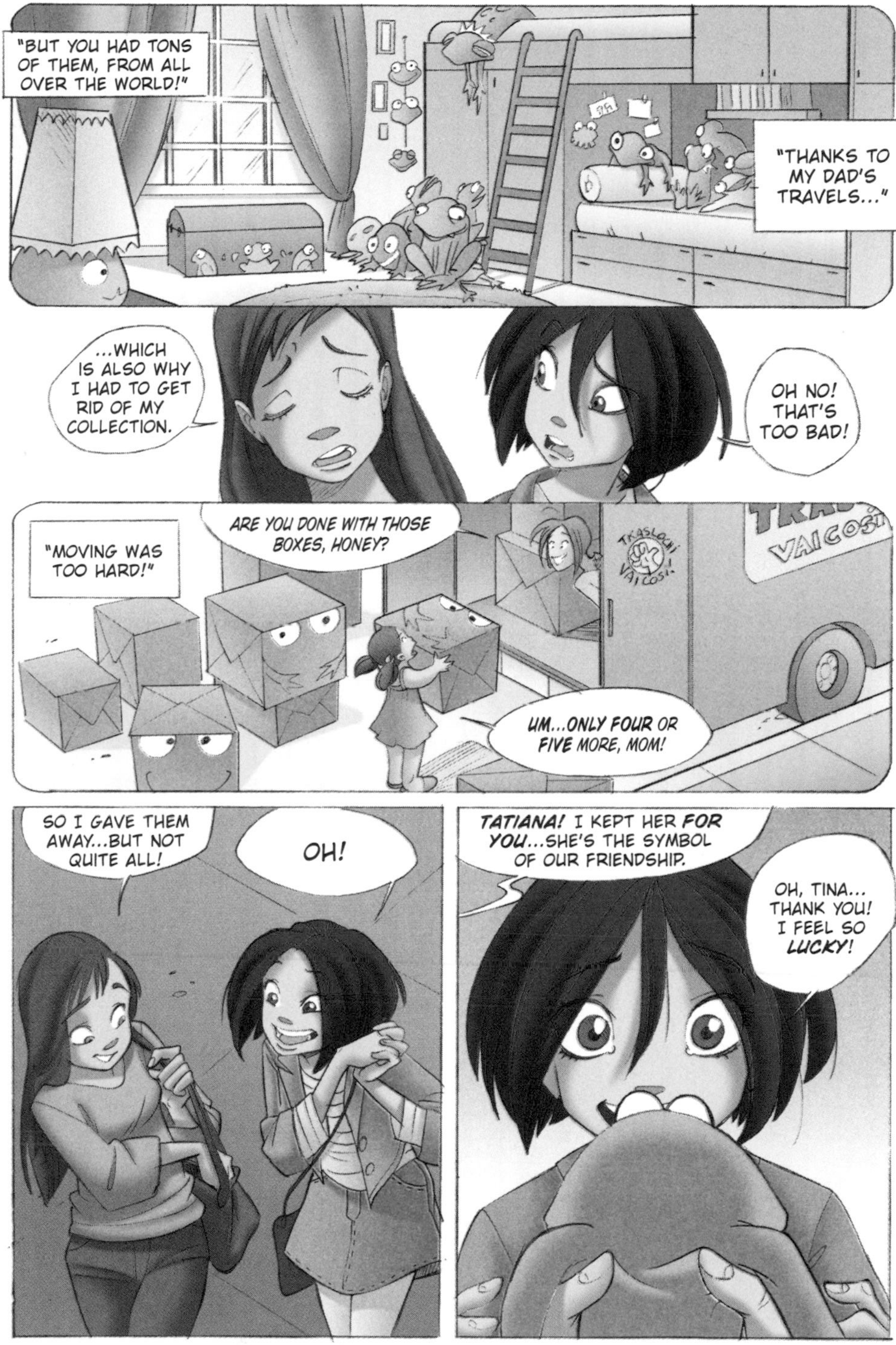
"BUT YOU HAD TONS OF THEM, FROM ALL OVER THE WORLD!"
"THANKS TO MY DAD'S TRAVELS..."
...WHICH IS ALSO WHY I HAD TO GET RID OF MY COLLECTION.
OH NO! THAT'S TOO BAD!
"MOVING WAS TOO HARD!"
ARE YOU DONE WITH THOSE BOXES, HONEY?
TRASLOCHI VAICOSI!
VAICOSI
UM...ONLY FOUR OR FIVE MORE, MOM!
SO I GAVE THEM AWAY...BUT NOT QUITE ALL!
OH!
TATIANA! I KEPT HER FOR YOU...SHE'S THE SYMBOL OF OUR FRIENDSHIP.
OH, TINA... THANK YOU! I FEEL SO LUCKY!

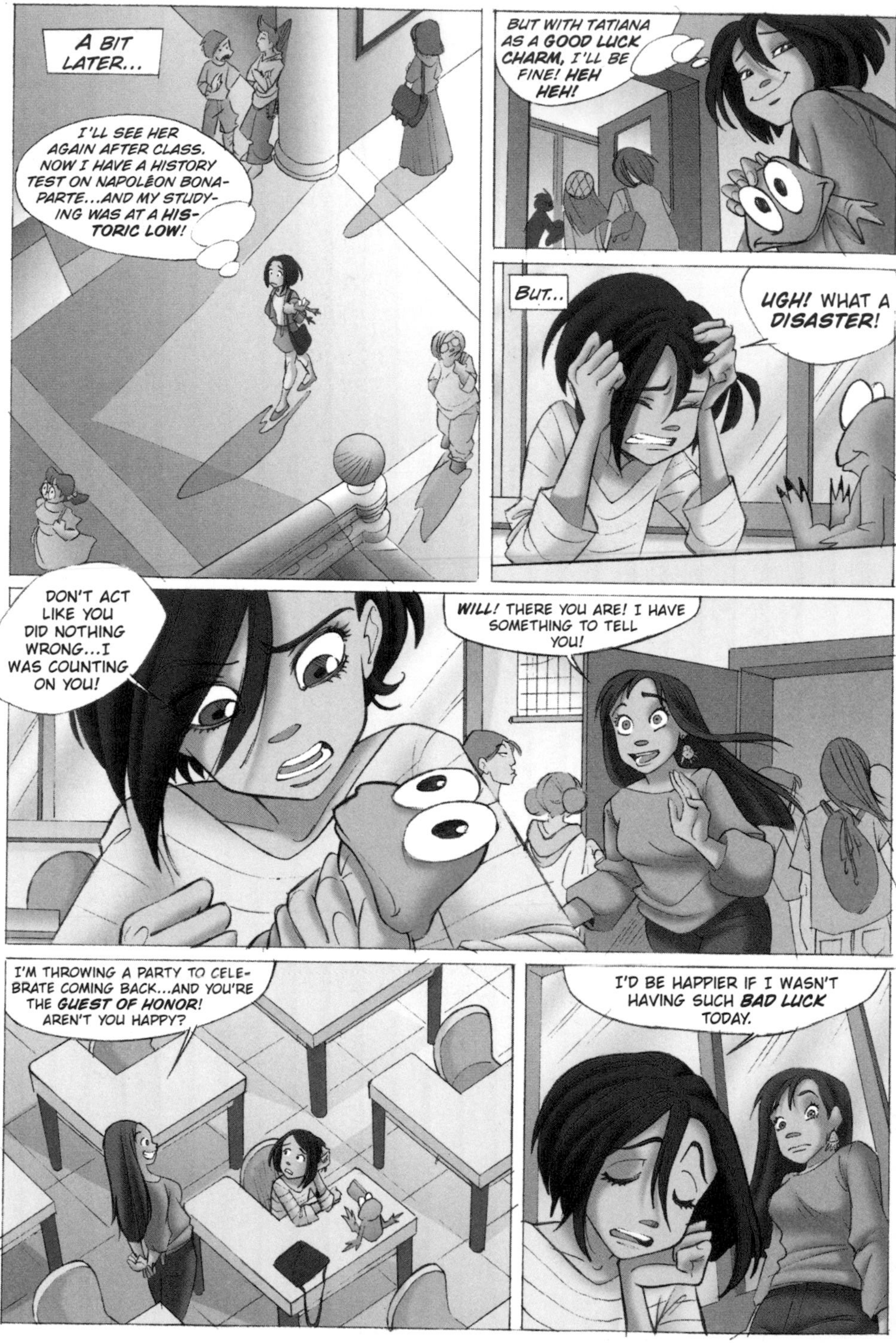
A BIT LATER...
I'LL SEE HER AGAIN AFTER CLASS. NOW I HAVE A HISTORY TEST ON NAPOLÉON BONAPARTE...AND MY STUDYING WAS AT A HISTORIC LOW!
BUT WITH TATIANA AS A GOOD LUCK CHARM, I'LL BE FINE! HEH HEH!
BUT...
UGH! WHAT A DISASTER!
DON'T ACT LIKE YOU DID NOTHING WRONG...I WAS COUNTING ON YOU!
WILL! THERE YOU ARE! I HAVE SOMETHING TO TELL YOU!
I'M THROWING A PARTY TO CELEBRATE COMING BACK...AND YOU'RE THE GUEST OF HONOR! AREN'T YOU HAPPY?
I'D BE HAPPIER IF I WASN'T HAVING SUCH BAD LUCK TODAY.

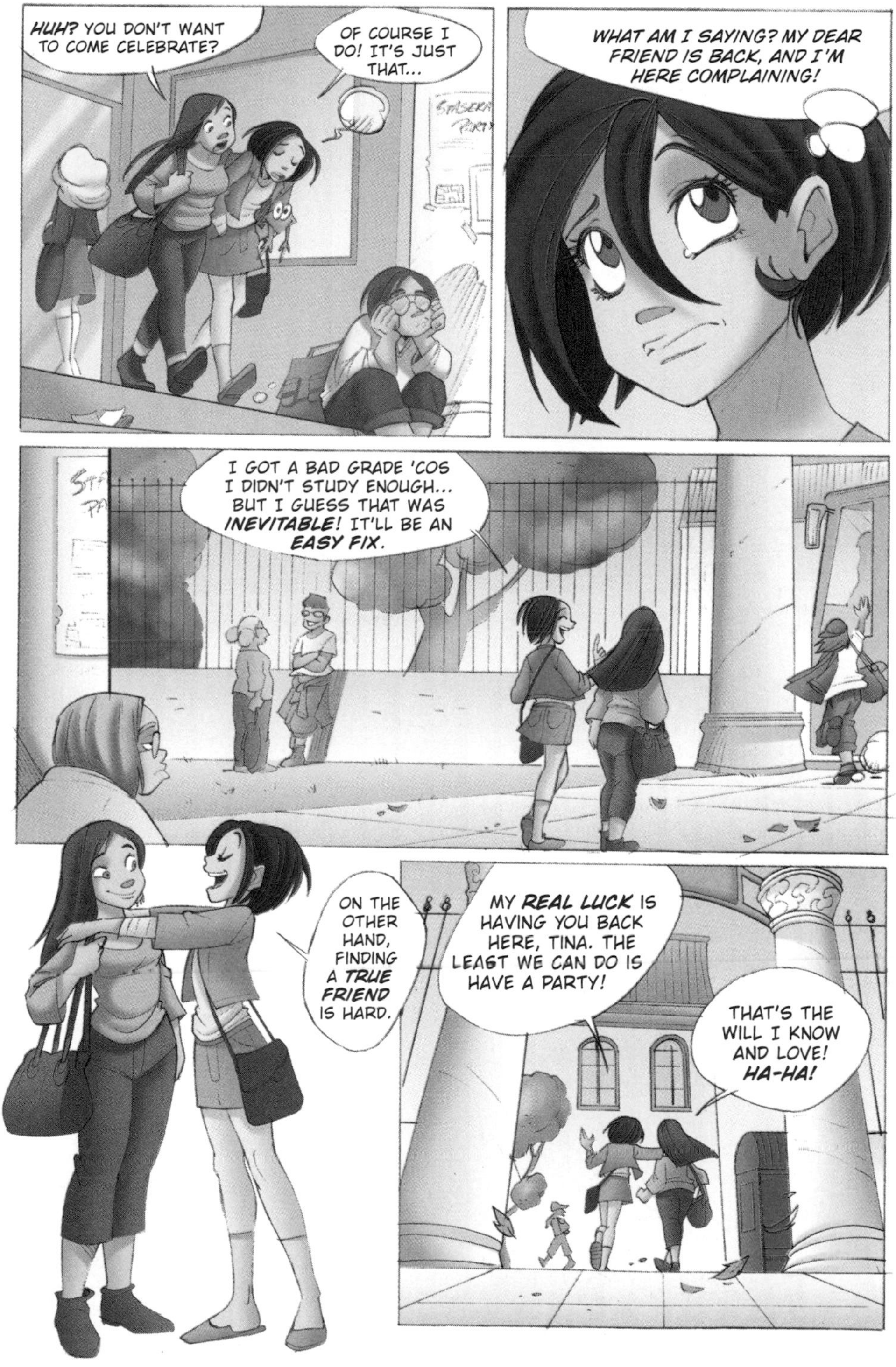
HUH? YOU DON'T WANT TO COME CELEBRATE?
OF COURSE I DO! IT'S JUST THAT...
WHAT AM I SAYING? MY DEAR FRIEND IS BACK, AND I'M HERE COMPLAINING!
I GOT A BAD GRADE 'COS I DIDN'T STUDY ENOUGH... BUT I GUESS THAT WAS INEVITABLE! IT'LL BE AN EASY FIX.
ON THE OTHER HAND, FINDING A TRUE FRIEND IS HARD.
MY REAL LUCK IS HAVING YOU BACK HERE, TINA. THE LEAST WE CAN DO IS HAVE A PARTY!
THAT'S THE WILL I KNOW AND LOVE! HA-HA!

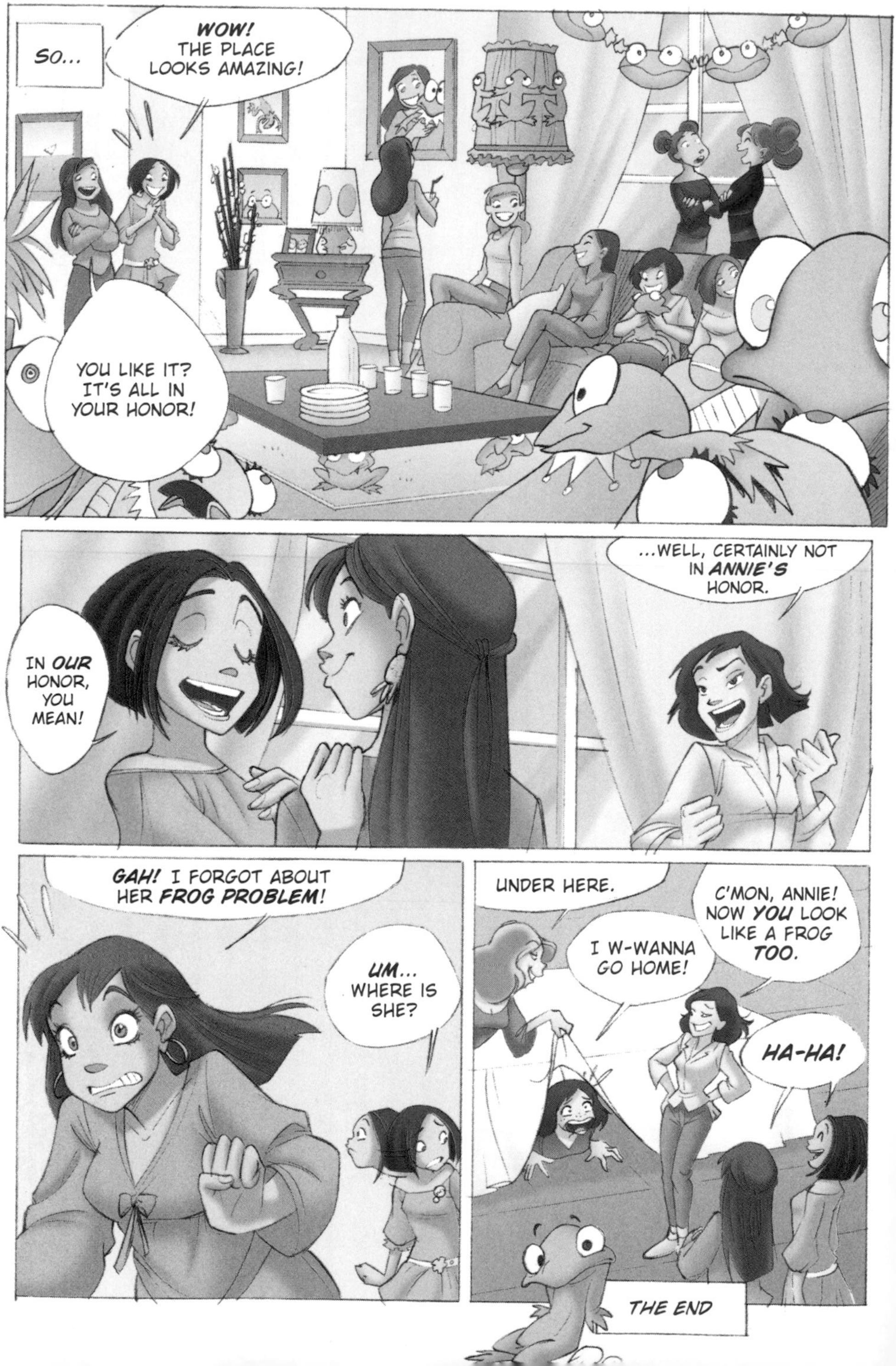

SO...
WOW! THE PLACE LOOKS AMAZING!
YOU LIKE IT? IT'S ALL IN YOUR HONOR!
IN OUR HONOR, YOU MEAN!
...WELL, CERTAINLY NOT IN ANNIE'S HONOR.
GAH! I FORGOT ABOUT HER FROG PROBLEM!
UM... WHERE IS SHE?
UNDER HERE.
I W-WANNA GO HOME!
C'MON, ANNIE! NOW YOU LOOK LIKE A FROG TOO.
HA-HA!
THE END

Read on in Volume 29!

W.i.t.c.h.

Will Irma Taranee Cornelia Hay Lin

W.i.t.c.h.

Will Irma Taranee Cornelia Hay Lin

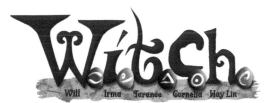

W.I.T.C.H.

Will Irma Taranee Cornelia Hay Lin

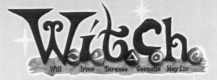

Part IX. 100% W.I.T.C.H. • Volume 3

28

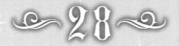

Series Created by Elisabetta Gnone
Comic Art Direction: Alessandro Barbucci, Barbara Canepa

This book is a work of fiction. Names, characters, places, and incidents are the product of the author's imagination or are used fictitiously. Any resemblance to actual events, locales, or persons, living or dead, is coincidental.

JY
150 West 30th Street, 19th Floor
New York, NY 10001

Visit us at jyforkids.com
facebook.com/jyforkids
twitter.com/jyforkids
jyforkids.tumblr.com
instagram.com/jyforkids

First JY Edition: April 2022

JY is an imprint of Yen Press, LLC.
The JY name and logo are trademarks of Yen Press, LLC.

The publisher is not responsible for websites (or their content) that are not owned by the publisher.

Library of Congress Control Number: 2017950917

ISBNs:
978-1-9753-2325-7 (paperback)
978-1-9753-2326-4 (ebook)

10 9 8 7 6 5 4 3 2 1

LSC-C

Printed in the United States of America

Cover Art by Giada Perissinotto
Colors by Andrea Cagol

Translation by Linda Ghio and Stephanie Dagg at Editing Zone
Lettering by Katie Blakeslee

THE GREEN TRUTH

Concept and Script by Alessandro Ferrari
Layout, Pencils, and Inks by Lucio Leoni

MAGICAL MOMS

Concept and Script by Augusto Macchetto
Layout by Alberto Zanon
Pencils by Federica Salfo
Inks by Roberta Zanotta

TEAMWORK

Concept and Script by Bruno Enna
Layout by Antonello Dalena
Pencils by Manuela Razzi
Inks by Marina Baggio

FIRST DAYS

Script by Augusto Macchetto
Layout and Pencils by Daniela Vetro
Inks by Marina Baggio and Roberta Zanotta

GREEN HOPE

Concept and Script by Maria Muzzolini
Layout, Pencils, and Inks by Lucio Leoni

WHAT'S TRULY LUCKY

Concept and Script by Maria Muzzolini
Layout, Pencils, and Inks by Giada Perissinotto